Ruaridh Nicoll was born in Arbroath, Angus, in 1969 and grew up in the Highland county of Sutherland. He travelled widely as a correspondent for the *Guardian* and the *Observer*, before returning to Scotland to write *White Male Heart* and now *Wide Eyed*. He lives in Edinburgh.

Acclaim for: *Wide Eyed*

'A quietly spooky tale . . . Part of the strength of the book as a thriller is the artful way Nicoll manipulates our sympathies . . . you have all the ingredients of an absorbing yarn . . . While the narrative is well-crafted and builds to a bravura climax, it is in the evocation of atmosphere, that elusive art, that Nicoll really earns his spurs. He is the master of everything from simple natural descriptions that have the limpidity of a watercolour to extravagantly gothic episodes in darkened churchyards. Weird events are set against equally weird backdrops: from RAF jets roaring across a cloudless sky to the burning pyres associated with foot-and-mouth disease. The result is a novel that is both unsettling and oddly exhilarating' *Sunday Telegraph*

'Nicoll writes intricate, accurate prose and offers alluring descriptions of the Scottish landscape . . . the landscape of *Wide Eyed* is beautiful and the situation is fascinating' *Guardian*

'A claustrophobically tense novel, *Wide Eyed* combines Nicoll's profound love of the Scottish landscape and its people with a journalist's eye for topicality. It also hints at a writer who intends to become as prominent a part of the literary landscape as the cliffs and mountains from which he draws his inspiration' *Glasgow Herald*

'Asked to condense a review of Ruaridh Nicoll's second novel into just one word, I would have to plump for atmospheric. I could also say riveting, or dramatic – or even entertaining. Indeed it is all of these but, for me, it is the all-enveloping atmosphere of Galloway that leaves the deepest impression on the reader. This is a truly grand second novel . . . his descriptive writing is of the highest quality . . . a beautifully told tale – and you will not be disappointed with the ending'
Scots Magazine

'The writing is lyrical and compelling and, for all the novel's emotive subject matter and intermittent violence, Nicoll's portrayal of grief, and the need to make sense of calamity is never less than convincing. Another triumph' *The List*

'An emotionally-wrought novel, in turn lyrical and violent, fable-like and gutsy, in which many of its characters are on a quest to find out who they really are' *Sunday Herald*

www.booksattransworld.co.uk

'At once both brutal and beautiful . . . The quality of observation is breathtaking . . . This is an absorbing and uncomfortable read, raising as many questions as it answers about what it means to be a young man in a territory where the roles are few and growing more limited with every passing year. But *White Male Heart* has far wider relevance than that. This is a novel that is both heart-rending and heart-stopping but which never loses sight of the importance of the blackest humour. It is without question a welcome and worthy addition to the growing sub-genre of tartan noir'   Val McDermid

'Eerily impressive. Like Sir Walter Scott ambushed by Iain Banks, Nicoll produces prose both rhapsodically beautiful and red in tooth and claw, marking out this modern gothic tale'   *Sunday Times*

'Nicoll's first novel takes us to the Highlands of Scotland, but this is not a gentle land, it is a place with a dark and sinister complexion . . . Though Nicoll is a journalist, he has a novelist's eye for the beauty of the landscape and the shape of its contours . . . This is a novel of startling originality, an absorbing psychological thriller as well as a deft portrayal of friendship and betrayal. Nicoll conjures up the pain of rejection and abandonment as convincingly as he describes the way in which a stalker stands downwind of a rutting stag. It is a long time since we have had a writer who is so at home with nature and hunting, and who describes them so vividly and fluently'   *The Times*

'In Ruaridh Nicoll's *White Male Heart*, Hemingway's ghost would seem to roam the Highlands. This is a tale of male bonding and competition, full of animal killing and proofs of masculinity. The blood is all in the service of showing that love, maybe even love of women, is a truer path. What's more, this journalist knows something Papa didn't; rural Scotland'   *Observer*

'Bracingly violent . . . beautifully told . . . this excellent, horrifying first novel'   *Evening Standard*

'The juxtaposition of civility and barbarity is central to Ruaridh Nicoll's *White Male Heart* . . . The structure of this novel creates an overwhelming sense of portent . . . Nicoll recreates the Scottish landscape with brilliance. He explores its latent violence and its remarkable beauty in a language which at times will leave you breathless. This is a bleak novel whose tensions build flawlessly into a shocking denouement'   *Literary Review*

Also by Ruaridh Nicoll

WHITE MALE HEART

and published by Black Swan

WIDE EYED

Ruaridh Nicoll

BLACK SWAN

WIDE EYED
A BLACK SWAN BOOK: 0 552 99904 0

Originally published in Great Britain by Doubleday,
a division of Transworld Publishers

PRINTING HISTORY
Doubleday edition published 2003
Black Swan edition published 2004

1 3 5 7 9 10 8 6 4 2

Copyright © Ruaridh Nicoll 2003

The right of Ruaridh Nicoll to be identified as the author of
this work has been asserted in accordance with sections 77
and 78 of the Copyright Designs and Patents Act 1988.

Set in 11/14pt Sabon by
Falcon Oast Graphic Art Ltd.

Black Swan Books are published by Transworld Publishers,
61–63 Uxbridge Road, London W5 5SA,
a division of The Random House Group Ltd,
in Australia by Random House Australia (Pty) Ltd,
20 Alfred Street, Milsons Point, Sydney, NSW 2061, Australia,
in New Zealand by Random House New Zealand Ltd,
18 Poland Road, Glenfield, Auckland 10, New Zealand
and in South Africa by Random House (Pty) Ltd,
Endulini, 5a Jubilee Road, Parktown 2193, South Africa.

Printed and bound in Great Britain by
Cox & Wyman Ltd, Reading, Berkshire.

Papers used by Transworld Publishers are natural, recyclable
products made from wood grown in sustainable forests. The
manufacturing processes conform to the environmental
regulations of the country of origin.

For Alison

SUNDAY

High tide: 00.45 (full moon), 13.00
Light south-westerly

I can walk through the shadows of my memories and feel nothing. Here in the garden I am tall, straight-backed, strolling like a gentleman. The reflecting sea spreads away to the horizon, offering a route out for the souls, while on the landward side, a thick forest blocks any way back. Shrubs and small trees, tilted by the southwesterlies, break up the sadness and protect the stones. Built into the wall is a granite temple to the memories of the Regos, reduced to the size of a cabin but still intimidating. The door has a small round hole at its centre. At the gate is Betsy's memorial, that lovely name Gillander. The boy has no place, having been lost, but I find I can never look for long; my eyes are always drawn towards the top wall, to a memory in the shadows. That one is mine. It is not that I fear it – I haven't felt such a thing for a long time – but I know respect. The moment will come and that is how it should be. I enjoy it here. Few visit, it is so hard to find. It is fresh in the garden, and I am so used to the forest, to the endless sound of dripping . . .

At the end of the promontory, with her fiancé crouched among the shards at her knee, Betsy Gillander looked out over the winter sea. 'Five kingdoms,' he had said. She counted, her gaze swinging across the dark landmasses that lingered at the edge of sight. The departing water reflected light back at her, the falling sun burning across its surface. She looked down. 'England,' she recited. 'The Isle of Man, Ireland.'

He picked up a small stone, black and sharp, showing it to her.

'Scotland?'

He smiled and shifted the stone in his palm, holding it so that his index finger could point towards the sky. The sea moved beyond him, drawn towards the slim channel through which it would rush out into the Atlantic.

Betsy shrugged.

'The Kingdom of Heaven,' he said. 'It was here, right here, where I decided to marry you.'

She had known that. She had been aware of the resonance as he had led her along the path. The proposal, which had come several weeks before, had already created a place for itself in her memory, in one of those galleries where the unforgettable lie. He had been in bed, she about to leave for work. 'You were thinking of heaven?' she asked now.

'Perhaps. Why not?'

'Heavens to Betsy.' The words had gone before she realized the tone wasn't quite warm enough. She added a smile and put down a hand to push back hair from his ears. She could feel her life, the old life, move away with the vast waters. Despite its blinding fall, the sun offered no heat and she shivered. 'Your knees will be sore,' she said.

His face shadowed as he rose, the sun behind him. 'We'll go in.'

'It's beautiful.' She had irritated him, and now tried to recover. 'It was a beautiful place to think of me.'

There was only room for one to stand in the surge of rock that formed this outward tip, and now he hung above her. 'This is what we came for,' he said. 'This is what you wanted to see.' He eased his way across the granite, climbing down into a flotsam-filled gully, then up towards the machair.

Betsy stood, blood seeping back into the places where the uneven rocks had pressed against her, a stiffness in her muscles. She had been deserted by her skill for saying the right things, the words that would keep him calm. He had mistaken her distrust of sentimentalism for callousness. The truth was that she felt removed, protected, despite the sucking of water in the crevices below. She felt at the edge of countries and her life.

She caught up with him at the top of the headland, and they paused at the base of a white, crenellated coastguard station that commanded a view of the firth. The village and the harbour lay below them, already making permanent patterns in Betsy's mind. She knew she was shifting his proposal to this place, combining the memories to exclude the image of him lying there in bed, her decision, as she accepted, whether or not to go to work. She was placing him in this tableau, with its perfect distance. Farmland rolled in from the north, then fell away to the east and west in mussel-stained shores. Distances were marked by the occasional homestead caught at points where wandering dykes converged. Trees were rare, huddling where the land fell out of the prevailing wind, and among them, small groups of sheltering cattle. The harbour was ringed by houses, wilfully independent in their design yet crouched together against a vast sky that seemed to stretch wider than was possible in this world. Apart from tenuous trails of smoke, the only movement came from the harbour. A fishing-boat was preparing to leave, while sailboats shivered on the falling tide, masts exaggerating their movements.

Betsy took her fiancé's hand, glad when he chose to accept it.

'You wanted to see,' he said.

'It's a beautiful place, it couldn't be lovelier.'

'I wanted you to see the place behind the thought.'

They walked down on to the pier. The fishing-boat rode high on the outgoing tide, the young crew passing supplies from the dockside, which were then carried down into the depths of the boat. The captain, squat and broad-shouldered in the way of the people in these parts but with clear features and white hair cut close, rested his back against the wheelhouse, talking to a man on the dockside, saying they would steam to the south-west. Betsy slowed to watch, her feeling of separateness still on her. The man on the dock was in profile and, in her mood, Betsy was caught by the cast of his face, with its long bones, the flat forehead leading straight to the tip of his nose. He had a thick mass of grey-black hair that fell back behind his ears to his neck, and shifted on his feet as he argued about some piece of equipment the captain wanted.

'Complaints,' he was saying. 'All I do is pamper you and what do I get in return? Nothing. *Nada.*'

'He's going foreign on us, boys,' the captain said. 'You're as generous as a Peterhead whore, Rego, and about as attractive.'

The crew whooped, and the man on the dock, who

12

Betsy presumed was the owner, offered a soft, thoughtful smile. 'Boys, you'll understand how your skipper knows so much about the Peterhead hairies? He came across one and asked her how much. She says, "Thirty quid," and he says, "Nah, too expensive, how much for a wank?" and she says, " 'Tis thirty quid whatever ye are." ' The crew, who had stopped to listen, cracked up, looking across at their captain.

'Don't listen to the dago, my love,' he said, and hopped on to the pier to kiss a tall, slight woman who had wandered up while the owner was telling his story. Dressed incongruously in summer colours, she offered an innocent smile to the captain as he put an arm round her. The man who had told the story grimaced at the rest of the crew and made a comic show of scuttling away.

One of the younger crewmen noticed Betsy watching and shouted up: 'You want to come to sea with us, love?'

Shocked out of the bubble in which she had enclosed herself, Betsy shook her head and laughed, as her fiancé pulled her hand in the direction of the inn. They walked away but stopped to look round when the owner shouted, 'Where's Priest? Priest!' An enormous man, round and bald but for a stripe of wiry hair around a swollen head, emerged from the wheelhouse in torn and filthy overalls, then scrambled up the side of the pier. He looked directly at Betsy, offering an empty stare that, even from such a distance, caused her to take a step backwards. She turned again and walked quickly towards the inn. 'For Christ's sake, come on,' she heard the man called Rego say behind her.

Betsy led the way through the empty reception area, up the stairs and down a corridor to their room. She walked to the window, past the floral bed-cover, the biscuit-coloured kettle, an old television, across the mustard carpet. One of the boys was releasing the boat from its moorings, throwing ropes down on to the deck and jumping after them. The woman stood on the pier. Gulls lifted off yachts as the black and red hull swung out and past them. 'That boat's leaving,' Betsy said, as her fiancé joined her at the window, standing close behind her.

'You could have been on it,' he said, reaching out to draw the curtains. 'They wanted you as their galley-girl.' He swung an arm under her and carried her to the bed.

Betsy woke to darkness. The memory of the large man climbing from the boat had followed her into sleep, his shadow scuttling up the harbour wall. She lay listening to the wind in the wires of the boats, then slipped from the bed to look out into the night. The weather had turned and a light snow swept across the sailboats that had grounded on the low-tide mud, yellow under the pier lamps. Unsure of the time, and needing comfort, she placed her hands on the glass, moving close to the pane so that she could see up the street to the harbour-master's office. The glass fogged, and in the mist she imagined her fiancé at work on the advertising campaign that had led to his discovering the village two months before. The building had been repainted and her eyes wandered from its glistening walls to the dark houses across the bay. These were memories chosen for her by him.

A draught negotiated the window's seal, and its chill sent her back to bed. She sought her fiancé in the covers, whispering in his ear until he murmured and enclosed her in his arms. When she woke again, he was standing at the window and she could hear sleet hitting the glass and the low whine of the wind. She crawled over to lie in the warmth of his departed body, seeking his scent before asking how the world outside looked.

'Dark,' he said, opening the curtain and showing her the sky: dawn had arrived, but little light with it. 'I don't think we'll be doing any walking.'

'Why would we want to?' Betsy moved deeper under the covers but he remained where he was and she sensed a slight disappointment in him. 'We'll find your cave tomorrow,' she said. 'This feels like an important day, our day. Let's spend it in bed.'

Her fiancé rapped his knuckles on the glass, then dropped back in beside her, Betsy moving towards him, coaxing him into making love. Later she rested her head on his chest, and looked out through the crack in the curtains while he fell into a gentle sleep, his breathing slow and, for once, untroubled. Listening to his heart, Betsy wondered how they would age. She liked his body, the way it fitted together, how he presented it when he spoke and his ease within it. In time she had grown used to the moisture of the skin, his captured breaths, the murmur of his thoughts in sleep. She would complain only when his restlessness woke her and he would reply by disparaging her quiet rhythms, her natural contentment, her restfulness.

They had met nearly eight years before, the memory causing her, as always, a stab of embarrassment. He had possessed a confidence, a self-assurance, that allowed him to use his insouciant wit to clever and cutting effect, consuming her twenty-year-old mind. Silenced by nerves, she had sought a voice in drink and ended up sleeping with his housemate, humiliated when the man she really wanted came into the bedroom the next morning to watch the

15

only television in the flat. Betsy now ran a fingertip across his belly, prompting a distant complaint. Of course, she had discovered that the self-assurance covered in-securities, the wit a streak of cruelty. These things had revealed themselves during those first years, yet there was much to love, not least his imagination and intelligence. She had laboured to get a good degree while he performed effortlessly. She had never questioned her desire to be liked, it seemed so natural, so she tried to make herself pleasing to him. Even after all these years his proposal, in some ways, had felt like a triumph. She allowed her fingers to run down past his belly button and into the hair below. Keeping her fingertips peripheral, she circled skin so sensitive that he stirred.

'Engaged couples have more sex than at any other time of their life,' she whispered.

'Let me recover.' He sighed, grumpily turning away so that she was forced to move.

She wriggled up behind him, leaning forward so that her mouth was by his ear. 'Now is no time for sleep,' she whispered, and goosed him.

With the weather closing in, they remained in their room, eating snacks they had brought with them or found in the complimentary basket beside the kettle. Occasionally Betsy's fiancé would stand and look out over the harbour, rain pushing past in the half-light, the atmosphere viscous with cold. They talked of the filming that had brought him here, of the advertisement he had written. Or of the other interests the area held, of the ancient religions that had touched this peninsula in the first days of wandering Christianity. Mainly they lay in bed, making the most of enforced idleness. Come evening, they went down to the bar for dinner. The storm was forcing the Irish Sea up the pier-wall, sleet and snow sweeping across the bay, and the rigging of the sailboats giving off a constant, background howl.

'Nasty evening,' Betsy said to the landlady.

'Very,' she answered, unsmiling. 'What can I get you?'

Betsy felt a sudden urge to force out the melancholy that had been dogging them. 'Champagne.' She turned to her fiancé, who looked uncomfortable. 'We should drink champagne.' The counter formed a circular island between two rooms, the public bar only feet away. The two men who were sitting there had stopped talking to watch her while the landlady glanced down to a glass-fronted refrigerator.

'We have Moët.' She looked up. 'You're celebrating?'

Betsy nodded. 'This is the creative young man who wrote that TV ad they filmed down here a couple of months ago. It's being shown for the first time tonight.'

'I thought I recognized you,' the landlady said, but the chill was still there.

'And it was here that he decided to marry me.'

She was a stout woman, who looked to be in her fifties. Finally she offered warm eyes but little more. 'Good for you.' She bent down to pick up the bottle. 'I'll bring this over.'

They sat in the corner, looking out into the gale. Betsy took her fiancé's hand, squeezing as the landlady arrived with the champagne, watching as she opened the bottle and poured a glass for each of them. A man came through the door of the lounge bar, soaking and whey-faced, and finding only them went back out and into the public bar. They offered the landlady a glass and, when she declined, ordered food, watching her pad away into the kitchen.

17

When she returned to the bar, she leaned over to talk in a whisper to those who sat on the other side.

The fiancé checked the slim watch that had been a gift from Betsy. 'Forty minutes,' he said. 'There's a TV on the wall of the public bar. They'll want to see it, don't you think?'

'Of course.'

'She didn't ask.'

'They'll want to see it, I'm certain.'

Their dinner arrived. Her fiancé's nervousness grew, and Betsy reassured him. He said it was his chance, that if he really was to make it as a freelancer, and not have to get a full-time job, the success of this slot was crucial. Betsy knew the territory well and quietly built up his confidence so that when the time came he surged through the two doors that led into the public bar. It was a bleaker room, the surfaces washable except for the worn green felt on the pool table. The men turned, their eyes weary, expressions distant but not unfriendly. They shifted so that he could reach the bar and talk to the landlady. 'That ad,' he said. 'It's on in a couple of minutes. On ITV. Perhaps we could see it?'

The landlady looked along the bar. 'Why not?' she said, reaching for a remote. Sound emerged from the box before the picture, Jon Snow talking: 'If disease is suspected, will the government be placing restrictions on the movement of livestock?' There was no answer – the landlady had flicked over.

'That's all we need,' said one of the men. 'A bloody plague.' Betsy saw his hands on the bar: big, dirty, bruised but elegant.

The ads started running, the first for a mobile phone, while in the bar the door opened and a man came in, shaking the sleet from his receding grey hair. There was a muttering of welcomes, his name Bunbury. 'Any news?' he asked.

The landlady shook her head as she placed a glass under the tap. Betsy's fiancé looked impatient as Bunbury shrugged out of the jacket that covered his lean body. His right arm was in a sling, the ruined hand – black and crushed – visible beyond it.

'Lucky I'm left-handed,' he said, catching her gaze.

Betsy smiled, reacting uncomfortably to the faintly sour presence of the man, his eyes too close together. Her fiancé hissed. Pictures of an urban street party being broken up by the police flashed up, then cars driving along rainswept country roads until they reached a village, this village, music erupting over the harbour. The texture of the film was rich, velvety and dark, youths writhing, storm-water everywhere, and a couple breaking away, along the deserted street, to where the boy pushed the girl against the harbour-master's wall, the camera pulling away to show a dark bottle painted up the entire reach of the building, the legend 'Any SPort In A Storm' in block letters beside it. As the ad finished her fiancé waited for applause, but the men at the bar sought out their drinks. 'Christ,' said the man with big hands.

The landlady switched off the television and gestured Betsy through to the other bar. There was no sound but the wind and the clatter of cleats in the rigging beyond the window panes. Betsy took her fiancé's hand and had to pull a little, breaking through his mortification, leading him away, an under-the-breath muttering rising from the men they left behind.

The landlady waited on the other side. 'Don't take it personally,' she said. 'The storm. We've got a boat out in

19

it.' She was speaking quietly, earnestly. 'We can't contact them.' She looked at one, then the other with clear eyes and went back to her other customers.

Betsy gazed at her champagne glass, until her attention was caught by the crippled man pulling a canvas slip from under his ruined arm. He unrolled it on the bar to reveal several long knives, one of which the landlady lifted to test the edge. 'One of your specials, this one,' she said. 'How much do I owe you?'

Betsy sipped at her drink.

'They hated it,' her fiancé said, and walked away.

Betsy sat on the bed, back against the padded headboard, watching her fiancé read. He was sitting on a hard chair by the window, pretending to be lost in his book. As he flipped each page his hand occasionally moved up to mark a paragraph. 'It wasn't your fault,' she said.

He turned another page and she sighed, reaching over to pick up her novel.

'You're right,' he said. 'It wasn't. You talked me into it.' Dark eyes had rolled up towards her; his face had soured. The reassurance Betsy had offered during dinner had been repackaged into the cause of this downfall, and the wrong now lay with her.

'No one thought anything bad of you,' she said. 'It's the storm. They have friends who are out there, in danger.' She pointed to the window, and her attention was momentarily caught by the violence of the weather. The sailboats were lost in the driving sleet, but she could still hear them, hysterical in the darkness. She wondered if those in danger were the boys she had seen the day before, and felt fear for them. 'Any port in a storm,' she said. 'I mean . . .'

'I'd have thought it was perfect.' He was speaking from behind his book.

'They don't blame you.'

He put the book down. 'Everything I do goes wrong.' He spoke softly but Betsy recognized the tone. It emerged from a pool of resentment he held inside, which she always managed to forget was there, and which was fed by her paying the mortgage and his credit-card bills. 'I get a break, it turns sour. Nothing works out. My reward is your sympathy. This wouldn't have happened to you.' She waited, attempting to draw the sting with silence, his sharpness showing he was annoyed by it. 'I'm sorry if it pisses me off sometimes.' He picked up his book again.

'Can't we try to have a nice time?' Betsy asked. 'Please?'

'It was you who wanted to come here.'

A memory triggered as Betsy watched him – perhaps it was the awfulness of the marketing book he was reading: she recalled their university days, her struggle to complete the Ph.D. She had treated the idea of marriage with disdain then, proud of a life she believed richer and more textured than those led by others, and one that had ultimately resulted in an affair apiece. Hers had been a response to his infidelity. She had spent a night with her boss, a scientist she admired. She was aware that her temperament was naturally staid – she had been told so often enough – and that he added eccentricities.

'*The Art of Positive Thinking*.' She read out the book title.

He would usually respond to this by saying that only the unimaginative needed novels, talk of *Madame Bovary* – one of only three that he had ever finished – as 'fantasy for cattle', but he clearly wasn't in the mood. He told her to fuck off.

21

Betsy wasn't offended: the insult was a commonplace. Still caught up in her memories, she laughed at the conceit of her early twenties. Now there was no one left to justify herself to. The group of friends from their days at university had dispersed, mostly to London, but even those who had skipped over to Glasgow were now strangers, and the traffic never came the other way. She wondered now if his eccentricity was the excuse she had used for wanting stability in this part of her life, his trickiness counterbalancing the prospect of marriage. A certain seriousness had crept into their relationship, and now that there were just the two of them she felt she wanted its security. She yearned for a time when their days were no longer a battle of wills. She supposed she wanted to relax.

He had not lifted his eyes from the book, so Betsy slipped off the bed and walked to the window, putting a hand on the glass, feeling it bulge under the assault of the storm. Wet snow coagulated on the outer side, then slipped along the surface, pushed by the wind. At the pier, detonations caused by repelled waves shook the navigation lights, great towers of whitewater catching the wind to be thrown across the harbour in a rush. The sailboats, the tide now almost in, strained at their tethers, backing away from the sea. A car's headlights showed from among the houses. The sleet had turned the land a dismal white and, as Betsy watched, the car rolled slowly from one street-lamp to the next, headlights picking out the church and the line of houses leading to the pub before swinging out over the water and dying there. A wave hit the pier, the water rose and arced over to ratchet down on the car's roof. When the internal light came on, Betsy saw the occupant reach into the back seat, an arm and the top of a pale-crowned head showing through the sunroof. The light went out as the next wave fell, and as the water ran off the car, the driver's door opened, a man struggled out and ran for the pub.

'Another guest,' said Betsy, drawing the curtains. Her fiancé failed to reply so she pushed aside his book and lowered herself on to his knee. His eyes rose as she leaned down to kiss him. 'I'm sorry that it didn't go as you planned. The ad was great, really great. It'll be a massive success, sell crates of that vile drink.' She pulled back. 'The timing was just bad luck. A pity, that's all. But it won't make any difference. This is our time, and we should enjoy it.'

He looked over at the curtains. 'You'd think they'd know what they're doing,' he said. 'Even in weather like this.'

She put a hand to his face, bringing him back, gently kissing him until steps sounded in the corridor.

'You're a brave man,' they heard the landlady say, as she walked.

'Stupid.' The new voice was English, the words exact, clipped at each end. 'Last hour trouble. Knew . . . didn't make it tonight . . . might take days.' The footsteps stopped outside the neighbouring room.

'Well, here you are. It's the only other room that looks out over the front but' – the landlady failed to lower her voice, keeping it matter-of-fact – 'you've got an engaged couple next door so if tomorrow you want one of the back rooms just let me know.' They heard the door open. 'Will this do?' He must have said yes because the key changed hands. 'Okay. Well, goodnight, Mr Boyle.'

As the footsteps faded, they could hear the man moving around his room. Betsy looked at her fiancé. 'I think we've been set a challenge,' she said.

*   *   *

Betsy stirred, her eyes opening to the miserable light of a bedside lamp in the pre-dawn. Her fiancé was sitting up, looking towards the night and the storm it contained. She reached across to him. 'What is it?'

'I think it's going to give.'

For a moment she thought he meant the weather, but beyond the curtains, the window shuddered and thumped in its mounting. She sat up. 'Go and look,' she said.

He pulled himself from the bed, approached the curtains from the side and slid one open. Beyond, the darkness seemed thick, a black sky rolling past, and then, in an instant, hazing white into a blizzard. A strong gust hit the building and the glass crunched, tailing away as a hiss of air pushed through. The bulb flickered and then they were in darkness.

Betsy reached for the lamp and, when she found it, flicked the switch.

'No point,' her fiancé said, from the darkness. 'There's no lights showing at all, anywhere.' The square of window gradually asserted itself, what little luminosity the night held revealing itself now that the electricity had failed. A burst of white light startled them as the moon showed for an instant between the charging clouds. 'It's mayhem out there,' he said. 'Boats are off their moorings. There's snow everywhere.'

Betsy sought out her dressing-gown among the bed-clothes then joined him at the window. She opened the other curtain, reaching out for it, careful not to stand in front of the bulging glass. Now that her eyes had adjusted, the weather took shape as it ground against itself, causing shadows in the atmosphere. It was only when the moon-light flared that a full image was revealed; two boats were

24

on their sides. Another, the biggest of the yachts, had dragged itself towards land. Out in the darkness, the whitewater, wind and sleet met high above the pier, showing in thunderheads of phosphorescence. Another gust hit the glass, and Betsy moved to encircle her fiancé with her arms. A flash of moonlight lit the world and, for a moment, Betsy saw a car parked in danger, close to the last house before the pier, a dim light showing from within. Then the moonlight was gone and, shockingly, so was the scream of the storm. A long, rolling explosion of water hitting the pier took its place, whitewater rising.

The car door opened and, in the faint light, they saw a yellow-clad man step out and wedge himself against the side of the vehicle. The wind returned to crack and hiss at the window, sleet removing him from view. 'It's the fat man from the fishing-boat,' Betsy said. She had recognized him instantly, the memory of his rise up the pier-side still troubling her. 'They called him Priest.'

'You can tell that?' Her fiancé was warm under her hands.

'That shape.'

The squall cleared, and in a brief glimpse of moonlight they saw the man running out along the pier, looping a rope over the stanchions he passed, the wind pulling at a large object he held in his spare hand. The light faded, but in the gloom the figure, now only a smear, appeared to be backing towards them. They heard the sea hit the harbour wall.

'Jesus,' exhaled the fiancé.

'Maybe we should . . .' Moonlight opened out again, revealing the object the man had been struggling to carry as a child's dinghy, now in the water, his bulk within, legs absurdly splayed over each corner. The fluorescence of the boat and the yellow of his waterproofs became a blur in the darkness, and monochrome in moonlight. He was caught in an eddy, a flurry of snow fringing a curtain of water that arced over him, and then they saw him paddling, paying out the rope he still held until the wind caught him and sent him skidding across the water and back into the darkness, a mad pendulum of colour sliding across the boils. Neither Betsy nor her fiancé spoke: they waited for sight as wind, wave and sleet soared and doused him.

He showed again, hanging from the anchor chain of the prettiest yacht, the hull bucking above him. He disappeared and then reappeared, shockingly, in bright lights: the driver of the car had switched on his headlights, a beam that revealed the full weight of sea and storm crossing its path. Priest was tying the rope to the chain, the sea testing it at once. He lifted his paddle from where it was wedged between his upslung legs and his gut and paddled hard to avoid the yacht. The car swung round to roll beneath their window and Priest was gone, a smudge of colour sliding across the water to wash up on the battered land. The headlights had lost Betsy her night-vision, and she caught Priest's movements only when he opened the tailgate of the car, threw in the dinghy and rolled in behind it.

She and her fiancé didn't speak until the car had pulled out of sight. Then Betsy put her hand to the pane, felt it move and, as if challenged by Priest's bravery, pressed her cheek against it to see if anyone else had watched this performance. Nobody was out, but her gaze caught on the harbour-master's office, its walls seemingly discoloured, the white giving way to darker shapes below.

*　*　*

Come lunch, the lounge was empty, a single candle throwing yellow light from the corner of the bar, a chill hard in the room. 'Only sandwiches, I'm afraid,' said the landlady, who was fiddling with a radio.

Betsy said it was fine, and asked about the fishermen.

She told them that the boat's emergency beacon – it was the one they had seen leave, the *Albatross* – had started to transmit the day before but nothing more had been heard. She didn't seem inclined to discuss it further. 'Both the British and Irish coastguard are searching for the life-rafts, but with the telephone lines down there's no further news. I can't even pick up the radio.'

'We saw a man risk his life for a yacht last night. It—'

The landlady tapped her fingertips on the bar, interrupting Betsy. 'Let me get you those sandwiches.'

Betsy watched her walk through to the kitchen, then noticed her fiancé was already sitting at a table in the corner. 'Cold sandwiches,' he complained, as she joined him. 'And then? What shall we do afterwards?'

'Perhaps we should go for a walk,' she replied, equally sarcastic. Beyond the windows the sky had closed in, curtains of sleet driving in across the harbour. She had tried to make the best of it. When they had woken that morning, within the warmth of the covers, she had suggested they huddle against the cold. But he had fidgeted and complained and eventually gone to run a bath, furious when he discovered there was no hot water. Then he had dressed in all his clothes and sat gazing out into the storm. Despite the bad light, Betsy had eventually picked up her book, once in a while glancing up at the irritating man facing down the crunch of the glass in its mounts.

'I thought there might be something going on down here,' she said now.

'There's nothing going on.'

Betsy sat and waited for her food in silence. She tried to avoid feeling resentful, but her memory kept dropping pieces of evidence into her thoughts. It was true that she had wanted to see where he had decided to marry her, to celebrate the impulse rather than the drab delivery of the proposal, but now he was crushing this. She remembered the years when she had worked so hard, while he was out getting high. She would ask him to let her sleep before major exams and he would tell her she was dull, go out and bring back strangers who would play music through the night, often the same song over and over again. A different reaction was assured when success came her way and she wanted to drink and dance. He would refuse to emerge from his 'projects' and say she didn't understand his creativity. She recalled that, on those evenings, she would sit feeling as miserable as she did now.

'Why don't we ask if they have any board games?' she said, as the landlady emerged with the sandwiches. 'We could even ask if she would light the fire in the other bar. We could get drunk.'

Her fiancé was still looking out of the window as the landlady put down the plates, and Betsy was about to ask her when the front door opened and a man pushed his way into the public bar. He looked over the countertops and was about to head their way, but the landlady held up her hand and went to join him.

'Fuckin' nightmare.' The man spoke loudly, deafened by the storm. 'I went right up to the point, landed on my arse a couple of times, and near went over the wall. Got a signal, but I couldn't hear a thing. No use. I reckon the mobile's fucked as well now.'

The landlady poured him a glass of whisky. He looked at it guiltily for an instant, then swallowed it in one go. His eyes focused briefly on Betsy and her fiancé, and his voice dropped. 'There's a wall over the road and it's too difficult to clear while the wind's running . . .'

'I think that's a good idea of yours,' said Betsy's fiancé. 'Let's get a fire going in there and play Ker-plunk.'

They ended up back in the bedroom, where the sound of the window grinding in its setting found open nerves in Betsy's temples. It didn't take long for a row to start. Even in the calm of everyday life, the mundane triggered arguments between them. Now Betsy's fiancé was explaining why he thought her practicality was useless in this crisis. In the usual way, point-scoring turned the bland acidic, and she was soon being reminded of how insipid yet dangerous her lack of imagination could be. This expanded into what bad company she was. Betsy tried to keep her voice down as the quarrel developed: she had heard their neighbour shift on his bed in the next room. She even tried to go along the corridor to a small room set aside for residents, but its small window gave little light and it was bitterly cold, reminding Betsy of a sitting room at an old people's home. When she returned to the bedroom, her fiancé said, 'You can't leave it, can you? You have to have the last word.'

Betsy chose not to reply. Fully dressed, she slipped under the covers and tried to sleep, but without success.

That evening, amazingly, the atmosphere in the bar had worsened, following the storm down into its bleak depression. The landlady watched Betsy's fiancé turn off the torch she had loaned them, and apologized that, once again, only sandwiches were on offer. 'You put out the candle in the room?' she asked. Betsy reassured her and was about to say more, but the storm let loose a long howl, distant and melancholic, and they all turned to look towards the curtained windows. 'You should go through to the public bar where it's warm,' the landlady said. 'I'll bring you those sandwiches.' Beyond the two counters a fire burned strongly in the grate, but the faces of the men who stood there robbed it of any joy.

It took nerve to face the public bar again, and Betsy had to set herself against the force of her discomfort to make it through the two doors, the night screaming at them in the gap between. The men clustered at the counter, their talk low and their hands full of weary gestures.

Having picked up their drinks, Betsy and her fiancé sat in the corner, not far from the fire. 'If we can, we should try to leave tomorrow,' Betsy said. Apart from their agreement to eat, those were the first words either had said for four hours.

The landlady passed a plate and a candle over the bar to a man, who brought them over. 'Storm rations,' he said. Betsy replied with a sad smile and watched as he returned to his drink. The men who stood there seemed powerless, and she realized that they must be at the periphery of events: men who would take any risk to save strangers were now impotent to help their friends. They shifted uneasily, muttering the occasional platitude. 'Willie's a good captain,' said one. 'He's got to get them out of there.' Betsy had never had a view of tragedy before and it allowed her mind to wander from her own misery.

They finished the sandwiches and Betsy took the plate to the bar. She brought back another drink for her fiancé.

'You're not having one?' he asked.

'I don't feel like it.' A man came in from the night, beating his hat against his leg to get the rain off, nodding to them as he left his coat near the fire. Betsy noticed that the others watched him hopefully, recomposing themselves when they saw there was no news.

'I thought you wanted to get drunk.'

'That was earlier. I'm happy with this.' She lifted her soft drink.

'You won't even drink with me.' He said this softly, a murmur in her ear.

Betsy couldn't bear to get drunk with such fear around her, but all she said was, 'I just don't want to.'

'You're worried about them.' He leaned back into the fake leather, his voice still deathly quiet, barely audible above the storm. 'We can't do anything that will make them feel better. And here we are, stuck. Engaged. Together.' They sat in silence. 'Why did you say yes, by the way?' he asked finally. 'You always laughed at the idea of marriage.'

'Love.'

'Oh.' He took a moment to think. 'I wondered if it was charity.' Another pause. 'But, then, you've always confused the two.' The door in the lounge bar opened and their fellow guest emerged. He spoke to the landlady, all the while taking in the two rooms by degrees, like a nervous heron. In the candlelight his head looked delicate and he carried it on a long, thin neck. His hair had receded, increasing the sense that he could be easily damaged. The landlady pointed and he came through the doors that led to the public bar, greeting the men, and smiling when he saw Betsy and her fiancé. He had high cheekbones and prominent eyebrows, to the point

31

where pupils and irises were lost in the shadows of his face.

'Another of the stranded,' Betsy said.

He grimaced, and she felt his gaze, all but hidden, take her in and move to her companion. The scrutiny passed quickly. 'Not nice,' he said, looking towards the curtained windows. He returned Betsy's smile and the delicacy in his features fell away. 'You the honeymooners?'

'Not yet.'

He nodded, not seeming to hear. He moved towards the bar, asking the landlady where he should sit. She pointed to a table on the other side of the fire, and he looked back. 'Won't disturb you, then,' he said.

Betsy watched as he walked to the seat, pushing himself into the corner where two benches met. He was wearing a well-cut but aged black suit with an open-necked shirt. Very tall, he wrapped himself up, one ankle pulled above the other knee. He retrieved a torn khaki paperback from his pocket, holding it at a distance so that it caught the candlelight. It took a while for Betsy to realize he wasn't reading but returning her gaze. She blushed and he grinned, once again losing that peculiar air of fragility.

Betsy turned back to her fiancé. 'Did you really think I'd say no?' She recalled being happy as she walked to work that day. Edinburgh's air had tasted somehow fresher than normal, fizzing in her lungs.

'No. In truth I knew you'd say yes.'

Betsy just stared at her hands. Finally she said she was going back upstairs. Her fiancé shrugged: he would join her later.

That night the storm grew into a hurricane, snow turning to sleet and then to water, coming out of the west as a deluge. Betsy approached the window tentatively and heard houses being stripped, the wind gripping at overlaps and gaps, using the leverage to tear in. She lay on the bed in the dark, wrapped in the red coat she loved, and listened to the fury. She only moved when a series of savage blasts penetrated the storm's howls. Then she went to the window. No moon showed. Only the whitewater, reaching skywards at the harbour wall, created an impression of light in the absolute darkness, suggesting an unseen wave rushing in to obliterate everything. People emerged from the pub and a car's headlights sent out a beam across the harbour, penetrating the driven sea and rain. The lights swung towards the land, and there was the yacht that Priest had risked his life to protect. It had broken its rope and was on its side, grinding against the sea wall that enclosed the church's whitewashed bulwark in the harbour. Betsy felt a terrible sadness.

Her fiancé knocked on the door, asking resentfully to be let in. They did not make love that night; they barely talked. For much of the time they sat in silence until he fell asleep. Unable to follow, Betsy rested against the headboard, candle out, tempest to the right of her, troubled breathing to the left. She was thinking back to why she had said yes that morning in the flat, despite her disappointment at being asked in that way. She wondered if he was right when he said she always confused love with charity.

For the next eight hours she sat in the same place, thinking over their life together. Despite her exhaustion, despite even the tears the worst memories mined, she felt clear-sighted for the first time. She rested there, feeling the empty misery open up inside her as she looked closely at the course of their relationship. For eight hours she searched for the light in eight years but little penetrated the pain, darkness sucking away any laughter they had shared. By the time he stirred, she had made a decision to leave him, and as he sat up and focused, she acted on her conviction. She didn't care about the neighbour, she didn't care about anything but finishing this thing now. 'I'm not marrying you,' she said, as he struggled from sleep. 'It's over.'

WEDNESDAY

High tide: 02.16, 14.34
Dead calm

Betsy's former fiancé lay in bed, his head turned towards the window. In the silence, Betsy heard a body shifting in the next room, the neighbour moving quietly about. At last her ex laughed and sat up, swinging his legs out of bed. His face was still turned from her and only the back of his hands showed as they rose to rub at his eyes. Then he stood to waddle through to the bathroom where he lifted the toilet seat and pissed. He shouted over his shoulder, 'My breathing been bothering you again?'

'No,' Betsy called. 'You told me to examine our relationship and I have.' She had always resented hearing him empty his bladder: it compared badly with a scene in a Marquez novel where a bride takes fright at the sound of her new husband urinating 'like a stallion'. This dog-drain only engendered a mild disgust. 'I don't want to spend any more of my life with you.' The flow faltered, then stopped.

There was a flush. He returned to the room and walked to the window. Betsy caught his nervous glance as he passed. 'Have you been sitting here stressing?' he asked.

'Stressing?' The word riled her. 'No.'

'What, then?' The edge hardened in his voice.

Again, there was movement from the other room, the faintness of the sound suggesting care. Betsy realized that the storm had broken, and that her long search for a decision had coincided with calm falling on the world outside. She could hear gulls. The sky glowed with passing sunlight. From where her ex was standing he would be able to see the chaos, but from the bed all seemed peaceful. 'Thinking. As I said.'

'Remind me.' He turned now and looked directly at her, his face at rest but his eyes sharp.

Despite herself, she found she couldn't return his stare so, in an effort to appear relaxed, she examined her nails. The varnish was chipped. She wondered how to make it easy, how to ease out gently, but then she remembered the surge of anger she had felt in the night and allowed it to return. 'You make me unhappy.' Finish it, she thought. 'I've made my mind up. I don't want to marry you.'

'You're in a temper,' he said dismissively. 'You need time to get over it.' He pressed the switch on the bedside light and it worked. 'The electricity's back on. I'm going to have a bath.' He strode across the room, lifting his towel from a chair, then stopped as he was about to close the bathroom door. 'You said yourself that this is supposed to be our time,' he said. 'Stop spoiling it.'

Betsy returned to her nails, smiling at his gall, but when he had gone she rolled into a foetal position, pulling the covers over herself. She sat up only when he re-emerged, but studied the opposite wall. She did not want the neighbour hearing any more of this. 'How is it outside?' she asked. 'Can we get home today?'

He dried himself ostentatiously, standing in front of her to wipe down his body before he sat on the bed beside her. 'We've got another three days,' he entreated. 'The weather's better. I'm sorry if I've been difficult, it was that thing with the ad. Let's have some fun.'

Betsy rolled off the bed and stood in front of the window. Boats had been tipped on to their sides, the debris scattered across the low-tide mud, yet the harbour was calm, sunlight offering it an air of shifted normality. In the centre lay the yacht Priest had tried to save, crushed half-way along its deck by the corner of the church's sea wall. The flooding rain that had been the storm's finale had washed away the snow, and it was only as Betsy's eyes adjusted that she could pick out the damage along the harbour's edge: a roof torn away, a crumpled shed, a car pushed into a garden. Gulls picked at the kelp that had been thrown up on to the rocks while a line of jackdaws watched from a rooftop.

'Look,' he said, coming up behind her, 'you're upset. I hate it when you're upset. I rely on you, you know that. If I'm feeling down, I rely on you to get me out of it.' He tried to put his arms round her but she slipped away.

'I mean it,' she said, frowning. 'This is the end.'

He appeared confused. 'How can it be? Just like that? We're engaged. Betsy, I agreed. I offered to spend the rest of my *life* with you. That's commitment.'

Betsy's eyes were on the wall. 'Let's not talk about it now. I want to get out of here.'

The sound of several cars rolling slowly along the harbour road reached them.

'I want to stay,' he replied.

'Fine.' She started to throw clothes into her bag. 'I'm leaving.'

He was at her side, holding her wrist, and she glanced down at his hand, wishing she had dressed when he was in the shower. Her eyes shifted up to his face and he let go. He picked up a coffee cup and threw it at the wall. It bounced off and rolled on the bedroom carpet, the move at once pathetic and contrived. But there had been real anger when he grabbed her arm. There was movement from the neighbour.

'Sit down,' her ex said, pointing at the foot of the bed.

Outside cars were pulling up. Betsy counted them in: one, two, three, four. She put on her dressing-gown and went to the window. People, lots of people, were stepping out of the vehicles, each full to capacity. More cars passed the church, moving slowly towards them.

'Betsy, sit *down*. There are a few things that need explaining.'

The faces, hard and soft, old and young, were exhausted. From the expressions the news was bad. She couldn't even begin to imagine what they were feeling.

'Betsy. *Sit down*.'

She felt stronger, ready. She walked back to the bed where she sat, gazing up at him. It was going to hurt, but she'd felt this before. She had often joked that there was nothing more hurtful than an advertising man telling the truth, but those people outside, moving into the room below them, would be feeling so much more than her. Their pain mattered.

She made a final effort. 'Can't we do this in the car?' She was sharply aware of the man in the other room, and of the slow talk beginning below.

'No,' he said. 'You're going to listen. This is about me and you.'

'But—'

'I don't know them, Betsy, I don't give a *fuck* about them, but I know you, and guess what?' He leaned back against the table and perused her while she fidgeted. When she raised her eyes, she hoped they met his with sarcasm. 'You're fat, Betsy,' he said.

She laughed in surprise, but he continued through it.

'And you know it. You say "shapely", but it's just another word for fat. What's that thing you like to think? That you're like your name suggests, half Victorian heroine, half bar-wench. That means fat, doesn't it? And heroine? Please. What a conceit. You're Victorian in some ways, in the uptight sense, but heroine? I don't think so. If that is supposed to suggest sexiness, well . . .'

'I said that once. Once. And I don't think this is taking us any further.'

'Who the hell *cares*? You've just told me that you want to call off our wedding. I think I'm entitled.' He moved towards her, close so she could feel his breath. 'What are you going to do if you leave me? You're pathetic. Remember when we met? You followed me around. People laughed. Do you have any idea what I sacrificed going out with you? I had to deal with all the friends who, just days before, had been laughing about you. It was *embarrassing*.' He stepped back, wincing. 'But this isn't about me. Think about it. That credibility you seek, I give it to you. Without me, what are you?'

He waited, but she couldn't think of anything she wanted to say. She was wondering how she would have dealt with the tragedy unfolding below.

'Right. Nothing. Except perhaps exactly what you are. Overweight. The daughter of some nice aspirational people. With your politically correct education.' The assault had yet to focus, but she knew it would soon grow needle-thin and penetrate. He was aware that her skin had grown thick with scar tissue. 'Do you think for a minute that if that school hadn't been good you would have stayed there? It was a social choice, not a political one. You see nothing, Betsy, because nothing unpleasant has ever happened to you. You had all the support you needed from those parents of yours, and all the company you could want from your sisters, all with their nice, untroubled lives. Your happy, untroubled but oh-so-aspirational family. You've no edge, Betsy, and that doesn't attract people.'

It was one of his bugbears, that posh education of his.

'You can't even *dance*.'

'How long is this going to take?' she asked, one hand propping her up on the bed, the other raised so she could look at her watch. 'It's a long drive.'

'You're not going anywhere.' He rushed forward again. 'I care about you, stupid though that is.' He had raised his hand for effect. She recalled a crack an old girlfriend of his had once made, that he was the sort of man who would throw himself in front of a parked car. 'What are you going to do?' he asked. 'I don't want you to be unhappy. You won't find anyone else. Are you going to start trying to pick people up in bars? In nightclubs? You're horrible to watch on the dance floor – you move like a politician.'

Betsy thought he could do better than that. None the less she had picked her comb off the bed and held it in her fist, forcing the teeth into her palm so that she wouldn't cry.

'Where was I? Oh, yes, your childhood. That logical mind, with your scientific qualifications. That's the thing, isn't it? Those parents, those oh-so-supportive parents, never actually pushed you in any direction that might trigger a sense of creativity, did they? Was that their choice, or did they recognize your lack of creativity as *innate*? I suspect it was the latter. You can count, but you can't feel. Rational, emotionless.'

'I think I'm getting the point.' The teeth of the comb hurt.

'So you'll stop this nonsense?'

When Betsy said nothing, he continued. 'Then you're not getting the point and I'm not making myself clear.' He had started to walk back and forth across the room but now he stopped and pointed at her. 'Let's stick with the impressions. A fuller picture will soon emerge.'

'Look, why don't you just apologize?' said Betsy.

He was sitting beside her at once. 'I already have,' he said. 'But if it helps, I'll do it again. I don't want to hurt you. I just want you to see clearly. But if it helps, I'll say I'm sorry.'

'It would mean we could get out of here.' Betsy looked at him with hope, but saw at once that it had been the wrong thing to say. The waters in the pool of resentment he held inside him boiled up to reveal a bed of hate.

He spoke slowly, though, carefully even: 'I need to make you see clearly right now. It would be too difficult in the car.' He stood up and looked out of the window, then came back. 'Betsy. You work in a laboratory, doing research on animals, in a place that one day will be remembered as a place of horror. And you accept the guff the people in charge feed you, that you're going to do the world a favour by torturing—'

'We don't—'

'You fall for it so much you fuck one of the old cunts – and what about me? Against all reason, I forgive you. I can't believe it even now. Your infidelity, it didn't even have any emotion. But you escape. Your cosy little world survives. Is that what you're planning? To take up with that boss of yours? Do you really think he's going to leave his wife?'

'No.'

He took a breath. 'It's shaming me, what you do, but I don't complain. I put up with all this, I'm even willing to marry you. Christ, it beggars belief right now. I agree to marry you, although your wizened imagination has always fought against my creativity. You even used your embarrassing job as an excuse to stop us moving to London where I could have prospered. I don't want to lay it out on you, but I only put up with this because, well, you're a really very good administrator. That's why you get on in that horrible laboratory of yours. You're like some prison guard. You take others' twisted ideas and make them happen.'

'Oh, please—'

'Betsy. I'm right. You know I'm right. We can start again.'

The comb stung, the teeth deep in her palm.

'If you don't believe me . . . if you really decide to end it, you'll be screwed. This protected little world of yours is going to fall apart. You'll be out there without anyone to go to. Our friends are my friends. You're expendable in your work, there are always other organizers, and imagine if knowledge of that affair spreads.'

'You'd do that?' said Betsy, startled. 'You'd reveal it?'

'I didn't mean that.' He backed off, changing tack. 'Look, Betsy, your dad is ill now. We shouldn't kid ourselves, he's probably dying. I don't think you fully understand what that's going to do to you. You've never experienced anything bad before, but I have, and I know you'll need me to get through it. So, why don't you have a little think about your position in all this? Just think about what it's going to be like, out there alone.' He sat down next to her and put his arm round her waist. 'We've been together a long time, and I've apologized, and I'm willing to forgive you too. I did offer to marry you and I mean it, I really don't want you to be crushed by what you don't know. What do you say?'

God, Betsy thought, the pain. The true, awful horror of it. She could hear the mass of them moving below and she imagined all those people whose friends and relatives were missing out there in the shifting sea. She could see those living rooms to which the loved would never return. She wanted to help in some way, but she knew that the best she could do would be to leave them to their grief. Then she caught her ex's expression – aggressive and worried. She laughed. She wiped her nose with her sleeve because, despite herself, a few tears had escaped. She looked at him sitting next to her, his intense interrogatory smile covering his concern, and laughed again. 'Oh, fuck off,' she said.

He stood up, shocked.

'I want to go. We've a long journey to get through.' She stood up to finish her packing, keeping her back to him, spinning only when she heard the sound of keys, the zip of his bag, the door opening.

His clothes had gone. Betsy threw on a jumper and some jeans and ran barefoot down the stairs and out on to the road. He had reversed, ready to drive off, and Betsy slapped her palm on the bonnet of the car. 'What are you doing?' she shouted through the glass. 'It's my car.'

He wound down the window, about three inches. 'So report me,' he spat, as he accelerated past her. She stood, hopping from one foot to the other on the freezing

43

ground, following the car with her eyes until it turned towards the church. There, her attention was arrested by the wall of the harbour-master's office. The paint had been washed away in the storm and now the advertisement shone out once again, a twenty-foot bottle of alcopop beside the words: 'Any SPort in a Storm.' She stared, her feet coming to rest. Then she became aware that people were watching from the lounge-bar window. She walked back towards the hotel, her head down. Just before she passed under the lintel, she looked up and, as she did, she saw the neighbour's face disappear from view.

She climbed the stairs and tiptoed along the corridor but found, when she reached the door of her room, that she'd locked herself out. She leaned against the wallpaper, head touching the surface, and stared at the ceiling. She tried to breathe through her nose, determined to hold it together until she had some privacy. Yet inaction felt like a refuge. She knew her neighbour was listening at his door to see if she was still there – the walls were so thin they could almost be drapery – and it was this intimacy that finally moved Betsy to action. In other circumstances she would have called on him for help, asked him to go to the bar and get spare keys, but after all his eavesdropping she didn't want his charity. She pushed herself off the wall and slowly, in bare feet, with no makeup, her hair crushed from sleep, her eyes washed red, descended the stairs to approach the bar door. She knew she couldn't hesitate, that if she did she would stand in the hall for ever, so, very quietly, she pushed her way in.

At once she was part of a crush. The room was full of people, warm in weatherbeaten clothes, thick-skinned faces under ragged hair, hands held in pockets, or in front of them, or supporting heavy heads. Smoke layered the ceiling. Weary eyes took in her condition but offered no sympathy. She searched for the landlady, but instead she saw the boat's owner, the man from the pier, standing on a table, his long face grey with exhaustion. 'The seas were terrible,' he was saying. 'It was a miracle they found the life-rafts at all, but when they did there was no one in either of them.' He paused. 'It looks as if the sea opened up and the boat went down. It seems there was no warning. But we shouldn't make any judgements, not until we know more. The Irish coastguard, our own navy, they asked me to say they did everything that was possible.' He stopped, waiting for questions.

'Might it have been a submarine?'

'The navy says there were none operating in the area.' He shrugged. 'We'll have to wait and see.'

'The families?' a woman asked.

'They're together. Which reminds me, we're getting calls from the press. I've no idea how many reporters will arrive, the *Record*'s local man is already here. If you're approached, just remember we need to act as one and protect the families.' When nobody said anything more, he was helped down into the crowd. People appeared confused, unsure what to do, and then one, followed by another, pushed past Betsy to get out into the fresh air. Others gravitated towards the bar. A man Betsy recognized from the night the advertisement aired in the pub spotted her and walked across. 'Where's that man of yours?' It was almost expectoration. 'The advertising wonder-boy? You'd better tell him to get up the road and paint that slogan off the harbour-master's wall, and not use emulsion like a damn fool this time. You tell him to do it at once.'

'He's gone,' Betsy replied, frozen by the aggression. 'He's left.'

The man frowned. 'Well, tell him to get back. Get him—'

The landlady was at her side. 'Go and get a drink, you,' she said to the man, pushing him away.

Betsy turned to her. 'I've locked myself—'

'I thought so.' The landlady showed her a key. She opened the lounge door, and they were through into the hall and the quiet. 'He's a drunk, that one,' she said, gesturing backwards. 'Bitter, but, well . . . I saw what happened outside. Are you all right?'

'It's fine.' Betsy felt immense gratitude. 'It's better for me this way.' There was the beat of their feet. 'The fishermen? They're still missing?'

They were on the stairs, the landlady having to speak over her shoulder. 'Well, yes.' The determination in her voice betrayed desolation. 'The Irish think they've found the boat on the sea floor and our navy found the life-rafts empty. They're still looking but there's not a lot of hope.' She clicked open the door to the room and let Betsy past her. 'It's not working out for anyone these last couple of days.'

'I'll try to get out of here as soon as I can,' said Betsy. 'Is there a bus?'

'Not today. The storm has disrupted everything. I'll be amazed if your . . . if he gets out himself. You should probably rest up too, you know. Don't worry, we'll look after you. I'll keep your room free. There's newspaper people calling – about the boat, you know.'

Betsy gave a weak smile. The landlady's eyes were kind. 'I don't even know your name.'

'It's Martha. Martha McCall.'

'Thank you, Martha.'

The landlady touched her shoulder, then turned to go.

Betsy went in and sat on the end of the bed. Later she lay down and curled up. A little after midday, Martha brought her a bowl of soup and some bread. She told Betsy there was a road open to the west side but the buses weren't running. After she had eaten, Betsy tried to read, and failed. She turned on the television, grew bored and stared at the ceiling. There were shouts from the harbour where men were trying to salvage boats from where the storm had washed them up the sea wall and she pulled up a chair to watch. From around the harbour came the sounds of sawing and hammering. A car pulled up and the locals watched the driver step out and look around. She guessed this was a reporter, and she gazed at her with distaste, feeling for the relatives. The picture window gave her the perfect view out on to the remnants of disaster, and while she found it distracting, Betsy felt the guilt of a voyeur. She thought about asking Martha if anybody was planning to drive out, but quickly realized she was incapable of dealing with strangers just yet. With the manner of her fiancé's departure, the room had become a sanctuary.

The window allowed her an escape. She watched gulls criss-cross the harbour, above the industry of the villagers below. Jackdaws hopped along the drier patches of ground, searching for food. It was as if a jigsaw that had been broken up was gradually being put back together. The journalist, whom Betsy heard coming up and down the stairs, appeared below her at the front door, then wandered along the pier, trying to talk to the men who worked there, receiving polite smiles but, it seemed, no more.

As the afternoon slipped away, Betsy saw Priest lope in across the fields that rose from the far side of the harbour to break around the base of a hill on the horizon. His weighty body might almost have danced as he negotiated the rocks on the shore. He waded out across a stream that spread on to the mud and pebble flats revealed by the falling tide. Despite the temperature he was wearing shorts, and even from across the harbour it was clear that the flesh of his thighs and forearms bulged from his clothes. He disappeared behind the bulk of the outflung church, reappearing at its base, his step delicate and agile for such a big man. Without stopping to survey the damaged yacht, he clambered over the hull, passing in and out of sight, cutting, tying and pulling. Soon he had the two ends of the snapped mast beside the road, with other equipment piled neatly at the side. The reporter picked her way carefully towards the yacht but Priest ignored her. She looked at her feet, then tried to take a step further, calling to him. When she received no reply, she gazed around in bewilderment. Priest crouched, sawing.

Betsy went to the bathroom, and when she returned, she lay on the bed, dazed from lack of sleep. She lay there for maybe forty minutes, rising only when she heard the sound of an engine. A tractor driven by one of the locals was dragging the hull of the once beautiful yacht across the flats and up to the high-tide mark, Priest walking beside it. By the road, Rego was dumping equipment into the back of his Range Rover. There was now a small group of reporters by his side. That night Betsy lay listening to the voices in the bar below. She was disturbed only twice, once when food was brought to her, and again when her ex phoned, a call she hung up on answering. That night, to her surprise, she slept dreamlessly.

48

THURSDAY

High tide: 02.51, 15.12
Light westerly

For the last few days, Betsy had ignored the flawed mirror that hung flush to the bedroom wall. Now she pulled off the shirt she had slept in, and stepped, with a certain regret, into its unflattering light. She had always tried to ignore the appeal of mirrors but her ex-fiancé's attack had necessitated a moment's reflection. The one important relationship of her twenty-eight years was over, and the morning, which had brought strength, also offered the first stirrings of uncertainty. She needed to begin the process of dealing with his criticisms.

Her skin was almost translucent from lack of sun. She winced, reached over to switch off the overhead bulb so that the winter light would flatter her, then started with her feet, their damaged toes, letting her gaze rise. It was easy to see the disappointments, the bad knees, the overly heavy shoulders, but she understood that they were inherited and not her fault. She saw only the faintest bulge to her belly, her bottom was fine. She hated herself for doing this. She tried to remind herself that happiness was

49

no one's responsibility but her own, a lesson learned through eight years of small criticisms, but her gaze sought refuge in the better part of her body, her long neck with its gentle curve up to the base of her skull, a gift from her mother. She also liked her head, although it was rounder than beauty dictated, the autumnal hair with its slight curl, the small, straight nose that took nothing from her big hazel eyes when a smile played there. A tiny crease between her eyebrows that reinforced the suggestion of laughter was a secret source of pleasure that she would occasionally touch, an action she knew people took as self-consciousness. As her gaze fell again she found that she was checking for the little signs that his hands once made on her, marks she had loved. There were none. They had already faded. To hell with him, she thought, she wasn't fat. She knew she wasn't fooling herself: her gaze had been honest. She turned and lifted the still damp towel from the bed and walked into the bathroom.

She bathed and dressed, choosing her clothes carefully, wanting to offer a sober, unfussy appearance, almost as if she were mourning but without causing offence to those dealing with real, unburied ghosts. Wearing a beige shirt and her darkest trousers – her flame red coat was hardly sepulchral but there was nothing she could do about that – she went downstairs. She would see if she could leave and, if she had time, take a walk. Just to be out of the room made her feel stronger. She had dealt with the first of her ex's criticisms, and although there were more to come – the image of her father, ill but not dying, kept sidling into her head – they could wait.

Martha was working on her books in the bar. She looked up and smiled as Betsy came in. There was a burst of laughter and Betsy spotted three reporters having breakfast in an alcove. Martha must have noticed her look of distaste. 'Oh, they're all right,' she said. 'They're just doing their job.' Betsy's silence must have suggested disbelief because Martha added, 'They've been pretty respectful on the whole. And, anyway, it might mean we find out what happened. D'you want breakfast?'

Betsy said coffee would be fine.

'We might be able to get you a lift out later, up to the main road, although I've no idea if the buses are running up there. You're sure you want to get out today?'

'I don't think I'm any help here.'

Martha smiled again. 'Maybe one of the journalists is going back. I'll ask.'

Betsy sipped at the coffee Martha poured for her, then, aware that the landlady was busy, said, 'I'll take this outside. It looks like a nice day.'

It was the first time she had been beyond the inn's door in twenty-four hours, and the chill air cut at her worries. The village was quiet, but for the gentle beat of a distant hammer that reached her on the breeze. Light streamers of cloud spread inland across the vast sky. She set off on to the pier, her mug steaming in the cool air. The pavement had a greenish tinge, and the low-tide stench filled her lungs. She looked along the pretty houses, keeping her gaze from the harbour-master's office wall and its unfortunate slogan. For the first time she felt truly alone, and was overcome with the sensation of being an adult, as fresh as the gusts of sea-breeze. She finished the coffee, dismissing other criticisms that had been lurking in her mind.

She returned the empty mug to the bar, fended off a journalist's approach by telling him she wasn't local, then went back out into the day and set off on a walk up to the promontory. The tragedy that had beset the village magnified her sense of isolation, and at the top of the hill she stopped, ignoring the rocks where he had made the decision to propose. She looked out to sea, to England, Ireland and the Isle of Man, to the horizon, and felt the loneliness stab. Yet her step grew stronger. She had thought of returning to work, using the concentration science required to get her through the emotional difficulties, but that idea now crumbled in the breeze. She grew bolder, setting off along the eastern shore, a thought taking hold. She wasn't about to fool herself, she had her job and her family to fall back on, but looking out across the Solway, at these other kingdoms, she felt that cosseted world he had spoken of break open. The future was all around her, and she could spend the sabbatical she had secreted, in case of a honeymoon, answering his criticisms, taking a journey into the world without his protection. She crossed a channel through which the tide would rise to caress the spine of the village, then picked her way along a track where yellow grass touched the black edge of the shore. She reached a wall of lichen-white rocks, flat stones emerging from its flanks to provide a stile that, once mastered, gave Betsy a fresh joy of discovery: she entered grassland, punctuated by rocky outcrops that rose to peaks of flowered gorse. Closer to the sea these upbursts grew exuberant, the bedrock jagged and raw, the foundations of Scotland exposed here at its end. Under crying seagulls a headland rose, patched with yellow.

Betsy gazed back on to the line of houses that now rested below her, precarious on the spit that narrowed under them before rising away to the white, crenellated lookout. The boats that had survived the storm rested on the mud in the harbour, a green navigation light blinking beyond them on the pierhead. She went on beside a wall, its surface a filigree of lichen and moss and, as she topped the rolling hill, she stared out to the east, up the firth towards the hills of the border country where the coasts of England and Scotland closed in to meet out of sight. The dark hills were white-tipped with snow in the pale sunlight, and Betsy stopped to admire them, nourished by their beauty. Looking back, she found the village had reduced into the landscape. The coast rose to the west, the land rolling around a small hill, then continuing to the edge where it fell in high cliffs to the sea. In the distance she could see a pine plantation seeking protection in the contours from the onshore winds, before strengthening and spreading inland. There was romanticism in such a landscape and Betsy tried to free herself from its grasp, knowing she had problems to think through before she could let her dreams take hold. And yet the logistics of splitting up might not be so difficult: he could move out of her flat while she was away – most of their belongings she had paid for, and were hers. She would be reasonable, generous, even, and it would be all right. She looked down. At her feet, beyond the gorse's arm-thick tendrils, the earth fell away into a fissure, a bay enclosed by cliffs, rocky points providing guano-painted perches for seabirds that now floated up from below to scream at her. Beyond, the twin buoys of lobster-pots rose and fell on a swell that hissed through the rocks.

Betsy walked round the fissure and arrived at a gate in a barbed-wire fence. Fields, enclosed in a network of dykes that led down to the rocky foreshore, lay beyond it, the cliff falling away, only to rise further up; and in the distance, on a horizon, an arch topped a headland, too distant to identify accurately. She hesitated. The fence had been designed to discourage further rambling, but with adventure colouring her blood, she climbed over and followed a stock path down to the foreshore. Here, the rocks lay broken and ruined, green-rimmed pools in the hollows above the waves, while between them, flotsam had collected: pallets, bottles and branches. Gulls rested on every point, rising at her approach. She crossed three fields, one dug up by the hoofs of cattle, negotiating walls by their cracked and broken stiles until she reached another promontory where her route was blocked by a bramble thicket. Forced close to the water's edge, she sent oystercatchers peep-peeping into the air and passed under a sloe so old and thick that it was all but devoid of thorns, its branches reaching inland, twisting and grappling together to form an outstretched claw.

The promontory was a low maze of thorn. Betsy followed one path and then another, only to be forced back by three-inch spikes. At last she chose a route that took her through a gap in a green mossy wall, two pigeons fighting free of the bushes, and then she was into a clearing, ruined sheds half hidden under thorn, a home reclaimed by the land. Despite its maudlin atmosphere, Betsy was looking across a bay that opened out ahead of her, at an immaculate blue and white cottage on the furthest shore. A path led down through the cottage's garden to a jetty that, at this stage of the tide, hung in the empty air. The bay was empty but for a large edifice that sat at its heart, barnacles shading it the same grey as the stones it rested on, yet its outline cut straight lines in the sea beyond. It seemed to be a concrete ark, under threat from the coming flood, and at odds with the vitality of the cottage beyond. Betsy took a step forward. Beyond the cottage, the ground rose into cliffs with the arch she had seen earlier on the horizon, while to her right grew an ancient oak, itself stark against the sky. She decided to sit below the empty branches and rest, then jumped in fright. A figure stood pushed back against the trunk, in a dress the colour of the bark.

'I can't talk to you,' the woman said, in a voice both high and clear. 'I don't mean to be rude but I just can't. I won't.'

Betsy recognized the wife of the fishing-boat's captain, and felt the horror of her intrusion into such grief.

'You write lies,' the woman said. She seemed shocked by her rudeness. 'I don't mean any offence. That's what I've been told. You understand, don't you? Why I can't talk to you?' Her face told of her thoughts, which passed instantly across it.

'I'm not a journalist,' Betsy called back. 'I was on the pier that day, the day your husband, the day the boat . . .' She stopped.

The woman tried to meet Betsy's gaze, but her eyes veered away. 'Why are you here, then?' she asked.

'I'm so sorry,' Betsy said. 'I was taking a walk. I didn't know you lived here, I was admiring your house.'

The woman's head swivelled towards her home. They were some distance apart and yet, as she spoke, her voice needed no volume: it carried easily on the breeze. 'I have to go now,' she said, but didn't move. 'He wasn't my husband. I never wanted that.' Her face, already pale, blanched further. 'He said it was all right that I never wanted that.' She crumpled, curling into herself, and Betsy rushed forward as she balled herself into the base of the trunk, the tears flowing silently, dripping over her nose.

Betsy bent down but the woman was so tightly coiled

that there was nothing to hold and comfort. She waited, watching as this stranger crouched, rocking on her heels, listening to the quiet sobs. When Betsy finally put a hand on her shoulder, the woman was instantly in her arms, head on her chest.

'There's no one,' she said.

Betsy was gazing down to the bay where the sea was creeping up the side of the ark. 'I'm here,' she said at last. The ark's prow lay angled towards them. The woman kept her head close, not speaking for some time, and then, slowly, she lifted away and looked Betsy full in the face for the first time. 'Tell me who you are,' she said.

'I'm Betsy. Betsy Gillander.'

'You were with a man that day. On the pier. Where is he?'

A weariness swept in. 'It doesn't matter,' she said.

The woman gripped at her coat. 'It does matter.'

Betsy studied her eyes, and saw terror lying there, black and shimmering. 'He's gone. To the city.'

'Why?'

Betsy wanted to comfort her but, despite the tragedy that had swept in, she was impossible to lie to. 'He asked me to marry him,' Betsy said. 'And I didn't want to.'

The woman looked away across the bay to the cottage. 'I have to go,' she said, standing up and brushing herself off. She began to walk away, but stopped after five paces. 'Will you be my friend?' she asked. She had wrapped her thin body in her long arms, probably against the cold, but also in resistance to the pain.

'Of course. Of course I will be your friend,' Betsy said.

'They say William was to blame. That it was his fault.'

Betsy was unprepared for this, and could do nothing but stare. 'I'm sure they don't say that,' she said eventually.

'They do.'

Betsy frowned. 'I'll be your friend. I promise.'

A small grateful smile touched the woman's lips, and she walked away along the path. Betsy noticed that a hollow had been formed at the base of the tree with room for two people. There was a rock, flush with the ground, where the markings of a grid had been scratched, half of the squares shaded into a chess or a draughts board. She glanced back at the woman, at her light-footed departure along the shoreline.

Martha was standing outside the inn when Betsy returned, twisting a cigarette in her fingers, taking a puff, twisting it again.

'Last one,' she said, as Betsy reached her. 'I have a theory. When everything goes wrong, give up smoking and none of the bad things will exist any more.' She raised an eyebrow. 'A photographer's going up tonight. He said he'll give you a lift.' She took another puff.

Betsy stood beside her, facing the harbour, hands by her sides, fingers tapping on her thighs. 'Can I help?' she asked. 'Is there anything I can do?'

Martha looked at her, sidelong. 'In your state, probably not.'

'I met a woman on my walk. The partner of the *Albatross*'s captain?' Gently the tide lifted the boats off the mud. She was already troubled by her promise to be a friend. 'She was . . .'

'Upset?'

'Yes, of course, but she seemed a little . . . innocent.'

'Helen,' Martha said, taking a last puff and stubbing out the cigarette.

'I haven't got a lot of reason to go home.' The words

were an escaped thought. 'There's nothing I can do?'

Martha raised her hands in exasperation. 'Who knows? Stick around. It'll mean one less reporter in the inn.' At last she smiled. 'But if you do want to go, be in the bar at six.' She went inside. Betsy heard her tell someone inside that she would only get them a drink if they stopped asking questions.

Betsy was propelled up the precipitous stairs by a surge of purpose, the thick carpet of oranges and reds a blur underfoot. She turned the corner and ran into her neighbour, who was coming the other way.

'Outside,' he said, after they had backed out of close proximity. 'Lovely.' He had outdone her in his sober outfit, a long black coat over his dark suit.

'Yes.' There was no room to pass.

'Bad moment, though. To visit.'

Betsy tried to suggest her need to get past by stepping to the side, but he ignored her.

Instead he leaned against the wall, one arm straight out, head held to one side, giving tilting presence to his shyness. 'Horrible.' Words struggled from him: a slow, staccato delivery that seemed to be scar tissue on a childhood speech impediment, binding his desire for conversation. He dropped his head so that, once again, Betsy could barely see his eyes under the shadow of his eyebrows; his skin was tight and unlined. There was no pleading in his face, no expression at all. She found herself wanting to close the conversation at once.

She pointed. 'I have to . . .'

'Course.' He smiled, but only the ends of his lips moved. 'I'm a . . . a walk. Don't suppose?'

'I've just got back.'

'Ah. Maybe later, then.'

Betsy smiled, and they stood for a moment. At last he backed against the wall and she slipped past.

Betsy moved the chair to the window. There she sat, watching the tide rise slowly up the harbour wall. She imagined the water entombing the ark in the bay, and saw the woman grieving under her tree. She was unable to shake the sense of terror she had seen in those eyes: it coloured the afternoon's chill light. Betsy had felt alone as she walked along the coast, and the woman had said that she, too, was without friends. The easy thing to do would be to leave, to hitchhike out, return home to the complications of the failed relationship. Yet Betsy felt she had tasted clean air during that walk. Her ex had told her that she had never been handed anything difficult by life. Now here it was. All that was required was for her to summon the will. Whichever way she looked at it, she had been asked for help. With a rush of fearful excitement she threw on her coat, ran down the stairs and out into the crisp air.

She retraced her morning's walk, standing once again beside the oak across from the pretty cottage on the other side of the bay. The ark had disappeared under the rippling water; a pair of shelducks floated where it had been. Having measured her own setback against the horror engulfing the woman who lived in the cottage, Betsy had dismissed her personal unhappiness as contemptible. Here was life. Her challenge was to do something useful with it. Her nerves felt as sharp as the air. It was impossible to confront such a landscape and not reject the cynicism with which her ex-fiancé viewed the world. She was capable of helping this woman – or, at least, offering to help her. She followed the path along the shoreline and climbed through the garden to the back door.

A telephone was ringing, and in the distance, she heard a voice raised in argument. Caught by indecision, she took a step back. At last she followed a path to the corner of the cottage. There were bushes, but no route to the front. The voice revealed itself as that of a journalist trying to argue his way in. Her sense of purpose returned, and Betsy ran back to the kitchen door and knocked. The argument quietened, grew desperate, stopped, and then Helen was at the other side of the glass. Her eyes widened when she saw who it was. 'I can't talk to you,' she whispered, through the pane.

Betsy replied in the same manner: 'You said you needed a friend? I want to help. If I can.'

There was a fit of swearing from the side of the house. From the rustling, the man must have snagged in the bushes. Helen's eyes darted towards the noise.

'I can't let anyone in, I've been told.'

A cry of pain was followed by more cursing. The telephone stopped ringing, then started again.

'I just thought . . . if you needed some help?' They were both speaking against the glass, almost conspiratorially. 'You said there was no one, and when you left, I thought if there's anything I could do . . .'

'Oh, please, and I'm the fairy godfather,' interrupted the man. He had made his way through the undergrowth and joined them at the back door. 'Mrs Kerr,' he shouted at the glass, 'this is what I was warning you about – the tabloids, they'll try anything.'

Betsy had confronted the reporter, and met gauging eyes. Laughter lines, momentarily out of use, fell down his face.

'We were not married,' said Helen.

The ringing was getting to Betsy. 'The telephone,' she said.

Helen looked behind her. 'I can't answer it.'

'You should unplug it.'

'But what about—'

'We really don't want to impose,' the man said, pulling a thorn from his hand. 'Sometimes it's easier to talk, though, at a time like this.'

Betsy was appalled. 'Don't drag me down to your level. I'm not one of you. I have nothing to do with you.' She was desperate to explain herself to Helen: 'I'm not a journalist. I have nothing to do with him.'

'Awful,' the reporter said, pretending to be disgusted.

'I was here when the boat went out—'

'Disgraceful,' said the reporter.

Betsy felt her brain push against her skull. She thought of hitting the man – he was the same height as her – but she inhaled instead, filling her lungs with the fresh salt air, bringing back reason. The telephone stopped and she let her lungs empty. She discovered amusement buried in the man's eyes, which sickened her. 'I promise you, I'm not from the media,' she said to Helen. 'I wanted to help, really wanted to help, but this is just . . .' the phone rang again '. . . awful.' She found she was on the verge of crying, Helen looking at her with a startled expression from the other side of the glass. 'I am so, so sorry.'

Her distress seemed to touch the other woman who leaned forward, opened the door and ushered her in. As the door shut, Betsy saw a change on the reporter's face, a look of intense suspicion matched by a lack of humour. A shadow of the horror had touched him.

'I hope you're telling the truth,' he said. Then,

sympathetically, he said to Helen, 'I'm sorry for your loss. I'll be waiting out front, in case you need to talk.' He hesitated. 'I think I'll go the other way.' He began to pick his way back through the garden in the opposite direction from the route by which he had come.

Betsy clenched a fist, pushing her nails into the skin until the mortification subsided. Her threshold for losing control was high; she had extended it over the years into a resilience against showing weakness. She was horrified that she was shuddering in front of this woman who had lost so much. 'I'm sorry,' she said at last. 'I shouldn't have come, but it seemed like the right thing to do.' The telephone was still ringing, and Betsy looked for it in the house beyond.

'The answer-machine,' said Helen, following her gaze. 'It ran out of tape.' The natural light that must normally have defined her face was dimmed by exhaustion and she moved unwillingly towards the kitchen. 'Would you like some tea?' she asked. 'Poor you. Your fiancé.'

'No,' said Betsy. 'Don't . . . please don't worry about that. I just wanted to see if there was anything I could do, but I've made a fool of myself. I certainly didn't come for sympathy.'

The ringing stopped and began again. Helen had been spooning tea into a pot, but her hand stopped midway between the two. 'You didn't want tea?'

'No . . . yes. Tea would be lovely.' Betsy felt like an idiot. 'Perhaps I should go.'

Helen's eyes were on her hand, the spoonful of tea in front of her.

The discomfort began to suffocate Betsy. She needed to take control. She stepped forward and touched Helen's arm. 'Let's have some tea. It's the phone. Do you mind if I hang up?'

Helen shook her head. She picked up the kettle to pour the water, while Betsy lifted the receiver and dropped it back. The ringing started again an instant later. She pulled the jack from the wall. A faint ringing could be heard somewhere within the cottage, but distant enough not to interfere. Helen offered a little smile and gestured to a seat at the kitchen table.

As she sat, Betsy studied the room. The kitchen was thin but ran the length of the building, long windows overlooking the sea, except where the small utility room, an alcove really, opened out on to the garden. The walls were painted white, with the sashes and doors a glowing Mediterranean blue. A range, also blue, stood at one end, handmade cupboards hugging the walls along either side. A polished clutter of shells and fossils had collected along the window-sills, and a telescope pointed out to sea. Pictures of Helen and William were pinned to a board. Betsy saw that these were the only ones: there was no one else.

'That reporter confused me,' Betsy said, as Helen sat down opposite. 'I really didn't want to impose. I just wanted to make sure you were all right before I go home.' She saw that, although there was probably ten years between them, Helen's features had an ageless quality; her fair hair fell to her collar, framing wide-open eyes, high cheekbones and an expression that seemed too open for the weariness it now carried. She had a nervous habit of resting her fingernails on the edge of the table and pressing them into the wood. A thin line ran parallel to the table edge where she sat, growing faint towards the ends, deeper at the centre.

'It's kind of you,' said Helen. 'It can be a little frightening here on my own.' She looked away towards the sea.

The phone continued to ring above them, stopped, then began again. They sat listening until finally Helen spoke. 'When the telephone used to ring, it was always him,' she said. 'We play games when he is away on the sea – would, was away.' Helen looked down at her fingers, and then out to sea again. 'You came along the coast?'

'Yes.'

'We'd play anything, really, often chess – he could play from memory, I'd have a board. But other things too, other games. They fill up my day when he isn't here, little things he'll ask me to discover when he's out there.' She was struggling with her tenses. 'He would hide things and I would have to find them, treats, you know, when he was away, little remembrances of him. And then he would come back.'

'There must be someone you can lean on. When you say there is no one else, you don't really mean it, do you?'

'I shouldn't talk about this. I'm sorry.'

Betsy reached forward and laid a palm on Helen's hand. Her fingers stopped their pressing and her hand sank to the tabletop. 'You should,' said Betsy. 'It's just that I feel like an impostor. You don't know me.'

'There's Mr Rego.' Helen studied the table. 'You may have seen him on the pier that day. He's the owner.'

The 'Mr' jarred, inappropriate under the circumstances. 'But a woman, perhaps?' asked Betsy. 'Who did you talk to when William was away to sea?'

Helen didn't reply for some time. 'I used to go down to the water,' she said, 'the rockpools on the shore and, this sounds silly, talk to the sea, ask it to keep him safe.' Her eyes swung across as she sought Betsy's reaction, and she must have misconstrued the response. 'You think I'm mad but . . .' The telephone reminded her. 'It used to be enough to talk to him. We didn't need anyone else. I try to call his mobile now – he used to keep it on night and day – but a woman's voice says it's turned off and to try again later.' Distress sent a shadow across her face. 'I want to answer the telephone. I can't help myself. I hope for a miracle – that when I lift the receiver it will be him, and he will be fine.' She raised a hand and, trembling, poured the tea. The cloud had passed. 'Would you like a biscuit?' she asked, waving at the worktop where a tin stood on the side.

'No, I'm fine.' Again Betsy placed her hand over Helen's. 'Tell me.'

Helen glanced down and then, for a second time, into Betsy's eyes. 'You *were* on the pier that day, weren't you?'

'Yes.'

'Well, the last time I answered the telephone a man screamed at me. He said William was a murderer.'

'No.' Betsy recoiled. 'Surely not. It's surely reporters calling.'

'I don't want William to stay out there in the sea.' Helen spoke in a rush, failing to hold back her tears. 'I want him to come back. I want him here with me.' The flesh on the back of her hand felt cool and soft. 'If he was here with me, I could at least visit him. Bury him under the oak tree. Lay flowers.' She was gazing wide-eyed at Betsy, tears running freely down her face. Sympathy was not going to be enough. Betsy had no idea how to comfort her. She had misjudged. It was a shock to hear a sudden knock at the front door.

'Ignore it,' Betsy said, 'unless you're expecting anyone.'

They sat, holding hands, as the banging grew louder. And then the visitor shouted, 'Helen, it's James, open up.'

Helen pushed her hair off her face as she stood up, then

disappeared to the front door. As Betsy waited for her to return, she felt a desperate urge to be gone. The embarrassment of her disastrous entrance had faded, but the newcomer would pitch all into confusion again. Helen came back with Rego behind her. 'You're not answering your telephone,' he was saying. 'I had to drive all the way over here.' He stopped on seeing Betsy.

She stood, and extended a hand. 'Hi, I'm Betsy Gillander.' She kept her hand outstretched, but her smile slipped.

'Betsy Gillander?' He ignored her hand, but kept looking at her. 'Really? Betsy Gillander?'

'Yes.'

'And what are you doing here?'

'Well, it's a long story—'

'You're a reporter?' he interrupted. He appeared, if anything, more tired than when she had last seen him. His thick hair fell back over his head exposing an expanse of his forehead, which had lined with his question. His skin was as grey as the dykes at the sea-edge, darkening under eyes that now watched her from an angle, his head turned slightly towards Helen, half profiling his heavy jaw. He was tall, and he stooped, having ducked to come through the door.

'No,' said Betsy. 'I'm not a reporter.'

He took her hand, fingers wrapping around hers. 'You know this lady, Helen?'

Helen was busy getting another mug, clearly nervous with Rego. 'She's my friend.'

'You've met her before?' He looked back at Betsy. 'You'll excuse me for asking?'

'Yes,' Helen replied.

Rego's face relaxed.

'We met this morning.'

Rego turned swiftly back to Betsy. 'I don't understand. What do you want?'

'I was walking this morning . . . and I came across Helen . . . and I thought I might be able to . . . help?'

'Betsy was on the pier the day the *Albatross* sailed,' Helen added quickly. 'You were there too.'

Rego observed one and then the other and, although Betsy was nervous, there was something in his stance that filled the room and settled her. He had the easy authority that some men carried, an assumption of control she would normally have resented, but here, in these circumstances, it seemed almost comforting. The reassurance shattered when he spoke again, his words tainted with disgust: 'You're being helpful? Are you religious?'

'No. No, I met Helen by chance and she asked if—'

'Betsy's been very kind,' said Helen.

For a moment Rego said nothing. 'And you're not a reporter?'

'No.'

'You can prove that? You can prove who you say you are?'

Betsy was still wearing her red coat. She reached into the pocket for her wallet and handed him her laboratory pass. Rego examined it, repeating her name under his breath. 'You're a scientist?' he asked, picking up the phone.

'A researcher.'

Rego, momentarily confused by the lack of a dial-tone, followed the wire with his eyes, then reached over to plug in the jack. There must have been someone at the other end because he tapped the cut-off until he had the noise he wanted. He dialled the number of Betsy's office and asked the receptionist if she worked there. When he had put down the receiver and pulled the jack from the wall, he asked, 'You're on holiday?' the distaste returning.

Betsy was about to say again that she was only trying to help but Helen had handed Rego a mug of tea, which took his attention.

'You don't have coffee?'

'Sorry.' Helen was flustered.

He put a hand on her shoulder. 'No matter.' He sipped and put the mug to one side, suspicion still lacing his eyes. 'How're you coping?' he asked Helen.

She shrugged and tried to smile.

'There are a few details we need to talk over, about what's going to happen. It might be better if we discuss them in private. Shall we go next door?' Rego offered Betsy a watery smile. 'You don't mind, I hope?'

'Of course not.'

Once they had gone, Betsy moved slowly along the length of the worktops. She didn't blame Rego for his suspicions and felt no resentment at her treatment; if the circumstances had been reversed, she would have behaved in the same way. She just felt out of place.

As she waited she noticed the love that had been put into the handmade units, the subtleties in the design. Drawers ran easily, opened by handholds cut in the wood, sanded down to avoid sharp edges. She could see the man in the photograph at work here, investing his love in the workmanship to get Helen through the days when he was away at sea. The wooden floor had been polished and worn by years of traffic, and she saw their life together in those steps. All was spotlessly clean. Each shell, rock or piece of wood on the ledge was carefully placed and significant. The tragedy of Helen's loss was on every surface, a shared life broken. Faced with this savagery, Betsy saw how paltry her own unhappiness was. Death now tortured Helen within her own home, a place designed to be a sanctuary from real life. As this refuge closed around Betsy, she began to believe, again, that she could be of use, assuaging some amorphous feelings of guilt that had taken root. She waited with her arms wrapped round herself.

There was another knock at the front door and she heard Rego emerge from a side room to answer it, then step outside to talk. Helen returned to the kitchen and gave Betsy a small, tired smile before she emptied Rego's still full mug and placed it in the sink.

'It's the policeman,' Rego said, reappearing. 'He'll stand out front and make sure the reporters don't bother you. It'll let you get some rest.' He looked at Betsy. 'You're staying at the inn? I'll give you a lift back. Helen could use a rest.'

Helen gave her a shy smile of affirmation. 'Should I drop by again?' Betsy asked.

'Yes, I'd like that,' Helen replied. 'Perhaps tomorrow?'

Betsy moved forward and awkwardly kissed her cheek.

Leaving the cottage, Betsy climbed into the passenger seat of the Range Rover, its cream leather soft to the touch, immaculate. The afternoon had passed and the sun had slipped away leaving a trace of red in the west. She saw the front of Helen's cottage, the pretty face it offered. It sat on a bend in the single-track road, where two reporters now stood smoking and talking to the uniformed policeman. Rego started the engine, and pulled up alongside them. 'There won't be anything out of here tonight,' he said. Betsy caught the eye of the reporter she had argued with earlier, and he nodded back, friendly enough. The other tried to ask a question but Rego accelerated away, the headlights reflecting off their parked cars. As the Range Rover topped a small rise, a shimmer of the day still showed on the distant waters, the village below illuminated in the last reflection. The warm interior of the car smelt of soap.

'So you're planning to stick around?' Rego asked. He drove with one hand on the wheel, the other lying in the well.

'If it's helpful,' Betsy said.

Rego offered no opinion on this. Instead he switched on the news. A presenter recounted the loss of the *Albatross*, saying an Irish navy vessel now maintained a position above the wreck. There seemed to be confusion over responsibility, as the boat lay deep, at three hundred feet, on the line where British and Irish waters met and there was the suggestion that the boat's captain might have been to blame for the disaster. Betsy looked over a newly moonlit field, to the rocky foreshore and the sea below. She found it calming to gaze out over the water, the moon sliding cold light from the east while the western horizon reflected the last of the sun. She was exhausted and desperate to pee, and decided not to ask about the blame that was attaching itself to William Kerr. The presenter turned his attention to the animal epidemic in the south.

The Range Rover slowed as it passed houses and Betsy let the strobe of the windows lull her further, the lights and televisions warm beyond the glass. They pulled up outside the inn.

'Helen filled me in on how you've broken off your engagement,' Rego said, switching off the news. 'I'm sorry to hear that.'

Betsy said nothing.

'Funny place to find yourself, under the circumstances. You're sure you're not just putting off the inevitable by not going back now?'

The nose of the car was out over the harbour. 'Your yacht,' Betsy said, indicating the wreck lying on its side in the yellow light of a street-lamp.

'A shame . . .' He spoke softly.

She looked over at him. 'I'd better go.' Her bladder burned. 'Thanks for the lift.'

'. . . but with the *Albatross* gone, I can't worry about that.' He turned in his seat. 'Are you sure you should be sticking around? Nobody would expect you to, and I think I can make sure Helen's okay.'

Betsy felt confident in her plans now. 'It seems like the most useful thing I can do right now.' She shifted on the leather seat. She needed to go, but she also needed to ask. 'She said some people are blaming her.'

'She said that?' Rego leaned forward to rest on the steering-wheel. 'I wouldn't worry about it. There's some blood running in the village. Some details of the accident have got people itchy, but I'll sort it out.' His breath smeared the windscreen. 'It's a bad business. I'm hoping to keep it sensible, considerate, at least until the reporters are out of here.' His face rose so that he could see the inn's sign. 'There is one thing you might be able to help with. There's a man staying in that room up there. I think his name is Boyle. Have you met him yet?'

'Briefly. I don't know anything about him.' The pain in her belly was now sharp. 'I'd really better go.'

Rego picked up a cloth wedged below the windscreen and rubbed at the condensation. 'I think maybe he is a reporter.' He checked the cloth for dirt.

71

'He arrived the night the *Albatross* left,' Betsy said, 'so it seems unlikely . . .'

'That's what makes me wonder.' He thought for a moment. 'He's asking questions. What do you make of him?'

'I really don't know. Strange, perhaps.' She felt uncomfortable with this.

'You've got no connection with him?' His attention enveloped her, a sudden stare, and she was glad she didn't have to lie.

'No.'

He stepped out of the car and walked round to open her door. 'I'm sorry to ask,' he said. 'It's just so important to know what's going on.'

Betsy's bladder almost stopped her getting out. 'What is it you think he's looking for?' she asked.

'I have no idea, but if you happen to find out, let me know.' He closed the door behind her. 'The way things are moving, what they're saying about William, I worry about people making too swift conclusions. Most of all I worry about Helen. In many ways I have a responsibility. And he worries me.' To her surprise he leaned down and kissed her, but he also whispered in her ear, 'As do you,' before backing off to look her in the eye. 'But I'm hoping you're telling the truth.' He smiled again, a little distant. 'If you are, then thanks for all you're doing for Helen.'

'It's not a problem.'

The cattle shift, turning to look at me as I ease their aching udders. Their bodies are thin, wasted from their generosity. Their lines are Cutter's lines, but I know their forebears, every one of them. The best give everything, the udders bloated pink fountains, so full the blood tunnels along the edges of the mass of flesh. As they move off, I tell them it is all right. When I leave, it is quiet, the moon rising above the house. I go into the forest with a soft touch, leaving no marks, drains washing away the traces of my passing. The wild animals are respectful, if they hear me at all. At home, rendered meat hangs from the frames, but no foxes have been drawn to the scent. All is quiet.

Betsy lay in her bath, letting the water ease the strain of the day. She was disconcerted by how inured against her troubles she felt, and wondered if she was in shock. Rego's surprise and suspicion on seeing her, and the farce outside the back door of the cottage, which even now made her tremble with embarrassment, had wiped her ex from her mind. She felt useful. There was plenty to worry her – the blame being attached and the lack of support – but Rego seemed so in control that Betsy could concentrate on offering emotional support. She relaxed in a cloud of scented steam that faded out the bathroom's tired yellow interior, and thought of the beauty of the walk that had taken her to Helen's cottage that morning, so different from the walks she had taken with her ex-fiancé several days before. The memory took her from this new world, and she saw the inevitable confrontations that waited at home. They were distant. She had missed the chance of a lift out and, if she hadn't been stranded without a car, she might have chosen to seek out another place, without the veil of tragedy hanging over it. But not now. At last she felt optimistic, taken from herself by a sense of purpose. Fear would come later, in sleep, with dreams of that strange, vast man climbing the harbour wall.

The reporter she had met outside Helen's cottage

approached her as she ate in the bar that night. He introduced himself as Euan and they spoke briefly, but long enough for Betsy to reassure him that he hadn't been blind-sided by a less-principled competitor. He tried to keep the conversation going but she demurred and slipped into a corner with her plate and a magazine; she had told Martha she would honour the original booking and stay for two more days. The food had improved dramatically, with fresh queenies landed earlier that day by Manx fishermen. Boyle was in the public bar, talking to the man Martha had called Bunbury. He was receiving little response, the crippled man's monosyllabic answers matched with a roving, disdainful scrutiny of the figure Boyle cut. Sometimes, when Betsy's eyes rose, she saw Boyle looking back at her across the bartops. She finished quickly and returned to her room.

She failed to read. Television was of no use either. The drink she'd had in the bar had triggered a taste for alcohol, but she couldn't face talking to the journalists, and didn't want to be seen doing so. Instead, she took her place at the window, watching the lights reflecting on the mudflats until a knock disturbed her. She wondered whether to ignore it, but there was another rap, nervous. 'Yes?' She sighed.

'Neighbour. Sorry, intrusion.'

'Yes.'

'Wondered if.' He was speaking to the veneer. 'If you're all right. I suppose.'

Betsy was about to say she was fine, but reconsidered. She walked across the room and opened the door. Boyle was standing awkwardly, holding a bottle of wine, which he now lifted. 'I'm fine,' Betsy said.

'Perhaps, drink?'

Oh, Jesus, Betsy thought. 'I'm . . .' She recalled Rego's question. 'Okay, why not? The residents' lounge?'

'Newspaper people.'

Betsy said nothing.

'My room?' He pointed back down the corridor.

'Your room?' Betsy felt exhausted.

'Convenience. I don't . . .' He lifted his hand as if unsure.

Betsy laughed. 'No, of course not. A drink. Why not? I'll be a minute.' She lifted a finger. 'A minute.' She closed the door. Returning to the window, she pressed her forehead against the pane. She needed to rest. Even the walk had been longer than she was used to and, now that she was standing, she realized she still felt cold, chilled by the shock of the break-up, her life adrift. She faced a choice, increasingly stark, of immersing herself in her surroundings, of helping Rego find out who this man was or of heading home. Betsy knew she wanted to go on here. She sensed that in this place there was protection from, and answers to, her ex-fiancé's criticisms. And so, although the idea of going into the next room deflated her, she felt the reward, her ability to give Rego something he needed and therefore be useful, was worth the effort. Her head rolled on the glass and she found herself looking along the harbour at the slogan on the harbour-master's office wall. Sorrow pushed her upright and she went to the door. At least it was his room and not hers: she could run away.

He answered her knock at once and ushered her in. The room was similar to her own, its gaudy curtains and carpets smelling of cleaning fluid and long-stale tobacco. The bottle of wine stood open on the sideboard, two glasses beside it. Her neighbour poured and handed her a glass. 'Best they've got,' he said.

Betsy sipped it. 'It seems lovely,' she said. 'I try not to drink expensive wine. I'm worried I might get a taste for it.'

He offered her a seat at the end of the bed, while he concertinaed into a chair near the window, his arm resting on a tabletop. Then, with a struggle, he pulled himself to his feet again, pushing one hand out towards her. 'Henry Boyle,' he said.

'Yes.' Betsy shook the hand.

'You know?' The difficulty he had in speaking allowed him no change in tone but Betsy knew she had unsettled him.

'I must have overheard it, maybe on the day you checked in.'

'I didn't think I told anyone.'

'You did, you told Martha. Anyway, it's nice to meet you, Henry. I'm Betsy – Betsy Gillander.' She remembered her ex-fiancé's criticism. 'It's a silly name.' At once she felt this was a stupid thing to say and found herself countering her own words as he sat down: 'Although I'm sensible.' She needed to shut up, and looked round the room, her gaze falling on a glass box that contained a stick of crystal, thick at one end, then splitting into smaller branches so that it seemed like a diamond glove. It sparkled brilliantly, even in the dull hotel lights. He had followed her gaze.

'Salt,' he said. 'Dead branch left in a salt mine, air crystallizes and . . .' He pointed.

'Beautiful. Where did you get it?'

He said nothing. Betsy noticed that his air of nervousness had disappeared. 'Get you anything?' he asked.

She took a sip of her wine. 'I'm fine,' she said. 'So, what brings you here?'

Boyle had slung one of his long legs over the other and

now scratched at the black hair that peppered his ankle. He looked up. 'Work.'

'And what's that?'

'Insurance.'

'You must be very good at it, I mean, to get here before the storm.'

He laughed and the sound, although it emerged and disappeared in an instant, seemed genuine and warm. 'Pensions. Life assurance. Boring.' He scratched again at his ankle, this time harder, and then viciously before suddenly relaxing. 'Saw you downstairs, surrounded by reporters.'

'Yes.' Betsy felt on edge. 'You were talking to that man with the damaged hand.'

'Terrible,' he said.

Betsy gazed at him.

'All devastated,' he said. 'By this.' He pointed out towards the harbour.

Betsy smiled and nodded. Perhaps he was a journalist.

'As you'd expect.' She took a sip of wine. 'So you're from?'

'Leeds.'

'And you're here selling life assurance?'

Again he failed to answer. When he lifted his face to drink, his pupils reflected light, but they were otherwise invisible. 'That fat man. Did you see him? Rowed to the yacht? In the storm?'

'No,' she said. 'Who's that?'

For an instant she thought he might be irritated by the lie, but he had an ability to cover his thoughts. 'Wondered if you knew,' he said. The lie seemed to have distracted him. It was difficult to tell, but she thought he might be looking at her breasts.

'So, this insurance?' she said.

'Complicated,' he repeated. 'Bad business. Bad timing. The owner. James Rego. What do you make of him?'

'Do I know him?'

'You were in his car.'

Betsy didn't respond, just looked back at this man, whose nervousness, his one readable emotion, disappeared with a smile. Next door, in her room, the telephone rang and she stood up. 'You're a journalist.'

'No.'

Betsy put down her glass. 'My telephone,' she said. 'Thanks for the drink.' She pushed the chair out of the way, walked to the door and let herself out. The phone was still ringing when she reached her room and she lifted the receiver, then dropped it back. Then, like so many others in the village, she pulled the wire from the wall and lay down on her bed in an effort at sleep.

FRIDAY

High tide: 03.31, 15.58
Stiff north-easterly

Betsy rested on a stanchion at the end of the pier, gazing out over the sea, the coast shadowed by the early sun. Off the promontory, a half-moon was slowly paling to nothing in the crisp sky. The tide was close to full ebb, sandbanks showing in the channel that led out from the base of the harbour wall, gulls taking advantage of the rare occurrence to hunt down creatures caught in the open. The sea reflected a twinkling, shattered light. In a better climate it would have been welcoming, but the icy wind reminded Betsy of where she was.

Although exhausted by the previous day, she had not slept; the night had left her tense. It had been impossible to be rational at three in the morning when half-opened eyes see nothing but the flash of the pier lamp. She had yearned for sleep, and then for dawn, and as the darkness turned to grey, she had finally relaxed, comforted by the thought that her anxiety had been for the future, not the past.

She had called her parents at seven, the traces of the night leaving the need for some familial understanding, but she should have known better. She found herself recalling a scene in a bad movie where a wounded soldier screams for his mother, knowing her own cry had been equally forlorn. Apparently her ex-fiancé had been in touch, and had convinced her mother that Betsy had suffered a breakdown. His theory was that the sinking of the *Albatross* had triggered some impulse that had caused her to discard an opportunity for happiness. Her mother searched for Betsy's error, probing with a blunt lecture on responsibility. 'Charity begins in public,' she said. 'Right now your responsibility is to yourself.' In the end Betsy had been forced to break the stream of unsettling advice by lying: she had grown tired of supporting the ex, she said. This news cheered her mother long enough to get her off the phone, but not before she'd suggested Betsy return to Edinburgh and face her responsibilities. There had been no offer of sanctuary in the family home in Glasgow, but there had been a brief conversation with her father – 'Are you coming to visit?' 'No, Dad.' 'So you're on your way, then?' – before she had rung off. Now she had made up her mind to stay where she was, at least until she was due back at work the following Monday. She was still thinking about her mother's need to see the worst in her decisions when she heard someone on the pier behind her. She chose not to turn.

She recalled the steps from sitting in her room and hearing the pacing next door, the hesitation and sudden advance, as if he walked in time to his thoughts. Refusing to acknowledge his approach, she allowed her eyes to lose their focus so the sparkle on the sea grew blurred.

'Sorry. Upset you. Last night.'

Her gaze sharpened, a gull wing-tipped the small waves before rising and crying out.

'Not a reporter, whatever you think. It . . .' She heard him shift. 'It is complicated.'

At last Betsy looked round, up at Boyle's long neck, his smooth features. 'You didn't upset me. The phone rang. If you say you're not a journalist that's fine.' She stood. 'I really don't care.' She walked back along the pier, hoping he wouldn't follow.

He spoke behind her. 'Came across badly. Wanted to . . . to be sure you were all right, with your man . . . leaving, you know.' The voice trailed away, but Betsy had stopped.

'I don't know you,' she said. 'Not at all.' Somehow he had been there in the background during this whole hellish experience. 'If you want to do me a favour, leave me alone.' She walked fast now, preferring not to see what he would do.

She ducked through the inn door and returned to her room where she lay down, letting the loneliness lie heavily across her. Remaining there meant a loss of the necessary activity that filled a day, and as the morning passed, she thought about taking a walk, perhaps to look for the cave her ex-fiancé had wanted to see. But the idea exhausted her and she didn't move. Instead she found herself thinking of her flat in Edinburgh, with its small and comfortable rooms painted in earthy colours that offered warmth through the harsh winters. She tried to imagine it without her ex-fiancé, which both saddened and thrilled her. Having never before experienced the breakdown of a serious relationship, she tried to see the sequence, the steps they would have to take. He would be sitting there now, filled with resentment. Or perhaps he had already begun his trawl for someone else to look after him. She knew he had spent the fee from the advert, and would be worried about money. Again she felt the sting of his criticisms. She didn't think to question them: she was aware that even a prick can make a point.

By chance she glanced into the mirror, and was shocked by her appearance. The energy that brought a freshness to her face had diminished, and she searched for a premonition of the future, looking for signs she had always vowed to ignore. She had to remind herself of her disdain for such insecurities. She thought again of pricks, and went in search of the journalist, Euan.

It didn't take long to find him. He was in the lounge, standing at the bar with a photographer, while one of Martha's assistants, a woman with tied-back red hair and a small, unamused smile, listened to his stories. Betsy looked down at the half-pint of beer and shot of whisky resting on the bar in front of him. 'You're not worried you might be a cliché?' she asked.

He offered a slow smile. 'I save my originality for my writing.'

'And his genius for the expenses,' said the photographer.

'Now, that was hackneyed,' said Euan. 'You want a drink?' he asked Betsy.

'A glass of water, please.' The barmaid poured it, then used Betsy's arrival to escape, heading for the kitchen. Betsy watched her go. 'I need a bit of advice,' she said. 'If you wanted to find out about someone how would you go about it?' She tried to avoid his grin. Light entered the bar through the picture windows, only to be absorbed by the dark interior. She had let the morning pass, but hadn't realized it was quite so late: the day was at its most lethargic.

'I told you,' Euan said to the photographer. 'Wait in the bar and the story comes to you.'

'Snaps don't, though.'

'So, who is it you want to find out about?' Euan asked.

'I'm just looking for some advice on how to go about it.'

'Well,' Euan said, as if prepared to play a game he had already won, 'if I was trying to find out about somebody, the first thing I would do would be to put their name in my computer and see if it came up in any newspaper articles published back to the eighties. But you can't do that. Unless you give me a name.'

Once in a while the laboratory where Betsy worked fell under media scrutiny, and she had attended a media training seminar. 'Smile,' she recalled the man saying. 'Smile and say nothing.' Betsy brightened. Euan continued to grin back at her.

The stand-off lasted only a short time. 'Is there another way?' she asked sourly.

'I'm hurt. I'd thought we'd already reached a level of trust.'

Betsy sighed. 'Henry Boyle.'

Euan lifted his glass off his notepad and flicked it open. 'How are you spelling Boyle?'

'I doubt it's like the growth, although it would suit him.'

'B-o-y-l-e, then.' He wrote it down. 'But I'll check a couple of spellings, and see what the system comes up with. So, what has Henry Boyle got to do with it all?'

Alcohol had burnt the flesh off his cheeks but Betsy saw no regret there, just plenty of life. 'I don't know,' she said. 'Nothing probably. He's that odd, gaunt bloke who's staying here, you know the one . . .'

'Who. Speaks. Like. This. Yes.'

'I think he might be a reporter.' She was now looking towards the door, worried he might appear.

'Why should I help you find that out?'

Betsy drank her water. 'You wouldn't want your story stolen by someone using subterfuge, would you?'

'Oh, please. That's a rubbish reason. What'll you give me?' Euan must have understood Betsy's expression because he sucked his teeth. 'Okay, I'll think about it. Maybe he is a reporter, or maybe he's just a freak. They turn up to things like this, tragedy junkies, you know. You should have seen what it was like in Albania before the Serbs withdrew from Kosovo.'

The photographer stepped away from the bar, picking up the camera-bag beside his feet. 'I think I'll go and get a picture,' he said.

'I'd better be going too,' Betsy said.

Euan looked unhappily at his drinks, then poured the whisky into the beer and swallowed the mixture, landed the glass on the bar and picked up his notepad, all in one long, smooth move. 'I suppose I'll have to come too.' He caught the disgust on their faces. 'What?' he said.

The photographer just shook his head.

The afternoon was slipping away by the time Betsy arrived at Helen's cottage, the sun setting behind her as she trudged along the darkening road that Rego had driven the night before. The press had gone from the gate, and the policeman dozed in his car. He emerged with a mug in his hand, greeting Betsy and walking her to the door. When Helen answered, he handed her the mug, and said that since she had company he might pack it in for the evening, then told her to call if there was a problem.

Once they were in the kitchen, Helen moved around with her head down so as not to show her face, wear visible on the soft skin. She spoke in bursts, about the way she had spent her day. 'I was going to put William's things away,' she said. 'Somewhere safe.' She searched for something on the window-ledge. 'But then I thought I would like to keep those things there.' Her eyes rose. 'Do you think that is a mistake?'

Betsy was looking out of the window, seeing a shadow on the water, the tip of the ark's prow. 'They are your things too.'

'He always complained that I cleaned his things too much. That I would wear them away. It's one of the things I remember when I look at them, that and where he found them.' She lifted a badge from the window-sill, a diving pelican with some Spanish name inscribed below. 'He used to say that being remembered was life after death. When I worried about accidents, he would say that we would never actually leave each other, that it's impossible to forget someone you truly love.' Helen laid the badge down. 'I thought I would put them away for safe-keeping. I didn't in the end. Do you want to know what I did do?'

'What's that?' said Betsy.

'I cleaned them.'

Betsy smiled.

'Would you like tea?'

'No. Perhaps a glass of water. Let me get it myself.' She poured water from the tap into a glass, still looking out across the bay. 'Helen? What's that thing in the bay?' she asked. 'The stone boat?'

Helen came over to stand by the window, but there was little to see now. 'It was something to do with the

85

military,' she said. 'During the war they made these float-ing harbours so that they could invade France. They practised here because the tides are so big, and they thought no one would notice, we're so far away from the world. They made them out of concrete because there was no metal. That one sank.'

'Not very surprising if it was concrete.'

'It must have worked, though. They won the war. The camp used to be in the bushes behind the tree, but most of it's gone now. There is still a big base over the other side of the village, a firing range.' She hesitated. 'I don't like all the military things.'

The tip of the ark had disappeared into the night and they fell silent. When Betsy spoke, she kept her voice low. 'It's not really my place to say, but you really shouldn't put anything away, not until . . . you know . . . for sure.'

Helen frowned. It seemed an unusual expression for her face. 'But I do know.'

Betsy misunderstood, thinking Helen meant that with fishing accidents the body would often never be found, that families would just have to believe they knew. She took Helen's hand, squeezing.

'They talked to me,' Helen said. 'The divers. A man called Oliver Finlay. He said they found Jim Orr on deck. Tied on, of course.'

Betsy's hand froze, eyes wide.

'He said that the diver didn't see anyone else, because he can't get into the boat yet.' Her face lost its composure. 'But I hope William's there. The life-rafts were empty. The sea is so cold. I know he's dead, and if he's there then maybe I'll get him back.' Helen let Betsy take her other hand. 'I wrote a letter today.' She was now speaking to Betsy's neck. 'To the council, asking if I could bury him

86

under the oak tree, if they find him. I was wondering if you would post it for me.'

'Of course,' Betsy whispered.

'I don't want to be any trouble.'

'Don't be silly, that's no trouble.'

Helen apologized, wiping at her face. 'We should go into the lounge,' she said. 'It's better there. I'd like to play a game. Would you play a board game with me? It takes my mind off everything.'

'If you like.'

'Very much,' said Helen, quickly moving down the corridor, turning through a door. 'I would like that very much.'

'I'm afraid I'm not very good at chess,' Betsy said, as she followed. She knew she shouldn't have been surprised by the living room, but she was. Despite the darkness beyond the window, it was dazzling, as bright and fresh as a villa she had once rented on an island off Greece. The walls were white above a varnished floor, the furniture handmade and then stained, but it was the upholstery that caught the eye. It was fresh in primary colours, the contrast forced by equally vibrant cushions. The paintings on the walls showed boats under clear skies. Lamps flooded the room with light and Betsy blinked. Helen adjusted a dimmer switch, which thankfully muted the effect. Betsy could tell she was waiting for a reaction.

She went with her original impression. 'It reminds me of being in the Mediterranean.' What she didn't say was that it was the sort of look she might want, for a week or two, in a very hot place. To have it all the time, in Scotland, would drive her mad. There was a sofa in the middle of the room, facing a yellow-tiled fireplace, a flat, oiled-beech coffee-table between them. An armchair, draped in

87

a fire-red blanket, stood by its side. An elderly television with a silver façade sat in the corner. Books and trinkets, the only darkening influence, were lined along low-level shelves made from bricks and scaffolding planks, which had been painted to match the blanket.

'I like things to be fresh,' Helen said. 'I hate mouldy colours, and it's so wet around here, everything can seem mouldy.' She stood at the coffee-table and pointed, with both hands, to a corner of the sofa. 'You sit there.'

Betsy was still taking in the room. As in the kitchen, the photographs were all of Helen and William. 'The furniture?' she asked. 'Did William make it? It's beautifully done.'

'His father was a carpenter.' She checked to see if Betsy was interested. 'That's how William started out, they were on the Clyde, in the shipyards. I don't think he liked it – too political. Although he believed in kindness and hated people being used, he fell out with the union. He liked to go his own way, but the jobs went anyway.' Helen curled up in the other corner of the sofa, slipping out of her shoes so that she could pull her legs under her. 'He came down here to build boats, but there wasn't much call for it. Fishing is in such difficulties, and we're so far off the tourist trail.' She leaned across and touched Betsy's knee. 'My little secret is that I'm not very good at chess either – it's all that planning ahead – but I love watching great players play and William was a great player.'

'You lost against him?'

'Sometimes. He said I was unpredictable, but he let me win, now and again, through the years.' These thoughts swept a shadow across her face that came and went like the passing of a bird across the ground. 'But I was always the best at Chinese checkers.' She reached forward to a shelf in the coffee-table and pulled out a box. Opening it, she laid out the board and placed counters across the star design. 'He never beat me at this.'

Betsy watched as Helen set up the board, her expression one of absolute concentration. There were questions that troubled Betsy, about the arrangements that Helen would have to make for the future, but evidently her companion didn't want to think about what was to come, or even what had happened. The shadows that passed over Helen's face were heartbreaking to see, so Betsy kept her questions to herself, letting time flow easily for this woman who wanted to escape decisions. She listened as the rules of the game were explained.

They played for an hour, with Helen showing Betsy the moves she was missing, her long fingers picking up pieces and sending them leaping across the board. There was no time-lapse in her game, her mind instant and apparently infallible. Betsy tired, but Helen seemed content just to win and win again, and at last Betsy was forced to ask if she wanted to eat.

Embarrassed, but also unwilling to leave the game behind, Helen carried the board through to the kitchen. She opened several cupboards and looked hopelessly at the contents. Finally Betsy asked if she could help. There was some dried pasta, tinned tomatoes, a couple of old onions. Against faltering resistance, Betsy put together a meal. All the while they continued to play.

As they talked, Betsy began to understand what an accompaniment to life these games had been. It seemed that William had patiently matched her, maintaining interest by changing only the game itself. Betsy saw love behind his patience: Helen's focus offered her pleasure, not because of the winning, although she was competitive, but rather as a distraction from her life. She wondered if he had played against her with the same interest, or whether he just enjoyed watching her move and think, for, as Betsy now realized, there was something calming about standing opposite such an intent creature with her flying hands.

They ate, then remained in the kitchen, falling silent, moving pieces. Occasionally Helen would correct a mistake Betsy had made, or express surprise at an outcome, but otherwise they allowed time to pass. It was getting late and Betsy knew that when she slept, she would again be troubled by the memory of the man climbing the pier. 'Do you know anything about Priest?' she asked.

Helen's eyes showed nothing; she concentrated on the board. 'He lives on the other side of the village,' she said. 'Close to the army range.'

'He's strange.' It was Betsy's move but she stayed still, hoping Helen would go on.

'He's an unhappy man.'

'Unhappy?'

'William said it's not his fault.' She had looked up.

'What's not his fault?'

'That he's frightening. He lives in the woods.' She added, in a fast flow, 'Like an animal.' Her attention fell to the board. 'It's your turn.'

'The woods?'

'William hated gossip.'

Helen's discomfort stopped Betsy asking more.

An hour later Helen offered her a bed for the night and, glad not to have to walk back to the village in the dark, she accepted. There were two single beds in the spare room. In many ways the decoration – the wallpaper was

90

striped blue and white, with matching curtains and colourful bedclothes – should have been as shocking as before, but Betsy was growing used to such vibrancy. She lay still until the sound of Helen moving across the floorboards in the next room died away and only the sea remained. The constant roll of the waves along the shore seduced Betsy's breathing into a slow rhythm and, exhausted, she fell asleep.

SATURDAY

High tide: 04.22, 16.58
Light north-easterly

On returning to the inn the next morning, Betsy discovered a piece of paper, folded and pushed under the door of her room. She struggled to read the tangle of pen strokes on the back but finally made out, 'Here's what's on file. Not a hack, but might be an angle. If it turns out to be interesting, let me know.' Euan had left his number and, as an afterthought, suggested a drink.

Betsy stripped, wrapped herself in her towel and ran a bath. As it filled, she lay on the bed to read the contents, a computer-generated story taken from a Nottingham evening paper dated three years earlier. A woman had been left forty thousand pounds by her elder sister although it was twenty-three years since they had last spoken. The reporter had tried to couch it as a feelgood story, but it appeared the sisters had fallen out on the death of their parents, the younger leaving the family home in the West Country for Nottingham. The ties had broken, but despite this, the elder sister had named the younger as beneficiary to her life assurance. When she had died the insurance company had been unable to trace the sibling, and an inheritance tracker had taken up the task. The photograph showed an elderly woman with mouth like an inverted U standing beside Henry Boyle. '[It's a] difficult job,' he was quoted as saying. '[On the] one hand you break news that someone once close [has] died, on the other you [are] handing over [a] legacy.' Betsy tried to recall the questions Boyle had asked, attempting to guess whom he was looking for. If it was Rego, it might mean yet more bad news, and why, she wondered, didn't Boyle just approach him? She read the article again, smiling at the writer's attempts to make Boyle comprehensible and then, realizing her bath was about to overflow, ran to turn off the taps. The article had described Boyle as a 'former policeman', which she couldn't imagine. She slipped into the water, feeling the exhilaration of knowing she had been useful.

The pleasure of being submerged overcame her, the warmth penetrating skin chilled by the walk back from Helen's cottage. She let herself drift, her thoughts with Rego, and lay long enough for the water to cool before she pulled herself from the deep. Whatever the result, she should let him know soon.

She dressed, then looked for his number in the telephone book and dialled. An answering-machine cut in and she decided against leaving a message. She surprised herself when, for the next hour, she sat on the bed waiting, rereading the article and dialling every few minutes. At last she felt ridiculous and went out to see if she could find him in the village.

The harbour was empty of water; an old man was on the mudflats pushing his boat towards the sea, a collie barking from the gunwales. Betsy walked up the street, looking for the Range Rover and finding, as she had the previous day, eyes turning towards her. Yet where, hours earlier, those leaning against the pebbledash walls, or standing on the stoops of their sea-front cottages, had appeared removed from the world, there was now hostility in the looks they threw, as if they had returned to their lives and found her waiting there, an unwanted trespasser. Everyone she passed fell silent at her approach, and she flinched when a group of jackdaws hunched over her from a rooftop and, blue eyes peering down, complained loudly and bitterly at her presence. In this street of propped anchors and windlasses, of model boats in windows, of 'Seaviews' and 'Gullstones' plaques, of silent groups watching, the jabbering felt like jeering, and Betsy stepped up her pace to escape. She slowed only on reaching the sign that announced the village where she settled on a bench placed to command a view over the houses below. She pulled her coat round her, the wind chilling her face.

She felt a long way from the warmth she had discovered hidden among the bleakly beautiful Georgian streets of Edinburgh. She understood the city. Her flat, although small and too far off the edge of the New Town to be fashionable, was her place, with her decorations and her surroundings. As she now looked over the houses and harbour, out to that cold, icy sea, she felt a sudden need to touch home. She walked down the hill to an old-fashioned phone box that stood at the corner of the first house and dialled her own number. The small panels of icy glass were smeared from years of weather, the floor cracked concrete. Her call clicked, rang and was answered.

'So you haven't moved out yet?' she asked lightly.

There was a pause. 'I've been trying to call you,' he

said, his voice level but tight. 'I was worried about how you were. I was wondering if I should drive down there and get you.' Each sentence was delivered in a rush, followed by a two-beat pause that seemed to let the words pile up. 'I've even tidied the flat in case you saw sense and made your way back. But there was no answer from your room. The woman at the hotel said you weren't in, even late last night. And now you call and ask if I've moved out yet.' A tremor was disrupting his delivery.

'I'd like to come home,' she said, keeping her voice as reasonable as she could. 'And it might be better if you had moved out by the time I get back.'

He exploded: 'I don't think so. You'll have to drag me out of here. Just who the hell do you think you are? This is my flat too.'

Betsy would later smile when she recalled being genuinely surprised. 'I own it,' she said, taken aback. 'I paid for it. It's my—'

'So fucking what? I've lived here for a long time and I'm not moving. I'm not *moving*. I have *work* to do, and you're disturbing that. You want to break up, you find somewhere else to live. And if you want the money from this flat, I'd suggest you keep paying the mortgage, because I'm not going to.' He fell silent, but she could hear him breathing. 'How dare *you*?' It was almost as if bile oozed from the earpiece. 'How dare *you* treat me like this? You need help, Betsy. You need *help*.'

'So, you're not going to move out?' She had cooled her tone to match the ice on the glass of the phone box.

'No, I'm—'

She replaced the receiver, opened the door and walked on to the road, unsure where to go. A flicker touched her eye, then a screaming roar above her head, an eye-closing, piss-inducing bedlam that brought her to her knees. The sound faded fast but left her shocked and shaking. Then she saw a jet, a sliver of steel, slice in a low curve to the west. A moment later she heard gunfire, a slow belly-felt pop-pop-pop. Her gaze fell to where a rusted estate had pulled up. Martha was unwinding the passenger window.

'You praying?' the landlady asked.

Betsy pointed after the jet. 'That plane just – just attacked.'

Martha laughed. 'Oh, it's the range. It used to be just tanks but now it's fighters. They're not supposed to come over the village.' When Betsy didn't reply, she added, 'I'm glad to see you. I was wondering if you'd run out on your bill when you didn't come in last night.'

Betsy watched the plane curve out over the water, a dot against the horizon. 'You live with that?'

'We grew up with it. You get so you don't notice.' Martha followed the path of the fighter. 'I suppose they haven't been over for a while. Anyway, how are you?'

'Apart from nearly . . . ?' Betsy laughed. 'Not so good. My ex is refusing to leave my flat.' There was no change in the half-smile on Martha's face and Betsy felt foolish. 'I spent last night with Helen.' She wondered whether to ask about Helen's lack of friends in the village. 'I spent the evening playing board games with her.'

Martha nodded. A car had pulled up behind them and, with a glance in the mirror, she lifted a hand in recognition. 'Do you want a lift to the inn?'

'No. I'm looking for Mr Rego.'

Martha's natural detachment fell away, and she gave Betsy a searching look. 'You won't get him today. The men from Maritime Safety are here.' Her half-smile returned. 'You're getting involved?'

96

'A little.'

She raised her eyebrows. 'Well, if you're brave, you can find him later, at the boneyard, after ten tonight.' She looked in her mirror again. 'He'll definitely be there.'

'The boneyard?'

'The boneyard. At the Castle Church.'

Betsy looked down at the church in the village, a bulwark into the harbour, into the sea.

'Not that one,' said Martha. 'It's not far from Helen's cottage, just keep along that road. You can't miss it – it's in the middle of a field.' She glanced into the mirror again. 'I'd better go.'

Behind, the man waited patiently for Martha to move off.

'Is it a church service? Wouldn't I be imposing?'

Martha actually laughed, a rare sound, as warm as a rich cough. 'No. They play dominoes. That's why it's called the boneyard. Be sure to take some money now, if you go.'

'But—'

'I'd better get going.'

'I'll ask Helen for directions.'

Martha straightened and pulled away.

Betsy stepped back and looked again to the west, towards the unseen land fired upon by those screaming aeroplanes.

Come evening, Betsy cooked for Helen: she baked a sea bass she had bought off the deck of a Northern Irish boat that had come in with the tide. She had begged ingredients off the cook at the inn, then carried her haul to the cottage. Helen, who at first had tried to stop her, was calmed by orders to retrieve what herbs survived in her garden at that time of year, then ate hungrily, stripping away the flesh of the fish, missing nothing.

'Have you been eating?' Betsy asked, fiddling with her own food, her appetite damaged by preparing the meal.

Helen was startled. 'Oh, yes,' she said, lying badly. When she finished, and as Betsy continued to pick, Helen told her of the Maritime Safety officials' visit. A man and a woman had dropped by in the morning, had asked a number of questions and left soon afterwards. They had told her it was inconceivable that the *Albatross* would be raised by the British as it was against government policy. 'The lady said the sea was a fitting resting place for a sailor,' Helen told Betsy, then asked if she could eat Betsy's fish skin.

Betsy handed over her plate. 'Surely they will do something, now they know where it is?'

Helen frowned. 'There's an argument between the British and the Irish. The boat is lying on the point where their waters meet, but the Irish want to raise the boat, because their coastguard, who were closer during the storm – well, some people are saying they should have saved William and the crew.' She stopped to eat the last of the fish. 'The Irish are paying these divers to go down. That man I told you about, Oliver Finlay, is one of them, they specialize in this sort of thing. But they can't get all the men out, and the Irish want the British to help fund the boat being lifted. The safety people said the Irish are playing politics. They said I should ignore it, not get my hopes up, that the Irish have no intention of raising the boat – they just don't want to be blamed for their coastguard's failure to help the crew. It's all so complicated.'

'And what do you think should happen?' Betsy was shocked at the discursive tone Helen was using until she saw that the intensity of feeling was in her eyes, rather than her voice.

'I think that if they can reach them they should. I want to be able to visit William.'

Betsy put out a hand. The serious questions felt too personal for her to ask then. It was still too early. She needed to be there to feed and comfort, rather than inquire. 'Have you seen anyone else?' she asked hopefully. 'Has anyone been to visit?'

'Mr Rego, just before you arrived. He wanted to know what the safety people wanted. He said they were right, that the Irish are being irresponsible, covering their backs. And I suppose that's what happened in the past. That letter, it was pointless.'

'Maybe not. I posted it.'

'Mr Rego brought me provisions so that I didn't have to go into the village. He says it's better to stay here for the moment because of the reporters. He has been kind.'

'I'm going to try to see Mr Rego later,' Betsy said, as Helen rose and lifted the plates. 'I was told he would be at the church down the road. I think it's called the Castle Church.'

Helen appeared shocked, in that flitting way she had. 'You're allowed?' she asked.

'I think so. Martha said they played dominoes.' Betsy paused. 'I can't really imagine Mr Rego playing dominoes. Is there something I don't know?'

'It's usually just men.'

'Like a club? I thought it was in the church. It's not the masons or something, is it?'

'I really don't know. They go there to have fun. I think they gamble. But it's for men. That's all William ever told me, because I like dominoes, you see, and wondered once.

99

But it's a spooky place to go at night, if you ask me.'

'Well, if Martha suggested it, it can't be all that bad. Did William go?'

'Oh, no. Never.'

Betsy stayed until eleven when she kissed Helen goodbye and stepped out into the night. They both looked up into the crystalline sky, the half-moon shining brightly beyond the eaves, a sweep of stars trailing away to the west. The air, while still, was cold enough that Betsy felt its touch like a hand on her face, the frost already forming, nothing seeming to move. Under such heavens the fields lay silky, cows motionless, dark in the ethereal light.

'I'd be scared to walk on my own,' said Helen.

Betsy tightened her red coat around her, pushing her chin into the warm folds of her scarf, hands deep in her pockets. Suddenly cheerful, she looked up at Helen. 'I'm supposed to be frightening myself.' She laughed.

Helen said nothing, her face still pointed towards the sky, then her gaze fell and she smiled softly. Betsy, aware how inappropriate that had sounded, stepped forward and hugged the older woman, her hold awkward because Helen's arms had remained at her sides.

'I'm sorry,' Betsy said. 'I didn't mean . . .'

'Don't worry,' Helen whispered, as she freed herself from the embrace. 'It's not the night that frightens me,' she said. 'It's the morning.'

'I should stay.'

'You're already doing so much. I'm grateful for your visits.' She smiled again, then shivered. 'Please be careful out there in the night.'

'You should go inside. You'll freeze standing there.'

'I'll watch you go.'

Betsy raised a hand, little more than a flick of the wrist, then swivelled and walked up the driveway between the bleak winter borders. She turned right on to the single-lane track that Helen had told her would lead to the church, then waved. Helen lifted her hand in return, then finally closed her door.

The night was very cold, and with the chill digging through her coat Betsy kept up a swift pace. Again the embarrassment of expressing her petty concerns, of mentioning, even obliquely, her determination to rob her ex-fiancé's denunciation of its venom, swept through her, and she lectured herself on the horrors facing Helen and this village. After her earlier telephone conversation, with her ex's words still hard in her ears, she wanted to feel stronger, surer of herself, before heading back into the fight that waited for her in Edinburgh. She drew comfort from the help she could offer Helen and Rego, her own unhappiness diluted by the tragedy around her. This was a truth even she found faintly unpalatable, and one she needed to keep to herself.

Dykes enclosed the lane. The tarmac was broken in the places where grass had pushed through before dying in the heart of winter. Out of sight of Helen's cottage, Betsy fought free of self-recrimination and looked to each side, into the rich night. A creature moved, the frost under its feet collapsing, and a lonely lowing rolled across the land. On the road ahead, moonlight threw shadows at jolting, threatening angles. Betsy tried to avoid searching for shapes, aware that to look for a presence in the darkness was to find one. She felt her fear and wanted to suck it in, to thrive on it in the belief that it revealed an imagination she had been told she didn't have.

She had never before walked alone in the country at

night, and now she wondered if her decision to seek out Rego had been wise. Used to making her way through the midnight streets of Edinburgh, she tried to distract herself with the differences. There, she kept to the main roads, preferring to risk the advances of the army of drunks that swept home late at night rather than the ill-lit closes and feeder roads that writhed at the feet of the capital's old town. Here, the few lights touching the landscape felt as distant as stars, their glow sucking warmth from the emptiness. The cow lowed again, and a night bird replied, and as she walked she assured herself that she felt refreshed, that her fear was exhilarating. She was certain there was no danger, knowing that even the dullest brain could conjure up ghosts on a night like this. With nerves burning from experience and flesh scorched by cold, she barely even thought about turning back, her walk steady, one step after another. She told herself that there were no other footfalls hidden in the sound.

The road crested and Betsy stopped to look to the east, to where the firth lay flat and black in the distance. She inhaled deeply and her lungs swelled, offering an oxygen clarity. She loved the moonlight on the metal sea, the murmurs of waves merely a notion from such a distance. She might have stood there for a long time but the sound of laughter brought her back. Further down the lane, a copse mushroomed in the middle of a field. Lights emerged from among the trees, and laughter rolled towards her again until she heard a door close. For the first time she felt truly nervous. With her comments, Helen had made these real people far more worrying than the spectres of the imagination that hung in the night.

A car approached from behind, headlights sweeping the field as it moved up the other side of the rise. After so long in the darkness, the idea of the vehicle appalled Betsy and she sought a hiding-place, running along the lane until she reached a beech, bare-boughed in the night. She scrambled in behind its trunk just as the lights showed, and watched the car pass, its rear lights fast pulling away. She remained at a crouch. She knew the car: it was normally parked under her window at the inn. Now it was pulling up beside the others parked at the point where the road drew closest to the copse. She emerged from her hiding-place and hurried on.

Boyle stepped from the car, a curved shadow in the moonlight as he moved across the dark field. With his arrival, Betsy felt a keen sense of disappointment, as if her part was being taken from her. Yet a resolution was about to occur, and she followed him, turning through the small swing-gate that let her into the field, curiosity pushing her on. A worn path led towards a high wall that encircled the copse, the church half concealed beyond tall gates. Here she slowed, the field open and exposed under the moon. She didn't want to be seen as Boyle hesitated at the entrance, the bars rising beyond his head. He turned to the side, and she saw him rise up the wall, presumably on a stile, then disappear from sight.

Betsy had expected something less frightening than this. Silence now returned to the shadowed landscape like heavy air. There was nothing welcoming about the bone-yard, only a miserable light emanating from somewhere unseen beyond the wall. The cold forced her across the field, but the steps came slowly now, and she knew she was being careful. Only as she approached the wall was the silence swept away, by the sound of a blow and an exhaled grunt.

The shock was so great, she might as well have seen a

body. After her initial surprise, she rushed to the gate and arrived to see Boyle being thrown, arms slack, against a tree by the huge figure of Priest. Part of each man was in moonlight, but most was in shadow. Boyle appeared unable to complain, winded by the first blow, the last of his breath taken by the impact of the tree-trunk. She could not see his expression: his neck was now held by one large fist against the side of the tree-trunk hidden from her. But she could see Priest's face, illuminated by a thin slice of a light falling through the empty branches. It was strangely calm, devoid of feeling or effort, with a slight licentiousness in that he held his tongue between his teeth. Priest drove his fist into Boyle's belly and Betsy screamed.

Priest, still holding Boyle by the neck, looked over at her then away, along the wall of the church and into the shadows. A door opened and shut, the light briefly flooding the trees further into the copse.

'Damn it, Priest. What are you doing?' Rego was at Priest's side, pushing him off Boyle, who slumped to vomit in the wilted grass. 'And what's he doing here? Look at the state of him. I said scare them off, not beat them up.' Hitching up his trousers, he crouched down and shook Boyle. Priest gazed over at Betsy, his expression empty. 'You,' shouted Rego, pulling at Boyle's jacket, careful to avoid the vomit. 'Are you all right?'

Boyle rose on to all fours. He spat, and lifted a hand to wipe his mouth. Betsy wondered whether she should back away but found she couldn't move. Priest's eyes, the adrenalin that surged through her, a weight that seemed to hold her feet, all kept her at the gate.

'Sorry,' Rego said to Boyle. 'Our fault. An over-reaction.' He appeared to look at the vomit. 'I don't want to make excuses, but you shouldn't sneak around. Not at a time like this.'

Priest hadn't taken his eyes off Betsy, holding her there. Boyle spat again.

'There's no story here,' Rego continued, 'so unless any real damage has been done, I think perhaps you should go. Come and ask your questions during the day. Like a normal person. Can you walk?'

Boyle got slowly to his feet, helped by Rego putting a hand under his arm. 'You're lucky you scream like a girl, otherwise I wouldn't have heard you, and God only knows what would have happened. Priest, apologize.' Boyle's birdlike head turned towards Betsy. Rego, seeing the other men look away, followed their gaze, his mouth falling open. It took him a moment to close it again. 'You brought a friend?'

'No,' replied Boyle, his voice hoarse, very quiet. He was leaning against the tree.

Rego looked at Priest, who said nothing.

'No?' said Rego to Boyle.

'No.' Boyle's voice was a little stronger.

'This is confusing,' said Rego.

Betsy spoke, finding the words difficult: 'I walked from Helen's.' She lifted a hand. 'To see you. She said you'd be here.' She was still appalled by the violence. 'And I saw.' She tried to express her disgust in a gesture.

There was no breeze, and no sound but for an occasional burst of laughter inside the church. Only the condensation from the breathing showed that time was passing.

'Well, then, you arrived in the nick of time,' Rego said, with a smile. He turned to Boyle. 'Time you left, I'd say. And you, Priest. You've disgraced yourself. Go inside.'

No one moved.

'Go!' Rego's rich voice betrayed frustration. Boyle pushed himself off the tree and, still holding his belly, walked to the wall. Betsy now saw the stile, the flat stones emerging from the mortar, rising away to a vertigo-inducing height. Boyle appeared at the top, then descended. He glanced at Betsy and then, hunched in pain, walked back towards his car.

She watched him go until, startled, she felt a presence on the opposite side of the gate.

'You'll be needing a lift home,' Rego said.

'Yes,' she said, and shouted towards the departing figure. 'Henry? Do you need a hand? I could drive. Back to the inn.' She had taken a step or two after him when a cloud must have drifted in front of the moon because he slowly disappeared from view. He must have ignored her, though, because his car started, reversed into the lay-by, then headed back along the road. Betsy felt an incapacitating fear surround her. When she turned, she found that the only light in the darkness emerged from a long, thin slit in the wall of the church, illuminating a few frozen twigs hanging in the air.

'I meant that I'd drive you,' Rego said, from the night.

'I'll walk.'

'Why would you want to do that? When you came to see me.'

'I only came to tell you that I haven't found out any-thing about him.' Her reticence was instinctive, trust had fallen away, and she wanted to think.

'Long way to come to tell me . . .'

'I couldn't find you today.' She felt impatient. 'And I wanted – I wanted to see what this place was like.'

'Don't be angry with me,' Rego said, his voice calm. 'I really didn't mean that to happen, but he came sneaking around here looking for a story. What do you want? Priest overreacts. I told him to watch out for reporters, and he went over the top.' The moonlight fought its way back, and she saw he was pushing a hand through his hair. 'But let's not waste too much sympathy on Mr Boyle. You said yourself that he was creepy.' Rego looked at her. 'But then again, maybe you know him.'

Betsy rolled her eyes. He must have missed it, because the silence drew out. 'I *don't* know him,' she said at last.

'I'm just trying to be honest,' Rego continued. 'It's odd that you turn up at the same time, first in the village, and now here. Look at it from my perspective.'

'I arrived before the *Albatross* sank.'

'Perhaps that's not what you're after.'

Betsy looked at Rego with distaste. 'What, then? What about Helen?'

'Are you and Helen becoming close?'

Betsy felt her anger grow, and began to walk away across the moonlit grass.

'Wait,' said Rego. 'As I said, look at it from my perspective.' The frustration had returned to his voice. 'Why are you still here unless there's something else going on?'

'Because I want to help,' Betsy replied, her voice strained.

Rego was silent but Betsy had stopped. He stood at the gate, and she heard him sigh. 'Come and I'll show you why I'm so paranoid,' he said. 'It's just a few people trying to get a little enjoyment, that's all. But if I tell you? And you're helping him? That will make me look a fool.'

'I'm not with him.'

'I believe you. I believe in coincidence. Come over and I'll show you.'

Betsy stood where she was.

'The gate's locked. Come over the wall.' He turned away. 'But don't expect anything exciting.'

Betsy peered up at the forbidding wall. She didn't want to go any further. The attraction had dissipated with that punch. She was about to tell Rego this, but he had vanished, and she no longer felt safe in the darkness. With Priest nearby, it had become apparent that the spectres weren't imaginary. She approached the steps. They climbed so high that she worried about pitching off the top. She felt the salt underfoot where the stones had been gritted, reached up to the top of the wall and climbed. Rego had waited at the other side to help her down. He raised one hand, his grip steadying her. She stepped on to the frozen grass under the wall. The trees now reached overhead. Another burst of laughter came from within the church. She took her hand from Rego's and shivered.

'You didn't tell Priest to beat him up?' she asked, hope in her voice.

Rego's face was touched by a slash of moonlight. It had taken on the quality of ebony, reinforcing Betsy's impression that it was like a mask. 'What kind of man do you think I am? I told him to chase away snoopers. I'm just glad Boyle got here before you.' He laughed, the sound sudden, and when it died, Betsy felt he had tired of the incident. 'Come and meet the boys.'

Betsy hesitated. 'Are you sure this is all right?'

'Of course. You came to see me.' He took a step towards the church. There was a presumption in his tone that bothered her. 'You walked from Helen's. On a very dark night.' The humour masked something Betsy couldn't fathom. Although she felt no imminent danger, she sensed that he was enjoying how completely she was

108

in his hands. She had no idea of what was happening in the church, only that men were there, and those men seemed unconcerned that someone had just been beaten in the woods outside. 'Come,' said Rego, taking her elbow.

Betsy stayed where she was.

'There's nothing to worry about.'

She felt like an idiot for putting herself in this situation.

Evidently seeing her fear, he laughed again. 'Okay, look, I'll get my coat and then I'll drive you home. At least that way you won't have to worry out here in the dark. You'll wait?'

Betsy nodded, distrustful of her voice. Rego walked back to the church and pushed his way in, the door, its aged surface pockmarked with studs, swinging back. She couldn't see into the depths, but she could hear Rego talking to the men inside. 'Sorry, boys, I have to go. Continue as long as you like. Priest's in charge, which should make sure you'll all pay at the end.' There was a stream of abuse as he stepped outside and closed the door. 'Shall we go?'

'You look a little shaken,' said Rego, as they drove back towards the village.

'I shouldn't have come.' The moonlight rippled off the sea. A breeze must have got up. She could see the lights of England far away in the distance.

'Still, I'm glad you did.'

Betsy caught him looking at her and he turned back to the road. 'I like that you were brave enough to walk along the road at this time of night. It showed guts, an adventurous spirit. Even I think it's a funny place back there.'

Betsy let herself sink into the seat. 'I didn't know that. I was told you played dominoes.'

Rego laughed. 'We do. We play dominoes.'

'I expected a . . .' she couldn't think of the expression '. . . a church thing, like a beetle drive.'

'And look what you got. Devil worship. A sacrificed outsider.'

'Don't joke about it. Priest beat him up.'

Rego fell quiet. 'We do play dominoes,' he said eventually. 'All sorts of varieties, but for money. We also play a bit of poker, Texas Hold 'Em, if we have the numbers. We gamble. It's not so innocent.'

'Why there?'

'It's tradition.'

'It's a bit Gothic.'

'We call it the boneyard, which sounds Gothic.' He looked for understanding but Betsy let him go on. 'It's the name for the dominoes left in the middle after everyone has taken their hand. The church hardly gets used, once every few years for a wedding, maybe, but not properly since the MoD took over this area back in the war. The Americans, when they were based here, used it as a casino because the parish minister had demanded a ban on gambling and it was the GIs' way of sticking up two fingers. It started something and even though the Americans left a long time ago and the boundaries of the range rolled back so that we don't have to drive through it any more, we were drawn in, and never got out of the habit. Of playing, and playing in the church. It's just that we play dominoes now.' Betsy said nothing. 'And, as I say, the occasional hand of poker.' They turned the corner beside Helen's cottage, the dark windows suggesting she had gone to bed. 'I suppose it is odd, but I've grown up with it, and most of the fishermen who come in know about it, and some of the farmers, and there's a haulier based up the road a bit, and even the retired head of the old D-SS, so there's always people prepared to play.' He chuckled. 'As cultural invasions go, it's more interesting than McDonald's.'

The lights of the village welcomed them and soon they were among the houses, turning right, down towards the harbour-master's office.

'Or alcopops,' said Betsy, seeing the slogan.

'Our own invention, I think. Is that one really made with port?'

'I'm afraid so.'

Rego pulled up outside the inn. 'It's funny driving into the village now,' he said. 'Everything has changed.'

Betsy's fear had burned off with the lights, although she felt weak. Rego's calm manner had lulled her, and it was the memory of his humour outside the church that now took precedence in her mind.

'That's why I'm paranoid about the church,' Rego said. 'If the reporters hear of it and put it in the papers they'll build up a view of us that doesn't do us justice. The outside world loves to look down on places like this, make out we're . . . well, whatever they choose – hicks, victims or even degenerates. People won't understand that we're just trying to deal with the stress, looking for release – and a little continuity, of course. And as for me, they'll think I'm being callous, that I don't care. And that's not true. It couldn't be further from the truth.' His face was troubled. 'You see that?'

Betsy nodded.

'Would you like a drink?' he asked.

'It's after midnight. The bar will be closed.' Betsy looked at the pub windows. A light glowed behind the curtain.

111

'Not in this morally corrupt place. Not on a Saturday night.'

Rego put a hand on Betsy's arm as they reached the door. 'Let's go into the lounge bar,' he said. 'I don't want to get caught up in the local chat.' They turned right. The room was dimly lit and empty, the reporters gone. Boyle's car had been parked in its usual spot outside, but he wasn't in the public bar. He must have gone to his room, Betsy presumed. There were three men sitting at a table by the fire, who glanced over but said nothing. Bunbury stood at the bar, staring at them. Rego ignored him.

'Evening,' said Martha to Betsy. 'I see you found him.'

'Are you still pouring?' Rego asked.

'Well, yes, especially since you have a resident with you.' She lifted a bottle of wine from the chiller, pulled the cork and poured him a glass. 'But I'd like to be out of here by one, if that's all right.' There was reservation in Martha's welcome, which faded as she turned to Betsy. 'Would you like some wine too?'

Betsy had been about to order a beer. 'Is it good?'

'Very,' said Rego. Then his voice dropped. 'Martha, did you tell that man Boyle I'd be at the boneyard?'

'No.'

Betsy noticed Rego's gaze had switched to Bunbury.

'I did tell Betsy, though,' she added.

'That's fine. It was Mr Boyle I wondered about.'

'Not me.' Martha showed no interest in why Rego might ask.

Bunbury was smiling. Some meaning had passed between him and Rego, which Betsy couldn't make out. Even Martha seemed to have grasped it, looking at one man then the other. Rego relaxed. He gathered up the bottle and the two glasses and walked over to a table at the window.

'That plague's coming,' Betsy heard Bunbury say behind them.

She was about to turn, but Martha replied, 'Is that what the telly's saying, Joe?'

'Have you met Joe Bunbury?' Rego asked, when they sat down.

'We passed maybe a word,' said Betsy. 'Looks like he's been in the wars.'

'That's what I mean when I say the press could make what they like of this place.' Rego took a sip of his wine and appeared cheered by it. 'This is a very good wine, you know,' he said. 'I won't bore you, but it's actually the best white Spain has to offer, and it's not too expensive. It's about finding the right . . .' He stopped, watching Betsy drink.

'It's lovely,' she said, without much interest.

Rego laughed. 'Bunbury, then. Joe Bunbury's from the village but for most of his life he lived over in Dumfries working at the big rubber plant there. It's where they make wellies, and carpet underlay and things. His job was to turn a big lump of rubber into a long, thin sheet by feeding it through huge, superheated drums. Have you ever made pasta?'

Betsy shook her head.

'Quite right. I need to get out more.' He put down the glass. 'What happens is this lump of boiling rubber falls from a hole in the ceiling on to these superheated rollers, and it was Bunbury's job to mix it in this mangle, cutting and folding it in on itself until it reached the perfect consistency when he would feed the strip into another machine. Everything in the process happened at more than a hundred degrees, so he's a very brave and skilled man. And the men who do this job are a clique, with all

113

these traditions, the most important one being to make their own knives for cutting the rubber. It's part of the mystique, a symbol of the skill – you know?'

Although they could see through to the public bar, Bunbury had his back to them, leaning on the counter. He seemed to be watching the television, although the sound was down.

'Well, a few months ago one of his hands got caught. He was quick to hit the stop button, but it was too late. He won't let them amputate it. It's against his beliefs. Somewhere over the years, in all that heat and noise, dealing with all that danger, he was touched by the Almighty's love, if you hear him tell it. I just think he was touched in the head. He's a scary man now. Way back we used to be friends.'

'Hence the look?'

'It's a strange place you landed in,' Rego told her. 'No doubt you thought it was just a pretty harbour. Well,' he took another sip of wine as his long face swung towards her, 'what about you? Is it really just Helen keeping you down here, or is it something to do with your break-up?' he asked.

'None of your business.'

'Come now.' His hand was lying on the table and he raised it so that he could drum his fingers. 'Here you are, looking after Helen, visiting my game in the middle of the night, asking all these questions. The give-take ratio . . .'

'You've told me about Mr Bunbury.' Betsy was caught by the elegance of the bones that showed at his knuckles. 'And about your dominoes.' Hair extended down over the wrist and on to the back of his hand, yet there was a delicacy that reminded her of a pianist. 'And even how welly boots are made.' She followed the line of his arm until she met his eyes. 'But not much about yourself.'

'I think I'm trusting you more than you're trusting me.'

Betsy thought about this. 'My ex said some things that have made me think.' She looked again at his hand, but there was no further question, the silence drawing out. 'He told me I haven't really done anything in my life,' she went on. 'That I have been protected from reality. So I thought if I tried to do good here, help Helen, then I was, I don't know . . .'

'Helping yourself?'

'Don't mock. This isn't a new-age thing. I just want to know that he was wrong, that the accusation is rubbish.'

Rego was staring at Bunbury's back across the bar. 'It's a funny thing, isn't it, that you can't measure the pain you feel by the suffering of others?'

'Oh, I think I can.'

'Then you're wrong.' Now he was watching one of the men who had been by the fire come through from the public bar. He was young, but his face was aged by weather, his head shaved close to the skull. He stood over them. 'Any news?' he asked, ignoring Betsy.

Rego looked carefully at the newcomer before he spoke. 'Nothing at the moment.' A pause. 'It's difficult to tell what will happen.'

'Did you see the Maritime Safety today? They saw Cathy this afternoon.'

Rego sucked his teeth. 'They were a touch rude, but I think they might have a point.' He lifted a hand towards Betsy. 'Kenny,' he said, 'this is Betsy. Betsy, Kenny Orr. Kenny's cousin Jim was on the boat.'

'I'm sorry,' said Betsy.

The man looked at her for an instant, then turned back to Rego. 'What about these divers, this Oliver Finlay?

Jim's on a harness down there, floating. Nothing about getting his body off?'

'The Irish are paying their bills, so we don't know yet.'

'And lifting the boat? Finding out what happened?'

'Maritime Safety say it's not the British government's responsibility.' He shrugged.

Orr's face was bitter. 'Christ. And what do you think?'

'It would be good if they can bring Jim up.'

'And the boat?'

Again, Rego sat for some time, Orr's eyes intent on him. 'I think you know what I think,' he said.

'Fuck Helen Kerr,' Orr spat. 'William Kerr killed my cousin. I want that known. Fuck her. She's not that backward. She knows exactly what she's at.'

Betsy was about to protest but Rego's hand was on her arm at once. 'To what end?' he said. 'What good can it do?'

Orr looked away, now biting his lip in agitation. 'There's a lot of folk very angry about this, James. Very, very angry. They don't want to feel angry, they want to feel sad, they want to mourn, and they can't do that unless the world knows the truth.'

'I understand, Kenny, I really do, but right now? We need to stand as one. We need to be united. There will be no truth if we fight each other. The press will love it. So let's try to take this one day at a time.'

'What are you taking one day at a time?' Orr now spoke quietly, but with the sharpness of threat. 'You just lost a boat.' He was square on to Rego, his body thrust forward.

Rego raised his palms in submission. 'If you don't want me to help, I'll back off.'

'I don't want you to back off. Just don't give me the

116

twelve-step.' With that Orr rejoined his friends, who were now waiting at the door. They followed each other out into the night.

Betsy tried to speak, but he shushed her. 'Have another glass,' he said.

They didn't speak for several minutes, and it was Rego who broke the silence. 'There's nothing wrong with feeling bad about your break-up,' he said. 'You can't help it mattering to you, even if there's a holocaust across the road.'

'Even if that was true, I care about Helen now.' Betsy pointed at the door. 'What was that? What's going on?'

A weary bitterness swept across Rego's face. 'They think William Kerr ignored an opportunity to head for harbour. They think he kept going in the face of very bad odds. They think he lost the families their men.' He was leaning forward, close to Betsy, his eyes unblinkingly on hers.

'And what do you think?' she asked.

He leaned back. 'I don't think it matters, to be honest. I think, for the sake of everyone, that it should be left alone.' He picked up his glass. 'Most of the families want the bodies back, none more so than Helen Kerr, and that I can understand, but if that means raising the boat, well, the cost to Helen, to this village . . .'

Betsy gazed across the bar at Bunbury and thought of Helen at home in bed. She wondered how ignorant she was of the hatred that Orr had just expressed. She must know something of it, and with so few friends . . . Betsy felt smothered, felt the village turn against Helen, almost as if it were a physical shift.

'I really hope you're not a journalist,' Rego said.

'I'm not,' she replied.

'I'm glad. I would look a fool. You know, I can under-stand why Helen likes having you around. Perhaps we all need someone who's not involved at moments like this. I'm glad you've decided to stay.'

'Thank you.'

'But,' Rego squinted at her, 'please take any suggestions I make seriously. I need you to be with me to get Helen through this.'

'Of course.'

'And keep me informed of how she's feeling. I've got so much on, I don't want to miss anything.' He swallowed the last of his wine. 'I should get home. Thanks for having a drink with me. Home's a cold place just now.' He stood up and pulled on his coat. 'Let me ask you something,' he said. 'That laboratory you work for. The one you showed me the card for. I've heard of it. It deals in genetics, yes? You're interested in bloodlines?'

'I suppose.' Betsy had been watching Bunbury say goodbye to Martha and leave. There was no one left in the public bar. 'Yes.'

'Well, have you ever seen a prize milk cow?'

She laughed. 'No, I can't say I have.'

'Come over tomorrow. I'll take you on a tour of the farm. Introduce you to Hirondelle. She's a three times gold-medal winner at the Royal Highland Show and she knows it. She's French, you see.'

'That's quite an invitation.'

'Don't smirk. I have a prize dairy herd, some of the best milk producers in the country. It'll be an honour. For you.'

'I'm sure it will. Okay, I'd love to.' She put out her hand.

Rego took it, but leaned forward to kiss her cheek.

SUNDAY

High tide: 05.34, 18.22
Flat calm

The Sabbath dawned as yet another day of weak sunlight angling in across the frozen earth and salt-washed shores. It was as if the vast and murderous storm of the week before had robbed the heavens of strength. Betsy opened the curtains and looked out over the harbour where the surviving boats hung stern to the sea, resisting the pull of the ebbing tide. Although her muscles ached, she felt a vibrancy in her blood, which now ran heavy with oxygen. She was due at the laboratory in Edinburgh in twenty-four hours, yet she could already feel ties to this place that resisted the pull of home. Her friendships with Rego and Helen might as yet be threads, but they were holding. She knew, as she placed a hand on the glass, feeling the chill, that she had reason enough to call her work, make her excuses and stay a day or two more. She left the room before she saw the sea sweep out, leaving the boats in the harbour high and dry.

She had decided to talk to Henry Boyle – she had seen him from her bathroom window as she washed. He was in the village graveyard, a small plot on the slope that ran landwards from the coast, not far from the start of the path that led to Helen's cottage. To reach him, she followed a track that led behind the houses, passing small back gardens, at one point ducking under the stern of a boat that sat rotting on stilts. On the hillside, Boyle was silhouetted, moving from one stone to the next, bent over to see the inscriptions. He spotted her when she opened the gate, paused and, perhaps remembering himself, returned to his task. As Betsy walked up the slope, she passed through the decades, the tended ground spongy under her feet, until she caught up with him in the 1960s. He ignored her, rubbing the surface of a gravestone in an effort to make out the surname – 'Allan John Carruthers, Died 9 September 1966' – then straightened, moved on.

'Sorry about last night,' she said to his back.

Boyle scratched at the stone with his hand. 'Why? Probably saved me . . . from worse.'

'I mean I'm sorry it happened.' Betsy took another step. 'I wanted to say that, because I think I know why you're here.'

'Thought . . . I'd told you already.'

'Yes.'

He was stooping, perhaps so that he could see an inscription, or from the pain of the punch to the stomach. He peered up at her. 'Yes?' he asked, then continued. He reached the end of a row and rose to his full height, gazing across the memorials.

'That you're here searching for someone's relative.'

Boyle's attention settled further off, far into the east. Nothing changed in his face, the skin so tightly stretched over his bones that any expression would have to be intended and he seemed to have chosen, long ago, to

120

avoid revealing anything. Only the bitterness in his words revealed his fury. Following his line of sight, Betsy saw that Helen's cottage was just visible through a distant tree line, and that Rego's Range Rover was parked out front.

'I think someone here has been left money,' she said, 'and that you're tracking them down.'

Boyle went back to checking gravestones, saying nothing.

'That was why I was at the church last night. I was on my way to tell James Rego about it.' This made her sound like a spy, she thought, and added quickly, 'But only because he thought you were a reporter. I was too late.'

Boyle checked a stone, took three steps and checked again.

'I didn't tell him,' Betsy said at last.

Boyle rose, resting a hand on a gravestone. In the cold his head was the colour of weathered bone. 'Why?'

'There was something about seeing you hit.' She had been studying the palm of her glove but now looked up. 'It made me think I shouldn't interfere until I had spoken to you, until I made sure I wasn't putting my foot in it.' This was genuine: she had wanted to tell Rego but it seemed only fair to discuss it with Boyle first.

He looked down at the stone he was leaning against. 'Appreciate that.' He swung away and began to move along the line of stones again.

'What name are you looking for?'

He ignored her.

'Is it a relative of Mr Rego?' She had noticed cars beginning to pull into the village. There was a gap in the line of houses, and she could see movement on the road beyond. Helen's cottage was now out of sight. 'Could I help?'

'Who else knows . . . about me?'

'No one. I found out from a reporter. He had a news-paper article, about a woman who died in Nottingham.' Betsy couldn't see his face, but suspected it would reveal nothing anyway. 'But he's gone now.'

'Why . . . you staying?'

Betsy took a moment to reply, and in that time he had risen to face her again. 'I think one of the widows could use my help,' she said, a little defensively.

Boyle took a step towards her. 'Generous.'

'Ah, well.'

'An idiot,' he said.

She thought he was insulting her. 'What do you mean?'

'Your boyfriend. You deserve better.'

Betsy looked at the road, where the Range Rover was rolling slowly towards the village, the memory of being overheard in her hotel room reigniting the anger she had felt. She wanted to know what Boyle was up to. If there was a way in which she could discover any bad news or, better still, good news, it would help the man in the car. She bit her tongue. 'Well, that's something else. I could use a project. Let me help.'

'Don't tell. Anyone. Tricky if people know. Relatives don't want neighbours knowing . . . about a windfall. Excites interest, jealousy, fear.'

'But I'm an outsider. It would be better with two. Can I help you look for a name on these stones?'

Boyle smiled, which lost him the last vestiges of her sympathy. 'Nothing here, looked three times already. Never changes, day to day, but . . . let you know.'

With his refusal, Betsy's irritation blossomed. She now felt he had taken the beating too easily, and felt sus-picious. She had trouble pretending friendliness, but

122

forced a smile as she gazed over the rooftops to the harbour's far rocky shore. 'I'll keep quiet,' she said. 'But if there is anything I can do, please let me know.'

Boyle nodded.

'One last question. In the article it referred to you as a former policeman. That doesn't play any part in you being here?'

Boyle laughed, the sound shocking in its resemblance to the jackdaws' mockery. 'No. Long time ago, during miners' strike. Left with no love lost.' He tried to appear sympathetic but failed. 'If . . . you need . . . to talk? I'm . . . good listener.'

She lifted a hand in farewell, as she began her walk back down the hill. When she reached the gate she turned to find him looking after her, but then he waved and continued along the stones, past the Orrs, Bothwicks, Hunters, Simpsons and Renwicks, unable to find what he was looking for. Betsy felt a sense of desperation in her inability to read him. The Range Rover, which had stopped briefly, now rolled on through the gap in the houses and out of sight.

By the time Betsy reached the road that encircled the harbour, groups of people had appeared, all dressed in dark clothes and moving sleepily in front of the white walls of the village church. The Range Rover was parked on the pavement, and Rego stepped down as Betsy walked up. Life was slowly seeping from him. Betsy half expected to see Helen but the passenger seat was empty.

'How was he?' Rego asked, studying the villagers as he spoke.

'Sore stomach, bruised ego.'

He lifted a finger to rub the flesh below his left eye.

'I'm glad you're here,' he said. 'I'm losing perspective.'

It was clear which families had lost men in the tragedy: they formed cores in the crowd – young women either pregnant or with babies, protected on all sides by mothers, brothers, sisters, uncles, aunts and friends. She saw Kenny Orr with a woman who could only be the girl-friend, Cathy. She was heavily pregnant. Another couple, short with round faces worn by weather, huddled over two boys of barely fourteen, each parent with a hand on one of the children's shoulders, talking to friends or relatives. By another group, a girl of about six was receiv-ing an embrace from a slate-haired man with a thin, triangular face.

'The world is falling in,' said Rego. 'And I can't do any-thing.'

'I expect you're doing a great deal.' She hesitated. 'Is this . . . ?'

'First service since the sinking, a sort of memorial service. This church only gets used about once every two months, but there's nothing like tragedy to bring the clergy out of their rafters.'

Betsy noticed that the couple with the two boys were leaning against each other. 'Is Helen not coming?'

'Some reporters have come back for this, and it's better if there's not a scene.'

People were staring at them and Betsy roused herself. 'I'd better get out of the way. I'll go and make sure she's okay.'

'She'll be fine. I've just been there.' Rego laid a hand on her arm. 'She didn't want to come, but if you've an hour, I could use some support. Would you sit with me?'

'I'm not dressed for it.' She felt out of place in her red coat.

124

'It'll be fine. Come. I'll walk you in.' Betsy was caught unawares by the certainty with which he moved her towards the church door. Faces nodded at him, but were blank as they watched her pass. Conversation died, then swelled behind them as they entered the church, and was muffled and dulled by the walls. She was surprised to find that the place was already half full.

Bunbury waited at the head of an aisle and Rego hesitated on seeing him. 'Joe,' he said, the words coming faster than normal, 'this is Betsy Gillander. She's going to sit with me. Would you find her a place?' His hand slipped from her elbow and Betsy realized she was about to be left. 'I won't be a moment,' he reassured her. 'I have to check on the other families.'

Appalled, Betsy watched him go until she felt Bunbury handing her a hymn book, his expression one of disapproval.

'Gillander, eh? There were Gillanders around here at one time.' His voice came in a whisper that would penetrate walls. 'Indeed, I think one of them was named Betsy.' He led her to a pew close to the front, standing at the end to usher her in, ignoring her plea to be placed further back. 'I think she was the last.' He had gone before she could reply.

The people in the pews behind appeared funereal, although there were no bodies to bury. They shifted in their seats, coughed or talked quietly. The church itself was sombre, a rectangular box with no decoration except a simple plaque to a former minister above the annexe door. The pulpit was central, rising behind the altar. The only nod to the sea, which rose twice daily to enclose the building on three sides, was a tiller from a small boat on which the hymn numbers were hung. The room was a cool but faded blue. There was movement and Betsy turned to see the Orrs coming up the aisle, small frowns touching their faces as they saw her sitting there. They filed along a pew two in front of her, other groups coming behind, the two parents still leaning into each other as they settled, the father with one hand braced on the pew in front. Betsy squirmed as these families filled the space immediately in front of her, flinching as they glanced round at those behind. She was desperate for Rego to return.

The church was full now, the breathing, moving and coughing bringing life to the cold, dank building. Betsy searched the back and saw Rego talking to a tall man near the door. Three reporters sidled towards him. He ignored them, nodding gently as the other spoke.

Betsy heard a creak and turned to see the minister emerging, Bunbury holding the annexe door open for him. He was small, overweight and clearly overcome. He read out the names of the dead, starting with William Kerr, while Rego slipped in beside Betsy, taking her hand and squeezing it. Betsy returned the pressure. The families moaned as the other six names fell across them, and by the time the minister was done, his head was bowed. When the congregation stood to sing, the voices were choked and breaking. The minister recovered with a sermon in which he described taking a walk along the coast and seeing a school of porpoise travelling under the cliff. He said that while it was hard to understand the cruelty of the world with such beauty all around, he felt certain the victims of this terrible accident were with God. He imagined their spirits travelling across the waves like those porpoise, carefree now that they had been freed from painful life. At the last, he asked for kindness and understanding for all who suffer.

Betsy felt adrift on the emotions that rose and fell with the minister's words. The community was sharing a room with the families of the lost fishermen and the effect was of being in the belly of a great injured beast. The peripheral lashings of this creature, directed in the main towards the reporters, felt distant from here at the centre where the families hunkered in their pain. Here, the suffering was absolute and crushing, the outrage so pure and internal that it coloured the depths of its victims' eyes. It was here, at the centre, where an act, the slightest gesture, could send messages to those who waited at the edges, those desperate to overcome their impotence, triggering cruel and terrible responses. Yet these unwilling stars of pain, whom Betsy was sitting behind, obviously wished for none of this fame, but their glow held the community in desperate longing. Betsy, looking between the heads of the Orrs, stopped seeing the fixtures of the church and perceived what was really there: an emptiness between the altar and the pulpit. The minister, finishing his sermon, stood high above this void where the bodies should lie. Betsy realized that this space, with its grey flag floors, must torture the families. For now these people's relatives hung in the winter sea, far from the gaze of warm sun or a familiar eye. Betsy thought she understood why Helen had preferred not to come. How was it possible to feel steady as the bodies of those you loved were at the whim of passing currents? The minister now moved into that gap. He stood behind the altar and raised his hands to the living, blessing them. The small organ in the corner struck up and the service was over. Betsy noticed that she was gripping Rego's hand far too tightly. She released the pressure.

Rego stood at the end of the pew, greeting the families as they left. He motioned Betsy to follow them out, the rest of the congregation feeding into the aisle behind. The minister, talking to one of the Orrs, shook Rego's hand and smiled at Betsy, who stepped off to one side. 'A fine sermon,' she heard Rego say.

Seagulls clamoured over the spreading crowd, and the sound caused Betsy to feel again that the building was a creature, alive when its dark intestines were intact, but dying now that they spilled out across the road. She saw that Bunbury was watching her and she turned away, shivering, unused to her mind throwing up such imagery.

The sun cuts through the cataract and slices into the wound. I lie still, clearing my mind, the bodyaltar revealed and prone in its temple. It is not for me to think, but to feel nothing. It is the same when violence is needed. Yet there was something about the boy, something that disturbed the calm. It is difficult to see into that soul. But what do I know? Nothing. I must clear my mind. The Saint has yet to stir, but the world is trembling. Trouble approaches from all directions, and Cutter needs my trust. I empty my head, but the news that Cutter has given, of a plague across the water, plays in my mind, the reflection of fire in an eye. It is a betrayal of the Saint, but I rise and cover the altar, leave the temple and head into the forest. It is so difficult to feel nothing.

Hirondelle proved to be a Prim Holstein heifer, a Friesian if she changed citizenship. Rego had turned off the road and pulled up in a concrete yard between several flaky-white steadings. Beyond the slate roofs were larger barns that ran back into a stand of mature beech. He had loaned

128

Betsy an old pair of red wellington boots, which, while slightly too large, gave Betsy a sense of childlike adventure and put the memorial service at one remove. He had unknotted his tie and exchanged his dark blazer for a suede jacket, his brogues for black boots, and had then led Betsy through a series of stone passageways, filled with the strong smell of cereal feeds, milk and manure, to the cattlesheds.

'These boots match my coat,' said Betsy, as they walked.

'Little Red Riding Hood.'

'Not so little.' They entered the shed, a vast, modern expanse, split in half by a raised concrete walkway wide enough to take a tractor. Feeding troughs ran along either side of this platform, where the dairy herd moved with steamy, shuffling bellows over a thick straw bed. 'What lovely cows you have,' said Betsy.

Rego opened a gate, and swung himself down. The cows turned to watch, as Betsy hesitated. 'What if they get frightened and stampede?' she asked.

'Come on.' Rego lifted a hand and she climbed down.

It was intimidating to be in an enclosed space with so many large creatures, but Betsy's new concern was sinking into the muck. Rego explained that it was safe, and began to walk among the cows who stood and watched, unmoving.

He stopped a few yards from a beast that was facing away from them, its rump scrawny above thin, straight legs, hoofs rising as if leaning forward on broken heels. Its tail was a frayed white mop that tightened into a sleek pink cord, a hip joint jutting out from the bony back where the tail turned into her spine. A number, 21 06, was branded across the rump, but Betsy's eyes were on the large, plump udder that squeezed out from between the two thin legs. The tail frayed exactly half-way down its swollen depth. The cow's body, although slick with health, seemed to be emaciated at a cost to that udder, as if everything she was rested there. The creature raised her head towards the far wall, then her face swung round on her long neck and she looked directly back along her length. Her ears were out, although the one closest to her body was lifted to avoid her flank, the crown of her skull rising away like a tiara. The eyes were patient, eyelashes expansive in her long face.

'*Salut*, Hirondelle,' said Rego. '*Ici* Betsy.'

Hirondelle shifted sidewards and her flank was revealed, her head white but for a patch of black on the jaw, and then a great sweep of darkness over her shoulders breaking up into islands as it moved back towards the all-white haunches.

'You're very beautiful, Hirondelle,' said Betsy. 'I presume I can speak to her in English?'

'Not if you want to be understood.' Rego walked forward, putting out his hand. The cow sniffed and ignored it; her tongue emerged and ran up the side of her face before it slipped away into her mouth. 'It's a cow, after all.' He waited forlornly for a smile, then walked down her flank, running his hand along her hide.

'I didn't know you could get so close,' said Betsy.

'They're handled twice a day.' He crouched beside her rear legs. 'And this is what it's all about. This is a money-box – or was until prices fell and transport costs rose.' He pointed to the thick, full veins that ran along the surface of the swollen udder. 'These are milk fountains and this one's as good as they get.' The pink skin was covered by the faintest sheen of white. When Rego put out a hand to touch, the cow flinched away. 'Easy now,' he said, shifting back and rising. 'I hope you're impressed.'

'You should be proud.'

'This is how genetic modification should be done. Years of good breeding'

'I'd rather think of her as just a beautiful creature,' said Betsy, glancing over and jumping. Priest was standing nearby, eyes swivelling deep in his fat face as he looked from Rego to the cow. Betsy tried to recover, but she felt a little unsteady. She had not yet seen him so close in good light and she noticed, and smelt, the filth on him. His dark blue boiler-suit was smeared with dirt, his hands and face were grey and the whites of his eyes tinged with blue. Again, he held the tip of his tongue between his teeth. At Betsy's gasp, Rego turned. 'Oh, hello, Priest,' he said. 'Bit early for the milking, isn't it?'

The man didn't reply, just crabbed sidewards to Hirondelle. Although it was impossible to read him, Betsy sensed his resentment at their presence in the barn. She felt as if she had been caught trespassing. The cow had allowed Priest to take her head in his hands, and now lifted her nose to sniff his face.

Rego seemed a little irritated. He gazed around the building, as if hoping to find fault. 'Give me a second,' he said to Betsy, and motioned Priest out of her hearing.

Betsy stood still. Many of the cows had turned towards her. She didn't like being the centre of attention, now that she was on her own.

'Okay,' Rego said, returning. 'Shall we go? Let's leave the two of them together.' He led her back the way they had come. 'I won't show you the milking parlour,' he said. 'Priest does all the milking and he can be a bit sensitive about people traipsing about in there. I've got to respect that. After all, I don't want to get up at five thirty in the morning.'

'So you're just responsible for the bloodlines, then?'

'Again, from a hands-free perspective. It's our friend there who gets dirty. He likes it, he's fond of them.' They had returned into the daylight and Rego seemed cheered. 'I just take the credit.'

'Convenient,' said Betsy.

'So, this work you do. Are you going to create genetically modified cows that will put me out of business?' He was washing his hands under a standpipe in the yard.

'That's not really my area.'

'No?' They reached the car. Rego dried his hands with kitchen towel he kept behind the seat.

'I deal more in theory.'

'More dangerous yet.'

Ice-filled potholes crunched under the wheels of the car as Rego followed a track that ran along the edge of a plantation. It was the same wall of trees Betsy recalled having seen in the distance on that first day, as she walked back to the harbour with her ex-fiancé. A small loch curved away to their left returning a little further on, the surface edged with ice, waterfowl keeping to its watery centre. Sunlight slanted over the trees, hitting the water out from the shore. Betsy's attention was caught by the silhouette of a fighter slicing through the sky to the south. There was a roar after the plane had passed out of sight, penetrating even the Range Rover's noise-proof exterior. They drove in shadow.

'The firing range?' Betsy asked. 'It's on the other side of the woods?'

'It starts about a mile that way.'

'Don't you worry that they might drop a bomb on you by mistake?'

Rego smiled. 'The targets are much further over. They used to fire tank shells just over there, though. We were worried then, especially about Priest. His place is in the wood.'

'There's a house in there?'

'It's more of a ruin, I think. I'm embarrassed to say that I don't really know. I never go in. It's his choice, though. He likes living in a place where nobody can find him.' Rego sounded tired.

'That seems a little odd.'

'You didn't notice that he was odd?'

Betsy laughed. 'Yes, but I mean . . .' She bit her lip and found herself studying the darkness at the base of the wood. The sunlight passing over the treetops enriched the shadow.

'He . . .' Rego seemed to struggle with what he wanted to say. 'When he was eleven, he . . . he hurt himself, in an accident . . . and he's never really been right since. But he's fine if he's left alone. That's all he really wants, to be left alone.'

'What happened?'

Rego said nothing but Betsy waited. 'It doesn't matter,' he said at last. 'It's embarrassing, and it really doesn't make any difference.'

'That's fine. I understand.' Betsy didn't mean it. She looked again into the darkness of the forest. 'You're good to him, though.'

'We grew up together.'

They came to a fork in the track, took the left turn and passed a sign: 'Howe Hill Strictly Private'.

'Because of the pilgrims,' Rego said.

'Pilgrims?'

'They go all over the place, leaving their little crosses. On their way to the cave.' He paused. 'You don't know about the cave? I thought that was why everyone came here.'

Betsy felt a shift, as if the landscape reconfigured itself. 'My ex wanted to visit it. It's near here?'

They were rolling through outbuildings now, then through a last clump of pine, out beside the chicken run, a walled garden directly ahead. 'I'll show you. We should take a walk – it's such a beautiful day and it might clear my head.'

'He said it was historically significant.'

'Yes. Very. It's where Christianity first touched down in Scotland. You're clearly not a Catholic.'

In front of them stood a Georgian house, the façade shaded from the sun. The straight lines and perfect angles seemed a civilized eye's response to the anarchy of the surrounding nature. A set of steps led up to a double door, with a high thin window at either side. Above were two more windows of the same proportions, then the eaves, the gentle descent of the roof. It was truly beautiful, a grand house by any description, yet smaller than its effect suggested, as if the architect had been ordered to trick and please the visitor simultaneously.

Rego let Betsy admire it for a minute, then led her through the garden, the paths bordering winter earth that had been turned under heavily trimmed shrubs. It was clear that the garden was resting, waiting for summer. They walked in silence, Betsy stopping to look back at the house from the different perspectives, enjoying its proportions. The only protuberance was a thin set of stairs

134

that climbed the side wall, the only curve a bow emerging from the front, taken up by long, elegant windows that seemed to suit the face of its owner. The windows kept watch on the firth, which sounded maybe half a mile distant but Betsy was unable to see the water from where she stood. They walked towards the sea, moving under empty trees, towards a gate overshadowed by a crippled oak. The bleakness touched Betsy, but the cold on her face, the crispness in the air, the clarity of the light lifted her further from the morning's gloom.

She broke the silence by asking about the house, and as they passed through the gate and followed a path down to rejoin the main pilgrims' track, Rego told her how in the grand days it had been his grandmother's house and then, later, his parents'. At last, they stood at the edge of a cliff, sloe and bramble keeping them from the precipice. The sea stretched out in front of them until dark landmasses broke surface on the horizon. 'You're very lucky to have all this,' said Betsy.

'Was lucky.' He looked at her and she saw that the weariness was in fact a profound sadness. He stepped back and began to walk to the east. He stopped a hundred yards further on, where the path led into a small gully, a flat stone showing a small cross. He had recovered, and beckoned her after him. They scrambled down the shale, and into a rocky bay.

A stream that had accompanied them formed a pool in a bank of fist-sized stones, sinking away to reappear further down the slope where waves whispered on the shore. Round and smooth, these stones were hard on the ankles and Betsy stumbled across them. The bay, which swung inland in a gentle arc, had been saved from the main force of the storm: the shoreline was clear of the detritus that lay piled along much of the coast. To the south, black rocks, painful-looking shards even from such a distance, jagged into the sea. Looking north along the scrub wall of the cliff, Betsy could pick out the route of a wide path, as if built for processions, that led up between outcrops of massive, leaning rocks. There it met what could only be the cave, a cut that fell into the shade, like darkness in a fold of flesh. As they walked she saw wooden crosses stuck into the earth wherever grass tufted the slope. A light trail of cloud had cast a haze over the sunlight, silvering the air, and she felt a presence, not malevolent or benevolent, but pervasive, stronger than that of an old house. Rego had not spoken since his words on the cliff edge.

As they passed more crosses, Betsy was struck by the simplicity with which they were made, out of branches and twigs, the lengths held together with twine. There were other markers: every ledge had been filled with stones from the beach, each with its own small crucifix scratched into the surface. The effect, added to the sense of presence, was of another time, earlier and savage. They climbed up to the natural portico, its smooth floor trodden flat by centuries of feet. The cave's opening, a wound in the rock, struck Betsy at once. It resembled a cut in tightly drawn skin, like an eye or, given the orientation, a more intimate orifice, scarred by thousands of scratched crosses.

'This is where the saint who brought Christianity to Scotland used to kneel,' Rego said. 'Or so they say.'

Already flooded with an image, Betsy was startled by Rego's words.

The sun seems sick. The plants will not grow. With plague on the land, I believe the dry cattle should be in from the fields, but Cutter refuses. He tells me not to bother him, to do what I'm told. He has enough to worry about, he explains, and orders the fishing equipment cleaned. The milk cows are restless, he has troubled them.

Rego led the way up the steps to the side door of his house and stood aside to let Betsy into a long kitchen. A dresser ran the length of one wall, matched by a table in the middle, with a range at the end. He asked her if she would like a sherry to see off the sun and, glasses in hand, they padded through the house in their socks. The dining room, reached by climbing three steps, fed into the great bay windows, the sea opening up beyond the leafless trees. There was a large mahogany table and old portraits that hung on walls as rich as the darkening sky. They walked through into the drawing room, which took up the entire side of the house with windows facing in three directions and a vast fireplace in the fourth wall. As in the dining room, the furniture was aged but immaculate, comfortable sofas covered in worn fabrics, with patterns that showed game-birds walking. Here, the faded corn-yellow on the walls held landscapes. Touched by a sense that she was in another era, Betsy asked if he had changed anything since he had inherited the house. Rego shook his head, with an unusually reticent smile. They walked through into a tall, square hall, and climbed a narrow staircase that led up to a balcony. He showed her his office, a room set against the upper levels of the bay windows, with a vast dark desk facing the door. Then they moved through into the bedroom. It took up the front corner of the house, one window looking down to the sea, another towards the forest. The bed, a carved expanse of oak, white linen and threadbare, earthy counterpane, was positioned for the view.

Rego grew awkward. 'It's the best spot to see the sun set,' he said, leading her into the corner where a daybed reclined perpendicular to the setting sun. 'It's where I watch the sun set.'

'Of course,' Betsy replied. They sat next to each other, sipping their drinks, watching the sky burn. Despite the flirtation she had let slip into her reply, Betsy remained careful to keep the conversation on the further edge of personal. It was unusual for Rego to lose the self-assurance that gave him poise and a quiet authority, but Betsy had begun to discern the need in him. As darkness filled the room she sensed that he had moved closer and, aware of being corralled, she stood and suggested they go back downstairs.

As the evening passed, she started to get a fuller picture of the monumental weights that pressed down on him. It was as if he, too, was caught in a storm, and blows could come from any side. In Betsy's eyes, he stood alone, and in that lay the need she had felt, a yearning – deeply hidden – for the comfort of touching someone. They ate a quiet supper, accompanied by a bottle, and then another, of Spanish wine. Betsy had been determined to keep him at arm's length, despite a growing awareness of her own desire. She wanted to retain her separation from her usual life, to enhance her sense of exile in which she was certain she would find the answers to the questions with which she had been presented in the break-up of her relationship. Yet the elusiveness of that need in him, the way it could only be glimpsed, was getting to her. An hour passed after dinner, then two, and she felt a carelessness take her.

'You being here,' he was saying, 'it makes such a

difference. On my own, the wine had been tasting bitter . . .' The phone rang. He didn't move until the answer-machine clicked in and they heard Helen's sobs. Then he dived for the receiver, saying her name and listening. 'I'll come right over,' he said at last. 'Yes, right now. This very minute.' He put the phone down. 'Something horrible has happened. Someone's done something horrible to Helen. I need to go over there.'

'Is she okay?'

'Physically yes, but no, she's not. She's scared.'

'Let me come.'

He thought for a moment. 'Okay.' He glanced at his watch as Betsy put on her jacket. 'Jesus, it's nearly midnight.'

They drove fast through the stand of pine and pulled up outside the outbuildings. He jumped out. 'I won't be a moment.' As he was about to close the door he had a final thought. 'Hit the horn.'

'What?'

He reached in and took her hand. 'Lean on the horn.' He pushed down and the car howled, a sharp sound in the night. 'Just keep at it. Don't let go.'

Betsy sat with her hand on the horn, looking into the darkness. A light came on in one of the buildings and Rego emerged, pulling a trailer, a shovel in his other hand. 'Keep pushing,' he shouted, as he attached the trailer to the towbar at the back, then threw the shovel on to it. When he returned and had put the car in gear, Betsy removed her hand and sat back. The Range Rover smooth-rolled over the bumps, yawing as Rego tried to avoid the potholes. The purr of the engine was shattered every few moments as he pummelled the horn, and he pulled up where the track turned and ran up along the edge of the forest.

'Won't he be asleep?' Betsy asked.

Rego pointed into the darkness. Priest rose out of the forest and scrambled over the fence, his big, dirty face passing Betsy's window before he jumped into the trailer, both hands gripping the bar at its front. Rego took off, Betsy looking back. Priest was bracing himself, staring past her and out into the distance. He showed no surprise at either the late call or her presence. She glanced at Rego and he caught her eye, then looked up at the rear-view mirror.

'Loyal manservant,' he said.

'Don't be mean.'

Once on the metalled road, Rego drove swiftly, lights swinging across the fields, rabbits running stupidly in an effort to escape the tyres. The street-lights glowed in the village but the cottages were mostly dark, and then they were out into the night again, moving fast along the small road until Helen's cottage appeared. There was a silvery reflection from between the gateposts, alien in the matt shades of the night. Rego pulled up and leaned on the steering-wheel to look at a large pile of fish, three feet high at its centre, tapering away in a gradual slope to all sides. Scales reflected light from the ditch and under the hedges that bordered the gates. He opened the door, and the smell hit them – sickly and sour.

'Oh, God,' said Betsy.

'Right,' agreed Rego. 'But it could have been worse.'

'Really?'

Priest was standing beside Rego's window, but peering into the night. Rego shooed him to the side, and then, holding open the door, deftly reversed the trailer into the entrance of the field, swinging it round so that he could back up to the fish. He stepped out. 'Over to you,' he said to Priest.

Priest lifted the shovel from the flatbed and began to load the mess into the trailer. There was a mixture of ugly-looking creatures, a slurry of sea-life. The smell was overpowering as they were disturbed, and Betsy put a hand in front of her face as she watched Priest work.

'It's the rubbish,' explained Rego. 'They wouldn't have wanted to use anything that could have been sold.' He walked round the pile but couldn't find a way through. Helen had appeared at the door of the cottage, fully dressed, and, for once, in a thick coat. They waved. 'A bit stuck here,' Rego shouted. 'We'll try and find our way round the back.' He pointed at the field.

Helen nodded, just visible under the light above the door.

Rego led Betsy through the gate. She felt quite drunk, but made her way safely up the side of the house. Rego looked for a spot to negotiate the barbed-wire fence.

'This is awful,' said Betsy. She felt a giggle rise, a re-action to the booze and the cruelty of the situation, and wanted to control it before she embarrassed herself. 'Is Priest all right doing that?'

'Oh, yes.'

'I can't believe you make him travel in the trailer.'

'Trust me, he smells worse than the fish.'

'That's terrible,' said Betsy, feeling complicit.

The light from the cottage spread across the garden. To Betsy's query about how they were going to get over the fence, he lifted her and dropped her gently on the other side in the rockery. She brushed herself down in an attempt to regain a little dignity, while Rego vaulted across beside her.

A seriousness enveloped them as they followed a path to the back door where Helen waited, hugging herself. Her

141

expression – a complete lack of comprehension – sobered them further, and Rego, then Betsy, embraced her. She had been crying and, leaning into Betsy, began to sob again. 'Why? Why would they do this to me?'

'Come inside,' said Rego, 'out of the cold.'

Helen was still holding Betsy as they entered the kitchen, but then pulled away, apologetic. 'I'll make tea.'

'No,' said Betsy. 'I'll make it. You sit down.'

Helen sank to the table, pressing at the edge with her fingernails. She looked nervously at Rego, who lowered himself on to the chair opposite.

'So, tell me, what happened?'

Helen glanced at Betsy, worried.

'Helen?' said Rego.

'Well, I don't know.' She was shivering, even though she had her coat over her shoulders and the kitchen was warm, condensation streaking the window. 'I was asleep. The phone rang.'

'And you answered it?' Rego said.

'I'm sorry.'

'Go on.'

Helen began to cry again. 'This voice said . . .' Her sobs were the same as those Betsy had heard the first time she had come to visit, her voice emerging taut, adding emphasis to an unnecessary attempt to imitate the caller. 'This voice said, "Willie wants to give you a gift, a remembrance of him." I asked what he meant, I was frightened, but whoever it was said, "He's left it for you out front. It's something he liked more than life." And then they rang off.' The kettle had boiled but Betsy stayed beside the table, stroking Helen's hair. Helen, eyes wide open, threw a look from Rego to Betsy, then back again. 'Well, I went down,' she continued softly. 'I went out there.' She

142

stopped, and crumpled again. Betsy knelt so that she could hold her.

'They're bastards, Helen,' said Betsy.

'William didn't do anything wrong,' Helen sobbed, through her tears. 'He would have done nothing wrong.'

Rego sat, his chin on his fist. 'I know,' he said. 'I know.' He looked at Betsy. 'This is a bad business,' he said. 'I'll go now, find out who did this and put a stop to it.' He looked back at Helen. 'Did you recognize the voice?'

She whispered no.

'It shouldn't be too difficult to find out. We'll get it stopped.'

Helen struggled to recover and Betsy left her to make tea.

Rego followed her. 'I'll have to go and do this on my own.'

'I'll stay.'

He smiled. 'Priest is clearing up. I'll leave him the trailer, then pick it up later. By morning the mess will be gone.'

Helen raised her eyes from the table. 'Mr Rego? William was a good man, wasn't he?'

'Yes, a good friend, and a good husband. But I can't just sit here. I need to go and sort this out right now. Betsy will look after you. You'll be all right now, won't you?'

Helen nodded.

'Betsy, walk me to the door, will you?'

They moved down the corridor. Rego opened the front door and stepped out on to the porch. In the lights from the cottage, Betsy saw Priest working away, tireless. He had already cut a dark path through the dull shimmer of the rotten fish.

'I'm sorry,' said Rego. 'You have no idea how sorry. I

enjoyed tonight. For a while I almost forgot.' He had placed a hand gently on her arm.

'Will they listen?' she asked.

'I'll tell them Priest had to clear it up.'

'Then go and find them.'

He looked into the darkness. 'Terrible. Look, I'll come by in the morning.'

Betsy shifted her face a little so that his kiss landed on her cheek, but she watched him all the way to his car.

MONDAY

High tide: 07.05, 19.51
Light easterly

Betsy followed the thin, indented line along the table edge with her eyes. It dimmed near the corner, picking up again after the turn. She watched Helen's fingers work. Catching her gaze, Helen dropped her hands into her lap. They looked at each other, Betsy holding the receiver to her ear, the line connecting with a click. 'Hi,' she said. 'It's me. I've got a small problem.'

'Lucky you,' her boss replied, his voice dark with its Jedburgh accent. 'I've got a big problem.'

'Oh.' Betsy, hungover, sighed at his self-absorption. 'What's that?'

'You see the papers yesterday?'

'No, I'm in Galloway. I was busy yesterday. It's been a bit of a disaster.'

'Yes.'

Helen was smiling at her, but pressing at the edge of the table again.

'You know?' said Betsy.

'Your man called.'

'Called *you*?' She felt a bee-sting at the temple.

'Yes.'

Betsy waited. 'Oh, come on,' she said finally. 'Talk. Please.'

'He called to say he resented our . . . our mistake, and that he planned to write to my wife about it.'

'Oh, Christ.' Betsy sighed. 'I'm sorry. But your wife knows already – you told her, didn't you?'

'Yes. And that's what I said to him. Foolishly, as it turns out.'

Betsy's boss was a master of saying little and allowing others to fill the spaces until their nerves made them babble and humiliate themselves. After long and difficult years, Betsy had found that silences of her own could defeat the tactic, and the habit had finally grown on her as well. She said nothing and eventually he spoke again. 'You see, he decided to tell a tabloid instead.'

Betsy was confused. 'But why? Surely they wouldn't have been interested.' It was then that she saw the brilliance of it, and felt sick.

'They were very interested when he told them that I had signed the deal with Life Sciences. It gave them a lovely story. "Meet McFrankenstein. He tortures chimps, cheats on his wife and seduces his staff." The editorial said it had thought people like me died out during the eighteenth century.'

A chill seeded in Betsy's chest and expanded outwards. She kept quiet, this time because she had no idea what to say. He spoke again. 'I take it the romantic week didn't work out?'

'I'm so sorry.' Betsy looked up to see that Helen's smile had been replaced with concern. She turned away. She had only been calling in sick but now she felt

146

sick and wished she had been making this call in private.

'I know that,' he said. 'Where are you?'

'Same place.'

'You should stay there. The papers are looking for you – your boyfriend seems to have chosen not to tell them where you are. Surprisingly considerate of him.'

The irony of having been among reporters was not lost on her. 'What are you going to do?' she asked.

His naturally laconic style reasserted itself. 'Well, Comrade, if you've got a simple way of explaining what I do, of pointing out that I don't actually touch the chimps myself, I could use it right now, try to justify my work at least, but for the moment I have police protection, as do my family.' She heard him take a sip of a drink. 'Betsy, you're suspended. I think the chief will sack you, but you need to talk to him. You should have known not to talk about the Life deal. This couldn't be worse.'

'You *need* police protection?'

'There were protesters outside the front door of the lab this morning, and there have been threats and abusive phone calls to my home. We haven't had the first letters yet. Of course, there are already questions about the need for taxpayers to protect me. McFrankenstein seems to have caught on. All the papers used the description this morning.'

'What can I do?' Betsy was too shocked to say more.

'Give me a number.'

Betsy told him the name of the inn.

'Will you be all right there?' he asked.

'Yes,' she said. 'Fine. I'm very sorry, boss.'

'Well, it could have been worse,' he said, with a bitter laugh. 'You could have married him.'

'I'm so, so sorry.'

'Goodbye, Betsy.'

She replaced the receiver and looked at Helen.

'Bad news?'

'Horrible.'

Helen waited, and finally Betsy stood up, meeting her half-way so that they embraced, held each other close.

'Just trouble at work,' whispered Betsy, feeling stupid. 'It's you we need to worry about. It's you we need to look after.' She pulled away and held the other woman's hands, her mind jammed with the white noise of awful thoughts.

Betsy waited for Rego to arrive, playing a game with Helen that involved rhyming from the names of the seabirds they saw passing outside the window. It was a tough exercise, a complicated I-Spy, and one at which Helen seemed practised. The need to concentrate made Betsy wonder if the game was a trick of Helen's to take her mind off difficult things. She wondered if, having seen her distress after the call, Helen had turned to it as a form of comfort. If she had, Betsy was grateful; her mind was still a mess and she was keen to get back to the inn so that she could wait for any calls. She needed time alone to think. It was a relief when she heard Rego shout from the front door.

He surged into the kitchen, his big frame ducking under the lintel, and sank into a chair. He grinned first at Betsy, then Helen. 'You've seen the fish have gone?'

'Yes,' said Helen. 'Thank you.'

'I don't think it will happen again. I couldn't find out exactly who was responsible but I've a good idea. I've had a word with a few people. Told them that this sort of thing helps no one.'

Betsy picked up her coat. 'I've got to go back to the inn. I'll see you both later.'

Rego's good humour vanished as he stood up. 'Wait a little and I'll drive you. It's cold out there.'

She walked round to him and touched his arm reassuringly. 'I need the walk. Let's meet up later.'

There was confusion, a wariness, on his face. His eyes flickered to Helen.

'Something's come up at work,' said Betsy, 'and I need to have a think. Can I tell you about it later?'

'I could give you a lift back now. It will be icy on the path. You could hurt yourself.'

'No. Please. Stay with Helen.'

'I do need to have a word with her . . .' He looked at the other woman, then back at Betsy. 'Okay, be careful. I'll drop by later.'

Betsy kissed Helen, then let herself out of the back door. Remembering herself, she stepped over the flower-bed and looked through the window. 'I've tried to speak to the Irish, to do what you said . . .' Helen was saying. Rego gripped her hand and pointed to where Betsy stood at the window.

'Helen, I'll see you later too,' Betsy said, through the glass. She waved again and stepped back. She assumed Rego was helping Helen to claim William's body. As she walked towards the tree at the other side of the bay, her mind turned to her own troubles.

Martha was outside the inn. 'You must have been up early,' she said, as Betsy approached.

'I stayed at Helen's again.'

The direction of Martha's gaze was fixed on the fields opposite; a group of sheep stood close to the shore edge. 'How is she?'

'Put upon, I think. There was a nasty incident last night.'

'Oh, yes?'

'Somebody dumped a load of rotten fish at her door.'

Martha turned to study her but then the landlady's attention fell away. 'How long do you plan to stay?' she asked. 'It's just the bill – I might get you to pay weekly if you're going to be here much longer.'

The change of subject was as blunt as the question. It put Betsy back on her heels. 'I suppose that depends on how long I can afford it,' she said.

'Which is why I would prefer it if you could pay weekly.' She was joking, but the words still held a cold edge. 'I'll do you a deal, though. Seven days for the price of six. Call it a hundred and fifty for the week. How's that?'

'Good.' A jet flew low across the firth, the sound chasing it through the sky, and they were silent until it had departed, the popping of its cannons a distant staccato. Then they briefly discussed mundane matters, such as laundry.

'Did Helen say anything about the divers finding the others?' Martha asked, when the arrangements had been made.

'No.' Betsy was shocked. 'Have they?'

'They managed to get through this morning.' She pulled herself upright, even though she hadn't been noticeably slouching.

'And William?'

'No. Not yet. I'd better call Helen.'

'James Rego's there. I'm sure he knows.'

Betsy now saw the movement she had missed: Martha settling into herself.

'This weather,' Martha cried, with an anger that had been hidden moments before. 'It's an insult. It kills men, and then nothing but blue skies for days.' The flash passed. 'It's enough to make anyone superstitious.'

'What does it mean, their finding the bodies?' asked Betsy. 'Will they take them off?'

Martha frowned, her brow corrugating. 'I don't know. You'd hope so. The Irish want to lift the boat but the British government is refusing to pay its share. They say the sea floor's a fitting grave for sailors. They're not being a lot of help.'

'James says it's better if it's not lifted. He feels it'll raise more bad feelings towards Helen.'

Martha produced a small, gall-sour laugh and drew herself up. 'Yes, I'm sure he does.' She left it at that and headed for the door.

The walk back had been easier than Betsy had expected. The air, while painfully cold, was salty enough that it had protected the path from freezing, and the concentration required had helped to keep the worst of her thoughts at a distance. Now, as Betsy followed Martha inside, those thoughts returned. She sat on the edge of her bed with all the prim demeanour of a guest at a dance, the awfulness of the situation in Edinburgh sweeping in like an unwelcome approach. Despite being a researcher and a solid member of the team, Betsy had become, over the years, something of a protector to her boss, and now she had let him down. A lapsed Communist, he barely ever called her by her name, preferring the 'Comrade' he still reserved for the closest of his small team. Thinking back to the telephone conversation she realized that the weight had been the other way. She felt humiliated. She knew his failings, they extended over every aspect of his character, yet his talent was such that she was prepared to pander to them. It was a constant battle to put up with his laziness, but she knew that his reliance on her made her feel wanted in a way her ex-fiancé never had. The balance between work and home had, in many ways, been perfect, but now, having upset one end, all had gone. In the past when things went wrong, she had protected her boss from colleagues, friends, funders and even the press, so that his work could go on. This time she was the cause of the trouble, and powerless to do anything about it.

It all seemed so unnecessary. The affair, if that was what that one miserable night had been, had hardly rippled their working relationship. Apart from the irritation of realizing that the whole event had occurred to quench some curiosity in him, with the insulting addition that the thirst had been sated by one experience, she had felt none of the uncomfortable shifts that office sex is supposed to cause. She had known why she was doing it, even at the time, although the regret as she sat astride him (this was his idea of good sex) only arrived with full penetration. Ultimately she had been reassured that a man's behaviour doesn't change much between the office and the bed, a theory proved when, after she had done all the work and brought him to orgasm, he had sighed and said, 'Well, I hope that got it out of your system.' He claimed later that this was to make her laugh, an antidote for the guilt he was sure she was feeling. While she didn't believe this for a moment, it had ensured there would be no altitude sickness when she returned from such heady heights of passion to the mundane realities of the office. None. Her boss lay on his back in more ways than she could count, in all ways, in fact, but one. And that was his job, where he was like the most wonderful conversation possible, an eternal revelation, and it was here she found the stimulation she needed. When she put information in front of him, results she had studied and manipulated in as many ways as she could, he would slide into the figures from a direction that had been invisible to her. He was a generous lover of this work, happy to draw her in, make her understand. So when they had reached the laboratory after that night, when they had returned to the ideas that a group of results had offered them the night before – the ideas that had led to sex – Betsy felt the relief that most mistresses would feel when their paramours announced plans for divorce. Somehow the experience of fucking him had made no difference at all.

Which could not be said for the reaction the betrayal had provoked in her boyfriend. The whole point had been to let him know. He had made a virtue of their so-called open relationship, holding up his absences to her as if they were other women's underwear. He would never name names but, rather, waited for her shock so that he could mount a furious defence of his 'rights' under their 'agreement'. He would tell her that her interest in the details was sad and he was withholding them only to protect her from her own nature. As a result, when she left the laboratory to pick up a sandwich and found her boyfriend standing at the front gate wearing an expression of the purest fury, she had no trouble in telling him she had had 'other plans' the night before and had been 'far too busy' to answer the 'ludicrous number of calls' he had placed to the receptionist that morning. He was genuinely shocked, asking what other plans she meant. To overcome her natural nervousness, she replied, with a certain boastfulness, 'I was having sex.' Saying those words was as much fun as telling her girlfriends about her first proper kiss when she was twelve. He looked as if his brain was trying to escape his skull. He couldn't speak. She began to worry whether he might hit her, and whether it would hurt, and result in an embarrassing scene outside her workplace. She walked away, and didn't turn until she had made the corner of the building. Alone, she ducked down into the lab's underground car-park and regained the safety of the seventies façade. She never managed to get lunch but she was content none the less, even when Security called to say that her instructions to repel any attempt by her boyfriend to get in had required force.

That day, as evening had approached, and with it the moment when she would have to head back to the flat, a soft fear had moved in. During the walk back along George IV Bridge, high above the old catacombs of Edinburgh, across a Royal Mile that was a sea of festival colours, she had been preoccupied with what she might find. As she stepped down into the heart of this city of wide horizons, into the view of the New Town and Fife beyond, she had begun to understand the damage her point-scoring had inflicted on herself. A little of her ease with life – others might say innocence – which several years later her ex-fiancé would attack with such devastating force, had disintegrated, and scars had formed on her soul.

By the time she had reached her flat in Comely Bank, her concerns grew immediate. A locksmith was removing the dead-bolt from her front door. 'You might want to finish up,' she had said, to his friendly greeting. 'There's going to be a row.'

He fussed for a while, asking if she had seen what the intruders had done to the place, but by then the boyfriend had appeared out of the bedroom, yelling at the workman for the time he had taken. Betsy wandered from room to room, surveying the damage. There was little of hers that he hadn't attacked, and although she had admired his ability to pick out the things she cared most about – he'd stamped on the architectural model of a wendy house her father had designed but never built – it would take years for her to understand the cool-headed thought that went into his fury. Despite the spittle-flecked screams of outrage, the locksmith appeared and handed her the keys, asking if she was sure she would be okay. She smiled reassurance, said she would be fine, and offered payment, which was refused. When he had gone, she turned to her boyfriend and went on the offensive. That evening had been truly terrible and it took some weeks to get over it, but although her infidelity was an open sore from then on, the lost nights to other women never reoccurred. A year or so later a slip by a drug-dealing Turk he went clubbing with suggested that there had never been any other women.

As Betsy's eyes lost focus on the inn's walls, she saw the awful monstrosity of his behaviour, and grew furious. She felt another part of her sour; this happiness of hers, this innocence he accused her of, struggled under the assault of his revenge. She stood as she picked up the telephone and rang her home number.

'You bastard,' she said, but her voice was greeted by one long howl of an obscenity, a vastly extended 'fuck-you', that ended with the phone hitting the floor. There was an explosion of glass and then he was back, whispering, 'The television, bitch,' and the line was cut. She didn't feel like trying again: her strength would be needed where she was. She felt like the bird that had just risen from the last available branch over a rising flood, all beneath her gone.

Her life in the capital was disintegrating. Her ex was destroying the contents of the flat. She saw her job swallowed up, her projects moving into other hands, her relationships turning to a call or two, then a falling out of touch. Her memory had always been good – she turned to the window and looked out at the cold landscape beyond – but a physical distance was involved here, and her old life now seemed to calve off like an iceberg setting out to melt somewhere in warmer distances. She turned on the television at one o'clock to catch the news. With the self-absorption of being in a crisis, she wondered if the story would appear on the screen in front of her. It didn't, which only added to her feelings of exile. The news was all of the animal plague: a market in the Borders was a well of disease from which farmers had unwittingly drawn, and images of greasy smoke hanging over pyres flickered out at her. The flames darkened the film's exposure, causing the melting carcasses to appear black and medieval. She switched off, lay down and tried to sleep.

Towards the end of the afternoon the telephone rang, rousing her from a half-dream in which she was fleeing spectres. She rolled over on the synthetic covers and looked at the handset, not sure whether to save herself anguish by ignoring it. When she finally reached out the line was dead. She slumped back, and returned to the unworldly space she had just left.

The phone woke her again and she rose, looking at the clock. It was almost six. She wondered if she was depressed. The idea made her smile. She lifted her legs off the bed and reached again for the handset, this time catching the caller.

'I wondered where you'd got to.' It was Rego.

'I was asleep.' She yawned, relieved. 'Did you try earlier? The phone rang but I didn't get to it in time.'

He said he had, and asked if she was okay. 'Helen said you had a bad call with your office.'

'Do you ever have good ones if you're away?'

He was silent. Then he said, 'I don't know. I've never worked for anyone else.'

Betsy failed to laugh. 'It was fine. I thought they might need me back but they don't.'

'I was wondering if we should get together later,' he asked. 'I enjoyed yesterday.'

'I hear they've found more of the fishermen.' She was finding it difficult to get the remnants of sleep out of her head.

He spoke his affirmative slowly, a drawn-out yes. 'They were mostly in their bunks.'

'But not Helen's . . . Not William?'

'No. He's probably there but it's dangerous, the way the boat's lying, they have to be careful.' He waited, then added, 'I'm trying to get them to take the others off.'

'Poor Helen. Is that what they're going to do?'

'They want to bring the bodies off in the next few days. But they're still talking about raising the boat to get to them all. I'm hoping it won't be necessary. That's why if we met it would need to be later. I've got a few things to discuss with some people first.'

Betsy scratched her leg. 'It's all right. I'm feeling shattered. You must be as well. I think I might just get a bit of rest tonight. Perhaps we could hook up tomorrow?'

Again, he took a moment to reply. 'It's a pity,' he said at last. 'This thing's getting to me. I could use your ability to listen.'

'It wouldn't be much good to you tonight.'

Another hesitation, then he spoke slowly: 'It's funny, you know, the people involved, that's what's important, the families. But I've just glanced at my accounts and, you know, this thing might ruin me. There's nobody I can talk to, nobody who'll understand, it would seem so insensitive.'

Betsy tried to pull herself together, extract a little energy from within. 'I really want to help, but can we leave it until . . .'

'Okay,' he said, as if his mind was already elsewhere. 'Goodnight.' He was gone before she could reply.

She replaced the handset and looked out across the harbour and up at the lights of the houses on the hill. Tonight she was not going to feel guilty. She couldn't shoulder Rego's troubles, not this evening. The water in the harbour moved sluggishly, thick in the cold, while above the air was clean and the sky was ablaze with stars. She tried to empty her mind, to feel nothing, to take no responsibility, and for a short while she managed: the beauty of the view from this room in which her life had begun its disintegration calmed her, this picture of a village in mourning.

After a bath, Betsy dressed and went down to the bar to ask Martha to make her a sandwich. The lounge was silent and barely lit. She had wondered if she would see her neighbour but the corners of the room were empty. Bunbury sat on the far side of the bar, leaning against the counter, smoking with his one good hand and eyeing her, his gaze rude and direct. Since Martha had gone into the kitchen, she was alone with him, despite the counters and bottles that separated them. She tried to ignore the stare by leaning against the bar and looking out of the window, but this meant she had to feel his eyes rather than face them. Finally, turning back, she was ill prepared but determined to make a remark. As she opened her mouth Martha returned with her food and Betsy let her lips meet again. She took her sandwich, thanked the landlady and threw one last glance towards Bunbury. He was stubbing out his cigarette while continuing to stare. As she turned away, she saw the beginnings of a smile break up his grey, hollow face.

With the reporters gone and the year barely staggering into life, Boyle was the only other guest, and Betsy felt safe enough eating her sandwich in the residents' sitting room. The colour scheme was the same as much of the rest of the inn, relying heavily on yellow, but it provided a relief from the claustrophobia of her room. She switched on the television, watched a quiz but turned it off when she tripped over a geography question. It reminded her of her inadequacies. There was little in the room beyond the lounge chairs, the television, and a half-hidden stash of board games, all requiring two players or more. There was only one window, and it looked on to the back, on to a roof between two walls.

She had changed her mind, despite her exhaustion, and wished now that she had gone to talk to Rego. Yet she reminded herself of the previous day, and the possibilities it had raised between them, the implications of which she did not feel strong enough to answer. Instead she tried to contain a growing sense of panic, of her life floating away from her, by thinking about his problems rather than her own. She walked back to her room, the thought of his financial difficulties worming its way towards the knowledge of Boyle's search. If there was money, she realized, then perhaps an immediate worry could be lifted, and

Rego's burden could be lightened. She picked up the phone, but punched in Helen's number instead of Rego's. There was no answer, Helen was presumably asleep, so Betsy left a message, wishing her goodnight, telling her she was sorry she hadn't returned but that she would see her in the morning. So tired she was barely able to undress, Betsy crawled between the covers, but she couldn't sleep. The night passed in shifting states of despair, desire and the occasional troubled dream.

TUESDAY

High tide: 08.30, 21.07
Easterly

I

I wake screaming, my hand a thrashing paddle on the boards. I have to choke my voice. Crush it until the silence of the trees surrounds me. It is lucky I can't dream of the moment itself. All I can hear is the whispering, Cutter's voice in my ear. Soon the redness in the east will turn the sky from black to blue, and sunlight will cut into the trees, making the icy branches crackle and tinkle. When the light touches the forest floor in the open areas, a mist will rise. The strange and beautiful days are bringing back unwelcome memories but for now, in the darkness, the trees are white-edged, even here in the depths of the forest. The bodyaltar quivers with goosebumps despite its health and I have to rub it down with fat, rendered from the heifer that died before Christmas. As I spread, I feel the ridges under my touch. I will go down to the cave today and wipe clean my memory of the night. Some day, by the Saint's grace, there will come a time when the incision will be a perfect match, and I will be lifted into the Kingdom above. Perhaps it will be today.

Betsy knocked on Henry's door, and heard a shuffling from beyond. When he answered, he had a towel round his waist, his shirt hanging open. 'Up early,' he said.

The time hadn't occurred to Betsy. She glanced at the window beyond him and saw that dawn had yet to arrive. She had been kept from sleep by the thought that Boyle might solve Rego's immediate financial problems. 'I had no idea it was still so early,' she said.

'Up anyway.' He opened the door further.

She had bathed and dressed without opening the curtains. 'I must be going mad.'

'You, me, everyone,' he said. She followed him into the room, at once noticing several more objects lined up on the dressing-table. It was a little shrine which, from the indentations on the bed, he must have been contemplating.

'How are the kidneys?' she asked, as she looked down. The crystallized branch sat on the edge of the dresser, marking one end of the row. It seemed duller than she remembered. Where at first it had exploded with light, the crystals had grown opaque. Although it was still beautiful, she could sense the darkness of the wood underneath.

'Sore.'

'What's happened to—?'

'Opened the box. Sea air. Stupid.' For once he hadn't let her complete a question.

She leaned over and looked at the branch closely. 'Can you save it?'

'Could leave. Go home.'

Betsy studied his face to see if he was serious but found nothing there. He was fastening the buttons on his shirt, unrolling the sleeves to cover the dark hair that

162

spread over his chest and lay heavy on his forearms. 'No one will talk,' he said. At last, she caught a suggestion of emotion: frustration, his head flicking on his long, extended neck.

'Why don't you let me help?' Betsy's hand moved towards the paperback lying next to the branch, the book she had seen him with in the bar, its cover old and worn. She saw now that it had been wrapped up, like a child's schoolbook. She never reached it. He picked it up first, so she moved on to a round stone, the third item in the line Boyle had placed so religiously along the veneer top. 'From the cave,' she said.

'Cave?' He stepped over.

'The saint's cave.' She was shocked that he didn't know this and stared at him. 'You must know about it. Along the coast. The place the saint used to go to meditate, the saint this place is famous for. It's a shrine now.' She looked again at the stone. It was definitely from the beach: the colours were the same, the cross scratched on its surface, but the surface seemed different, less smooth, as if it had been taken away and kept in a warm place. 'Pilgrims go down there all the time and scratch the rocks and leave them beside the cave. You didn't know this?' She laughed. 'Some sleuth.'

He took the stone, turning it over.

Betsy wondered if he was playing with her. 'Where did you get it?' she asked.

'What do?' he asked, with difficulty. 'You want?'

'I want to know who you are looking for. It could be important. It could even be a blessing.'

He looked surprised, but she understood this was intentional: his face gave away only what he wanted it to. 'That way?' he asked, pointing across the harbour to where the far rocks were showing, as dawn approached.

'The cave?'

He nodded.

'Yes, but . . .' Betsy hesitated. 'Tell me who you are looking for. The cave, it's near James Rego's house. Is it Rego you are interested in?'

'How far?'

Betsy tried to reach for the paperback, but he held it tight to his stomach, a curiously precious gesture. 'What's the book?'

'Love.'

Betsy fell silent. She knew she was intruding. She had objected to his unctuousness, and now she suspected he was tolerating her questions because of some residual interest in what had happened to her. 'That doesn't tell me anything,' she said.

He was gazing out of the window at the dawn. 'The land,' he said. 'Being closed off. Should go. While still the chance.' He shifted, turning his head back towards her. 'Please. Excuse me. Need to dress.'

Betsy watched the yellow light push across the pale land-scape, listening to the movements from the neighbouring room. The dismissal had not been rude, but it was clear that a sudden sense of purpose had taken Boyle. His door opened, and she heard his feet on the stairs, saw him pass through the front door below her and move through the village with an ungainly roll to his step. He turned between two cottages and followed a track across the field on the far side of the harbour, disappearing as the coast swung inland from an outcrop where cormorants perched. The land was lighting up in the horizon-skimming sunshine. Betsy made a choice, and followed him. She stopped at the edge of the field where Rego had hung a sign telling walkers that the land was private, but decided it was in her friend's interest that she trespass. The sunlight had strengthened, shadows focusing before the morning's swing to the north. The recurrent winter days had touched the landscape, drying and bleaching the deadened earth. Betsy looked back at the village but her eyes caught on the daubed slogan on the harbour-master's wall, and she flinched at this connection between the city and her. Again she wondered if it might not be better just to tell Rego about Boyle's mission, in the hope the information might allow him more time for Helen, but it was too early in the morning to visit him. More than that, there was an effervescence in the air that played on her as she walked, and she felt the adventure catch her. She kept low to the shoreline, following a path that wriggled between the boulders, enjoying herself.

She crossed a dyke, and when she looked back she could see sunlight showing through the gaps between its stones. Oystercatchers and gulls darted along the seashore, the water falling away as the land climbed. A stream snaked between two buttresses, flowing beside gorse and thorn to arrive in a pool that was wide and black, the surface punctured by boulders, then left it through a series of smaller waterfalls that were rhythmically drowned by waves from the rising sea, whitewater reaching up and lapping at the mouth of the pool. The cormorants had gone from their perch. Betsy was careful as she rounded the promontory but Boyle had disappeared, only the long, weaving incline of the coast rising into vertiginous cliffs, the plantation that struggled up from the wind-ravaged outer edge dramatic against the still dark western sky, the cone of the hill to her right. Rego's house was hidden in a dip.

The path, the faintest of tracks, lay along the cliff edge and Betsy followed it with difficulty. Boyle was ahead of her, appearing and disappearing with the dips in the landscape. She tried to stay low. At last she reached a wall, built up to be hard to cross, but on the other side, she recognized the turn where the path from the other direction began its descent to the cave. The bay below was out of sight, and Betsy chose not to follow Boyle. Instead she made for Rego's house, turning, after a short walk, towards the perfect lines of the Georgian roof, showing among the bare branches. She reached the gate at the bottom of the garden, and the oak that, come summer, would spread leaves wide over the entrance.

Here she gazed around the copse. The previous summer's leaves had broken into mulch where they had drifted, and the storm had left a bed of sticks. To walk further would be to set the ground crackling with alarm. In the distance several trees had fallen and the trunks lay prostrate and dark. Betsy stared up at extremities of the oak above her. The twigs shattered the blue beyond. Although stunted, the tree's thick, knotted trunk gave it a certain permanence, enhanced by how it opened into a cradle of branches that spread above the gate. Betsy noticed that they offered an entrance at the top of the leaning trunk. She unclipped the latch and stepped through to take a better look. Knots at the base showed signs that they had been used, long before, to climb. Betsy dawdled, her gaze passing through the empty spaces below the other trees, and then she clambered easily up the oak into the hollow.

There was a little pool of dirt, and a gap between the two seaward branches, which opened to allow a protected view of the coast. The bark was heavily scarred with symbols and letters, and Betsy let her fingers run across the marks. She felt warmth overcome her as she discovered a 'James', and she imagined the boy who had scratched the letters. The wood had long discoloured, bark-edge swelling and ridging at the slash giving the mark a calligraphic style its author could never have hoped for. When she looked again towards the coast the warmth went, and a chill spread over her skin to take its place.

A figure had broken the horizon, rising from the edge of the precipice. For a moment Betsy wondered if Priest had crawled directly from her troubled dreams. With a look east and then west, he began a slow lope towards her. A hand crossed his chest – he was holding his opposite shoulder and his head swung continuously, as if linked to the rhythm of his legs. Betsy sank down, the marks now an impenetrable babble around her.

Priest arrived below her, his footsteps feline for such a large man. She could hear his gentle panting, the murmurs between inhalations, half formed words oozing from him. She sensed hesitation in him and the murmuring fell away as he drew the bolt in the gate back and forth two or three times. She felt the air move slowly into her nose as she drew breath. He passed underneath and was now behind her. She couldn't risk turning for fear of making a sound, and had no idea whether her back was exposed, whether he was now watching her. Her knees ached, her eyes barely focused on the letters in the wood; all she thought about were the twigs that lay scattered under the trees, and the absence of sound. The pain in her joints built up until she couldn't bear it any longer. She rose and revolved slowly. Priest was nowhere to be seen.

Betsy rested against the branches, letting the discomfort drift away. Nothing stirred. The conifer plantation slid in from the west, pushing past a few hundred yards away. The spaces beneath the tall trees were empty in the soft light, a quiet landscape in which she picked out the hen coop, the garages, and the driveway. The air retained the freshness of early morning, the landscape still asleep.

She turned again, and found Boyle looking up at her from a few yards down the path. The shock registered in her belly but she was already so tense that she managed to suppress a cry. He put his index finger to his lips, suggesting silence. She leaned back against the cradled branches, trying to find equilibrium by concentrating on the letters and symbols that surrounded her. Among the doodles, the Js of different sizes, there were an M or two and a cartoonish penis. The absurdity of this childish picture allowed her to smile and capture herself. She stood up, backed out of the cradle, and paused as her eye returned to the M. She stepped down on to the ground.

'What are you doing here?' she whispered. She didn't want to be seen with Boyle, and led him behind the tree-trunk. 'You gave me such a fright.'

'What I'm . . . doing here?' He looked up at the tree, apparently calm. 'You.' He pointed. 'In a tree. And I frighten *you*?'

Betsy felt a nervous itch under her arms. 'What *are* you doing here?'

'Looking.' He smiled. If he was trying to reassure her, he failed. 'You?' He had moved closer to her.

His proximity irritated Betsy. 'None of your business,' she said, wiping moss from her coat. She took a couple of steps towards the sea.

'This? It's James Rego's house?'

168

She heard a twig break under his foot and stopped to look round.

'Saw Priest at the beach,' he continued. 'Thought I'd . . .' he gestured in the direction Priest had taken. When Betsy failed to reply he looked upwards. 'Why the tree?'

'You should be careful, you might get beaten up again.' Betsy was aware of the closeness of the outbuildings, the rising walls of the house, its big bay window. She was thinking about the marks on the bark, and the book Boyle had held. 'The person you're looking for?' she asked, deciding to take a gift of chance where she found it. 'The name doesn't begin with an M, does it?' His expression remained fixed, but he didn't reply. 'Come on, why not let me help?' She stared at him, but his eyes were shaded. 'I can keep a secret.'

He swallowed. 'You're sweet,' he said, in his strangled fashion.

'Sweet' was not a description Betsy was used to, and his reply conjured up an image of his body, with its mat of piggish hair. She tried to disguise her revulsion. She waited. A minute passed and she turned again towards the coast.

'Mary,' he said.

She stopped.

'Mary,' he repeated, and then, 'That's.' He choked. 'It.'

'I don't believe you. You must have more than Mary.'

'Army man. In the 1960s. Policyholder. Writes "Mary" on form. Gave the address as this village. That's it. No surname, no home address, nobody notices at the office.'

'That's it?' Betsy felt uncomfortable, the details made her feel as if she was trespassing on a personal history, but she overcame the sensation. 'How does that bring you here? Why Mr Rego?'

'You,' Boyle said. 'Your turn.'

'You'll tell me, though?'

He nodded.

'In the tree, up there . . .'

'About you.'

'No.' Betsy's tone was dismissive. 'No. Let's stick to this. In that tree, there are letters carved. James's name, lots of Js and – I said I would help – an M, perhaps for Mary.'

Boyle stared at her, then looked into the branches. He walked towards the oak.

'They're very old,' she said, following, reaching the gate. 'Mr Rego must have used it when he was a boy.'

Boyle climbed easily into the cradle. She could hear him moving around, finding the cuts.

'You see them?' Betsy asked.

Silence had returned to the woods. There was no sound from the tree.

The grease fills the grooves, my fingers running over each mark, blood bubbles rolling on the fat. I squat in a clearing, the sun rousing a mist around me. I cover the bodyaltar with my hands, touching everything. I reach for the original stig, looking for sensation, the rapture to roar in my head but, nothing. Night has unsettled me. I recall the whispering. I had tried, as I do, to cover my ears, but a voice can inhabit a dream so there is no escape. Long ago Cutter's voice moved into my skull. Insistently it explains that purity comes only with the knife. 'It's the old way,' he says, 'the only way to be certain of a clean soul.' He waves his arm at the world, at the five kingdoms, and ignores my tears, asking what use carriers of the faith have for such earthly agents. He calls them rocks, and says, in

his still squeaky voice, that teachers of faith endanger
themselves through cowardice by not hacking them off.
The force of his voice moulds my beliefs. I know he is
right. 'Their power is terrifying,' he whispers. 'They make
men rut, not just with the females, but with boys, little
boys, like us. You don't want to be like that, do you? Cut
them off.' Like the cold, his voice is clear, it appears at the
centre of my head. It's my comprehending of what I've
done.

Betsy waited impatiently for Boyle to return to earth.
When he finally did so, she asked him what he thought,
but he said nothing and headed off towards the
plantation. Feeling slightly foolish, she followed him,
wanting to know what he would do next. He seemed to
accept her company, and they walked along the deer fence
at the edge of the forest. The outbuildings were on their
right, their order shifting as they moved: the garage now
side on, hen coop showing, Rego's Range Rover just
visible through the intervening trees. There was no sound,
no sign of Priest, although Betsy's skin tingled at his
possible presence. Only the chickens looked at them and
then, uninterested, returned to their pecking. Sunlight slid
in from the south-east, further confusing the angles with
its shadows. Boyle stopped where Priest's stile led into the
plantation. 'The range,' he said quietly.

'Yes?'

He climbed the stile.

'You're not planning to go in there?' Betsy asked,
incredulous. 'Look how thick it is.'

'You go back.' At the edge of the wood, the layered
sweeps of needles fell as a uniform barrier against Boyle.
'But thank you.'

Betsy saw that she was about to be left alone, and didn't like it. She looked back at the house through the trees, the unearthly morning light, and followed Boyle over the stile. There was a path – curiously light, given that this was Priest's route into the forest – that led to the wall of spruce. There Boyle crouched, then pushed his way through. He disappeared. Betsy was about to follow but scratched herself on the needles, the pain sharp enough to make her curse under her breath. Gingerly, she felt for the branch and pushed it aside, moving into the gloom.

The ground was barren of all but fallen needles, a rust-hued dirt floor to a razor web of branches. Needles grew only on the outer edge where the trees sought the sun, but with a density that excluded all but the most exhausted light. The interior offered the sense of a cavern long deserted. The ground was dry, but a faint tinkling filled the contained air, the sound of millions of the tiny, oily needles breaking free of their icy surrounds. They stood in a space where the lower branches had been sliced from the trunks. A cleared break followed a run of trees that headed west from the fence. Boyle set off along the row, the only possible route into the centre.

Betsy followed, increasingly spooked. The wood held them, all sound from without dampened, all noise from within amplified. Now and again a tree had fallen, usually against another so that it hung at an angle, and they struggled to find a way past a dying trunk. Betsy's uncertainty was deepened by the shifting impression created by the uniform lines of trees. As she walked, the patterns reconfigured as the rows of trunks lined up, then returned to disorder with the changing degrees. With each step trees would slip past trees and in the gloom, where all was grey and brown, this movement would catch the edge of her eye and offer a perceived figure, either darting away or, worse, charging in. Boyle was moving ahead of her and she hurried to catch up, clambering up the small rise and on to an unused track, stepping out into shocking sunlight. The grassy road led through the trees before it turned out of sight, boulders pushed up to the bank between machine tracks now long grown over. The air was fresh, but warmer than beyond the borders of the forest.

'Firebreak,' Boyle said. 'Presume.'

Trees, older than the ones they had travelled through, rose again at the other side, the canopy higher but the rows underneath visible as they disappeared into the darkness. Betsy's eyes had readjusted to the sun, and she was unable to read much in the murk. 'This is Priest's wood,' she said quietly. 'And it's spooky enough without thinking he might be in there, watching us. Are you sure this is a good idea?'

'We'll go,' he said, but he didn't mean back. He turned left down the track, watching the west wall of trees, and when, within a few steps, he found another break, he struck out that way, taking them further into the forest. This time they were accompanied by an old stone dyke.

'Will you be able to find your way back?' Betsy whispered, to his back.

Boyle didn't reply. The wall was very old, its stones green with moss, and in places it had fallen. He stopped to help Betsy cross a dry drain, its uniform sides giving way to a base of quartz cleared of earth by passing water. She waited on the other side while he peered up and down the stream.

'What is it?'

He jumped over to her side. 'This way.' He pointed ahead.

'Where to?'
'Other side.'

Cutter says the plague is closer, coming out of the east. He says there are fires burning, pyres where the fat runs down staves and into the flames. I imagined I saw them when I visited the temple at dawn, their lights across the water. The fires are a sign, a reoccurrence, and my thoughts must have taken me back into those dreams of the ordination, of that sanctified pain. I dreamt of Cutter finding the knife – the Saint's blade, he said, since all the other stones in the bay were worn smooth and round. He ground its flinty edge – until running it fast down a finger produced blood – then scratched a cross on the flat of the blade. He must have been telling the truth, I know that now, for what would have been the point of that pain if the Saint had not willed it?

I have tried to avoid these memories and remember the truths. It took time for Cutter to convince me. He behaved like a child, performing a pagan ceremony to consecrate the knife, making some idiot intonation. When I said this, he pointed out that it was I who was grasping for purity, not him.

And there were the greater truths. Each time I went to the temple, that beautiful cave, the Saint seemed so disapproving that I had not yet heeded his voice. I was failing. Cutter knew that. He said I was choosing not to turn my body over to the Saint's mercy. To remove the temptation, to slice them off, would be to discard my fear, he said. He was right, Cutter is always right. Never have I had an urge that shamed me, never have I had an urge at all. If only I could match the cave, and rise up, it would become my sanctuary, no longer a place to fear.

I shiver despite the sun, and wonder if I can hear voices.

Betsy and Boyle had laboured for more than an hour. Passageways petered out where one ruined wall met another and they were forced to turn, finding firebreaks, traversing and turning again. At one stage, in his frustration, Boyle jumped down into a dry stream and they followed it under the branches. Betsy was now lost, utterly reliant on her companion, hoping he would get them out of the guts of this inhabited forest. They reached another firebreak and emerged from the darkness.

'You're putting a lot of effort into this,' she said bitterly, stopping to feel the sun on her. 'Why not stay in an office and make calls?'

'Freelance. For difficult cases.' He was searching the trail with his eyes. 'This, right direction.'

She wanted to rest, and tried to keep him talking. 'So you get paid? The company pays you, if you find someone they owe money to?'

He shook his head, a small sharp movement. 'Beneficiary.'

'Why would they—'

'Know which company.'

'People pay you to find out which company legitimately owes them money?' Her antipathy to him increased.

He nodded. She could only see the back of his head, the pale crown.

'How much?'

'Percentage.'

'How big?'

'Not your business.' He was walking along the firebreak now, the gradient increasing as they climbed. At one stage they disturbed a fox asleep in the sun. Betsy, content to be out from under the canopy, had allowed the light to

175

calm her, so the fright was worse than it might have been minutes before. There had been a frantic scrabbling, the fox leaping up from where it was hidden in a stand of dead bracken and bolting away, head and tail extended in a streak of colour. Once she had recovered, Betsy sighed wearily. 'Are we nearly there yet?' she asked Boyle, with as sarcastic a smile as she could manage.

Cutter had wanted to kill a lamb, that bright summer when the breeze came warm off the sea, but I told him that enough would be sacrificed that night. I had bathed in the ocean to clean and chill my body, the shivering walk to the temple, lying facing the mouth of the cave, lifting the flinty stone. Oh, sweet Saint, the agony. Cutter vomited, of course, and cried, and looked with rabbit-eyed idiocy, biting his fingers, as I took up the twine, the sheep-needle and made four fast stitches before I passed out. The hospital restitched it, ruining my work. Perhaps, this time, the cut will heal and I will hear the sound of the Saint calling, the key will turn in the lock.

A fox has moved under the canopy. Something has frightened it.

The firebreak straightened and followed the pattern of the plantation so that the wall of spruce on either side became a uniform avenue of spaced trunks, lining up on each side in their thousands. Betsy and Boyle walked for ten minutes before the break ended in a circular clearing, empty but for beaten earth and one small boulder pushed to the side. She decided to say nothing, but she suspected Boyle didn't have a clue where they were. She hadn't eaten, weariness and hunger were chilling her, and she felt bad temper take her. She sat on a rock and watched as he squinted through the trees at the other side. The clearing was large enough that a curtain of needles reached the earth and he was forced to push aside branches so that he could see. He beckoned, then disappeared again. Betsy hurried after him.

They were in darkness again but for the first time without any path. Betsy had to fight through the uncleared wood, sharp lengths scratching her hands and face. They had to crouch and crawl; her clothes were torn. She cursed but Boyle ignored her, pushing ahead to where light showed. A last effort took them into the open, a gap between the trees and a wall, a deer fence running beside it, beyond which lay the great open range, vast and desolate all the way to the sea. Betsy felt relief at being able to see a whole landscape, and only then realized how trapped she had felt in the forest. Her anger evaporated, and she found she was smiling. She coughed as she inhaled the chill air. With immaculate timing, two fighters sliced past to the south, the roar of their engines changing as they fired their cannons into land that was just beyond the horizon. Betsy noticed a Ministry of Defence sign attached to the fence in front of them and, on a rise out in front, a red flag hanging limp on its pole. The claustrophobia of the forest was replaced by a different fear.

II

Boyle leaned against the wall, studying the sweep of the land through a small pair of binoculars he had pulled from his pocket. The peaks and folds lay like worn khaki in the quiet light. There were a few broken-down buildings in a tattered stand of trees, the target the fighters were attacking several miles further on. Boyle offered the glasses to Betsy but she refused them. 'What are you looking for?' she asked.

He shrugged. He seemed to be examining the gap between the tree line and the fence, because he swung round to check the other way. 'Better sense. Where we are.'

'I think I know. We're probably about to get arrested as spies.'

He smiled. 'Come,' he said.

They walked away from the sea, along the inner edge of the wall. The ground was a bed of tussocks and the footing was difficult. Betsy put up with it in the hope that it would take them back by a route that didn't involve scrambling through branches that stung like lashes. The wall drew closer to the plantation and they pressed through the buckled remains of the previous year's bracken, past the occasional birch that had used the wall's protection to escape the attentions of grazing animals. The bank fell away to a dry watercourse, the wall spanning the gap in a cantilevered arch, the grille on the fence pushed to one side to allow a route into the range. Boyle dropped down and moved under the fence.

'Oh, come on,' Betsy complained, stopping half-way down the bank. 'It's a firing range. A clearly active firing range.' She looked back at the wood. 'Really. Don't.' She intended to sound pathetic in the hope of generating sympathy.

'Not far,' he said. She heard him scrabbling up the bank beyond the wall.

Again Betsy studied the wood. The wall of pine cleaved where the stream cut a route under the branches. It was a route in, but there was no way she was going alone into that darkness. She stepped under the wall and peered up the bank to where Boyle was sitting at the top. The sun hung beyond him, causing him to glow. She found a hand-hold and hauled herself up. As she did so Boyle put his binoculars back into his pocket, opened the small canvas bag he had carried over one shoulder and removed a flask and a packet of sandwiches. Betsy sat down beside him, resting her back against the stone.

'You're calm,' she said.

'Hungry,' he replied. It might have been a question because he held out a sandwich.

She thought they would probably be all right beside the wall, and the possibility of food cheered her. Boyle tried to pass her the binoculars but she refused to take them.

'Should,' he said, still offering. 'Things you wouldn't expect.'

Relenting, she put the sandwich on her lap and took the glasses as he unscrewed the top of the flask. The country, uncultivated for decades, had returned to moor, and she saw that it might look as it had in ancient times. Yet here and there, in gullies and on hilltops, hung black machines: beetles to the naked eye, which revealed themselves, through binoculars, as burnt-out tanks. She swung towards the stand of trees where the remaining wall of a large building with Victorian gable-ends rose amid broken pines. A smashed tank perched precariously on a mound of rubble, its gun-barrel pointing towards the sky. She was only two or three miles from the village, in a nation untouched by conflict for nearly three hundred years, yet looking out on a battlefield. She lowered the binoculars, horrified, wanting to get back to more familiarly scarred earth. When she returned them, Boyle passed her a cup of coffee. She put it on the ground and chewed slowly at the sandwich. It was one of Martha's – she recognized the chicken filling.

'Cleared land.' Boyle spoke between one bite and the next. 'Everything . . . is in the past.'

'So why are you interested?'

'Policyholder. Was safety officer . . . here.' He finished each mouthful before he attempted to enunciate the next syllable. 'Missing the obvious.' With some discomfort, she sensed that he was admiring her, his eyes covering her. 'Romance, with Mary, happened out here.' He looked away. 'The book, it's inscribed. To this man, Roberts.' He was struggling now. 'With love.' The sun had given him a halo. 'Love,' he said. 'In this village. With this accident. Need to be very careful.'

At last she saw his concern. 'I suppose you do,' she said. 'Yes, I really suppose you do. Money and love. In a place like this.' She laughed to herself, the humour apparently lost on Boyle. 'So, why James Rego?'

'His sister, perhaps.'

'Sister?' Betsy considered this. 'But I've been to the house and there's no suggestion of a sister.'

'Gone, perhaps, or, dead?'

'And Mr Rego would be the beneficiary. But how do you get to that – to a sister?'

He pulled the book from his pocket, bent the cover back to show her a page. He had found his place without difficulty, held it up but did not hand it over. The text was in French but pencil marks covered the typeface, an explosion of tiny words. Boyle's long index finger pointed to one, written in a small, curving hand: 'Howe Hill.'

Betsy looked up at him, lost.

'Rego's house,' he said impatiently, and Betsy recalled the sign. 'Perhaps nothing . . . but your discovery.' He

180

shook his head, its sweep greater for the length of his neck. 'I asked some of the older people . . . if they remember a Mary at Howe Hill.'

'And?'

'Turn away. Say nothing.'

Betsy looked out over the landscape.

'Perhaps nothing,' Boyle repeated. 'Nobody speaks to strangers, after . . . after the boat, the drowning.' He waved towards the sea, was silent, and then, 'Asked the landlady.'

'And what did she say?'

'Said if I have questions about James Rego, I should ask James Rego.' He was looking at Betsy again. She had been surprised by the sudden ease of his speech, the first sentence she had heard him speak without gaps.

'There must be records? Local records, the census?'

'Parish records? No mention. Ones I could see.'

Betsy had expected something easier than this, had hoped for some straightforward good news, but this had problems attached; invisible dangers hung on to this hope. Her fingers tapped out her irritation on her knees. 'Why can't you tell him? Why can't you say there is this money? I mean, is there a lot?'

'Not . . . too much.' The stumble returned. 'Can't say.'

Betsy fell silent. 'But enough to bring you here, a big enough percentage.' She saw his eyes briefly. 'Why can't you tell him?' she repeated.

'I am wrong? It's someone else. Have to be careful.' Boyle took her cup and knocked the drips from it, screwed the Thermos back together and returned the remains of their breakfast to his bag. He perused the landscape where the characters he was chasing had once lived and loved. Betsy let him think. A calm seemed to settle on

181

him as he gazed away towards the sea, almost a relief, like a man sleeping after fever. At last he rose and walked out into the firing range, pausing only as a jet screamed low over the forest, its breath-sucking force winding Betsy, a reflection from the cockpit momentarily blinding her. Once over the range, it rose, until it climbed vertically, then rolled over to fly back over them at height.

'Catapult bombs,' Boyle shouted back. 'Flick it forward – that way, avoid enemy fire.'

Betsy gazed out at the great plain of uncultivated land, with its swathes of bog myrtle and flattened coastal grasses, its bushes where burns cut through the folds. A thick layer of vegetation covered everything as far as she could see, and she realized now that there were no live-stock. With nothing eating it, nothing taking its cut, a landscape grew like this. Yet the beauty was paid for with aeroplanes catapulting bombs into its midst, and its surface defiled with ruins and burnt-out tanks. There was a more general irony here that wasn't lost on her, but she didn't dwell on specifics. She didn't see that to get away from her cluttered life would require such sustained damage. 'Where are you going?' she shouted, as Boyle started off across the plain.

'Take a look,' he replied, pointing at the wreckage of the house in the distance.

'No.'

'Planes way over there. Safe.'

'You've got to be kidding. We need to get out of here.'

'Want to look.' It was clear he wasn't asking. 'You stay?'

'No.'

'Won't be long.'

Betsy was incredulous. 'Why? Why do you want to go out there?'

'To look.'

'For what?' She had tried to remain calm but now her frustration showed. 'What could possibly be out there?'

'Some sign. Family plot, grave. Find Mary Rego. Prove everything.'

'Beside the house?' She was having to yell now.

'Happens.'

Betsy looked over the plain to the shattered walls of the house in the distance, the damaged and fallen trees. She recalled Boyle in the village graveyard – he must have been looking for the Regos. 'But no one has lived here for years,' she yelled. 'Far longer than you could possibly care about. I don't see how it helps, even if there is a grave-yard.' But Boyle, waving an extended arm, had walked out of earshot.

As the distance grew between them, the forest weighed in from behind. She glanced nervously at the wall, as if someone might be watching from the woods. At last, unable to bear it, she leaped up and hurried after her companion.

She cursed with each step, keeping the rhythm as she dropped into gullies and rose over ridges in her pursuit. Only when fighters cut through the sky to the south did she fall silent. Boyle had slowed and she caught up with him at the edge of what must have been the old policies, rotted tree stumps lethal in the undergrowth.

'Brave,' he said.

'Stupid.'

'Don't take easy option. Like that.'

She realized he was talking about the break-up.

'Think we're alike,' he added.

'I don't think so. If you don't mind, do what you have to do, and then let's get out of here.'

As they closed on the ruins, they passed the foundations of outbuildings, Boyle wandering off among them. The ground grew hard where driveways had disintegrated. From the forest fence the scale of the place had been dwarfed by the surrounding plain, but as Betsy moved past two large pines, one dead, the other alive but broken off half-way up its length, the remnants of the house rose into the sky, jagged and red. It had been large and ornate, utterly at odds with the elegant Georgian building on the other side of the woods. The red sandstone façade still held a trace of its once gloomy weight, but now many of the bricks lay in piles around its foundations, or sprayed out in the ragged grass. Betsy had never experienced war, but it was clear that the house had been blown to pieces. She turned the corner of the building and found the tank hulk rotting in the rubble. Its cladding was rusted, its tracks full of moss, the surface covered with fist-sized holes with smoothed-out edges, remnants of once superheated metal. Boyle was moving out across the grounds, searching for a family plot that she doubted was there.

The interior of the house was open to view: floors clung to walls but had slumped during years of wind and rain. Grass, moss and even small trees had taken root. There was a strange acidic smell, which she thought at first was due to the rotten contents, but then she noticed she was being watched. When she saw one set of eyes, others appeared, all around her. The building was full of cats, motionless until she saw them and then, as if aware they had been spotted, they rose from where they had been lying, sat up and looked at her. She counted at least eight on her first sweep of the ruins, then found another, only a few yards away, in the remains of a fireplace. The animal, finding itself under observation, moved up to the floor above in quick, languid leaps. There it sat beside one of its fellows, a fatter creature with almost identical grey and white colouring. 'Henry!' Betsy shouted. 'Come and look at this.'

He wasn't interested. He moved between the broken and felled trees, quartering the ground in his search. Betsy turned back to the cats. They returned her gaze, their interest lazy and distant. An initial silence was broken as they relaxed. There was a short spell of scratching when a ginger with a ringed tail sharpened its claws on a piece of exposed timber, then the faint whisper of falling dust as a grey with a flat face jumped up to the floor above. The grey and white cats she had seen first began a playful fight. And all of them appeared oddly healthy, coats bright among the rotten masonry. Several carried bellies that nearly touched the ground, yet walked like lions. The two playing cats tumbled down ledges to the first floor, but froze when she shifted her feet. She tiptoed further through the rubble, keeping clear of overhangs, avoiding a drop into a basement. She looked down to see another four cats looking up, one from within a box that Betsy could now see was full of straw.

'Henry!' Betsy shouted.

He appeared round the edge of the building. 'Nothing.' He was presumably disappointed, but she couldn't tell. 'Need to look further. Sorry.'

'Look at all these cats,' she said.

Boyle gazed at the building.

'They're healthy,' Betsy continued, 'as if they are being fed. And they have boxes.'

The cats, who had been watching the new arrival with curiosity, looked away as one, ears pointing in a uniform direction, their eyes on the wall. Several leaped up through the floors to perch silhouetted against the sky.

Boyle shifted around the building so that he could see out on to the plain, Betsy following. There, moving towards them, his shape dropping into gullies then re-appearing, was Priest.

Boyle lifted his binoculars. There was the sound of falling dust as more of the cats took to the upper edge of the wall. 'Seen us,' he said.

'He knows we're here?'

'Coming very fast.'

Betsy felt a surge of panic. Her armpits itched. She hadn't wanted to be in this empty place, with its ruins and its cattery, and now this strange and violent resident was striding towards them. She felt unprotected, in a place divorced from the laws she understood. Inside she was screaming – she wanted to get away without having to face a confrontation with a lunatic. She wanted to be surrounded by strangers she could trust.

'Should go,' said Boyle.

Betsy tried to keep a grip on her hysteria. 'Where exactly do you want us to go? He's between us and the wood. And even if we get there, it's his wood. He lives in there. We could go the other way, I suppose, where they're dropping bombs.' She realized she wasn't doing a very good job of keeping calm.

'Will be fine,' Boyle said. 'Go that way.' He pointed to the north-east, where an old road that led from the house was still visible from the drains that once accompanied it. This would mean that Priest, arriving from the south-east, could intercept them.

'What is he doing?' Betsy tried to control her voice.

186

Priest was still too distant for her to pick out any expression.

Boyle passed her the binoculars.

She lifted them and found she was shaking. Boyle put a hand on her wrist to steady her and she furiously shook herself free, the anger dealing with the tremor. She saw Priest's face now, a clear disquiet complementing the determination of his fast-moving legs. She shoved the glasses back at their owner.

'This way,' Boyle said, and led her back round the house. The pace he struck was fast, and Betsy found she had to jog to keep up. She didn't mind, she wanted to sprint. She found she was relying on her companion now.

They emerged from under the broken pine to find Priest only a couple of hundred yards away, walking fast. Boyle kept his eyes fixed on the forest, but Betsy couldn't help but look over at the other man, whose head was swivelling back and forth between the ruined house and them. When he noticed that Betsy had dropped the pretence that they hadn't seen Priest, Boyle waved, but continued his march to the north-east. Priest made no response. Betsy only felt the beginning of hope when she saw that he had not adjusted his route, but carried on towards the house.

They passed within shouting distance but no further acknowledgement was offered before the distance between them began to grow. Betsy felt the release of the immediate tension, a certain flawed relief.

Soon they were beyond the cleared parkland, following the remains of the road as it rose and fell on the plain proper, and there she turned to look behind. Priest had disappeared into the wrecked building from which she was certain he would soon emerge and follow them. Jets swung in from the sea, cutting over to bomb the west.

187

The track Boyle was following led inland, gently swinging into the edge of the forest where a gap opened up in the trees, a vehicle track leading through the wood. There was a chained gate, the fence at this point over six feet high and topped with razor wire. They found that if they pulled on the gate's bars, a gap opened up under which they could wriggle. On the other side Betsy looked down at the state of her clothes. 'Why did I follow you into this?'

'You wanted to.' Boyle didn't smile. 'Come . . . with me.'

'With you?' Betsy laughed. 'That wasn't my first thought.'

'But now?'

'We should go.' She began to follow the track. After the earlier effort of fighting their way through the depths of the plantation, the return journey was swift. Barely twenty minutes brought them to the end of Rego's driveway.

Boyle had been silent the whole way, and Betsy, unable to read his expression, wondered what he was thinking. She had used the time to conjure up ways to bring him and Rego together. She thought the most direct method seemed the most sensible. 'I could ask Mr Rego if he had a sister,' she said. 'I could say you asked if he had a sister.'

'No good.'

'I'll tell him I said I didn't know and the conversation stopped there.'

'No.'

'But it's a good idea. There's no harm in it. We've been seen together, Priest will tell him. And he asked me to find out what you were up to.'

Boyle threw a quick look at her, then peered up at the

sky; his gaunt black-clad figure seemed so out of place. 'Not the right time . . . for this.'

'It's exactly the right time. It couldn't be a better time. Say yes. Or I'll do it anyway.'

He was studying her again. 'Okay,' he said, the monotone unchanged. 'But only that.' He stepped towards her. 'Rego,' he said. 'You like him.' Again, he was too close.

'I'm worried about him,' she replied. She wondered if his ability to hide what he was thinking had been cultivated, or whether it was a defence. It crumbled only when he made his inept advances on her. 'I should get down there, to see what I can find out.'

Boyle held out his hand but Betsy simply raised her palm in goodbye, and turned to walk away.

'Enjoyed . . . our walk,' he shouted after her. And then, after a moment, 'Only name, no more. Mention money, I leave.'

She lifted her hand again, a final acknowledgement. When she eventually looked back, he had gone, and at once she felt the forest closing in beside her. The day was no more than half over, and she was exhausted.

III

Betsy found Rego leaning against the passenger door of his car, shouting angrily into his mobile. He hadn't noticed her approach. 'How am I supposed to run the game if you pull out at the last minute?' he yelled.

She wondered whether to back away, but realized she was unlikely to make it without being seen. Instead she circled the car.

'These are excuses.' Rego was quieter now, but clearly exasperated. 'Why don't you tell me what actually

189

happened? Why don't you admit Bunbury's got to you?' He caught her movement and his eyes swung towards her, the big forehead creased in concentration. 'Why not?' he shouted. 'There is a loyalty issue here. You are ruining the boneyard by doing this. Listen to me. This is bad. Really bad.' There was a pause. 'Tell me! What is it? Talk to me.' Whoever was on the other end barely got a chance to reply but during the brief silence Rego shook his head at Betsy in apology. 'I can control Priest,' he shouted, 'you know that, and, anyway, why listen to Bunbury? He's hardly stable. He sells knives, he's like some . . . Who does he think he is? A tink messiah? He's probably all geared up to use those blades of his.' Again the other had little time to speak. 'Okay, your decision,' Rego said, with sudden calm. 'But think carefully. You leave, there's no getting back. You're excommunicated. You understand. I've got to go, someone's here, so think about it and get back to me.' He took the phone from his ear, squeezing the button that would end the call, and stepped forward to kiss Betsy's cheek. 'The day I'm having,' he complained, and then, noticing her appearance, asked, 'What's happened to you?' His phone bleeped, and he looked at it. 'A message. Give me a second.' He dialled a number and listened, his expression changing, collapsing further. He lowered the phone and stared at the wood. 'Another of my players just cancelled.'

'They're pulling out?'

Rego leaned back against the car, running a hand over his face.

Betsy asked if she could help, spooked by the defeat that had shown in his eyes.

'Only if you know some hotshots for the boneyard.' He slapped the side of the car with the flat of his palm. 'Jump in.' He held open the door for her. 'I need to look at something.' As Betsy stepped on to the running-board, he stopped her. 'Your clothes? What have you been doing?' He had reached between the seats for a piece of cloth, which he was spreading over the seat as he spoke. The phone bleeped again. He moved away and Betsy sat down on the cover while he walked round to the other side of the car. He started the engine, phone clenched between shoulder and ear, and they pulled along the drive. 'Don't worry,' he was saying. 'It'll happen. I'll sort it out.' He dropped the phone into his pocket.

'How's Helen?' Betsy asked. They turned on to the road, towards the village.

'I'm not sure. I haven't talked to her today.'

'I was thinking I should move in with her, just for the moment. I've haven't seen her for twenty-four hours, and I don't think I'm giving her the support she needs.'

'We'll check on her.' The wood had given way to a field and here Rego slowed, lowering Betsy's window with a switch in the well. 'This problem with the boneyard,' he said. 'It's taking my mind off things. It's the last thing I need.'

He was looking past her, out over his land. There were small groups of cows and sheep in the field, some sniffing at the dry earth. A few beasts still searched over the remains of the morning's hay.

'What are you looking for?' Betsy asked.

'Everything needs to be in the right place. The government's putting restrictions on the movement of livestock because of the plague. We're being told not to move beasts across any public road, or any road at all.' He tapped the dashboard. 'I don't want anything to starve.' She saw how exhausted he was: all health had now been stripped from his face.

191

'It's going to be bad? Financially?'

'Oh, yes.' He laughed, a bleak sound. 'The farm's in debt.' He reached into his pocket for a handkerchief and rested it between his palm and the steering-wheel. 'There was no profit in it before this. The sinking of the *Albatross* . . .' He shook his head and they moved off again.

'Yes?' They had both forgotten the state she was in, the mud on her clothes. Even Helen had slipped from her mind. There seemed such a weight on this man. She reached out and felt the flesh under his sleeve.

'I'd borrowed against it.'

'Oh, no,' said Betsy.

'God knows when the insurance will pay out. And the yacht. Uninsured. Funny, you know, I won her from a day sailor in a bet, so I thought, well, easy come, easy go. I even nicknamed her Patsy. Well, now look who's talking.'

'James, I'm sorry.'

'My fault,' he said.

Betsy had no reply. She just looked towards the village, the few houses that showed towards the sea.

'That's the thing,' he continued. 'It's ridiculous but I have no one to talk to about it.' His mobile rang and he looked at the number on the small screen before pressing the receive button. 'Well?' The pause was short. 'What's happened? You've all got together and decided this. After all this time. It's not right, you know . . .' Again the lull was short. 'We can talk about percentages.' And again. 'Ah, well . . .' He shut it off, and brought the Range Rover to a halt at the top of a rise, the Galloway landscape opening up in front of them, the once low-rolling dunes now fields and dykes. 'This country,' he said. 'It's beautiful but it's too far away. They don't want our milk. They're quite happy to bring it here at fifty pence a pint, but to take it away, too expensive. And the fishing, even with a boat, it's all but gone. Tourism? We're stuck between countries and not even on the road to anywhere. And here's the village, at the wrong end of Scotland, its only local boat sunk, its boys . . .' He sighed. 'Gone. Ruined families. I barely even have a game left, and that was my last source of income. That's why I was so protective of it the other night. The boneyard is dying. Everybody's always liked the irony, you know, of holding a game in a church. It's probably the real reason we kept it there instead of bringing it into somebody's home. You want to know why they're all going off it? Bunbury. He disapproves. He wants to bring religion back, start a revival where it all began, where that bloody saint got off his bloody boat. Bunbury. The place is falling apart and he's spreading that sort of poison.'

Betsy felt a desperate need to offer Rego some hope. She had to look to the east, towards the dark, distant hills, to remind herself of Boyle's threat to leave if she messed this up.

Rego continued to talk. 'We always saw the game as part-payment for what we lost when the army came,' he said. 'We hoped we could make money from it, but nothing has ever been the same since they took our land.'

'What do you mean? What land did you lose?'

'The land to the west,' he said. 'The range. It belonged to my father. It's where we lived. Then the war came, the government took it from us. They said they'd give it back but they never did. All they offered was the small purchase price and gradual ruin for us.'

Betsy kept her eyes on the man beside her.

'That, and the constant sound of gunfire.' At last he laughed. 'Well, I'm sure I would have ruined it anyway,

193

given time. I am the last of the line – I always knew I would be.' Now he looked back at her. 'Any clearer idea why are you here, Betsy?'

Betsy recalled the terror of the morning, a fear she was utterly unused to. It added to the surprise she now felt. Unconsciously she had begun to absorb Rego's misery.

He noticed she was having trouble speaking. 'I didn't mean . . .'

She reached across and put an arm around his neck so that they embraced awkwardly. 'I wish I could make it better for you,' she whispered. 'There'll be something good out there. Let me help you find it.'

He held her close, then pulled his head back so that he could see into her eyes. When he came forward again, they were kissing, his lips opening against hers.

Betsy was ready for this, if not quite how it happened. They fought out of their clothes right there on that rise, Betsy shifting over to sit on top of him. There was the urgency of new sex, the self-consciousness slipping away and real sensation closing in. In such all-consuming desire, the pleasure was brief and James Rego cried out.

Later, with the sunlight dripping yellow beyond the windows of the house, Rego appeared almost boyish. He was wearing a dressing-gown he had retrieved from the upper floor, and Betsy had wrapped herself in a blanket. After his first pained exclamation, they had returned home and he had shown a little more generosity. Betsy felt the concerns of the past days lift.

'You choose to live alone?' she asked.

He was lying back on the sofa, her legs over him. She had wanted him to hold her feet but he had refused.

'I'm difficult,' he said. 'I never wanted children. I can't

194

imagine them running around out here. Or a wife in the kitchen. It's not for me. I have my habits, my tastes, and I'm getting old, you know.'

She laughed. She had a glass in her hands and sipped. 'You're not going to lose all this, though?' she asked seriously, sweeping the room with her hand.

He followed the gesture to the pictures on the wall, the furniture and carpets. Betsy saw that all these things had been squeezed into the house, presumably after the loss of the bigger place out on the range. 'I hope not,' he said. 'I have one last chance.'

'And what's that?' she asked.

He smiled. 'If you lose always double.'

'A bet.'

'We'll celebrate when the time comes.'

Later still, she had asked if she could wash and tumble-dry her clothes. 'I might have a bath,' she said, as they sat in the warm kitchen, picking at a little food.

'You never did tell me how you got so dirty.' The dressing-gown suited his look. His lined face was calmer than it had been for some time, and his long hair matched the louche comfort of the robe.

'I was having an adventure with Henry Boyle.'

He had a piece of bread in his hand but it had stopped on the journey to his mouth. 'He's still here?'

'Oh, yes.' She found herself under a sharply focused gaze. 'We went out on to the firing range.'

He pulled at the bread. 'Why?'

Betsy exhaled. 'Boyle left the inn early. And I followed him. He saw me . . .'

'You didn't tell me any of this.'

'I didn't get the opportunity.' Betsy hadn't thought

clearly about what she was going to say, and now, with Rego's big dark eyes on her, she was aware that she needed to get this right. She felt her way. 'He's interested in something . . . looking for something.'

'He didn't tell you what?'

'Well . . . I tagged along. We . . .' She was about to say that they had walked along the coast but changed her mind, wanting to keep to the truth as far as possible. '. . . went through the wood.' The path from the cave to the main road was a public right of way so she didn't have to say they came through his garden.

'Actually through it? Priest's plantation?'

'Yes.'

Rego switched his gaze to the window behind her, clearly amazed. 'He's brave, I'll grant him that.'

'Trust me, I wish I hadn't followed.'

'You met Priest?'

'Not then. We got to the other side and came out on to the range, and then Boyle said he wanted to go out to the ruin – the ruined house out there? Is that the house you were talking about? Your parents' house?'

He nodded.

'I didn't want to go. I mean, they are dropping bombs out there.'

'Right.' His eyes had widened; he appeared amused.

'But I didn't want to be alone near the forest either so I followed. We reached the house, and then we saw Priest coming.'

'What did Boyle do when he got to the house?'

'He walked around the grounds.'

'What was he searching for?'

'I think, perhaps, he was looking for a grave.'

'A grave? There are no graves there. Why would he be looking for a grave? He told you this?'

'Well, yes, but he didn't say much. He has that funny way of talking, you know.'

'Did he find anything?'

'No. I'm certain of that. He wanted to go further. But Priest arrived. And we left. Fast.'

He smiled thoughtfully. 'And you came back the same way?'

'No. Through the gate. Up there.'

'It just gets weirder with our Mr Boyle.' He leaned back. 'He shouldn't be wandering around MoD land – or my land, come to that – and certainly not while this plague is on the loose. The military would go nuts. *I* should go nuts. Whose grave is he looking for?'

'Well,' said Betsy, 'he asked . . . and this is weird, but . . .'

'Go on.'

'He asked if I knew whether you had a sister.' She watched but Rego didn't seem to register this; it didn't even touch his eyes. 'I told him I didn't know.'

When he replied, each word arrived slowly, as if his thoughts had deadened their delivery. 'Why would he ask that?'

'He didn't say.'

His gaze had not left her. 'Anything else?'

'A name, Mary.'

The eyes flicked away, and the long forehead wrinkled. 'And you said?'

'That I don't know. That I had no idea. Of course I didn't. I think he might have wanted me to ask Helen, but I wouldn't, of course.'

'Thanks for telling me,' he said, standing.

'I would have told you earlier but . . .' She smiled.

'Let me run you that bath.'

When Betsy stepped into the water, Rego handed her a glass.

'Did you see the cats?' he asked.

She nodded.

'He feeds them. Anybody who's wanting rid of kittens, is going to drown them or something, Priest takes them out there and feeds them. There's more than a hundred.'

He ran a hand along her cheek and smiled. 'Enjoy the water,' he said.

They sat in the Range Rover outside Helen's house, the engine idling. Betsy felt fresh, if tired. Her clothes smelt of fabric conditioner, her hair of apples. The morning's expedition had exhausted her, the sex had made her feel better, and now she felt warm and calm. Although she had been troubled by Rego's obsessive cleanliness – he had rid himself of the residue of sex with unromantic haste – just emerging pristine made her feel better than she had since arriving. Having pampered herself, she had stolen a look in his mirror and found she was drawn, had lost a little weight, but this, she felt, flattered her. Rego shifted in his seat. 'I think you're right,' he said. 'Helen would appreciate you staying.'

'I'd be more use to her here than at the inn. I'll need to ask her, of course.'

'I'd put you up myself.'

'I should stay here. You've got a lot on your mind right now, and while it would be good to be . . . well, near, I don't want to get under your feet.'

He didn't say anything.

'It was a lovely afternoon.' Betsy smiled. 'I had a really good time.' She opened the door and was about to step down from the car, but then she turned. 'Do you have a sister?'

He laughed. 'Not that I know of.' He leaned over so that they could kiss. 'You go and look after Helen. I'll see you soon.'

I have no authority, and the dogs hate me for it. They bring the sheep in lazily from the south field, easing them through the gate. Cutter watches, urging me on my way, using the same flick of the wrist. He has bawled at me for not telling him about the trespassers on the range, but now he is talking on the telephone, laying his bets, arguing odds, eyes following the sheep as they move on his orders, his decisions. The dogs return as if it had all been too easy. They prefer Cutter's disdain to my friendship. I follow them to where Cutter still argues the odds, offering money. He dials again and, looking up, waves me away once more.

WEDNESDAY

High tide: 09.37, 22.09
Calm

The ark rose beside Betsy, the tide at her feet. She lifted herself on tiptoe to look over the deck, but found the surface the same as the sides, an expanse of concrete, rough with barnacles. Lapping seawater filled the divots her toes had made in the sand and she stepped back, her attention caught by movement in the distance. To the east, where yellow-green fields rose from the cliff-edge to crest in a smooth, rolling horizon, three figures had appeared. She could tell they were children, not because of their size, which at such a distance was difficult to gauge, but by the way they ran around, looping and circling one of the round bales that dotted the landscape. Like birds in flight, they spun and disappeared into a dip. Betsy looked back to the ark, reaching out to it. It was sharp to the touch.

She'd discovered that Rego had laid a bet on a football match to be played that evening. She had found this out that morning when he had driven her and her luggage to Helen's cottage. As he waited outside the inn, she'd seen him polishing the dashboard of the Range Rover. When she had come down with her bags, the fluidity with which he normally moved was absent. He had hung forward to kiss her, a flicker touching the corners of his eyes. It was these little things that had given away the imminence of the gamble. He had tried to appear unconcerned, his natural authority a bluff.

Helen had accepted Betsy's suggestion that she move into the cottage with only the minimum of polite resistance.

The holes in the ark's hull gave way to a rank and salty interior, suggesting a cell that would be submerged twice daily, a place that inspired instinctive fear. Seawater now curled among the rocks at Betsy's feet and she took another step back. In the distance the children had re-appeared, tiny figures playing at the edge of the precipice, while over in the garden of the cottage Helen fussed around the small rockery.

Martha had been uncharacteristically sentimental when Betsy left. 'I can help, so don't hesitate,' she had said, as Betsy handed her the cash. 'I can't do much about any-one else in this place but you're a visitor.'

Betsy had kissed her and Martha had smiled. 'You know where I am.'

She had said goodbye to Rego at the cottage door, then used Helen's phone to call the laboratory, but her boss hadn't been available. His secretary, a woman who loathed her, had been left with instructions to transfer Betsy's call to the director. The resulting conversation had been uncomfortable. The director was a brilliant man who, Betsy knew, hated the distractions his genius had brought down on him. He had asked exactly what she had told her boyfriend, and decided on suspension rather than outright sacking. He had told her that reporters had turned up at her parents' house and, if she could, she should stay where she was. Then he had suggested she call her mother.

The tide had caught up with her again so she picked her way back to the path that led to the cottage. She wanted to see Rego again, which meant deserting Helen for a few hours. She watched the other woman work, feeling guilty. For two days now, unsolicited brochures had arrived at the cottage, suggesting a variety of courses from basic sailing to a master-mariner's certificate. The phone still rang in the middle of the night and, according to Rego, opinion had continued to turn against her. There was, he had said, a pool of bad feeling among those on the periphery – those impotent watchers – that he was struggling to contain. Yet, the memory of Rego's hands on her, and the look of fear in his eyes, beckoned her. 'I'm just going for a walk,' she called to Helen, and received a wave in reply.

I had noticed the girl earlier, looking at the trees, looking innocent, hands behind her back, looking up. She has become Cutter's bint. I ignored her, but still she found me. She cannot have noticed my presence before because she seemed surprised and put out a hand. She wanted something. But women are always wrong and cannot serve the Saint. Cutter is susceptible. I am immune. I left, though, to be certain.

With the sun half-way through its fall, Betsy followed the thin road through the village, and then on towards Rego's house. She was joined by a small flock of starlings, which moved ahead of her along the telephone wire, or filled any bare-boughed trees that grew beside the wall, scattering happily as she caught up. Their presence should have caused her pleasure, but instead the noise grated, and she felt she was being harried. She had been shocked by how much she craved Rego's touch. She had felt the lack of impressions on her skin since her ex had left. Her love of contact, the whisper of fingers on skin, or a gesture to reinforce a point, had grown out of her childhood. Her father had been tactile, her mother removed.

The thought brought back the other call she had made that morning. 'It's so embarrassing,' her mother had said. 'It's like having Monica Lewinsky as a daughter.'

Betsy picked up her pace and the starlings rushed into the sky and over her head, falling behind. Her mother's snobbery incensed her, because it had grown out of something good. Both her parents had wanted to change their worlds, but where her father's idealism had been tempered by the truths he had discovered, her mother's beliefs had grown parasitic to her rising place in society, so that she was forced to adhere to them to maintain her standing. Betsy's father had been humbled, but her mother had grown ever more sure of herself.

She turned down the driveway and tried to ignore the forest on her right. She let herself into the house, and climbed the stairs. She was disappointed to find Rego at his desk, his face creased over his chores. He seemed almost pained to see her, as if he was already battling anything that might distract him from the coming game. He asked for an hour. Betsy said she would see the sun go down from the gardens, although her legs ached from the walk.

She had not forgotten about the missing sister, and began to look for other clues. Instead she discovered Priest in the garage. He was sitting with a lawnmower engine resting on his knees. His small eyes were sunk deep within the bloated face, his tongue was gripped firmly between his teeth. He said nothing, just tilted his body forward, almost as if he was protecting the engine in his lap. Betsy had been hit by the smell of him, a rotten stench of rancid fat. His clothes were rank, the exposed flesh greasy, layered and meaty. 'I'm sorry about yesterday,' she said, trying not to gag or show her fear and revulsion. 'I didn't know about the ruin out there, I didn't know about the cats.' Nothing changed in his face: his expression remained a mixture of the childlike and the lewd. She took a step forward, and he moved so fast she could barely avoid crying out. She threw herself back against the doorjamb as he dropped the engine, lunged past her and out of the door, bolting for the plantation in his strange, sidewards scuttle. She felt the tickling of her nerves as she watched him cross the stile and disappear into the undergrowth. It took her a moment to catch her breath before she walked back to the house.

Rego was in the drawing room when she returned, surrounded by his ageing furniture. The tired landscapes on the walls, the overload of sofas, chairs and tables, the rugs under his feet were all spotless but drained of colour. In such surroundings, his long face held an edgy nobility, as if he were of another time. Everything about him – his stance, the bowed rigidity of his body, the grip of his hands, the muscle of his neck, the hidden movements under the drawn flesh of his face – all spoke of tension. He was barely alive in this dead environment.

'I met Priest,' she said.

'Was it all right?'

'Just gave me a fright. That's all.' She crossed to him, put a hand to his face, and he smiled, a small gesture. She didn't take her eyes off him. She shifted her hand to his shoulder, then down his arm, and raised her palm again to his face. She could feel the coiling inside him, the strain under his skin. She stood on tiptoe and kissed him, and felt the slow movement of his muscles. His eyes were on her, and where they had gazed into some distance, they now focused on her. He seemed to be coming back to life. An arm moved round her, and she felt the power of what she had begun. Somewhere inside him a shift had occurred and there was an irreversible energy in his movements. His hands passed over her, unfastening buttons, sliding across flesh. He moved her to where he wanted her, as her hands ran up the contours of his body. When he pushed into her, he was gentle. They took their time. She grasped his thigh, while he appeared to forget everything. He exhaled, holding her, then stepped backwards and collapsed on to the sofa. For the first time, he seemed unaware of the state he was in. The tension had left him, and he looked exhausted, almost unbearably sad. Betsy sat down. As they looked at each other, he started to recover and, apparently a little embarrassed, stood up. He attempted a smile as he went off to the bathroom. Betsy leaned back into the corner of the sofa, frustrated, looking out of the window towards the darkening sea that showed beyond the trees. The last of the sunshine felt unnatural, its lack of warmth leaving the landscape with nothing but a pale winter light that, with the passing days, had felt increasingly sickly. She rearranged her clothes.

Over dinner, Betsy watched Rego play with his food, a slice of potato moving across his plate. They had not spoken for several minutes, but she was still thinking about the subject of their conversation – her father, and the isolation he found himself in, of having no memory, his life now a continuous stream of unfulfilled wishes. Rego looked up at the clock, and Betsy reached across for his hand. 'Are you all right?'

'It's going to be fine. They'll win. It's a good bet.'

She shouldn't have, but Betsy was comparing the two men. Her father had struggled. Brought up poor, his parents had fought to get him into university. He had survived on nothing for years, and it had made him un-forgiving of waste. Rego appeared to revel in waste. She realized that if she was seeking insights from this fling, they had yet to reveal themselves, except perhaps that he was too old for her.

'Why architecture?' he asked suddenly. 'If he was having trouble paying his way. It's about the longest degree he could have done.'

She studied his face. The tension had returned, and the afternoon had passed without further intimacy. Now he appeared to be trying to take his mind off the forthcoming match.

'He was obsessed with council housing,' she explained. 'He had a theme, an ambition for the projects he took on – he wanted people to be able to see a long way, whatever the state of the community. When we were growing up, he told us that ambition is about being able to see beyond the horizon. He wanted the people he housed to see for ever.'

Rego's gaze had switched back to the clock. 'He should have gone to sea.'

'Then there's only a horizon. He never liked the sea.' She thought of her childhood, the endless competition. Her father had feared losing the tenuous grip he had on being middle class and made no apologies for pushing his daughters. She shouldn't have been surprised that he had married a snob. Her mother's career as a doctor had been equally impressive – she waged indefatigable war on the fat-filled Scottish diet, but she fought her battles proscriptively. 'We had to achieve. It would have been intolerable to either of my parents if we hadn't,' she said.

Rego had fallen silent again.

'What about you?' she asked, the thought of her career bringing sudden pain. 'What was your childhood like?'

He stared at her blankly as he tried to comprehend the simple question. 'It's what you see,' he said, after a moment.

'But your name? Rego?'

He smiled. 'Ah, well, we turned up here a while ago. The story goes that a man got off a boat, said he was a Spanish aristocrat, but never said why he had been forced to come here.'

'A black sheep.'

'If it's not a complete fabrication. I'd put money on our being as common as muck. Why else would he have stuck around? Anyway, that was a long time ago, he did well, and I'm as native as the next man.' He looked again at the clock. 'Talking of money, the football.'

'How much did you put on?'

'None of your business.'

They both stood. Betsy took the plates to the sink and rinsed them before loading them into the dishwasher. They cleaned the kitchen together, Rego wiping all the surfaces dry.

'Is this really your last chance?' Betsy said. 'This bet?'

'It'll be fine. There's always one more chance.'

They sat down to watch the game in his office, Rego behind his large desk, Betsy in the armchair they had pushed to one side. She recognized one of the pre-match pundits, although she had little knowledge of football. It was Rego's gamble that excited her interest now. The match had yet to start and so she asked him if he had ever lived away from the village.

'Home educated.'

'And the interest in sherry?'

His natural detachment had slipped, tension expressing itself in his lack of movement. 'Went to Spain once,' he said, a trace of irritation in his tone. 'Sanlucar de Barrameda – with William Kerr, in fact. It's a fishing village. We were looking at a boat. It has the best sherry in the world, manzanilla, and the best seafood. Willie and I, we had a good time.' The memory appeared to trouble him and he frowned.

They listened to the pundits for a while, then Rego reached for a bottle he had brought with him and poured them both a drink.

'How do you bet on this?' Betsy asked, as she took the glass. 'They all think Aberdeen will win.'

'Aberdeen are all but certain to win so it doesn't matter. For every hundred you put down you get forty back.' He took a sip. 'Plus the original hundred, of course.'

The players ran on to the field.

When it was over, Rego was silent. The game had been exciting, yet his only movements during the second half were a flinch at each goal. It was a tale of plucky under-dogs rising to a challenge. There was nothing in the game that offered him any joy whatsoever. Sweat touched his forehead as the minutes ran out, and he only shuddered when the third goal killed his hopes. Betsy studied her lover and understood that he had seen this coming all day, had known the world was continuing to move against him. Yet with the final whistle, his bet lost, a change came over him: he soured, lost life and hardened. He moved round the desk. 'That rule of gambling I told you about,' he muttered, 'that when you're losing, you should keep doubling and then all will be equal.' His eyes swung towards her. 'There comes a time when you've nothing left to bet.' He seemed to see the end, as if he was shifting his armature to set himself against that finality. 'A pity. A real pity.'

The mobile rang and he removed it from his jacket pocket, pressing at the fascia without looking at the screen, walking towards the door as he listened. 'Yes. You know where I am. Yes.' He walked back to where Betsy stood and looked down at her. She felt uncomfortable under the gaze. She reached out but there was nothing under her palm that gave, just contracted muscle. Those eyes looked at her as if she were something new, as if he was seeing clearly. Her concern for him grew.

'There are things I need to do,' he said. They had already agreed that he would drive her back to Helen's cottage because he was due at the church for the rump of his game, but it was supposed to be later than this. 'I'll drive you over now.'

'Is there nothing I can do?'

He shook his head. 'It's a setback. That's all.'

As the headlights of the Range Rover ran over walls and fields, sweeping fast across the starlit countryside, Rego existed in some other world. Only as they left the village did Betsy see that he was looking at her. She touched his arm.

'If you don't want to go back to your flat, why not go to your parents?' he asked. 'Or your sisters?'

Betsy felt a stab of hurt. She thought about her sisters.

The competition of their childhood had left bad feeling that none of them had shaken off, and they had yet to learn to separate each other's real nature from the way their mother represented them. 'There are a few things I haven't told you about my sisters,' she said lightly.

The Range Rover pulled up in front of the cottage but Betsy sat still. 'Are you going to be okay?'

His eyes were dark in the twilight of the dials. 'I'll be fine.' He leaned forward and they kissed, her lips pressing on his stony mouth.

'I'll be here. If you need me.' She stepped out, closed the door and watched the car turn out of the driveway. Helen was standing under the doorlight, waiting for her, a pamphlet in her hand, but Betsy left her there as she watched the tail-lights of the Range Rover disappear along the road. She knew that she could help. Her anger at being dismissed was directed not at Rego, but at Boyle.

Helen had tiptoed out to stand beside her and Betsy embraced her. She took the piece of paper, and read it in the faint light from the door. 'For peace of mind plan for your funeral with Armstrong Funeral Directors.' Betsy sighed. 'I told you to throw all this in the bin.' The cold was cruel around them.

'I did, but then I couldn't help but look through them, take them out of the bin. I thought there might be a letter, from the council, saying I could bury William under the oak, or, I don't know, something kind.'

Betsy propelled her gently towards the door. 'Come on, let's go inside.' The guilt returned. 'I shouldn't have left you for so long.'

It is too cold for sleep. The forest is quiet now, the freezing silencing the whispering of the trees. I am uncomfortable on the boards. The recent mark has soured and I can only lie on my back, in the manner of the Saint. The cow fat has seeped over the edges of the wound, and darkened it. I thought it might have been the last, might finally have been ideal. And perhaps it was. Perhaps that is why the flesh has grown angry, the edges tender to the touch. It is as if, having sought for perfection, something, somewhere, is burning it from my skin. There is an ache below. Perhaps this is it, what I always wanted.

I lie, hands across my chest, listening. Cutter has been worrying, he has been wide-eyed, and that can only be bad. The pain is too great for sleep and I take to the night. The trails are cold, the sweep of the branches chill on my burning face. I move, low and quiet, on the dry streams. I watch the animals; their activity has calmed me in the past, their nature helping me feel sure again, empty and content. A fox passes, careful of its surroundings, missing my stench. It goes on towards the forbidden lands to root after the voles in the night. In the old clearing, I see two small roe. I hope to see a badger, their determination pleases me, allowing rest, but there are no tracks and I move on.

I hear a vehicle, out beyond the forest. It is late, too late for people, and I think of Cutter's animals. I move into the pasture where the cows, those sent into the cold for their dry udders, stand silently in the night. A few lift their heads to watch me come, and swing towards me, but I pass them fast. There is shuffling from the sheds, the milk cows keeping warm, but then I am beyond the field, in the pine brake. It is full of birds and I have to slow. There are lights down by the road. I was looking for sleep, but I only find disturbance. The bodyaltar aches.

There is a shout and the lights go off. I move through

211

the brake without disturbing the birds, and bring myself close to the wall. I can relax, all is fine. Cutter is there. I had been confused as he is without his vehicle. There is a pickup and a man talking, swearing at the state of the world. I can see them in the darkness, under a moon waning to nothing, but there is enough light from the stars and the breath rises between them. Cutter watches as the man turns and opens the back of the truck. A torch shines, and I see a ewe, bound in the back. I crouch, unwilling to anger Cutter, but I shift closer, silent. Cutter curses. In one movement, the stranger lifts the sheep over the gate and into the field. I can now see the ewe's eyes, dull in their resigned terror. I am close to the wall. I could touch the man's hand as he reaches over to cut the ropes. The ewe struggles to its feet, and limps away from me, towards its suspicious fellows. I look back through the gaps in the wall and see money move.

THURSDAY

High tide: 10.33, 23.09
Calm

Betsy opened her eyes, and was blinded by the sun breaking over the Solway. She retreated beneath the covers,
trying to recall where she was, until the sound of sobbing
placed her. Helen had asked to share the spare room, and
now the cadence of her weeping would become an
accompaniment to Betsy's waking. Later, Helen would
explain that it was the shock of waking, the fresh realiz-
ation that William was dead, that brought the tears. Betsy
knew enough not to disturb her: this was too personal;
necessary before each day could begin.

She lay and listened, her eyes half shut against the light
on the blue and white wallpaper, reminiscent of a carnival
tent. She presumed the intention was to cheer the waking
guest to another seaside day, but it made her wince. With
the sun in her eyes she would have liked to roll away
from the window but she did not want to embarrass
Helen, whose sobs had fallen to a murmur as gentle as the
sea on the shore below. Finally, though, the glare became
too much.

Helen was lying on her side, her body pulled up into a small hillock under the duvet. Tears were running down her face, rolling on to her nose and dripping from its tip. Watched over a gap of only a few feet, she brought a hand out from under the covers and wiped the tears away. 'I'm sorry,' she whispered.

'Would you like me to hold you?' She watched Helen slip from her bed. Betsy lifted her duvet and took her in her arms, the tears wet on her neck. She seemed so thin, her body longer than Betsy's but curled up so that it felt like holding a large child.

'Thank you,' Helen whispered, the sobs quieting at once. Soon she was asleep, with Betsy very awake.

As the sun cast light against the wall, its surface glowed. She gripped Helen, and closed her eyes but her mind was running and she found herself waiting. It would be an hour before Helen woke again, and then only when Betsy, suffering from an arm starved of blood, shifted.

They dressed, Betsy leading the way downstairs, collecting the post from the front porch, removing a black-bordered letter before Helen had a chance to reach her. All that was left was a bill for some work carried out on the property by the council. As they made breakfast, Betsy saw how low on supplies Helen was, and said she would go to the village shop.

'I should come,' said Helen.

'Not unless you want to.'

Helen touched the back of her hand to her lips. 'Perhaps I'd better not,' she said, with a soft smile.

'I'm happy to go.'

Helen suggested Betsy take her bicycle, rolled it out from the porch and into the crisp blue morning. 'This weather,' she said, joining Betsy, 'sunshine, with no breeze

... William was suspicious of days like these. He was hopeful in all things but the weather. "It's only a lull," he'd say, on a day like this. It would make me sad.'

A group of cormorants flapped up the shoreline, following the water's edge. Only the tip of the ark was showing. Betsy hated the idea of a lull, she wanted this sunshine to bring on the first signs of spring. She wanted to see flowers rise from the earth, the snowdrops, blue-bells and daffodils. She wanted this sun to give life, not just cast choleric light across the countryside. The radio was on in the kitchen, the sound of the new hour beeping from an open window. She heard the news headlines telling of the spread of the plague, engulfing counties.

As always Helen was dressed too lightly, bones showing under her summer dress. Betsy tried to convince her to go back inside but she insisted on walking as far as the gate, then handed over the bicycle.

'I think I'll push it a bit of the way,' Betsy said, fearful she would make an idiot of herself. 'Get a bit of air.' She would have left it behind but the basket on the front would make carrying the provisions easier.

They said goodbye and Betsy began her walk, gazing across the countryside. The road was white from the salt that the council trucks had spread and the land had dried in a way that was unusual so close to the sea. A sign had been hung on every gate now, warning walkers from the land. A bird of prey hung over a distant dyke, hovering, its wings a blur.

Soon the bird shifted further along the wall and hovered again, then half swooped to the ground and flew fast towards the sea. Again it stopped, now hovering over the verge a hundred yards ahead. As she closed, Betsy could see the curve in its body, its back at an angle so that its wings beat towards the sky, neutralizing gravity. The attitude forced it to hold its head over and down so that it could concentrate on whatever was in the dead grass below. Betsy moved towards it, yet still it hung there, until she was almost under its beating wings. Its concentration was such that it ignored her and Betsy stopped and looked up, right up to its belly, and she shivered because it seemed to be staring right back at her. It dived, and the fright of watching this predator fold in its wings and drop towards her made Betsy cry out. It reacted in turn, giving way and planing over the fields, before beginning the rapid flap of its wings.

When Betsy reached the village, she turned towards the small post office and shop that took up part of a house on the main road out. She propped the bicycle against the wall and straightened her back. The shop door formed an intimidating wall of stickers and local messages. A car rolled down the hill, the driver looking out at her.

Self-conscious, she pushed her way in.

There was enough room for one, or two at a push, in front of the counter. Every space was stacked with provisions, all the mundane but useful goods: bread, cereals, sugar, milk, eggs. With no one there to greet her Betsy began to assemble the items she needed, but when she looked up again a man in his fifties had appeared in the narrow space on the other side of the counter. He had square glasses, his hair grey and tufting from the side of his head, thin shoulders covered by a windcheater, the words *Yachting Monthly* stitched on the chest. He had the weather-blown complexion of a man who spent all his spare time sailing. He packed the goods into plastic bags, writing down the prices as they disappeared. He cast a long look at Betsy and frowned.

'You're James Rego's friend,' he said, the accent from further north, central Scotland.

'I'm staying with Helen Kerr.' Betsy felt defensive, and furious because of it.

'Oh, yes.' He was studying her. 'How is she?' Betsy prepared herself to be short, but he kept talking. 'Tried to call, but no answer. Not even the machine. We – my wife and I – wanted to know if there was anything we could do, anything she might need. We could have delivered.'

Betsy didn't want to explain; Rego's advice had been to avoid getting involved in the politics of the village. 'The telephone, it's been off,' she said simply.

The man blinked. 'Will you tell her we're very sorry for her loss? And if there's anything we can do? Anything.'

Betsy found she was staring back, unsure how to respond. 'Of course,' she said at last. 'I'll tell her.' Wanting to change the subject, she looked around, a quick act because Martha had already told her the answer to her next question. 'You don't sell newspapers?'

'Used to,' the shopkeeper said, 'but the distributor didn't make it worth my while. It cost me.' A grievance. 'Did Helen say why she didn't go?'

'Go where?'

He appeared offended. 'To Wicklow. To see the boys come off.'

Betsy dropped her gaze. Once again, she had been left uninformed. 'She's not feeling very strong at the moment,' she said.

The offence fell from the shopkeeper's face. 'No, of course.' He finished his calculations and passed the bags over the counter. Betsy took them, and paid with her other hand. 'As I say, tell her that if Margaret and I can be of any help, she knows where we are.' He closed his cash drawer.

217

Once in the sunlight, Betsy tried to pedal her way back but swiftly decided against it. She was troubled that no one had told her that the families had gone to collect the bodies. A car passed her as the fields opened up on either side, cattle grazing on hay that had been spread in a line, seagulls making a racket above them.

When she crested the hill and saw the cottage in front of her, the car was pulling up at the front door. Betsy slipped back on to the bicycle and, with determination, pedalled down the hill. She reached the gate as a man in a grey suit rang the bell. He glanced round and smiled, then walked back, transferring a camera he was holding in his right hand to the left. 'Mrs Kerr?' he said.

The front door opened behind him, Helen emerging nervously, relief showing as she saw Betsy. The man looked back at the door, then from one woman to the other. They were standing where the fish had been, a glitter of silver scales underfoot, a sweet smell rising.

'Who are you?' Helen asked.

The man extended his hand. 'Alan Gordon,' he said. 'Gordon Dunsyre Estate Agents. Here to look at the property.' He had noticed the smell too, his eyes flicking down.

'Look at the property?' said Helen, glancing at Betsy. 'Why?'

The man turned to Helen. 'Mrs Kerr?' She was motionless, arms crossed. 'A Mrs Kerr rang on Tuesday and said she wanted us to sell her house?' His attention was still switching from one woman to the other.

Helen kept her eyes on Betsy. 'No,' she said.

'No,' Betsy agreed. 'I think there has been a mistake.' She had turned to the agent, taking control. 'Perhaps somebody has played a practical joke.'

The agent studied his schedule, then gazed at them. 'Not a very funny one,' he said. 'I've driven all the way from Castle Douglas.'

Betsy gestured at the fish scales. 'Do you remember the voice of the person who called?' she asked.

'Oh,' he said. 'Oh dear. My secretary took the call. I'll ask her.' He pulled a mobile from his pocket and quick-dialled a number. They stood looking at each other.

'Helen,' Betsy said. 'You should go in.'

'I'd prefer to stay here.' She had moved alongside Betsy. 'My home.'

The agent's telephone conversation was short. 'Not much use,' he said, as he closed the phone. 'She couldn't remember. Said it was a man, though – she remembers because he gave the name as Mrs Kerr. She thought it would have been your husband.' He had decided Helen was the woman he was looking for.

There was a pause as they stood looking at each other, and then the agent scratched his neck. 'Well, I'm sorry to disturb you,' he said. 'Unless you want your house valued I'll be getting back.'

'I think we'll be all right,' Betsy said.

'Okay, then.' He smiled. 'Goodbye.' An afterthought. 'I hope you find out who's doing this.'

They watched as he drove out of the gates and down towards the village. 'I'm sorry,' Betsy said. 'You shouldn't have to deal with that.' All the hope the shopkeeper's kindness had engendered had vanished with the estate agent's appearance.

'I love this house,' Helen said.

'And nobody's going to take it away.'

'It's all I have now.' She spoke fast, traces of panic lacing her words. 'I have always loved this house. William

219

wanted to move away, to a place where there was more fishing, but I couldn't bear not being here.' She had turned to the cottage. 'I never saw the sea when I was a child, never once. My aunt sent me a postcard. It showed a cottage by the sea, all bright and fresh colours like this one, so unlike the filth where I grew up. I still have the card, it was my dream, but this house turned out even better. When I met William and found out he was a fisherman, I knew he must live near the sea. He was a fisherman, and he loved me. I was so lucky. He was never unkind. He wouldn't have let other people be unkind to me. Now he's gone and there is so much unkindness, and now they want my house.'

Betsy put an arm around Helen. 'Come on,' she said. 'Let's go inside.'

Betsy made tea as Helen began pressing at the edge of the kitchen table. When she set the mug down, she put a hand on Helen's shoulder, feeling the agitation under her fingers. She took the seat opposite, and noticed that Helen's eyes were darting over the surfaces, moving from one object to the next.

'The man in the shop sent his best wishes,' Betsy said. 'He said to tell you that if there was anything he or his wife can do, you only have to ask.'

Helen accepted this with a passing frown. The response of the shopkeeper had troubled Betsy. She had wondered whether Rego was offering sensible advice, whether Helen's cutting herself off from all the others was the right response to the suspicions, but the appearance of the estate agent discouraged her from mentioning it. 'Nobody can take your house away if you don't want them to,' she said.

Helen picked up the mug.

'You're all right for money?' Betsy asked, suddenly concerned. 'The mortgage?'

Helen answered with unusual wariness. 'I haven't looked. I will, though, later.'

'If you want any help . . .'

'I won't.' The certainty left Helen as swiftly as it had arrived. 'I couldn't bear not being here,' she said. 'William found it for me.'

Betsy thought she would wait a while before she brought up the subject of the bodies being taken off. If Helen knew already, she had chosen not to tell, and if she didn't know, then Betsy wanted her to be less anxious before she found out. 'Tell me,' she said, seeing an opportunity to distract Helen from the latest assaults. 'Tell me where you met William.'

Helen shook her head, her gaze still moving across the worktops.

'Please?'

She lifted her hand from her pressing, signalling defeat. 'In Doncaster. I was in a chess club in Sheffield, the Steel City Knights, we went for the competition.' Her voice quietened, and the hard edge that had arrived with her fear withdrew.

Betsy had noticed that in the last couple of days Helen's almost constant chatter had given way to silences. She was about to get an explanation.

Helen fussed at the tabletop. Eventually, with a flick of her head, she spoke: 'Are you in love with Mr Rego?'

Betsy was so shocked that tea entered her nose. 'No.' She coughed.

But Helen kept talking. 'I think I was in love with William from the first time I saw him. I was watching him

221

play. He was a wonderful player. He reached the final. He had these big hands and yet he moved the pieces so carefully. I loved watching him. He was thoughtful and considerate, never aggressive with his opponents, not in any way that could be considered rude, even on the board. But he was so sure in how he played – he thought in ways I never understood. I watch a lot of chess, you know. I get this magazine and it takes you through the great games. Well, William, he played like an artist, I saw that. An artist who smelled of the sea.'

Betsy had recovered, but remained silent. There was a sense of weight behind Helen's words, and whatever barrier had been holding her back now cracked. She told a history which Betsy suspected had, until then, been shared only with the dead man.

'Our team had lost,' she said, 'and we were watching the others play. William was in the semi-finals, playing against a legend in the area. And you could sense the sea on him. It was there on his hands, in his face, but mostly in his eyes. When chess players concentrate they sit crouched over the board, their minds on the game, but William sat straight, there was no strain, he enjoyed himself. And now and again he would look up at me, and in those eyes, for the first time, I saw the sea.

'I didn't know much about men. I was seventeen, and I was scared of the boys at school.' Helen looked to Betsy for reassurance, and found it. 'There were two boys who always taunted me, who'd wait for me on the way home, push me against walls and try to kiss me. There was nothing I could do about it. The teachers said they'd help but they never did. And the boys would laugh and try again, and tell me I really wanted to. I barely knew what they meant, my mother told me so little. At

222

home it was even worse. My mother kept lodgers all my life.'

'Your father?'

'He left before I was born.'

'I'm sorry.'

Helen shrugged. 'I'm being dull,' she said.

'No. Not at all. Do you mind talking about it?'

'I shouldn't, really. Talk about it.'

'You should.'

'I forget what I am saying.' Each morning's weeping seemed to drain Helen: she looked empty of tears.

'You said your mother kept boarders?'

'They were horrible. Some of them. One was nice. But another would mess around with me, when I was very little. He would touch me. This one man, if I was crying, would touch me.' She shuddered. 'And ask if that made it better. "Is that better?" he would say, when he put his big hand down my front. And I would be so frightened I would stop crying, until later that is, and I can still feel the pain of the sobs when I escaped and found somewhere private. I told my mother, in the end, and she threw him out. It was horrible. She hit him and he hit her and she threw boiling water, scalded him, and some of it hit me. But he left.

'It made me trust her, until I was older, until I was sixteen, seventeen, and then there was another man, one she liked. He was nice until he was drunk, and then he would make remarks. Soon he was waiting outside my room until he thought I was undressing and then he'd come in, say he was coming to tell me something, apologize, but his eyes, they would run all over me. Eventually he offered me money to touch him. I said no, and he got angry, threatened me, told me he would have me thrown out, said I'd have to do it with other men for money, less clean men, in the street. Well, I told my mother. I hadn't until then, because he always made it seem like it was a mistake, coming into my room, into the bathroom. But she wouldn't believe me. She liked him too much.

'I would go back to my games. In school and at home, I would stay inside and play patience, or Chinese checkers or chess, which one of the teachers had taught me, a man who asked for nothing in return. He was the one who introduced me to the chess club, and there I felt as if I actually had friends. And at school the teacher would play chess with me when he could, but he was busy, so he taught me to read the moves when they were written down, and he would cut the chess games out of the newspaper so that I could play alone.'

Helen stopped talking. She had at last put her hands flat on the kitchen table. 'I shouldn't be telling you this. It's not of any interest.'

'Please,' said Betsy. 'Go on. If you tell me these things then I can understand.'

'Well, I'm finished, really. That's about it.'

'But the tournament? You were telling me about the tournament.'

'Oh, William? Well, William was different. I could see it in his eyes. He seemed so strong. He seemed so much older, he was only twenty-seven, but I was so young.' She looked up. 'He was very beautiful. It made me feel . . . well, I know now, in love.'

Betsy laughed.

'He won his game, and when he got up he asked me if I had seen any mistakes that he had made. He asked me. I couldn't speak – I couldn't believe he was speaking to me. The club was staying to the end, but as spectators, because we'd lost. William was to play the next day in the final, and that night I met him in the corridor of the hotel where we were all staying. He asked if I would help him practise. I said yes, and we sat in the lounge for most of the night, playing and talking. It was magical. I asked him about the sea, and he told me. I think he was surprised, because I asked him about the water itself, but once he saw I really wanted to know, he told me things I had never even thought of, about the patterns on the surface as the wind covers the water, about how a sea changes when it nears land, about how it moves at different temperatures, the phosphorescence, the shapes of the waves, the surges in the sea itself, the way you can see the curve of the earth on the horizon. And I told him about my life, and my dreams. I had never felt so happy.' She was studying the table. 'I asked him to take me away with him.'

The sun had swung round so that its beam coloured Helen's face, giving her a pale, beatific glow. She blinked, and shifted, but did not move to pull down the blinds or cover her eyes. The atmosphere was calm in the kitchen, the air still touched by the scent of breakfast, warm drinks. Only the sea moved outside, the world over-exposed.

'Would you like anything?' she asked. 'More tea. Biscuits.'

'I'm fine,' said Betsy. 'I want to know what happened.'

'Once I'd asked William? Well, he laughed, of course.' Helen laughed now, an echo of the past.

Betsy waited.

'I remember, after he laughed, he looked sad. I remember this because it made me feel hope. He looked at me for a long time – we had been talking for so long, and I was

225

so young, I had told him all I had to tell, all the things I had never told anybody – and he told me later that he had begun to love me then. He was such a kind man. But he said that these things were too complicated. That we couldn't just run away, because we would have to end up somewhere, and there we would meet problems.' Helen now seemed to look straight into the southern sun, gazing directly into its core. 'I asked him again. I knew instinctively that the moment had come, that I'd never meet another man like him, with such kindness, and such knowledge. I told him that even if there were problems, there would be the sea, and places beyond that.' Helen choked on these last words, her voice turning ragged. 'The sea. He did go there in the end. Alone.'

'He meant to come back.'

Helen had turned her head towards Betsy, pupils tiny in the sunlight. 'I remember, before we left that evening, he held me. I put my arms around him and did not want to let go. I could smell the salt then, the fresh air. And we stood like that for a long, long time, until we heard a group of drunk people come up the stairs. I didn't sleep that night. I desperately wanted everything to change.'

Betsy leaned back and smiled. 'The next morning?'

'Well, the next morning I couldn't find William anywhere. He was supposed to be playing at ten, that was when the final began, but he wasn't answering the phone in his room, and I looked over the whole hotel. I was up very early, but by nine, I gave up and went for a walk. I'm sure Doncaster is a nice place, but even at that time in the morning I felt scared. Everybody seemed so unfriendly, the city so big. I was reminded of the lodger's threat to have me thrown out on the street, so I made a decision and hurried back to the hotel, to the conference centre where the tournament was taking place. I went to the secretary of the club and lied and said I was going to see my aunt in Rotherham and that I would take the train back home. But my aunt had died years before.'

'And he was okay with that?'

'She,' Helen said. 'Yes, why shouldn't she have been? But she offered to drop me off. It's on the way back to Sheffield, and I had to think fast and say I had already arranged to be picked up off the train.'

'And your teacher?'

'He wasn't on that trip. He hadn't been able to make it.'

Betsy said nothing. She didn't want to disturb the flow of Helen's story.

'Well, I went into the tournament room and there was William, taking off his jacket. He looked as if he hadn't slept. He smiled at me, and I went over to wish him luck. I told him I meant what I had said the night before.' She fell silent as she remembered. 'Well, he lost the match. He was playing a very good opponent, but he had beaten a better man the day before. They weren't very good games, and although he seemed to be concentrating – he threw me none of the looks of the previous day – he made mistakes. Towards the end the club members grew bored with the inevitability of it and decided to head off, and I said goodbye. I remember being scared then, because I didn't have enough money to pay for the train. We'd all slept in this one big room, and my bill had been picked up, kindly, by one of the group, but beyond that I was alone. At the end of the match William was given this little medal for being runner-up. He saw me standing in the small crowd that had formed a semi-circle around them, my bag at my feet. He said later I looked like a nervous angel. I remember my knees were shaking, my heart was in my mouth, all those things they tell you about in books. He came over. He didn't look at me. Instead he gazed down at this medal he had been given. He said he had gone for a walk that morning, to think about the night before. He said that he had thought about it all night. He said I was . . .' Helen gasped, awash in her feelings '. . . what they used to imagine mermaids were like – pure, dazzling light in a sea of corruption. He said he would show me the sea. He said he could say nothing more, because it would not be right, but that he would show me the sea. I didn't speak, he didn't know I couldn't get home. At last, I asked him if he had a coin for the phone and I called my mother. I couldn't lie. William was standing a few feet away and I told my mother I was leaving, that I had met someone who would be kind to me and that I wanted to go away with them. I tried to explain as best I could and she made no argument. And just before I ran out of money, I put William on the phone. She asked him to be good to me. That was it.'

Betsy remained silent, as still as the landscape.

'I called again a few weeks later, to tell her I was happy, but she had already sold up and gone, with the lodger. That's what the man who answered said, although he couldn't be sure. She left no address.'

'But that's terrible,' Betsy exclaimed. 'Did you ever hear?'

'No. I don't know what happened. I hope she was happy.'

A car pulled up on the gravel at the other side of the house and Betsy put a hand on Helen's wrist, saying she would find out who it was. When she opened the door, she found a man emerging from a small car, a second estate agent, this time from Stranraer. It took skill not to explain too much, but she got rid of him.

'More idiocy,' she said, as she returned to the kitchen.

Helen seemed content not to ask. She was now stand-ing at the worktop looking out over the sea. The cold sun gave the air a clarity that allowed the distant coasts to show; a cormorant flapped in to land on the prow of the ark, but waited only a moment before flying off again. 'William kept his promise,' she said. 'He took me to the sea. We drove to the coast, to a spot he knew, the most beautiful place. I still don't know where it is, maybe over there.' She pointed at Cumbria. 'But he knew this place. It was very rural, just lanes and small cottages, and we parked on a passing place. I remember being stunned because I had never seen such a place except on postcards, and it seemed so different. When we got out of the car I felt this incredible air on my face, cold and strong, full of salt. I remember thinking there was nothing human in it. It seemed richer than anything I had ever tasted and I remember being frightened by it. I was so young.' She laughed again as she looked out across the water, the sparkling surface barely moving in the sunlight. 'But there was no sea, just a path across a field. A stile and then a path. I wasn't really dressed for this sort of thing, but he gave me his coat and, wrapped in it, I walked into the wind. As we walked I noticed the top of the gentle slope stayed the same, there was only sky beyond. I must have stopped because William put his arm round me.' Helen looked over at Betsy. 'I remember every moment of this. We went forward slowly, and I began to hear this crash-ing, but I couldn't see anything. I guessed that this was the sound of seawater, the booming of the waves. And then there, over the top of the slope, was the horizon, the curve of the earth on the sea. I could feel the waves hit under my feet, felt the ground shudder. I remember being so frightened. The land fell away into a cliff. William got down on his hands and knees and motioned me to follow and we crept forward until I could see this whole sea moving below me, the white rising as the waves battered the cliff right beneath me, the taste of it on my tongue, spray on my face. And it was so vast that I couldn't imagine this man going out on it, and yet it seemed right somehow, because what I felt lying there was an extension of how I had felt when I first saw William. I was in love. It took away everything, all the other stuff. When, some days later, William made love to me . . .' Helen, who now leaned back against the worktop, tailed off: for an instant she looked as she should, a woman close to forty. 'I always saw William as the sea, most of all when he touched me.'

The sadness on her face was fathoms deep. It took time for her to speak again. 'I was so terrified, there on the cliff. It really wasn't anything like the scene on the postcard my aunt had sent me, but after a while William nodded us backwards and we walked along a path that ran along the cliff edge. We walked without saying anything for a long time, maybe an hour. I loved that, being able to look out to the horizon, to see as far as that. And I loved the air, I so loved the air.

'We dropped down into a gully where we couldn't see the sea any more. There was a bay ahead of us, and the path took us down between some woods to a small beach. We sat there. It was lovely, the sound of the sea hitting the cliffs now distant. We talked for a long time. William asked all these questions about the future and I told him about my dreams. I showed him my postcard.' Helen made the vaguest of gestures, as if re-enacting the moment. 'He looked at it. He kept looking at it, and at last he said he knew just the place. A cottage near the village he sailed from, this cottage. That's when I said I wanted to live there, with him.'

'You were so young.'

'I was seventeen.'

In the pale sunlight, Helen looked at Betsy, and at last seemed to understand her concern. 'He never stopped loving me,' she said. 'He was the same with me from the first time he touched me to the last day I saw him alive. He always said I was what he wanted, that he needed something precious to bring him home.'

Betsy found herself tangled in her own thoughts. The stark realities of her own life, the compromises she had made with her ex, because that was how a realist should behave, seemed misshapen in the face of Helen's past. She felt Helen's story was an assault on her way of life, almost because it seemed too open, too vulnerable, to pursue dreams in that way.

Helen continued to talk. 'When I cry,' she was saying, 'I know I shouldn't cry for the rest of our lives, for the time we never had. I know I should be happy for the moments we did have. I know how lucky I've been.' The misery seemed to rise within her, bending her over. Betsy leaped to her feet and held her in her arms.

Later, Betsy and Helen wrapped up and went for a walk that ended under the big oak where they had first spoken. There they sat, Betsy in the indentation that had been formed by William, Helen alongside her. Several small clouds touched the western sky, turning pink as the sun fell behind them.

'Do you think it's a change in the weather?' Betsy asked.

'No.' Helen was leaning against her. 'Red sky at night, shepherd's delight.'

231

'These short days. It's hardly night, more like teatime.'

'Red sky at tea, shepherd takes a pee.'

They both laughed. With an outstretched hand, Helen was shifting pebbles across the chessboard scratched on the rock.

The cottage was already in shadow, and the dusk was spreading out from where they sat, enveloping the land to the east. Betsy would see a great swathe of beautifully illuminated land, look away and find, when she looked back, all in darkness.

Two more estate agents had arrived in the afternoon, at almost the same time. When Betsy checked the *Yellow Pages* she found that all of the firms in the area had now made their visits. Looking to the south, she realized that she hadn't seen a jet all day.

'It was lovely how kind the shopkeeper was, when I went in this morning,' Betsy said.

Helen looked up from the board and smiled.

'This nastiness,' Betsy added. 'It could be just a small group.'

Helen moved the pieces.

'I just wonder if it's the right thing to do, staying holed up here, not going out.'

Helen's gaze rose, then dropped back to the board. 'Mr Rego knows what's best.'

Again Betsy looked east, towards the hills and even Edinburgh, somewhere beyond the pink clouds on the horizon. Given the pressure Rego was under, she wondered if Helen was right. 'You didn't tell me they were bringing the bodies off,' Betsy said, at last.

She did know. 'Tomorrow, they think.'

'And the families? They're all out there?'

'They flew to Ireland three days ago. They have to wait there, they think it might be unsafe . . .'

'You should have told me. Didn't you want to go?'

'They haven't found William.' A pause. 'I wouldn't be wanted.'

'Helen, you should have told me.'

'Best to stay here. Not make a fuss. See if they find him.' Her tone had hardened again.

'You should have asked me.' Betsy ignored the stubbornness. 'I would have taken you.'

'It's better to wait. That's what Mr Rego says.'

Betsy knew now that she didn't think so. Even without William being taken off, she was certain Rego had made a misjudgement. Helen should have been there. She couldn't have gone on her own, but he should have thought to ask Betsy to go with her. 'James is under a lot of pressure,' was all she said. She found herself wishing he would call. She was worried about him, and wanted to see him, but she also needed to talk to him about Helen. The only moments when he had seemed to forget himself were when they had made love. Yet Helen's story had caused Betsy to think in a different way about this rebound of hers. In so many ways, Helen lived in a fashion that Betsy disapproved of, allowing herself to be defined by the man she was with. William had seen her as something precious to return to, and when he hadn't returned, she had been left exposed, with no one to help her. As Betsy looked back at the cottage, at the small dykes that made up the maze of garden paths, at the bright colours of the walls, its fairy-tale quality the achieved ambition of a childish dream, she realized that this was what it must look like from the sea. This was what William would have seen through his binoculars as he sailed home. She wondered if

233

he was any less defined by his part in the relationship. If he had returned to find her gone, would he have been any less lost than she? He would have been more capable, certainly, but Betsy now had the feeling that the investment was so large on either side that its failure would have been equally devastating. The difference between Helen and herself was not only the willingness to offer everything but to expect everything in return. It made her understand Helen's question about whether she loved Rego. She didn't, and now she felt cheap. But she still wished he would phone.

Helen had stopped playing with the pebbles and was watching the darkening sea. 'I mustn't leave here,' she said, almost sleepily. 'If that's what you're thinking. I must stay. As long as I live with the sea beside me, he's here and I haven't lost everything.'

Betsy put her arm around her and hugged her close.

'It's getting cold.' Helen sighed. 'We should go in.'

'Yes.' Betsy lifted herself up, stiff from the earth, and brushed herself down.

As they walked back, Helen chatted about the state of her hands in the winter, about the cream she used to fight the drying effect of the air. Betsy found herself wondering how Boyle was getting on. Already irritated by him, her mood turned her further against her former neighbour at the inn. It was almost as if he were waiting, watching to see what was going to happen. And yet she was certain his lax approach was causing Rego unnecessary suffering. Betsy didn't know how much Rego was due, but it must go some way towards relieving his concerns if Boyle was prepared to spend so much time confirming his identity. She decided to track him down the next day and chivvy him along. Which would mean a trip to the village.

'I think we should maybe get out a bit more,' Betsy said, as Helen opened the gate leading up to the cottage. 'Why don't we have lunch at the inn tomorrow?'

'Oh, I don't think so. No, Mr Rego would be furious.'

'I'm sure he wouldn't be – and, anyway, I can deal with him. Martha is lovely, and she won't allow anything horrible to happen. Come on, just imagine that it's not as bad as you think. If you're going to keep living here you can't hide from everyone for ever.'

Helen had stopped. 'No, I couldn't do it.'

'I'll look after you,' said Betsy. 'Think how much better you'd feel.'

Helen said nothing. Then, frowning, she went towards the cottage's back door.

FRIDAY

High tide: 11.22, 23.47 (new moon)
Easterly

We wait, the animals and I, for the new growth. The land
is dry and the sun seems sick as it rises. Soon beauty
should touch the garden, but there are no flowers yet. I
have prepared; there is nothing more that can be done
until the new shoots emerge. The memorials are clean, but
for a grey-black lichen I allow slowly to cover the surfaces.
The storm felled the cliffside wall but it took little to
repair. All is prepared, all is ready. Yet I dawdle. If I
allowed myself, I would say that there is no future at all.

At night other lights show to the south: the pyres burning across the water. During the day there is smoke. The
stream that should run from the forest is empty, its path,
a glistening on the waterfall's rocks, has dulled. There is
nothing left to do here and yet there is a need to wait. The
work asked of me causes my hesitation but I know I
should obey. There is no room for nervousness. If Cutter
knew he would be angry. And he would be right.

Spring must come, yet . . . memories are abroad, risen
from the garden when they should be quiet. I allow the

lichen to grow on the stones so the memories age, but slowly. There is only one I avoid. I do not want to walk to the top of the garden. There is one memory that the Saint wouldn't want me to tend, and it is better not to rub away the lichen once it has grown there. The falcon shows in the distance, disturbed. There is someone out in the military lands. It will be the boy. Despite everything, it is time once again to do Cutter's will.

For once the post had brought good news. The special dispensation to bury William under the oak tree had arrived in a letter from the council. The clerk had kept the letter personal, subsuming the standard warnings about water supplies within sentiments of regret that helped Betsy convince Helen to have lunch at the inn.

They made their way along the coast at a leisurely pace. Helen had spent as much of the journey as possible down on the shore. She moved easily over the uneven ground, crossing chasms exposed in the slowly falling tide, searching for washed-up items of interest. She had been disappointed: the weather had been so calm that it had left little flotsam and so, having convinced Betsy on to the shore, she had begun to teach her about coastal life. She was so good at this, chasing crabs and minnows around the newly revealed rock pools, that Betsy, slipping and staggering across the kelp, asked why she had never had children. The childlike enthusiasm disappeared. 'Don't ask questions like that,' Helen said sharply, her interest in the shore gone. She marched towards the village and, although Betsy felt a little guilty, her hunger made her secretly pleased.

Helen fell back when they topped the headland and the village revealed itself below. She let Betsy lead them down on to the harbourside. There were few people in sight – a couple of bird-watchers crouched on the promontory with a telescope pointed along the coast. There were only three cars parked at the edge of the harbour. With the tide still fairly high, an Irish boat was preparing to leave while sailboats rolled with a gentle clinking of their cleats. At the door of the inn Helen caught up, and reached out to stop Betsy. 'Let's not. Too soon.'

Betsy smiled and gave Helen a small hug. 'It'll be fine. Come on.'

'It will embarrass Martha, and I wouldn't want to do that. Martha's always been very kind.'

'And she'll want to see you're okay. Come on.' There was enough uncertainty for Betsy to get Helen through the door.

As they came in Martha was vacuuming. A few locals were drinking in the public bar and seemed not to hear Betsy and Helen arrive because of the noise. Martha reached down to turn off the machine.

'We thought we'd drop by for some lunch,' said Betsy, her confidence failing her.

The men had fallen silent and were looking at Helen. Martha stepped forward to embrace her. 'How are you?' she asked.

'I'm . . . I'm fine.' Helen raised a hand, laid it tentatively on Martha's back.

'I'm glad to see you. The news. It's . . .'

'The others? I haven't . . .'

Martha stepped back but kept her hands on Helen's arms. 'William? They've found him.' She waited, seemingly appalled by the role that now fell on her. 'You didn't know?'

Helen slowly shook her head.

238

'They saw him this morning.' She was whispering now. 'He's on the boat.' Helen gazed back blank-eyed: the news had either missed her, or left her without words. Martha hugged her again. 'Oh, God, Helen, nobody told you.'

When Martha let go, Betsy stepped in to hold Helen. She seemed so delicate, as if she might fall at any moment. She had paled further. With care, Betsy led her to a seat in the corner, where the wall offered protection from the men in the other room.

'Are they going to bring William back?' Betsy asked, as Martha followed them over. Helen pushed herself back in the seat.

Martha was agitated. 'This shouldn't be coming from me. Somebody should be telling you what's going on. Who—'

'Mr Rego.' The syllables cracked in Helen's voice. 'Betsy. They've found him.'

'They're planning to send out a salvage boat.' Martha delivered this piece of news hopefully. 'The Irish are on the brink of deciding to go it alone and pay for the *Albatross* to be raised themselves.'

Now Helen's relief at the first bit of news collapsed. 'Mr Rego?'

One of the men, hearing this, snorted and walked from the bar. Betsy waited to see if he would come through the door of the lounge bar. He didn't.

'I don't know if he's got much say in the matter,' said Martha. 'The salvage laws . . . I think it's out of his hands now. He should have told you this.'

'He's doing his best,' said Betsy. 'It's not easy for him either.'

Martha gave Betsy a long, gauging look. There was further shuffling from the public bar. 'Let me get you some lunch,' Martha said. 'Some soup – I've made a chowder.' She paused. 'Helen. I'm very glad you have come. I've been worrying about you, we've all been worrying about you.' She walked back to the vacuum cleaner. 'I dropped a bag of salt,' she said, an incongruous explanation.

The remaining men now spoke quietly among themselves, the occasional grumble audible across the bar. Helen had shrunk into the wall, but Betsy pretended the men weren't there and took her hand. 'Are you all right?' she asked. 'Of course you're not. Oh, Helen, what can I do?'

Helen said nothing. She was looking at the table, her fingertips pushing at the unmarked surface. Betsy changed seats, shifting round the table so she could sit on the bench next to her. She was aware that, with this news, had come the absolute certainty that William was dead. 'It does means he'll be buried properly, under the oak,' she said. Things had shifted again. Betsy had hoped that the warmth of the greeting at the small shop would continue, and in many ways it had, but she couldn't imagine a worse place to receive such news than a bar.

Helen allowed her head to fall on Betsy's shoulder. She was keeping her tears inside, but Betsy felt shudders under her arm. A short length of wall meant the men could not see her, and their conversation continued, unrecognizable but for the occasional sighs, intake of breath, or grim laugh. Betsy could almost feel the weight of their presence on Helen.

'It will be terrible,' Helen whispered.

Betsy held her, looking down on the blonde head.

'Terrible. When they raise the boat.'

Betsy said nothing, just held her tight.

'What they'll find.'

'You won't, Helen. You won't have to identify him.'

'No, not that. The boat. The blame for the boat.' Helen was whispering, her voice so quiet that if their heads had not been together, Betsy would not have been able to make out the words.

Betsy wondered whether there was something else Helen had not told her, something Helen knew about her husband's state of mind when the boat sank. She shushed her, stroking her hair.

'I will have to leave. To go away.'

'Nothing can be that bad, Helen, nothing. We'll deal with it, I promise. I'll help you.' She could feel the strain, could feel the agony under her hand.

'It will get worse. I'll not be able to get food.'

'Come on, now, don't . . .'

Helen looked up. The fear in her eyes was very real. 'You'll go. You'll *have* to go, even if you're willing to stay. They'll turn on you as well.'

'I won't do that.'

'Even if William is buried, they'll deface the grave. The attacks, they'll get worse.' Hysteria was growing in Helen. 'I've tried. I've tried to stop them raising the boat . . .'

Betsy knew she would have to ask, to find out what it was she didn't know. 'Have you told James?'

Helen's gaze had fallen to the floor, but now it returned. 'Told him what?'

'What it is that's worrying you.'

Confusion. 'But this is what Mr Rego tells me.'

'What do you mean? He tells you?'

'This is what Mr Rego says will happen if they raise the *Albatross*,' Helen cried, and the bar fell silent.

Betsy tried to take this in, wondering what Rego could

241

know that was so bad he would say such a thing. She was about to reply but Martha appeared with the soup, put the bowls down and said she would get them some bread and cutlery, but the atmosphere caught her and she peered at them.

'It's fine,' said Betsy, grimacing a small acknowledgement.

Martha raised her eyebrows, but turned away. The silence in the bar remained until she returned with the spoons. 'Thanks,' said Betsy. 'It smells delicious.'

'It *is* delicious,' Martha replied. She went over to stand between the two bartops. 'What are you lot gawking at?' she asked the men.

'But do you know anything?' Betsy asked Helen, in a whisper. 'Anything about what happened that would make him think that?'

'No.' Helen was shocked. 'Of course not. All I know is the boat shouldn't be raised. That it's better down there.'

'It can't be as bad as that. It just can't be. And, anyway, you're hardly going to be held responsible. Even if it were . . .' She didn't know how to continue.

Helen was studying her again. 'They want my house,' she said simply.

Betsy recalled the face of each estate agent. 'Do you feel up to eating?' she asked, her voice betraying the sadness she felt. She began to feed Helen, as she might a child, all the while trying to summon up convincing reasons why Helen's suffering would soon be at an end. It was almost impossible to get past the persecution that had already taken place, the sense that Helen was utterly isolated from the people of this small community. Betsy felt her hand shaking as she lifted the spoon, her mind turning over the reasons why Rego might be prepared to terrify Helen, and why he insisted on dealing with this himself, refusing to call the police. She could only guess that whatever he was attempting to protect her from must be truly terrible. And yet, despite these efforts, a salvage boat would leave a small southern Irish fishing port, probably not unlike this one, to raise a boat and reveal secrets that would clearly change lives here. She was glad when Helen wanted no more, because she felt she might have dropped the spoon.

Helen spoke. 'William will be buried at the cottage,' she said. 'If I have to leave, I won't be able to visit him.'

'You won't have to leave, Helen.' She heard the strain in her own voice, and tried to control herself. 'I promise. I promised I would be your friend. I'll keep my word. I will do everything I can.'

One of the men in the public bar leaned over the counter to peer at Helen and Betsy. He pursed his thin lips, stepped back and left, reappearing through the lounge door, approaching them, his step high on the balls of his feet. His jacket was scuffed and dirty, and his long, thin hands were held together as he stopped at the table. Helen retreated further into the wall, her back pushed flat. Betsy tried to catch the man's gaze, to warn him off, but his eyes passed over her, frictionless.

'Mhairi and me, we're sorry for your loss, Helen,' he said. 'Anything we can do, you know where we are.'

There was a long silence. Betsy realized that his posture, aggressive in the way he leaned forward, was in fact his discomfort. As the silence opened up, his unease expanded into it. 'Well, I'd better be away home. But anything, you let us know.' As he stepped back, seemingly unwilling to turn his back, Helen whispered a drawn-out 'Thank you.'

'Whatever we can do, mind. Anything.' He waited to see if Helen would say any more, then walked away and out of the door.

Betsy sprang to her feet and rushed after him, emerging to find him zipping up his jacket. The cold breeze off the sea hit her. 'That was very kind,' she said. 'Thank you.'

He gazed at her with a look of such hatred that she stepped back. Then he walked away down the road.

Betsy stood and watched him go, then looked out over the harbour. There, Rego's smashed yacht lay on the fore-shore, the sailing boats and tenders rolling on a wave, the outgoing tide flowing round the pier. An old man was at the water-line, kicking at the mud with his boot, his collie happily trailing him. He bent down and then, from his crouched position, looked up at her. Embarrassed, Betsy went back into the pub.

Martha was standing over Helen, smiling. Her expression slackened when Betsy appeared at her side. 'I haven't had the chance to ask how you are,' she said.

'Helen's looking after me very well.'

The residue of Martha's smile was kind, a salve after the experience on the harbourside. She asked if they wanted anything else as Betsy sat down.

'The soup was enough,' said Helen. 'Thank you.'

'Perhaps just the bill,' said Betsy.

When she had dropped enough coins on the plate Betsy asked Martha how Boyle was getting on. The landlady shrugged. 'He went for a walk early this morning, and I haven't seen him since.'

'He's a strange one for a tourist,' Betsy commented. 'I wonder what he's up to? I can't work it out.'

It was a crass and inappropriate attempt to question Martha, who responded with disapproval. 'Well, there are a few strange tourists about,' she said at last. And then, 'Nobody wants a nosy innkeeper.'

As Betsy smiled, she knew that Martha listened. It was just that she didn't talk.

It didn't take long to walk back to the cottage. Although the tide had fallen, the shoreline no longer held any interest for Helen and she led the way, with Betsy following. Above them fingers of cloud pushed out to sea, faint and unthreatening. The sun fell through the gaps, slanting in from the south, the wind on their faces. Betsy wasn't tripping so much on the uneven ground, and found she had learned to watch and work out when she could afford to raise her eyes from the path. She wondered if Rego had called.

Helen, who had reconnected the answering-machine before they left that morning, must have been thinking the same thing because she checked as soon as they reached the cottage. There was a click and then the sound, perhaps recorded from a film, of screaming men, howling in fear. Betsy rushed to the machine, pressing buttons until it stopped. When she turned Helen was sitting.

'You see?' Helen said. 'Even if the boat is raised they won't stop. Not because I am resisting, but because they want me gone.'

Betsy knelt in front of her, holding her knees. 'It's just some idiots, Helen, it's not everyone. Look at what happened today, that man, he offered to help. It's just a few idiots, that's all.'

It seemed to have no effect. Helen looked back in fear.

Betsy stood and walked over to the telephone, dialling Rego's numbers, at home and on the mobile. The first clicked to the answering-machine, the second rang and was cut off. She called the house again and left a message, telling him Helen needed his help. Then she sat, reaching

245

out instinctively to push down on Helen's hand, stopping her pressing at the table. She wondered if the man in the bar had been kind for the sake of appearance, and that his eyes had shown his true feelings outside the front door, within smelling distance of the sea that had killed the men. Betsy wanted to help, to look after Rego and Helen, but she didn't know enough. She had expected to offer comfort without needing to know the others involved, but she was no longer sure that was possible. She had thought that knowing Rego would mean knowing everything.

'I feel a little tired,' said Helen. 'I think I might go and lie down.'

This seemed uncharacteristic, but Betsy helped her to the bedroom, then sat on the bed, talking quietly while Helen curled up under the bright duvet.

'Let me alone,' whispered Helen. 'Please.'

Shocked, Betsy backed off at once and returned to the kitchen, where she walked back and forth until she couldn't bear the silence any longer. She stepped outside and locked the back door behind her.

She followed the path down through the gorse to where the tide was retreating, the ark showing half its height. There she turned west, herding gulls and oystercatchers in great bursts up the rocky beach. Small birds picked at mud-pools.

She felt a growing resentment, not, she convinced herself, because of any perceived rejection by Rego but rather because his retreat was damaging Helen. She could see the depression eating at her and wanted Rego to control it. She had always imagined it would be all right, that together they could comfort Helen and bring her back into the world. With Helen's recovery, Betsy had thought her own strength would return, preparing her for the troubles that waited at home. She looked up to see the gulls shriek and mock her from the sky. Boyle must soothe Rego's financial worries.

She returned to the cottage and found Helen exactly as she had left her. She whispered that she was going to the village, and received a nod in reply.

Boyle answered her knock, opening the door only when he heard it was her, stepping back to let her in. He was holding himself gingerly, testing the length of a rib with a finger.

She entered warily, asking if he was all right.

'No.' The answer was sharp.

'What happened?'

He refused to reply and Betsy looked around the room. The curtains were half drawn so that it was gloomy, and it smelt of unwashed clothes. She noticed the salt on the branch had been dripping: the dark, dead wood now visible, emerging through the holes in the once-beautiful veneer. 'Your branch.'

'Yes.' The taut face was tighter yet, skull stretching the flesh. His head had fallen back, revealing his eyes for a moment.

'Is there anything I can do?'

'No. Leaving.'

'What happened?' She added, more in hope than expectation, 'Did you find the link?'

With some difficulty Boyle leaned over to pick his shirt off the bed, and there he held it, clearly too sore to attempt putting it on. His pain summoned Betsy's sympathy, but only a trace. He was holding his shirt by one finger, under the collar, and he had half turned to her. 'Why,' he asked, exasperated, 'are you here?'

Betsy had been ready to move forward, to take the shirt and hold it for him. She knew that he was not asking why she was in the room, but in the village itself – for once he seemed to be all there, not detached and watchful. He wanted to know why she was involved.

'I'm trying to help,' she said quietly. 'Is that not enough?'

'Liked you. Pity.' With a wince he extended his arm, holding out the shirt. 'You're a fool.' Although he was balding, the hair on the back of his neck extended down to spread along his shoulders. The muscles of his back were touched with a hint of weight so that they emerged in smooth, dark rounds.

'For trying to help?' Betsy took the shirt and held it open. He slipped one arm into the sleeve and then, with a groan, the other. She lifted the shirt on to his shoulders, keeping her hands away from the hair, his slim neck reminding her of something but she couldn't pin down what. She turned away. 'Perhaps. Worse still, I need you to help,' she said. 'You can't leave.'

He laughed, but the noise got caught in his nose. 'Wrong place. Wrong time.'

'It can't be.' Betsy tried to sound determined. 'The marking on the tree. You know you're right.' She saw that he had been packing – there were clothes on the bed. He travelled so light that at first she had thought it was a change of clothes. 'Tell me what happened.'

'Mistake,' he said.

She stood close to him, his shirt thankfully buttoned up. 'It's not a mistake,' she said, trying to keep the concern out of her voice, 'and you know that. You've shown me enough that I know there's no mistake. You can't leave now. Too much is resting on this. Finish the job.'

'Resting? What?'

'James Rego needs us.'

Boyle's gaze dropped to her hand, and Betsy realized she had taken hold of his shirt. She pulled back. The shadowed eyes moved upwards.

'Does he?' There was bitterness in his voice. He turned to the bed, carefully lifted his few clothes and put them into a holdall. 'You know him well.' He looked over his shoulder. It was infuriating not to be able to see his eyes clearly.

'I like him,' she said, ignoring the sarcasm. 'He's doing his best for Helen.'

Boyle said nothing, but he was watching her.

'Can't you tell me what happened?' Betsy shouted suddenly. 'Did he hurt you? He doesn't know who you are. You're sniffing around, oblivious to the pressure he's under. Everyone's under.'

'Oblivious?'

'Yes, oblivious,' said Betsy, at last animated. 'People are being hurt, lives being changed. People are dead, for God's sake. I understand you have your job to do, but do it. Look at you, no wonder people are freaking out under these insane circumstances, but now, at last, here you have the chance to do something good. To help. To ease the pressure. And what are you going to do? You're going to leave. That's great.'

Boyle was calm. Betsy's outburst had restored the placidity that irritated her so much. 'Money?' he asked.

'He needs support.'

'Financial?'

'Of all kinds. His boat has sunk. People have died. His captain is being blamed, and Helen is being persecuted. He's in real trouble. Why don't you just tell him?'

'No.'

'Then I will.'

'Time you do,' he swept a hand towards the north, 'gone.'

'Why? Why are you making this so difficult?'

Boyle rested against the dresser, and ran his hand across his lips. 'I . . . I'm no help. Come back. Better moment.'

'It'll be too late. It'll all be over by then.'

'Why?'

'Trust me, it'll all be over.'

They stood looking at each other, Boyle resting against the dresser, Betsy in the middle of the room. She had found some traction, she didn't know from where, but she could tell hope wasn't dead. Boyle shifted, a stab of pain showing around his eyes.

'What happened?' Betsy asked again, quietly.

'The firing range.' He was dismissive. 'Priest.'

'Priest hit you? But that's not James. Priest is out of control.'

'Out of control?' Boyle laughed, again through his nose. 'In total control. He pushed me. I. Faced him up. Strong bastard, stinks. Covered.' A wince. 'In fat.'

'And you blame James Rego for this?'

Boyle raised his hands. They fell into a brief silence.

'Did you find anything?' Betsy asked at last.

He shook his head. 'The end,' he said.

'It's not. I'm going to see James. I'll see him tomorrow. I'll go to his house, I'll find something. Something for certain.'

'Won't work.' Boyle raised himself from the dresser, the pain in his ribs making the movement slow. 'What could you find?'

'A sister.'

250

Boyle groaned. 'Picture?' He seemed to be mocking her as he pointed at his own little altar on the dresser, none of which had yet been packed. 'On his desk?'

'Why not? The place is a museum. It hasn't been changed for years. I'll look,' she said. 'I will look. Don't leave, not yet.'

Again he ran his hand over his lips. 'How are . . .' His gaze moved up her until she saw the shine of his pupils, his eyes on hers. '. . . things in Edinburgh?'

But Betsy shook her head. She wanted out, away. She didn't want this man in her personal life. 'I'll look tomorrow. I will find some evidence of this sister. Okay?'

'I, too,' he coughed, 'want to help.' He waited, but when she said nothing, shrugged. 'Tomorrow. Then I go.'

There is no forgiveness. Cutter came round the door of the workshop, kicking things, cursing, booting me. I have done what he asked, made the boxes as he said, but it makes no difference. The change has come, and although I do not understand what it is, I know that it is unalterable and my fault. Perhaps he sees that I am starting to feel. The boy was brave, it hurt to hurt him. Cutter would hate to know this and I would burn away these feelings with another cut but the last adulation has turned black, and is beginning to weep. The Saint requires devotion, not my pity, and must be displeased. He stabs at me but I don't know what is required. I don't understand, and I must not guess.

Cutter is cursing and I have to jump, not wanting to be kicked again. He grabs my head but the rendered fat causes his fingers to slip and he slaps me hard in the face. He tells me that everything is burning, and that soon nothing will remain. He tells me that they will come for

251

me, that I can only cheat the memories so long, and soon a stone will stand on my head.

I welcome it. The Saint is sending fire through my body. I want to tell Cutter about the flames that already lick at the altar, beginning its destruction, but he has calmed and I shouldn't rouse him. Our chances are slim, he tells me, the plague is on its way. In time it will arrive and may even save us. He kicks at the boxes, and nods, finally approving. 'Later,' he says, and goes. I continue with the work, weeping for the creatures who will die. More feelings! The Saint must have heard my complaints because the cut screams.

SATURDAY

Spring tide: 12.07
Strong south-westerly

There was no knock, just footsteps, and then Rego entered the kitchen, his face a smear of fury. Helen curled up in her seat. 'I've done all I can,' she whispered. 'I have.'

He looked from Helen to Betsy and back.

'They won't listen. They're determined.'

'Keep trying,' he snapped. 'Never stop trying. You.' He pointed at Betsy. 'Come with me.'

Betsy, who had hooked her heels up on the crossbar of her chair, put her feet on the ground. 'I'm sorry?' She was appalled by Helen's fear and spoke in the slow, warning tone she used when people irritated her at work, but Rego ignored this and gripped her arm. She stood in surprise and, aware that her dignity was at risk, let him walk her towards the door. She nodded back to Helen who, a touch disloyally, seemed relieved that his focus was elsewhere. In the corridor, Betsy pulled herself free. 'What do you think you're doing?' she asked quietly. The violence had unsettled her.

Rego strode ahead, opening the front door, ushering her through.

'What?' she asked, in exasperation. Although the weather had held, the wind had got up and was whining in the eaves. She stepped out, and was punched by the gusts.

'In the car,' he ordered, pointing to the Range Rover.

She climbed in, the thick door shutting out the breeze, sun pouring through the glass. Rego sat on the driver's side, big hands resting on the steering-wheel. 'You're damaging my efforts to protect Helen,' he said, a vein showing beside his eye.

'How?'

'You took her into the village.' A short pause. 'That was irresponsible.'

'Really?' Betsy felt her own annoyance. 'I didn't think so. In fact, I think you were wrong.'

'Wrong?' he shot back instantly, an intimidating darkness shadowing him. It emerged with every word, every move.

Having experienced her ex's overt anger, Betsy was used to dealing with this sort of thing. 'Yes, wrong,' she repeated. If she had found herself troubled by the low and violent fury, she now marshalled herself in the face of it. 'It isn't so dangerous for her to go into the village. Everybody we met was worried about her. It did her good.' The contrast between the steering-wheel and Rego's hand caught Betsy's eye: his grey skin made the white of his knuckles shine brighter. Beyond, traces of mud showed on the upholstery, and this unsettled her further. 'I'm not sure that isolation is the best thing for her.'

One hand came off the steering-wheel and Betsy flinched, a fingertip close to her face. 'You've no idea.' He became aware that she had recoiled and his tone lost its

254

threat, if not its anger. 'I'm trying to protect her.' The fluidity had gone from his voice. 'There's very bad feeling in the village. You don't know how it works. They'll be nice to her face, but when she's out of sight . . .' The next words rumbled in, loud and furious. 'You don't understand it here!' He looked at her closely, his natural presence turning to threat. 'I need you to be an extension of me here to help Helen. We need to act together, as one. You want to know what you could do to help? The Irish are going to lift that bloody boat. Get her to make calls, get her to stop them doing that.'

'But why? What could be so bad? If it means they can get William off, why shouldn't they? He's dead, and you've got Helen terrified in there. *He's dead*. What could they find there that'll make it worse?'

'You don't understand!' They were shouting at each other now, the noise dampened by the interior, the wind silent beyond the windows. 'There are things that are better left at the bottom of the sea. I'm not going to repeat them. You have to believe me. If that boat comes up, Helen loses everything. Don't take her to the village. Don't take her anywhere. Get her to make those calls. They're getting the other bodies off without raising the boat. If you have to go out, don't go further than the beach.' At last his voice had fallen and he looked at the palms of his hand, marked from gripping the steering-wheel. 'God knows, with the plague coming, you don't want to go wandering about anyway.'

Betsy looked at him, then down at the floor. She sighed and stepped down from the Range Rover. As soon as she had closed the door, Rego reversed fast through the gate and, spinning the wheel, was off. Betsy hurried in out of the wind that came up off the sea.

Helen was waiting for her in the kitchen, pressing hard on the table edge, staring out as if blind. 'I've tried,' she cried. 'I told him I've tried. But the Irish, they're so unhelpful. They say they've got to clear the matter up, for all the families. The marine-accident people, they were happy to leave William there, on the bottom.'

'James has been getting you to call the Irish?'

'Only now. Before it was just when they asked.' Helen looked at her, eyes searching for understanding. 'Now he wants me to call them and say William should stay where he is, say that's what he would have wanted.'

'And is it what you want?' Betsy tried to keep her voice steady and soothing, but she needed the answers. Her certainties were crumbling.

There was silence and it was then that Betsy realized what she had become in Helen's eyes. An extension of Rego, a widow-sitter. It was just what Rego wanted: unity.

'The tea's cold,' Helen said. 'I'll make some more.' She was on her feet, at the kettle.

'Helen?'

Helen stopped.

'I'm your friend,' Betsy said. She had stayed in this place to learn what it was to be independent. 'James and I, we're not in this together.'

Helen didn't move. 'If I can stay here, then that is what William would have wanted.' She bent down and looked through the telescope. 'The sea breeze has blown up some flotsam. We should go and have a look.'

'But you said you wanted him here, buried under the oak.'

Helen looked round accusingly. 'William would have wanted me to stay here.'

Betsy moved towards her. 'Do you know why James is so worried about the boat being raised?'

Helen straightened, trying to make out whatever she had seen with the naked eye. 'No.' She seemed distracted. 'But it must be terrible.'

'Was William capable of doing anything terrible?'

Her head flicked round. 'I'll go and see what's down there. It's a shame when you see things wash up and the sea takes them away again. You never know what you've missed.'

Betsy watched Helen pull on her boots and coat. She couldn't work out if she had changed the subject on purpose or whether she was just moving from one thing to the next. She left her to it, and went through to the sitting room. She had planned to phone her boss or her ex, but neither offered the sort of familiarity she needed after such a tense half-hour. She found herself picking up the receiver and dialling her parents' number, all but the last digit, then stopped. If she could be assured of getting her father she might have pressed it. But he would no longer answer the phone: the television was too loud, the interaction too confusing. She would get her mother and be lectured. With the receiver to her ear, Betsy sat with a finger on the cut-off. Even if her father did answer he would be unable to offer any advice, would only ask when she was coming to visit. Even the confusing questions that for a time had troubled him were gone. For a while he had taken to asking her if she was happy, the question more frequent as his illness worsened, until it had become an obsession. His persistence overwhelmed her, but finally it had broken like a wave, receding until all that was left was the refrain of a hoped-for visit. How would she explain this mess to him? He would listen and ask, 'Am I to see you soon?'

Betsy replaced the handset. She wondered what her father would have said. She hoped he would have told her to do what was right, and stand up for those in difficulty, but in truth, he would have been confused. His view of good works was grand, to create worlds in which others could live better, happier lives, not to involve himself in those lives. Once she had explained, taken it detail by detail, he would have wanted her to do the right thing by Helen, and she still believed the right thing for Helen was to help Rego. Despite his behaviour, she was certain that his financial worries were affecting his judgement. If she could solve those then he could concentrate on looking after Helen. She thought again of her father, and knew she couldn't have told him about sleeping with Rego. That, she understood, changed everything. It was why Helen's trust in her was haemorrhaging. She felt a sudden fear in her stomach, and wanted to be away. Her ex's criticisms filled her head. Fuck him, she thought. She was facing challenges he couldn't even comprehend. She needed to be strong, and she needed to end it, to find Henry his proof. Resolute, she picked up the phone and called her office.

The news wasn't good. Her ex had taken to standing at the barriers in front of the laboratory, part of the protest, pointing out relevant figures as they emerged. The death threats were coming in with every post. Her boss told her that there had been questions in the Scottish parliament, but despite a few idiots the politicians had been supportive. 'I've yet to hear a positive word about me, though,' he said, his tone sour. 'The big man was even told by some politico to get rid of me, to quieten the whole thing down. It had to be explained that I wasn't expendable, given that I'm in the middle of a ten-year research project.' When Betsy asked if she could be of any help, he said she could. 'Don't get found, Comrade. Stay low. The media's losing interest, this plague is now filling the pages, and all they've got is some ancient picture of you from your schooldays, which, while more attractive than the burning cows, shouldn't give you away.' Betsy was listening to this when she heard Helen return, the pad of her feet as she went down the hall and up to her room. She was relieved that the tone of the conversation with her boss had been warmer than before; she sensed him leaning again, the weight comforting. She wanted to speak for longer but there was something in the speed of Helen's passage down the corridor that worried her, and she brought the conversation to a close. It was only later, when thinking about the call again, that she realized her boss had failed to ask one question about how she was getting on. For now, though, she was following Helen upstairs.

The curtains were drawn, the fabric struggling against the light, the room in a twilight gloom. Helen was curled up in bed. 'You're worrying,' Betsy whispered, as she sat down beside her and stroked her hair. 'But it will all turn out. We'll make it work out.' She hoped it was the truth.

Helen rolled away, her face now sunk into the duvet, and Betsy, who had been distracted by the call, felt a change in her. 'Helen?' she called quietly, but there was no reply. She touched her shoulder. 'Has something happened?' Helen wouldn't speak, just lay still, and Betsy could feel her shaking. She gripped her. 'Helen?'

Helen's response was a quiet exhalation, long and slow. 'Please.'

Betsy stood and backed away through the door. She

dropped down to the kitchen so she could scan the land and sea beyond the window, looking for a figure, or something that might have caused this. There was nothing, only the waves rolling in, foam spitting up from the rocks, England in the distance. The sun was falling through clustered cloud, and the wind seemed to be spreading silver across the sea.

Betsy dressed for the outdoors in her coat. Outside, the fresh breeze burned her lungs and she had to breathe hard to catch herself but once she was used to it, it was effervescent on her tongue. She walked down the path, seeing the shadows on the beach, the flotsam Helen had gone to investigate. She felt the crushing obviousness of it, her stupidity at not checking first. She wanted to hurry but knew there was no need, that it was already too late, and, in truth, trepidation slowed her. There was salt on the wind.

Two large boxes were being pushed up by the tide, rumbling across the rocks. They were long and thin, and made from cheap wood. As she closed, revulsion swept in as she recognized them as coffins. She stopped and looked back at the cottage, so bright and fresh on the hillside above, the curtains of the spare bedroom pulled tight. She hoped for a twitch, to see Helen peer out, but there was nothing, just the wind. She turned back to the beach, and its bleak flotsam. They had joined the mess of seaweed lying on the foreshore, and Betsy scrambled down to them. The first she reached had been thrust up on to its side and she pushed it over with her foot, relieved to find it empty. On the lid was William's name, written in marker-pen alongside the date the *Albatross* had sunk. The coffin was roughly built, just planks and chipboard, a nasty joke. Betsy walked over to the second. The same hand had scrawled Helen's name and, beside the word 'died', a big question mark. Betsy looked up. The sea and sky became oppressive planes leading to a crushed horizon. It was winter, cold and bleak and Arctic. Here on the beach with the coffins, the future she had just promised Helen was shutting down. There was no mistaking this threat: it was time to call the police. Betsy ran up the beach. By the time she reached the cottage, the telephone was already ringing. She answered, and heard Rego at the other end.

The wind cuts across the bleak summit of Howe Hill, the world below. Cutter snaps his telephone closed and says, 'Okay, then, I think we might have gone a little bit too far there.' He seems cheerful, and is about to throw a friendly slap on to the bodyaltar, but pulls back. He says I am rancid, that he's lucky he's upwind. I am glad. The fire burns in my shoulder, worse than before, for the image has swollen and blossomed. I sweat and fear all touch. Cutter seems curious, studying the perspiration that washes my face and asks after my health, but I just shrug. He looks closer, sniffs and frowns. He wants to know why I do not wash. It is the end of his good humour and he switches easily to the bad. He complains that the boxes were probably too late, that the Micks will raise the boat against the cries of the fisherman's widow. He calls me a pig, and tells me that it's all my fault. 'You'd better take an axe and go down there and smash those boxes up,' he says. 'Make sure it's all gone, do it so it looks like we're furious. And do it fast.' He looks out towards the cottage by the sea. 'The woman's walking over to the house,' he says, 'so be sure to avoid her.' We look over the village to the sea, as he puts his binoculars in his pocket. 'Go,' he shouts, and I do.

Betsy walked with her head down into the breeze, her skull aching from the cold and her fury. Rego had told her the local bobby was related to one of the families that had lost a boy, and if she involved the police, the story would be picked up by the papers within the hour. She resented having to walk to his house, angry that he had refused to come and pick her up, and worried at having to leave the cottage at all – although Helen had welcomed this. Further attempts to involve the authorities had been refused. Helen did not want to talk about the coffins and seemed to side with Rego, once she had heard his promise to make the flotsam disappear. The opportunity to stand up to him in front of Helen had fallen flat.

Now she wanted to fulfil her promise to Boyle. As she had left the cottage, she knew all intimacy was over; that she had compromised herself. All the natural beauty around her now was subsumed under the deathly pallor of the land. She ignored the wildlife, the starlings in a tree beside the road, the wheedling gulls. She had considered Helen's bicycle but there was levity in its old-fashioned looks, its basket, that she could not cope with. She walked fast.

Only now, when she was in such a hurry, did she grasp how far it was. Still suffering the aches and pains from all the walking she had done in the two weeks since arriving, she winced at the blisters on her heels. Instead of growing fitter, stress and uncomfortable beds had left her with painful shoulders and a stiff back. She passed a field in which cattle stood at a feeding ring, pushing at each other in a dull-witted fight for place, and felt the creeping sensation that she was being watched. She stopped and looked across the fields, at the ragged trees, gorse and brambles that lined the path, and at the warnings to walkers that now hung from the wires. The dykes, with tight-packed stones, could hide anything, and not wishing to investigate she hurried on, feeling the presence pass, looking over her shoulder but seeing nothing. She passed through the village, and went along the road that led to Rego's house. The sea was blocked from view by the rising hill, the wood opening up on the right. Cattle and sheep looked back from where they sheltered from the wind.

Betsy pulled the bell-chain and, receiving no reply, opened the front door. She removed her boots under the hall's seascapes, hearing Rego shout a welcome from his office. She padded up to hear him finish a phone conversation with the word 'disappointing'. He was sitting behind his desk, the vast top now covered with junk where just a few days before it had been neat and ordered. The house, which until then had exuded the weariness of unchanging twilight years, now appeared lived-in, as if the finale had pushed dust into the air.

'I've sent Priest to deal with the boxes,' he said. 'He'll smash them up, get them gone.' He stood. 'I think that perhaps I should have him watch the place. See if we can catch whoever is doing this.'

Betsy recalled her unease on the walk and was glad she hadn't met Priest head on, glad he had hidden to watch her pass. It felt strange being in this house again. Rego was leaning back in his chair, exhaustion showing in his greying features. That he had allowed the place to grow messy disturbed her: she sensed it might be the start of a collapse. Her anger, her growing dissension from his actions deserted her, and she felt compassion for him. Trouble seemed to lap around his desk. He, too, seemed drained of his earlier fury. 'I shouldn't have spoken to you like I did this morning,' he said, his voice grave and repentant. 'It was awful. I know how much you're doing.'

'I'm worried that my help is causing trouble . . .'

He shook a hand and stood up, moving in front of her. 'No, you've been wonderful for Helen.' He ran his hand across her face, fingers slipping into her hair. 'And wonderful for me.'

Betsy stepped back. 'It's so confusing. I . . . We probably shouldn't have . . .'

He came after her. 'Don't say that.'

She was going to back off further, but he ran an arm round her, lifting his other hand to her face. She felt his breath. 'It confuses things,' she said.

'The only moments when I have forgotten all these troubles, when nothing else exists for me, have been with you.' His hand had fallen to her side, a thumb running over her breast. She hated herself for it, but she felt need in his touch and was excited by it. She tried to remember being angry, the awfulness of the distrust in Helen, his lack of contact. She found she wanted him, believing yet again that, with her help, he could solve everything. She liked his exhaled breath on her throat, his lips. She felt the arm tighten round her waist, the hand move down. 'You have been my escape.' He was pushing against her and she felt she might fall, staggering back a step. He backed her up against the desk, unbuttoning her, his mouth on her shoulders, moving down, hands tracing the contours of her flesh. 'I lose myself in you.' He spoke now into her belly. He was inhaling as he covered her body and she was up on the desk, the papers under her. His desire was feeding off her scent. Betsy let him take over, lying back and accepting his searching hands, and inquisitive mouth. There she lay, head back, as the glow of the day made only murky progress into the room, and all faded as she concentrated on the sensations. His attention changed as she shuddered, his grip tightening as he turned her over. She moved willingly, but too slowly for him and he forced himself on her with a violence that made her cry out. She was still caught in the sweeping sensation of orgasm, with no strength, but even so, the violence was too much: her legs, belly, pushed painfully against the edge of the table. All the delicacy, the infused beauty of his earlier act now disappeared and it became apparent he was taking out his anger in power. He was caught up, too consumed to stop, and she threw a hand back to the edge of the table, but he was too strong. She felt a nail break, felt bruising, felt she was back in the world and part of something ugly and brutal. She tried to move but he was too fast now. She tried to speak, tell him she was being hurt, that she was caught against the table, but he didn't, or refused, to hear. She yelled but there was no change, just the power and the agony it caused. She had to brace herself, trying to keep the pain to a minimum, and let it go on. He cried out as he came, and breathing hard, backed off, falling into the armchair that faced his desk. Betsy remained where she was, letting the pain subside, and then she twisted round to look at him. He sat, legs apart, trousers round his ankles, staring back at her without expression. She pulled up her jeans. The flesh around her stomach and the top of her legs felt raw, burned and angry.

'You needed that,' she said, her voice level and cold.

'You sounded as if you enjoyed yourself.' He wasn't cleaning himself, just sitting with legs apart.

'To begin with.'

He laughed, lifting a hand to push back his hair.

'You were . . .' she was speaking slowly, trying to pick her words '. . . over-exuberant. I felt . . .'

'As you said, I needed that.'

Betsy pursed her lips. 'It hurt.'

He said nothing, just looked back at her with a sated smile.

'Excuse me,' she said, and went to the bathroom. She sat on the toilet seat and examined herself. Of course, she regretted the squandering of her best intentions. It wasn't the desire, the passion, or even the violence. She understood when he talked about life being subsumed in grief, of needing to lose himself. It was the knowledge that when she shouted for him to stop he had not. She had hated that the feeling of being overwhelmed, pleasant enough, had been twisted into a horrible powerlessness.

When she returned, she found him back behind his desk, buttoned up. The telephone had rung and he was listening to a man leave a message, asking him to call back. He eyed her. 'Are you wanting to get back?' he asked, when the machine clicked off.

'Do you think I came over for sex? We have to talk about Helen.'

The mobile rang. Rego looked at the number and answered at once. 'Any news?' Betsy leaned against the doorjamb. He watched her as he listened. 'So another, how many days?' His eyes fell to his desk. 'Okay,' he said. 'Keep me informed.' He flipped the phone closed. 'There's dissent among the Irish,' he said. 'It might take another couple of days for a decision to be made.' He saw that Betsy was confused. 'To raise the boat.'

'And the bodies?'

'It's become a separate operation now that they've stabilized the boat.' He had become businesslike, the personal withdrawing from their conversation.

'They can get to William without lifting the boat?'

'So they say.' He leaned back. 'That's why there are questions about paying for a salvage crew. I need to do some work, see if I can encourage this change of heart. What's on your mind?'

'I'll wait,' Betsy said. 'I don't want to deal with it in a few sentences. I want to talk to you properly.'

He seemed suspicious, which insulted Betsy. 'Okay,' he said at last. 'Lunch. Can we talk over lunch? I'll work for an hour.'

'I'll be downstairs.'

He was flicking through papers. 'You should go for a walk.'

'You forget I just walked over here.'

His attention was elsewhere, so Betsy headed down to the drawing room.

The sun slanted in through the windows, seeking colour in the worn furnishings and rugs. The room was exactly as she had seen it last but for one newspaper, carelessly left open, its pages askew over the cushions of a chair. Betsy could tell that it had been thrown aside as James walked towards the bay windows. She picked it up, but whatever had caught his interest had gone, the page torn. Again, she felt the presence of the family who had created the room; the decoration the untouched remnant of something greater, long gone. She looked over the possessions, trying to imagine a sister for him, the parents sitting by the window. A bureau stood against one wall, a cabinet against another, and around the room were various bits of furniture that contained drawers and compartments. Betsy moved between the sofas and ran a hand along the bureau, nervous now that the reality of snooping was upon her. She felt the pain where the desk had dug into her, and sat on the arm of a chair, listening. Then she reached down to a small table beside her, sliding its drawer open to find cards and chess pieces. She closed it again and stood, wanting to try the bureau, but it seemed the most dangerous of all the possibilities, as if still protected by the mother who once wrote there.

She walked over to the door, tiptoeing despite the absurdity of it, and listened for James. The door of his office was shut but she could hear the murmuring of his conversation. She made for the cabinet. The front was a wall of thin drawers and she pulled out the first, the action sliding without a sound. A thin pile of maps lay inside, charts of the coast and the seabed. They were old, beautifully executed and, for a time, Betsy forgot her original intention. Her journey through the twelve drawers took her round the Irish Sea and up into the Hebrides. She lingered because she thought she could explain if caught among these charts, head off accusation by exclaiming at their beauty. Yet time was passing and she wove her way through the furniture, opening the drawers she passed, finding music books in one, embroidery in another, checking for names on the books and the half-finished needlework, but there were none.

At last Betsy stood before the bureau. She listened again for movement from above but now there was nothing. She tried the pull-down desktop but it was locked. She pulled the lower of the two drawers. It slid open but, to her disappointment, all she found were ancient games: Monopoly, Scrabble, dominoes. When she tried the drawer above, it gave without a creak, and here she found the photograph albums she had hoped for. She returned to the door to listen but there was not even the sound of talking. Her nerves itching, she pulled the first album from the pile: its dark card cover seemed the most recent. She opened the pages and at once noticed gaps. The album, long and thin, was old enough that the pictures were held in by four little corners, white frames on the black pages. The monochrome prints showed this house with a late-1940s car outside, the borders all full of flowers. There were photographs of James's parents, instantly recognizable, his father with the same thick, dark hair, his mother, a touch unfortunately, with her son's long face. And there were pictures of James as a boy, mostly on his own but sometimes with another, not a sister but a friend. Flicking through the pages, watching them grow, she realized with a start that the other boy was Priest. Looking closely she could see the faintest traces of the child in the creature who had troubled her dreams. As the pages turned and the boys grew, the images of Priest stopped appearing. There was only James, getting older, looking more confident, until these, too, ceased. Something about the photographs of Priest troubled Betsy but she couldn't yet see what it was. Most of all, the missing photographs disappointed her. Nearly one out of every five pictures was an empty space between the four corners, pictures she guessed must show the sister. She checked the other albums but they were older, a complete book of photographs of James as a baby, recognizable even then. Betsy had the third album out, looking at a portrait of his parents as a young couple outside the now ruined house on the firing-range, the monstrous Victorian mansion behind them, when she heard the door fly open upstairs. She was about to throw the albums back into the drawer but he was down the stairs so fast she froze. She waited in horror, the evidence of her search open by her knees.

He didn't come in. Instead, with a crash, he left the house. The Range Rover started, the spray of gravel like hail. Betsy waited. Then she rocked back on to her heels, carefully put the albums back into their rightful place and closed the drawer.

She walked to the front door. The car had gone, the engine no longer sounding through the wind, which rubbed against the building. The blue sky was lightly dusted with cloud, a group of starlings gossiped from an empty tree between her and the dark outbuildings. Knowing she would hear the car return, Betsy summoned her nerve and returned indoors. She climbed the stairs and entered the office without touching the still open door. To her left was a cabinet of bookshelves with drawers below, but she ignored this, and headed for the desk. The top was a mess of papers, cuttings and manuals: some on maritime law and salvage, others on insurance and warnings about the transport of animals. She began to open drawers, starting on the right. As each slid open, it appeared to relate to a part of his business. Bank statements were layered with letters, showing overdrafts and demands for payment. The fishing drawer was the same – letters, friendly at first, increasingly hostile, from chandlers, suppliers and engineers. The same again with the farm – letters, demands, a bitter labourer gone. She was trying to hurry but each letter had its story, and caught her attention. The centre drawer contained tools, pens, a cheque-book and a photograph, but after an initial beat of hope, it turned out to be an old picture of his parents, their arms round each other on some holiday abroad. Starting at the top of the left-hand tower of drawers, Betsy worked her way down. This stack was very different, each drawer lovingly kept. Where those other papers had been pressed down, folded and abandoned, the top drawer on the left contained a pile of folders, each identified with names written in calligraphic marker on the front. The first read 'Foxchapel King'. Inside, she found press clippings, scraps of form books, all relating to an Irish racehorse. She closed the drawer and opened the next. Again she found immaculate records, this about his collection of wines and sherries. Rego, left-handed, seemed to have kept this side of his desk for the worlds he loved, the activities he did not consider work.

She continued down, handbooks on card-play, card-counting, ace-tracking, casino-running, and notebooks with scrawled observations written in the language of aces and deuces. She reached for the bottom drawer, pulled, and found it locked. Her eyes rose in search of the key, and she found Rego watching her from the door.

'I'll just get Priest,' he said, his voice very quiet.

'No.' Betsy was so shocked, the word got lost in her teeth.

'It would be for the best. I wouldn't want to . . .' He licked his lips. 'Myself, you know. It's a pity. I was coming to rely on you, Helen was coming to rely on you.'

'No.'

'Betrayal. Everywhere.' He seemed to look through the window behind her. 'But not from Priest.' He paused again. 'He just got back, so I'd better get him.'

'It was for you.' Betsy had seen enough now to feel very frightened. She had seen what Priest had done to Boyle. What she had said sounded absurd, even to her.

'For me?' His expression hardened. Walking slowly, as if punched, he reached the armchair and slumped down. His eyes belied the hurt: the anger in them was savage. 'For me?' he repeated. For some reason the smell of Priest

271

had returned to her. 'Or for Mr Boyle? I presume this is something to do with him.' Again the glance at the window beyond. 'It's probably my fault for falling for it. I'm a fool, I suppose, on top of everything else. Stupid.' He chose that moment to shout, 'You had sex with me! I thought you were kind, not some damned Mata Hari.'

'I was trying to help,' she said.

'You're mocking me.' He grew reflective. 'I suppose I'm doomed anyway, so I might as well make it good, let it all collapse.' He waved a hand at her and winced. 'Do you know what Priest will do to you?'

'I was trying to help.' Betsy felt her face glowing as she tried to keep her composure. She took the press clipping about Boyle from where she kept it in her pocket and unfolded it, holding it over the desk, hand shaking. 'Take it,' she shouted.

He leaned forward and accepted the piece of paper. Betsy fell back, fighting the fear that the remembered stench of Priest had inspired. Rego's expression did not change as he read and, worried he wouldn't believe what was in front of him, she tried to make him understand. 'I found that when you told me to see who he was. It was from a newspaper.'

'So?' he said.

'He's looking for you. He works for an insurance company and he's looking for you.' The confusion on his face appalled her. She wanted comprehension. 'He wouldn't let me tell you. I was going to and then I saw him getting beaten up, outside the church, so I asked him about it and he wouldn't let me tell you.'

Rego had refolded the paper but now he flattened it out, reading again from start to finish.

'I don't understand,' he said, the words spaced, hard.

'He knows about a life-assurance policy. Money. For you. That you're in line for. I'm sure of it.' Betsy saw she was getting nowhere so she tried to pull herself together, sucking in air. Although making him understand was what mattered, she couldn't help but speak fast, the sentences emerging without gaps. 'A man who used to work on the range left a life-assurance policy to a woman called Mary, who was from this village, and Henry is trying to gather clues but he wouldn't ask you outright and he was about to leave because it was such a bad time and I knew how much you need some . . . some good news and he all but knows you had a sister called Mary who died which would make you the beneficiary.'

The anger in Rego's eyes died. He looked down to read the newspaper report one more time. 'How much?'

'I don't know.'

'I still don't understand.'

Betsy found herself shouting: 'I was trying to find evidence that this Mary is your sister.'

He tapped the arm of his chair. Then he began to ask questions, starting with the first conversations she had shared with Henry, continuing until she admitted she had been looking for the missing photographs from the album. When he fell silent she asked, desperation touching her voice, whether he did have a sister. He said nothing, just gazed back at her, his head still for several minutes.

'It went wrong,' he said finally. Betsy waited. When he looked at her again, he seemed surprised. 'Bad.'

'*Is* she alive?'

'No.' He stood up, and came round to her side of the desk, his movements fluid again. For a moment Betsy didn't know what he was doing and looked up at him

273

fearfully, but then she understood that he wanted his seat. She slipped away from him sidewards and he gestured towards the armchair with his hand, then sloughed down behind his desk, a move that restored a degree of benevolence to him. 'You really don't know how much?' he asked.

Betsy shook her head rapidly. 'But it must be sizeable. He's been down here for a while, so he must stand to make a bit.'

'He makes a bit?' Again the frown, but Betsy felt the threat receding.

'He gets you to sign for a percentage, and then he tells you about the policy. That's the way it works.'

Rego again appeared caught in thought, eyes scanning Betsy's face.

'I think that's probably the real reason I wasn't supposed to tell you, in case you tried to track down the policy yourself. He says it's so others don't hear about the money, the need for confidentiality.'

'And why is it that you didn't you tell me?'

'He said he would leave.' Betsy grew uncomfortable under his stare and raised her hands. 'What?'

'I don't believe you,' he said.

Although the first wave of fear had abated, this provoked a second. 'Would I make this up?'

'Perhaps I should talk to him.' Rego looked away. Out of the window, empty branches shattered the sky. 'Or perhaps not. You say he needs proof?' He took keys from his pocket and swung back to unlock the bottom drawer, leafing through papers until he lifted a small white envelope. From it he pulled a pile of photographs. He looked at each one until he smiled. Then he held up a small monochrome print between his fore and middle fingers. Betsy stood and took it. It showed Rego pushing a small, grinning girl in a home-made buggy. 'James and Mary, Howe Hill' was written on the back in pencil. 'Will he need more than that?'

'I think so. He's been spending a lot of time looking for her grave. That's why he was out on the firing-range.'

Rego flipped through the rest of the pictures, pausing, uncertain, over one. Then he looked up and added, almost absentmindedly: 'She's in the family plot. It's on the coast, beside the wood. But there's no marking on the grave-stone.' He had returned to the photographs. 'She disgraced us,' he said at last. His voice had hardened again. 'She was wrongheaded. She died in another place, but I brought her back, and buried her.' He looked at the wall beyond Betsy. 'I brought her back for sentimental reasons, but I wasn't going to put our name on the stone. My mother would have spun if I did. What are you going to tell him?'

Betsy, aware she was on uncertain ground, decided against asking further questions. 'That I found this picture.'

'And?' He stood and moved over to the door. 'I'm going downstairs to get a drink. Do you want one? A sherry?' He took her exhausted silence as a yes and left. Betsy stayed still, feeling ill from the retreating adrenalin. When he returned, he handed her a small glass and carried his own to the desk. 'What you should do,' he said, 'is tell him you lifted that photograph, but were too worried to take anything else.' She was impressed by how focused he was after only a couple of minutes away from her. 'But tell him you saw the death certificate, and that she died of pleurisy, in a place called Workington.'

'Workington?'

275

'Ugly name, ugly place. It's a port across the way. You can see it on a clear day, across the firth. And that's true. That's what happened. If he's so keen to see the graveyard, say you looked at the satellite photograph. Say there's something strange, and you think it might be the graveyard.' He walked over to the black photograph on the wall, motioning Betsy over. She saw now that it showed the whole area, undefined from such a height. Rego was pointing things out. 'This is the house and there's the wood, although it was younger back then, and if you look down here . . .' He indicated a clear space at the top of a cliff with a small building just showing grey against the black. '. . . this is the graveyard. It's surrounded by trees and bushes, but there is a track if you look for it. It comes in next to the wood. You could try to lead him to it.'

Betsy tried to make sense of the landscape. 'So how . . . ?'

He took her arm, his touch gentle although she flinched, and lifted her finger to the photograph. 'If you follow the fenceline towards the sea, you'll see a path leading away where the spruce turn to larch. It's easy – the spruce are evergreen, the larch have no needles. Once you start along there, the trees turn to birch and then sloe. It'll lead you down to the graveyard. He'd never have found it. And see if you can find out how much money we're talking about.' He smiled. 'So Ty Roberts left our Mary money? After all that.'

'Why he couldn't come straight to you, I don't know.'

'You should have told me, but you'll do a fine job now. I think you should hurry over there.' Rego was looking more cheerful by the moment. 'I'll give you a lift.' He winced. 'But I can't. I've got Priest loading the Range Rover at the garage.'

'He really is back?'

'I wouldn't have done it. I was just scaring you.' He shifted the subject. 'It went fine at Helen's. The boxes have gone.'

'I should get back to her.' The threat had felt very real. 'I'm happy to walk.'

'But you'll go and see Boyle?'

'Yes. I'll get my coat.'

'Go over the fields. It's faster.'

'Is it safe? The signs.'

'You've been here since the beginning of the outbreak, you'll be all right.' He kissed her lips. Betsy had to force herself not to jerk away. 'I'm so glad we got this straightened out. I hope I didn't appear too fearsome.' He didn't allow her a chance to reply. 'You'd better get going.'

Betsy found his new-found enthusiasm distressing, but she had committed herself, and she needed to see this thing out. She stepped back, put the photograph in her pocket and turned towards the door.

'Go out through the walled garden, that's the best way,' said Rego. 'Good luck.' He had the cheek to pat her bottom.

The plague was on the far shores of the firth, and approaching from the east. Not only had restrictions appeared on the field gates, farmers were now refusing to let even the postman into their yards. On the road across, Betsy had negotiated four barriers of disinfectant-soaked straw, and although she now took Rego's advice and walked out into the field, she felt at once exposed in these prohibited lands. Exhausted from the morning's fear, the shock of looking up from the desk to see Rego came back to her. Although she had witnessed Boyle's beating, she had somehow never conceived of being threatened. She needed to think, and the fields seemed too exposed. Instead she doubled back towards the oak. She decided to take a look at the graveyard before she said anything to Boyle, especially as Priest would be occupied. The walk would give her an opportunity to consider and, more importantly, calm down.

The afternoon hung round her as she passed under the oak. She followed the dyke, and then the fence until the spruce gave way to sickly-looking larch. She turned into the plantation. The wind died away to play with the branches above her. As promised a thin path entered the forest, no more than an indentation in the earth. For a moment Betsy worried that it was a wrong turn, the memory of being lost in the trees with Boyle coming back, but she steeled herself and fought a way through the fence. Now surrounded, the nerve-twitching claustro-phobia returned. Again she reminded herself that Priest was back at the house. She became aware of an absence. The jabbering that accompanied so many of her walks had died away, the birds gone, and she was relieved when the trees grew smaller, and clearings appeared. Here and there gorse blossomed, at first small plants, then large clumps with yellow flowers bright in the increasingly salty air. She crossed a dry watercourse, a plank providing an unnecessary bridge, and followed the track through sloe, sharp points defensive on each side. The bushes created a tunnel that gradually reduced in height until she was startled to find herself at the edge of a drop, punched by the wind off the sea. The graveyard lay below.

It was larger than she had imagined, walled into the contours of the ledge, rising at its western end to a height all but level with the point on which Betsy now stood, then falling away to the east and its gate. Wind-blown firs grew at various levels, covering groups of graves, and half-way up, inset into the wall, was the roof of a squat mausoleum. Beyond the furthest wall the cliff fell again, more than a hundred feet down to the sea, giving a view to the ancient kingdoms east and south and west. Betsy climbed down the steep track, joined a path that led in grand style to the west, its grassy passage a straight line between a carefully spaced avenue of rowan. She guessed that this would have led to the now ruined house on the range, the family seat. She turned left and followed this avenue to the gate of the cemetery, looking up to see where she had paused, at a point where the stream, dry at the moment, should have tumbled in a long waterfall.

The gate had been freshly oiled and opened smoothly to Betsy's touch. The grass was short and untroubled by bumps, indented only where the dead lay. The headstones were clustered rather than regimented, some sheltered, others looking out across the wide views. All faced the gate. Betsy felt the wind tingle on her flesh, and was dazzled by the sun, white on the grey lichens of the wall, the neat runs of moss in the grass. She walked over to the first group of memorials and started to read the inscriptions. Another shock awaited her, and this one chilled her heart. On a stone that seemed both ageless yet new was the name Betsy Gillander. She threw a look to the top of the cliff, and around the perimeter. Nothing had changed, all seemed quiet. She read: 'Betsy Gillander, selfless in life, peaceful in death, faithful retainer of the Rego family.' Betsy Gillander had died over a hundred and ten years before, yet with her scalp itching, her nerves prickling under her skin, the living Betsy recalled Rego telling her that a Betsy Gillander had worked for his family. The sea air poured oxygen into her blood, feeding her body and mind. It took effort to move from her namesake's resting place further into the memorials.

Although beautiful, the graveyard never regained the peacefulness Betsy had felt looking down on it from the ridge above. The stones, belonging to those who had worked for the family, were all old, yet a sheen gave the impression they had been freshly planted. The mausoleum was ugly, with the Rego name carved above the door. Some of the huddled stones had been skewed by expanding roots, but the bushes offered only a dead shade. Yet as Betsy moved up the slope, away from her namesake's grave, she felt a certain liberty return. The wind was fresh, and the sea was audible far below, the water shattering light beyond the cliff edge. At the top of the slope, where the walls met, stood a small stone cross. Unmarked, it had collected a greater covering of lichen than those she knew to be far, far older, an impression undermined by a small badge, nestled into the moss at the base that read, 'Just sleeping'. Betsy had to raise her eyes to the sweep of the horizon, to feel the wind on her face, to look on the upturning strata of rock that seemed to seek the sky, before she felt a surge of achievement. She felt certain this was Rego's sister, the woman whose photograph she now held in the pocket of her coat. As she stood at this furthest point, buttoned up tightly against the wind, she knew she had done her part. She could forget her concerns about Rego's behaviour and pass on this information. The criticisms levelled against her were being buried; she had made a difference. Rego would survive, Helen would keep her cottage. As she rested a hand on the top of the gravestone, the sharp edges of a creeper that grew there must have stabbed her for she lifted her hand at once, as if stung.

She stepped forward to look over the wall, at the plants of the furthest edge reclaiming their position as the ground staggered and fell to the black rocks below. There were no gulls, just emptiness, and the sensation of standing on a cliff with the graves behind caused her to jerk round and search the stones. She realized this visit to a graveyard on her own was a first for her, and that the experience did not bring solitude. Rather, a curious unease fed in. She began to walk fast downhill, passing through the gate without offering another glance at her namesake. She looked back only when she reached the top of the small cliff. All was as it had been when she first gazed down.

She avoided Rego's house by cutting down to the sea and using the cliff path to walk back to the village. She wanted to pass on the information to Boyle quickly so that she could get back to Helen. The sun was falling behind her as she walked round the bay, a firestorm above the fields to the west. A figure sat at the end of the pier, watching her come. As she passed the houses, she saw Boyle stand.

They met in the middle of the village, the sky colouring his face, weariness showing on the taut skin. His eyes were just about visible in the light, the skin below them grey.

'I have news,' she said.

'News.' She could tell he was on edge: his long neck was stretched forward, his face tilted a little towards the light. She pulled out the photograph and passed it to him.

He held it carefully by its edges, looking at the picture for a long time, then turned it over.

death certificate,' Betsy said. 'She died in I think it's over the other side of the firth. She contracted pleurisy.'

'Buried there?'

'I don't know.' Betsy felt a rush of surprise: the decision had been barely conscious. 'That's all I could find out. I had to look in the drawers of his desk. I need to go now. I've left Helen on her own.' The truth shocked her: she hated the idea of no longer being involved, and wanted to show him the graveyard personally.

'Workington?'

'I think it's on the Cumbrian coast. Over there.' She pointed, and although there was a house in the way, he understood. 'Is that enough evidence? It seems pretty conclusive.'

He looked again at the photograph, then out to sea. 'I'll go and see if I can trace her. Day or two.' He waved the picture. 'Thank you. Grateful.'

'But don't you have enough?' Betsy hadn't foreseen this. She wanted him to speak to Rego now. 'It's surely enough to go to him with?' She would have to tell him about the graveyard.

But Boyle was walking away. 'Day, maybe two, no difference,' he said, over his shoulder. 'Thank you.'

Unable to think up an explanation for her lie, Betsy had to watch him go, appalled by the thought of how much difference this delay could make. She cut through the houses, walking quickly along the road that led to the cottage.

Helen was where Betsy had left her, curled up in bed. There was a lethargy in her form that fought the colours of the room, a huddled figure under the covers. She showed no interest in any food Betsy made for her, and ignored any questions.

Betsy had checked to make sure the fake coffins had gone, but when she spoke of them, Helen shivered. With the gloom giving the impression of a child's room, Betsy thought of singing a lullaby, but her voice wasn't up to it. Instead she tried to think of a story to tell, something from her own life that spoke of a security that Helen could grip. Nothing came. She searched her memory for the happy times of her childhood, for warmth in the cosseted world in which she stood accused of sheltering. There had been trips to the west coast, and while they had been idyllic in many ways, no memory remained unsoured by the constant competition with her sisters. At last she recalled a walk she had taken with her father on the coast of Ardnamurchan, and she began the story at once, in almost a whisper, filling it with detail of the mountains and the sea and the autumnal smell of heather. She told of the white cottage with a red tin roof where they stayed, and of how she had been feeling sick, her mother impatiently (although Betsy omitted this) taking the other children off to play golf, leaving her father unsure of how to look after his daughter. As the day passed, Betsy had felt better and, to her father's evident relief, had agreed to a walk. To Helen, she now described all the things they had seen, the seaweeds, grasses, birds, trees and stones. Most of all, she tried to describe the smell of the warm earth, a comfort rising from the ground. They had rested, without speaking, at a spot where the sea lay in front of them, and there her father had noticed a bumble-bee trying to stand on a leaf. He pointed it out to his daughter and told her it was exhausted from all its work, too tired to fly. She had been struck by the sadness of it but her father had said that maybe if they took it home it would be all right. He laughed when Betsy had asked how they would find its home. 'We'll take it to the cottage,' he had said, 'and see if we can make it feel better.' He had picked up the leaf and held the bee in cupped hands and they cut towards home. There he had spooned a dab of honey on to a plate, put it on the window-sill and left the bee. Betsy was lifted on to the worktop so she could sit and watch, open-mouthed, as the bee slowly came back to life, pumping its legs to the intake of sugar.

As Betsy sat beside Helen, telling her story, she heard a car pull up outside the house and recalled that it was at the same moment, all those years ago, that her mother had returned, disturbing the vigil. It was the only act of kindness she had ever seen either of her parents extend to any creature. She didn't say this either. Instead, in response to Helen's grip, she told her the bee had flown off into the warm afternoon, a honey-drunk flight. In truth she hadn't seen it happen: it had gone by the time she returned from greeting her siblings.

Downstairs, the doorbell rang.

Betsy made to stand, but Helen had taken hold of her. The door opened and they heard Rego shout, his footsteps pounding into the kitchen, the living room and then up the stairs. He swept through the door. 'Helen?' he asked. Getting no reply, he spoke to Betsy: 'How is she?'

'A little tired.' She winced to show it was bad.

Rego collapsed on the bed. Helen was on her side, the covers rising over her thin form. 'I had Priest destroy those boxes,' he said, patting her hip. 'I'm going to have to get tough but I'll stop it, even if it kills me.'

Betsy felt Helen shiver again. 'She knows they've gone.'

'Who?' Rego asked.

284

'The coffins, of course.'

'Oh.' He sat for a moment, then looked at Betsy, raising his eyebrows. When she refused to give him the satisfaction of comprehension, he asked, 'Did you see him?'

She nodded.

'And?'

Betsy frowned and motioned at Helen.

His gaze dropped. 'We'll get you through this, Helen,' he said. 'You've just got to hang in there. And there is good news. William is off the boat, there's no reason for them to raise the *Albatross* now. Everything will be fine. The families are flying back from Ireland tonight. Tomorrow they will fly William home.' He waited, but Helen said nothing. Finally he pursed his lips. 'She needs some time,' he said to Betsy. 'Come on.' As Rego spoke, Betsy felt Helen's grip tighten.

'I want to stay with Helen tonight,' she said, disgusted by his almost gleeful manner.

He eyed Helen again, then looked at Betsy. 'Sure. Of course. Just come and have a word outside.' He stood. 'Try to get some sleep, Helen. I'll drop by and see you tomorrow. We need to talk about arrangements.'

Betsy tried to get up but Helen's hand tightened again on hers. She leaned down, and whispered, 'I'm not going anywhere. I'll be back as soon as I've seen him out,'-and stepped away.

Rego was leaning against the wall of the corridor. 'I thought I might have received a visit by now.' He was so close that Betsy wanted to move back, but he had lifted a hand to touch her face.

'He's gone to Workington.'

He was holding a strand of her hair between his

forefinger and thumb. The good humour fell from him like a blanket.

'He'll be back in two days.'

Rego stepped back, withdrawing the hand, using it to punch the wall.

'James, I tried, but he was off so fast.'

He studied his fist. Betsy took a step back. He looked at her momentarily, then rushed down the stairs.

She waited for a moment to settle herself, then went back in to Helen. There she stayed all evening, unable to get Helen to eat or speak. At last, exhausted, she lay down in the next bed and switched off her lamp. With darkness, Helen slipped across the space and under the covers to rest her forehead against Betsy's shoulders.

SUNDAY, MONDAY

High tide: 00.31, 12.50; 01.12, 13.31
Flat calm

Betsy looked down at her badly bitten nails as she cradled the telephone on her shoulder. Her hands had roughened with the cold weather, her scrambling walks. 'It's not good,' she said miserably. 'I can't get her to eat.' There had been no one else to call.

'I'm sure you're doing your best.' He sounded distracted.

To avoid snapping at him, Betsy bit at a painful cuticle on the little finger of her right hand, transferring the phone from one shoulder to the other. 'I got a call this morning.'

'Boyle?' The question was too fast, irritating her further.

'No. They said they were – I might have got this wrong – Manxmen.' It was high tide. The sea was close and flat, the ebb yet to pull water back out of the bay, the ark hidden under the faintest roll.

'Manxman Disaster Specialists, they're the divers. They retrieved the bodies.' He waited, and when she didn't speak, asked, 'They want to know what's to happen to William's body?'

'Yes. They're coming tomorrow.'

'Coming? Why? They've already spoken to her. He's to be buried at the cottage. Isn't that what Helen wants?'

'I didn't know they had already spoken to her.' Another detail she had been unaware of. 'And I don't know why they're coming.' Betsy resented having to discuss anything with Rego after his behaviour the day before, but there was no choice. 'I didn't ask.' She raised her eyes to the sea in the hope it might calm her.

'I suppose I'd better send Priest over to dig the grave.'

'I wish I could get Helen to talk to me.' Betsy couldn't get used to how much the sea rose and fell with each tide, that the vast ark could be so completely submerged. 'What about a service?'

'That shouldn't be necessary. It's only going to be us.' He seemed to be doing something else – she could hear the paper rustling. 'Someone could say something over the grave.'

Betsy had once read an article about the sea in which the author said that he had never seen it as cleansing but rather as a soup of tepid, briny effluence, full of disease and hidden death. 'I wish Helen would speak,' she repeated.

'So you don't know what's happened to Boyle?'

'I promise I'll let you know as soon as I hear anything.'

'I'd better go.' He rang off without waiting for a reply.

Betsy poured a glass of tap-water, climbed the stairs and sat down on the bed. When Helen failed to take it, Betsy asked if she wanted something to eat, but there was no reply. At last she swept back the lank hair, letting her hand rest on the thin shoulder. Helen was fading now, and Betsy didn't know what to do.

The rest of the day passed in the same way. There was

a book about Russian chessmasters on the side table and Betsy sent herself to sleep by reading it aloud. By the time she woke, night had fallen and she felt disoriented. She tried once more to interest Helen in food but was again rebuffed. That night she lay awake, with Helen at her back, thinking about the sea. She couldn't love it, like this other woman. The movement of the water scared her. The ragged holes in the ark came back to her, and she recalled looking into the sodden recess where little light penetrated, and which filled with brine twice daily. It horrified her because she saw herself stuck there, the water rising around her. She saw her own water-bleached face trapped within the concrete hull. 'You'll go back to Edinburgh,' Helen had said, and she was probably right. The thought of settling in this place was to see her decaying face look back from the sunken ark. She listened, trying to rid herself of the image, but there was no sound from beyond the windows. The sea would have retreated and would now be whispering its way up the rocks once again, filling those holes. The high thin clouds would barely mask the glitter of the stars. Everything was absence here, the lull all-encompassing. Betsy had done her bit for Rego and found no recompense. As the hours passed, she thought of Edinburgh and her life there. She missed the restaurants, and the classes she took. She wondered what films would have come and gone. There were galleries she too often neglected, and the room at the Museum of Scotland that had first inspired her towards a career in science. Where once, in the misery surrounding her break-up, she had imagined there would be no friends who worried about her, she found herself missing people who were probably, even now, concerned for her. She slept just before dawn, and woke again to the earliest traces of grey beyond the curtains, feeling Helen's tears on her back. She felt embarrassed by her earlier thoughts, light bringing the knowledge that the next few days held terrible fears for the woman beside her. As the 1970s clock flicked its leaves towards seven, she lay still, allowing her companion to grieve.

The alarm sounded at eight and Betsy slipped from the bed. She showered and dressed, then bent close to Helen's ear, and asked if she wanted anything. Helen shook her head, the acknowledgement itself encouraging.

'Those people are coming,' Betsy said. 'About William.'

Helen pushed herself up.

'You could see them in here, or not see them at all, if you're not up to it. If you tell me what you'd like . . .' But Helen had put her feet out of the bed, and was looking out of the landward window where the unseen sun leached light across the fields. Betsy watched her as she stood up. Her hair had lost its lustre and any vitality in her skin had gone. There was a hollowness to her face that seemed but a step from the grave. She held herself as if condemned, gazing on the stake, her nightgown a shroud. 'Oh, Helen,' said Betsy, making a move towards her.

Helen blinked. 'Can I have a minute?'

'Of course. Can I get you anything?'

'No.' There was the faintest trace of a smile.

'I'll be downstairs.'

The visitors arrived promptly. Betsy saw from the kitchen clock that it was exactly half past nine as their car pulled up. She called up the stairs to Helen, then went to the door. The bell sounded as she reached it. She was surprised to find the minister standing on the doorstep, behind him two tall, striking men.

'Come in, please.'

The minister, shorter than Betsy, the flesh of his neck pushing out from his collar, squeezed past.

'I'm Betsy Gillander. I'm . . .' she hadn't thought about this before '. . . a friend of Helen's.'

The minister nodded; the other men shook her hand. One was broad with a shaved head and very pale blue eyes, the other seemed Hispanic, dark, thin and angular, with a high flat forehead. The first introduced himself in an accent she now recognized from the Manx fishermen who came to the pier: 'Oliver Finlay,' he said. 'I'm a director of Manxman Recovery. We spoke on the phone.' To Betsy's nod, he added, 'This is Si Hurtado, our chief of diving.'

Betsy smiled at each in turn and shut the door, all of them close and uncomfortable in the passageway. The minister was rubbing his hands, looking around, and Betsy pointed the way into the living room.

'Helen, how good to see you,' she heard the minister gasp, as he passed into the room. 'I wish it was under better circumstances.'

Hurtado stopped and turned to Betsy, his black eyes dry and compassionate. Finlay was also looking at her. 'It's not good,' she said, guessing at what they wanted. 'It's been very hard on her.' They followed the minister through the door. Finlay cut him off, reminding Helen of the times they had spoken on the telephone.

Helen had taken her place on a high-backed chair that until now had acted as a shelf for her chess magazines. The others settled, the two specialists perching on the front lip of the sofa, the minister relaxing with a sigh into the armchair until he seemed to remember himself and sat forward to begin the conversation.

Finlay interrupted: 'Mrs Kerr, as you know we represent a company whose aim it is to return the irrecoverable. We know how important it is to get a family member back after a tragedy yet, while it was our job to recover William's body, it was the Irish government who employed us to do it. We have been asked by them to answer any questions you have – any questions at all – but I should tell you that we have found it best to be absolutely straight and not try to cover up any detail to spare feelings. We will answer your questions truthfully and to the full extent of our knowledge. It is up to you to decide what to ask.' He rested his hands on his knees.

'Would you like tea?' Helen asked nervously.

Finlay laughed. 'Honestly and truthfully, I'd love some tea. And I expect Si would as well.' When Hurtado nodded Finlay turned to the minister. 'Reverend?' The minister declined.

'I'll get it,' Betsy said, and walked through to the kitchen where she had left the teapot ready on a tray with cups and biscuits. The kettle had boiled but she heated it again. She had noticed that Helen no longer objected to being called Mrs Kerr, despite the lack of a marriage certificate: she had accepted her place as William's widow. Finlay was talking in the other room, his words unintelligible through the wall. Having filled the pot, Betsy carried the tray through, and knelt in front of the coffee-table to pour.

'. . . it was definitely sudden,' Finlay was saying. 'It looked as if it was there one minute, on the bottom the next.'

She handed Helen tea. Her friend held the cup for warmth but did not drink. 'Would you like me to light the fire?' Betsy asked.

Again, Helen had clothed herself inappropriately, the sleeveless dress hanging off her, thin arms mottled, her knees together, feet tucked back against the chair. She had washed and combed her hair but its colour, which now reminded Betsy of the dead grass beside the roads, accentuated the deathly face. She tried to smile a yes, then turned to Finlay. 'How did you find him?' she whispered. 'How was he?'

Betsy slid over to the fire and put a match to the kindling. She listened to Finlay before she poured tea for the guests.

'He was in the fish hold. Which was why we had a problem. The way the boat was lying, it was impossible to get to him until we had lifted the hull a metre or two off the seabed.'

'But how was he?'

Finlay looked carefully at Helen. 'We found him dressed in boots and a sou'wester, and below that a white and brown sweater. He had a screwdriver in his pocket, along with an adjustable spanner tied by string to his wrist. The panel covering one of the bilge lines was off.'

'What does that mean?' asked Betsy.

Finlay looked at her, and then back at Helen. 'We're not investigators, but it seems likely that there was something wrong.'

'Would that be William's fault?' Helen's voice had grown quieter still.

Finlay took his time in answering. 'I really don't want to pre-judge any investigation. As I said, we're not experts in this.'

'Looked to me like he was trying to save the boat,' said Hurtado, in a rasping voice.

'Si brought the bodies off himself,' Finlay explained.

'He's been diving since the day they found the boat, from the moment the sea was calm enough. At that depth you go down in a bell, for eight hours at a time. You get involved.' He opened out his hands. 'It depends how much you want to know.'

Helen twitched, the smallest acknowledgement for him to continue.

'When the Irish navy found the *Albatross*, they contacted us at once. She was just short of three hundred feet, on her side. It's very tricky at that depth.' Finlay inhaled. 'One of the fishermen, Jim Orr, had been working outside. He had a harness on and his body was in the doorway.' He stopped to watch Helen's reaction and when she continued to sit forward, holding her cup and saying nothing, he continued. 'This provided a problem, which was one of the reasons it took so long to bring them off. Every time Si wanted to get into the boat, he had to push past Mr Orr. As I explained on the telephone, our first objective is to account for the entire crew and not to touch anyone until we get orders from the authorities – but . . .' Finlay sighed.

'Difficult,' said Hurtado.

'Yes,' agreed the minister. 'I imagine it was.'

Betsy looked at Helen. 'Are you sure you're up to this?' She nodded.

'It's better to know everything,' said Finlay, his voice soft, clear and calm. 'Si wanted to bring Mr Orr's body up there and then, but the Irish fisheries minister decided, and I agreed, that everybody should come up at once. What we did was take down a bag and put Jim Orr in it, strapping him to the side of the boat until we were ready to bring up the whole crew. Of course the main problem with doing that turned out to be accounting for William.'

Again Finlay stopped, and Betsy saw that he wanted to make sure Helen was able to deal with the description. She seemed untouched, leaning forward to put down her still full cup of tea. But she asked Betsy for a glass of water.

In the kitchen Betsy ran the cold tap, looking out over the sea, imagining the job Hurtado had performed beneath the icy waters. The image of her face stuck in the ark came back to her. She shuddered at the idea of pushing past a drowned boy of seventeen to get into the interior of a corpse-filled boat. The face became Priest's, and Betsy had to shake her head to dislodge the image. The water ran cold now and Betsy slowed the stream to fill the glass. There was something terrifyingly human in the description of the clothes that William Kerr was wearing. She sensed it was Finlay's way of making it real. When she returned to the living room and passed the glass to Helen, Finlay was listing the places where the bodies had been found. Three were in their cots, another was in the galley, another in the engine room.

'There was no one in the wheelhouse?' the minister asked, then looked guiltily at Helen.

'Jim Orr was in the doorway,' was Finlay's curt reply.

Helen sipped her water. 'Did William look frightened?' she asked.

'No,' said Hurtado. 'None of them did. Three must have been asleep.'

There was a silence, which Betsy broke by offering more tea. It took the specialists a moment to register what they were being asked and hold out their cups to be filled.

'We deal with many disasters,' Finlay said. 'I was involved in Lockerbie. We both were with the explosion on the Piper Alpha oil platform. Both occurred swiftly but you could see the terror – it showed in scratchmarks and broken nails. On the *Albatross* there was nothing like that. When the investigations are completed, whatever they say, you must remember it happened so fast they wouldn't have known about it.' He leaned back so that he sat straight.

'Extraordinary,' said the minister. 'You'd have thought they'd have known something.'

'Sometimes,' replied Hurtado, his accent twisting the words, 'the sea opens up. And that's it.' He flattened his hands to show the waters closing.

A silence grew in the room, surrounding them. 'Were there any fish in the hold with him?' Helen whispered.

'You mean that they had caught?'

'Swimming.'

The minister puffed but Finlay looked to Hurtado.

'I do not think so.'

Again they waited, but Helen stood and walked to the door. 'Thank you,' she said. 'You've been very kind.'

Finlay twisted in his seat to look up at her. 'We have William's body up at the airbase,' he said. 'Would you like to visit him there?'

Helen shook her head.

'Have you plans for his body?'

'This is where I come in,' said the minister. 'I thought we could bury all the men in one service. I thought we might conduct all the funerals in ascending order of age. That would mean William would be last, the finale if you like. Maybe on Thursday at the village church.'

Helen looked at Betsy, eyes fearful.

'No,' said Betsy. 'I don't think so.' She turned to the minister. 'William is to be buried here. The council have given Helen dispensation.'

'Well, okay, certainly. But it would be better if they all

had the same service. They sailed together, worked together, were all taken off the boat together, as Mr Finlay said, so all the funerals should happen at once. And then there is the issue of the press. They'll come back and we want to be able to control them.'

Betsy could see traces of blood in the minister's eyes; he had the face of a secret drinker. She wondered if he saw salvation in presiding over such a grand ceremony. She was about to snap at him, but Finlay was ahead of her. 'Two of the crew were Catholic,' he said.

'But that leaves five,' said the minister.

Betsy noticed that Finlay and Hurtado were watching Helen, waiting to hear what she had to say, but she couldn't speak.

'The Irish government,' Finlay said at last, 'instructed us to do whatever you wish, to offer you any support we can and work with you until you are satisfied that your wishes have been fulfilled to the letter. Would you like a service?'

'Not in the village.' It was almost an exhalation.

An idea touched Betsy and she spoke without thinking. 'What about the church along the road? You know . . .' She didn't want to refer to it as the boneyard. 'You said it was still consecrated.'

'It hasn't been used for two years,' the minister interrupted. 'And that was for a wedding.'

'Perhaps it's time for a funeral,' said Finlay.

The minister looked at Helen. 'When?'

'Soon.'

The minister shrugged. 'Friday?'

'Tomorrow?' said Finlay.

'Too soon,' the minister said. 'I'd need to get it ready.'

'What about Wednesday?'

'I suppose I could. I haven't been inside for a long time.'

'We could check it over now.'

The minister glanced at the people in the room with him. 'And afterwards?' he asked. 'You would like him buried here?'

'Yes,' said Betsy.

'What about the grave itself?'

'James Rego's dealing with that.' Betsy saw Finlay and Hurtado glance at each other.

'What about telling people?' the minister asked.

They all looked at Helen who was leaning on the door, shaking her head. It was the most vigorous she had been since talking to Betsy about how she had met William.

'Are you sure?' asked the minister.

She nodded.

'I suppose. Certainly, if that's what you'd prefer.' The minister leaned back again. 'It will certainly make it easier to organize.' He smiled unhappily at each in turn.

Helen disappeared.

Betsy saw the men out, then followed her friend upstairs. Once again Helen was curled up in her familiar position on the bed. She was still wearing the dress.

'They're going to see the other families,' Betsy said, sinking down next to her. 'Amazing people, really, a terrible job to do.' Helen took her hand. 'Did you find them helpful?'

Helen said nothing, but she was crying.

Betsy stroked the now clean hair. 'We'll get you through this, Helen, I promise.' She stood and walked to the window, pressed her face against the glass. In the distance she could see the tops of the clump of trees that hid the church.

'They'll hate me once they've spoken to the others,' said a voice from behind her.

'Cut it,' shouts Cutter, pushing me towards the wide-eyed ewe. Now he is angry at the mess on his hands and kicks at the bodyaltar in frustration. He knows nothing of animals: if he did he would see that the sheep is sick and this serves no purpose. I refuse and he takes the knife. I look away as he cuts its throat, hearing the breath spill with the blood, and then he drops the knife at my feet, his hands out to keep the gore off him, making unhappy sounds. 'You're ill,' he tells me, as he leaves. That's the concern he offers. I act fast despite the pain, pocketing the knife, lifting the sheep and carrying it away until I have it in the trees. My mind plays tricks now. The pain is eating at my brain, the Saint burning on my shoulder. I try to serve him but I don't know what he wants. Branches occasionally touch the cut and the Saint screams with anger. The fire is spreading across the bodyaltar. I feel weary, an unimaginable sensation among other feelings I thought long gone. At my quarters I string the carcass up from the frame, nothing must be wasted, too much blood has already been spilt. I will render the creature into what can be used, but I don't understand. The mouth of the sheep is a mess, it is why Cutter wanted it killed. I don't understand why he bought this sheep, why he paid money for it, when plague is on its lips. Cutter should know best but I fear now. I fear so much that the pain slips from my head. Sensations I believed long gone return. Fear. Anger. Shame.

Betsy stood on the seashore, looking east along the cliff-edged coast to where, in the distance, the arch disrupted the horizon. To the south, sunlight lay on the water. She had noticed a warmth in it, a taste of change. Despite the restrictions – the plague leaped towards them along the coast – Betsy decided to walk along the cliff-top. She had not moved from the village since the outbreak began and must, as Rego had pointed out, be clean. She wanted to see the arch up close. From where she stood, it seemed to cut a hole in the blue sky, like an escape.

At first her path was difficult, stones and gorse barring her way. The cliff had yet to rise, and she dropped down beside a pool, putting up a snipe that twisted down to the shore and along the coast, in turn disturbing shelducks, which lifted off, black heads outstretched as they swung round to settle behind her. The sky was a blanket blue. Once over a dyke, the stone stile old and broken, she found her step lifting. The nervousness of trespass would soon be on her, but the air had revived her spirits.

She had been impressed by Finlay and Hurtado, by the directness of their approach, and now wondered if she had failed in her efforts to be a friend to Rego and Helen. She was so close to the centre of the disaster that she had no idea what was happening on the peripheries, out there where Helen's fate would be decided. It was only in the last few days that she had realized that those people she had watched act impotently in the face of the tragedy were actually Helen's jury. As she considered her efforts to comfort Helen, she wondered if they had been useless: poor balm like a priest's blessing for a condemned man. Perhaps she should have actively sought clemency. She had expected Rego to be there for the meeting that morning, but when she had called, he had said he'd other things to do. He told her Boyle's car had not yet returned to the inn and had started to complain – that his boneyard group had collapsed, that there was pressure for him to remove the wreck of the yacht from the foreshore, that movement and sale of livestock were prohibited, and that the decision to raise the *Albatross* would be made for certain that week. 'How can they be allowed to do this?' he had moaned. 'It's my boat. Where the hell is that friend of yours?' Betsy hadn't answered. Instead she tried to ask about Finlay and Hurtado's visit, but he had shown no interest.

As the cliff rose, she paused to look over the landscape. The fields ran away to her right, walls cutting them into shape. Round silage bales, large and black, peppered the landscape. The undulating land cut off in space, falling away in a cliff that dropped through the colours of the lichen – grey-green, orange, black – until it met the sea below, tearing the milky-green depths to white with its black fingers. Here on the upper edge there was no fence, just the brambles with their drooping heads, the gorse, the biblical thorn. Reaching a spur, she looked out to a sky of screaming gulls hanging over a dark rock. Cormorants dried themselves, black against black: only streaks of guano and snakelike kelp added colour. With each of her steps the gulls, seeking out nesting places, screeched at her, furious at the interference.

A ridge rose on the landward side, masking her passage from the road. A fox, which Betsy presumed had been sleeping beside one of the round bales, emerged to bolt into the brambles and, apparently, over the cliff. She climbed, rising to join the ridge as it swept round to end in a precipice, the arch at its very end, larger than she had imagined, hanging against the sky. As she closed, she saw that it was all that remained of an ancient castle, held up with a rusty iron frame that must have been added much later to stop its final collapse. It topped a pedestal of rock that was surrounded by cliffs on three sides; the upsurge in the strata showing this was where the rocks finally turned towards the sky. Betsy stood in front of the arch, peering out to where a seagull floated in the air beyond, captured in the frame. She felt she was being sucked through, then a wave of terror, and quickly moved back.

Once away from the old stones, Betsy recovered her composure and looked for the fox's hole at the edge of the cliff. She found its tunnel in the gorse, the small track leading down and out of sight. There was a rock beside the opening, offering a comfortable prop to sit against with a view over the bushes and the sea. She tried to make out Workington on the Cumbrian coast but the haze blurred her view. She allowed the sun to warm her face, and felt peaceful enough in this broad hollow to forget her troubles and doze, the hill rising away to shield her from the world.

She woke to the sound of children's laughter. Looking up the hill, she saw three small figures lying on the ground, a large black bale rolling towards the sea. She stood. The children spotted her and jumped to their feet. The bale rumbled towards her, picking up speed. The uneven ground caused it to bounce this way and that, a curve in its path that seemed, once Betsy could take it in, to exaggerate and diminish so that, first, it veered away from her and then back towards her. She felt a strange calm until she glanced behind to where gulls hung in the void and she heard the sound of its approach grow, and a scream rose to meet it in her head, drowning reason. She stepped to one side but the bale, bouncing high now, followed her. She took another two steps, and ran, but stopped. Only twenty feet now, and the sound of its passage sucked at her. At ten feet, it appeared vast, lifting high, on top of her, but then, bouncing to the left, it rushed past. With a tearing of polypropylene it ran through the gorse and out into air, gulls lifting in a great clamour of noise. There was a curiously muted popping and then a splash as the bale hit the rocks and the sea below. Betsy crumpled to the ground, watching the children run away over the top of the ridge. She lay flat in the grass, unable even to cry.

After a while she pulled herself up, feet under her like a girl at a picnic, looking up the hill at the blue sky beyond. Colours shone vividly, almost too real. She could still hear the children's laughter in her head, and see them running over the hill, her mind replaying the image. Only when she tried to stand, in an attempt to shift the colours, did they disappear. She began to cry, tears of fright burning paths down her cheeks, then turning to far more visceral sobbing for all she had taken over the previous two weeks. The wave hit. She fell back on to her hands and knees to gulp and gasp for air. Painful surges hit her, all her fears disgorging snot, spit and salt. She wept for everything. For Helen and Rego, for herself, even for the families she had ignored. It took time before she felt empty enough to sit. Longer yet before she rose unsteadily to her feet. The day was the same as it had been before the bale had rolled towards her, but Betsy felt exhausted and relieved. She followed the children to the crest of the hill on unsteady legs, no longer concerned about trespassing.

At the summit, the Galloway landscape opened up in front of her, the sweep of the slope falling away to the road. Even at this height there was no breeze to touch her face. The children were gone, but to the left, in its desiccated copse, stood Rego's church, its simple slate roof showing among the empty branches. Her intention to follow the children and find their parents died away with her adrenalin. Instead she decided to go to the church. It was time to complete her duties as Helen's friend.

She had to traverse the hillside to find the stiles that allowed her down. A car that she had seen in the village stood parked in the lay-by, and as she approached, she heard the sound of scraping from beyond the high wall that enclosed the copse. Assuming that the minister was preparing for the funeral, Betsy followed the wall until she could look through the bars of the chained gate. There was nothing to see, the door was hidden at the side, so she climbed the stile, topping the six-foot wall. Still unable to see what was happening within, she descended into the copse.

The sunlight barely touched the mat of grass that covered the ground below the bare trees. In the few places it did, clumps of snowdrops had appeared, bracketing lengths of sawn timber that lay piled towards the back. The church walls rose straight, slits the only windows. The studded door was open, the interior hidden in gloom. There were steps, then the sound of furniture being dragged across stone. Betsy moved forward to peer into the dusty space, light coming from the thin casements, east, west and south. The man who was heaving the trestle table into the corner turned. He had one arm in a sling. Under wiry grey hair, tight-set eyes now held her. It was Bunbury.

After a moment, he asked what she wanted in a voice that was harsh and dismissive. Three small children watched her from the gloom. 'Well?' he said, irritated. He walked back through the church and Betsy stepped inside, her eyes forced to adjust. The walls were made of thin-piled rock and the floor was paved in the same stone, each flag's irregular edges carefully matched. Three gravestones rose in the centre, on one the clear image of three stags' heads. It was here the children waited, but they backed off under her approach, moving beyond an arch that split the room until they were behind an ancient, tilting font and the altar itself, its piled stone topped off by a monumental rectangle of rock. She looked up to the slatted roof, and saw that it had been maintained in perfect condition. She had the impression she had strayed into an ancient and secret place, preserved for private rites. Bunbury lifted a last chair from where Rego's games must have been played, and settled it beside Betsy, leaning on it, impertinently close, waiting for an answer to his question. Despite this, she felt no need to bring down his wrath on these children.

'I wanted to have a look,' she said. 'William Kerr, the funeral, it's supposed to take place here on Wednesday.'

Bunbury looked her up and down. 'And you, you're Helen's friend, are you?'

'Yes. I hope so.'

He lifted the chair and headed for the corner. 'And if you're Helen's friend,' the last word seemed to slither from his mouth, 'what are you to James Rego then?' He was facing her again, and let his gaze linger on her body.

'What are you doing here, anyway?' Betsy said, annoyed. She wasn't scared of him – she'd had enough of fear for one day.

He looked at the children and smiled kindly before placing the chair he held beside the others. Then he picked up a broom, using his good·arm to lean on the handle. 'I'm an elder of the church,' he said calmly. 'I am preparing everything. For Wednesday.'

Betsy felt a fool, and didn't know how to respond. 'I should have realized,' she said at last. She took another step into the church. 'Can I help?'

'Yes.' His tone seemed to have softened, but she was mistaken. 'By leaving.'

'But your arm. I could sweep.' She held out her hand for the broom.

'By leaving.'

'I don't understand.'

The children watched from beside the altar. 'No,' Bunbury replied, with sudden menace, his tone oppressive in such surroundings. 'But that's just as bad. Go.'

Betsy blinked and backed out of the door. She looked at the church again from the top of the wall. She really didn't understand.

TUESDAY

High tide: 01.52, 14.10
Light south-westerly

The chickens peck at my feet as Cutter leaves his house, and I wait for a shout that does not come. He puts his telephone into his pocket and walks down the path that leads to the sea. I know he's ignoring me, and recognize his route. He is going to where the memories are. I move to the forest and travel swiftly along the dry stream, reaching the garden before him. All is peaceful, the memories calm, the lull lies across the sky. I slip round the wall, the cliff at my feet, and there, close to the precipice, I wait.

Time passes slowly now. The pain that clings to my shoulder makes my mind turn in strange directions, shifting thoughts blurring in the agony. In my stupidity, I am still unable to understand the Saint's screams: he grows angrier by the hour now. I see him in my dreams, a vivid figure, red and soaked in sweat. Even the memories that stand on the other side of the wall offer no comfort, and the cave has become an agony to reach. I feel the flames lick the bodyaltar as I watch through the gaps in the stones, waiting for Cutter to appear at the ledge above. In

*time, he does. He stares down. Perhaps he is surprised by
the condition of the garden for he never visits. I shift, the
Saint screams, and I put a hand to the cut, feeling the pus
seep through the fat I have layered on, fresh rendered
from the slaughtered sheep. I feel the sickness rise and
almost swoon but I cling to thorn, the cliff behind me, the
wall in front, the memories near. I wait for Cutter to come
down the ceremonial path, but he chooses not to. Perhaps
I have misunderstood, perhaps he heads for the military
zone. Shifting along the wall, I search through the gaps. I
should follow, I fear . . . but a sound stops me. The others,
the boy and girl, are on the ledge and I find I am gripping
too tight, the Saint bellowing at his altar. I do not want to
hurt this boy again, even if I were able. I do not want
to. I crouch. They stand. Cutter hides.*

Boyle seemed caught by the tranquil beauty of the graveyard that lay below them, its lawn rich against the
blinding sea beyond. The breeze was off Ireland, warm on
Betsy's face and playing gently on the gorse around them.
She wondered where Rego waited, or whether he planned
to follow them in. She was keen that they should be in the
graveyard when he arrived.

'Come on,' she said.

'Grateful,' replied Boyle. 'Leave me.'

'Don't even think about it.' She tried to laugh. 'Here am
I doing all this investigating for you, and you tell me
nothing.' She pulled at his arm. 'Tell me what you found
out.'

'I . . . take it . . . from here.'

Betsy tried to stay friendly. Rego had called the previous
night to tell her Boyle had returned, that his car was
parked outside the inn. They had decided it was time for

a proper introduction. 'I found this place,' she said. 'While you were away, I discovered this and I think you could share, just a little.' She tried to read him, almost certain that he was unsettled, his head jerking a little to the side.

'Why?' he asked, in the usual strangled way. 'Why you need to interfere?'

She laughed at the irony. 'Do you remember knocking on my door? Do you remember approaching me?' She was about to add that he had eavesdropped as her relationship collapsed, but decided it wasn't the moment. 'I found the photograph. I found the marks on that tree. I found this place. If it wasn't for me, you'd have nothing.' She was making her way down to join the rowan avenue. 'I think, despite yourself, you could do something useful, and I want to make sure you do.' She heard him following.

'This path leads to that ruined house,' she continued, as he joined her on the avenue. 'I haven't been along it, but you can see it on the satellite photograph.' She led him to the gate, swung it open, feeling the warmth of the sun. 'Everyone who ever worked with or for the Regos must be buried here, even, as I said, a Betsy Gillander.'

He read the inscription, with its talk of her being a faithful friend to the Regos. 'Appropriate,' he managed.

She leads him into the garden, pointing out the stone that carries her name. The memories are stirring, change is on its way. His head is swinging, his eyes unseen. I crouch behind the wall and feel the slope break away below my heels. My forehead touches the rocks, the holes between them my view. I shift sidewards as they climb the hill. He seems reluctant to move fast, pausing at the repository of Cutter's personal memories, dallying at those of the retainers under the trees. She is impatient, wanting him to go with her, up towards my stone. I shift in time with them yet I feel their approach as if I were in that other place. I flood with sensations, the screaming of the saints. My foot goes backwards, I swing out, the fall under me, the altar teetering on the cliff-edge, grabbing thorn, spikes slicing through my hand. The pain catches me and I extract the sloe, careful to remain low, to move with thought. I bring my foot back and eye a gap. It seems they did not hear. They stand together, in the sunshine, looking up the hill. The gate opens at the bottom of the garden but there is no sound and they do not notice. I cannot see, but I know Cutter has arrived.

Betsy stood in front of the simple monument, its surface a bruised crucifix of lichen, moss and granite. 'The only one without a mark,' she said. She looked back down the hill and jumped despite herself. Rego was half-way up towards them. 'Oh.' She exhaled.

'Damn you!' Rego shouted. 'What are you doing here? Don't you know there's a plague? Are you completely irresponsible?'

Boyle ignored the approaching fury, his attention on the stone.

Rego reached them, Boyle's indifference confusing him. He threw a searching look at Betsy. 'Excuse me?' he asked sarcastically. When Boyle continued to ignore him he looked again at Betsy. 'Is this where all the misunderstandings come from? Is he deaf or something?'

'Who? Buried here?' Boyle said at last, looking over his shoulder. He was asking Rego, but it was Betsy who found herself under the shadowed gaze, eyes there in the murk.

'Sorry?' The word emerged as a false laugh. 'That's

none of your business. How about you stop skulking around and tell me what it is you want. Before you bring the plague down on us to cap everything else.'

'To know who is buried here.' Boyle was still studying Betsy but he turned as Rego hissed.

'You're on my property.' Rego spoke slowly, as if matching Boyle's staccato. He stepped forward. 'Tell me what you want. It's time you did.'

The intimidation failed, Boyle facing him down. 'You know already.' His face revolved towards Betsy. 'Much for promises,' he said softly.

Rego seemed to relax, but Betsy looked to the ground, realizing as she did so that she had just confirmed Boyle's suspicions. There was a trace of rancid flesh on the breeze – Priest must be somewhere nearby, she thought.

'You know what he's up to?' Rego sniped at her. 'And you didn't tell me?' If this was convincing, it didn't matter, for Boyle was already walking down the hill. Agitation showed on Rego's face. 'Okay,' he shouted after him. 'Okay. This is the grave of my sister.' Somewhere a branch snapped and Rego swung round. 'Priest?' he shouted. 'Show yourself, Priest!' Boyle had stopped. 'I can smell you, you sick fool. You're supposed to be digging a grave, not skulking around here.' He turned back to Boyle. 'My sister. Her name was Mary. All right?'

Boyle began to make his way back up the hill again. His black coat, thin body and bird-skull head were horribly appropriate in the graveyard. He looked like a cleric hunting bones.

'No name?' he asked, reaching them.

'She was a disgrace.' The truth allowed Rego an anger he seemed to trust. 'Her name . . . Look. She lived, she died, she's buried here. I've got documents. What else do you want? You're raking up a past that is painful. Tell me what you need so that we can do what's necessary, and then you can go. I'm sure you must want to.'

'The child,' said Boyle, looking up at Rego, his eyes still hidden to those standing above. 'There was a child.'

Rego coughed, a rasping sound in his lungs, and he leaned on the grave. Like Betsy a few days before, he must have been stung because he recoiled at once, looking at his palm. He sought deeper breaths.

Betsy had felt the chill of this question. She could tell Rego was having trouble keeping control. 'No,' he said at last. It sounded as if the word had come from the detritus that lay at the bottom of his lungs. 'There was no child.'

Boyle stood below, the pale crown of his head just visible. 'In Workington. Old landlady. Said there had been a child.'

Rego seemed unable to say anything more. He stared at Boyle as if he wanted to suck the thoughts straight from that delicate skull. Again Betsy remembered the ark, the salty interior, and her feelings of being out of her depth. She saw now that Rego might gamble, but if there was ever a man with a poker face, it was Henry Boyle. Nothing showed on the taut skin, no truth, no lies, no emotion.

'Mrs Price. Old lady now.'

'A child in Workington?'

'Before.' Boyle was staring at the grave, Betsy thought, but it was difficult to tell. 'She said your sister . . . talked of it, made her ill.'

Rego gazed away to the faint line drawn by the English coast on the horizon. A fighter had finished its run and was heading back across the southern sky. Betsy realized that she hardly noticed them any more. 'That was the disgrace,' Rego said quietly. 'An illegitimate child. Back then, they said she had to go.' He added, with a callousness that at once seemed false, 'The baby didn't live. It makes no difference. The baby didn't even exist.'

The silence that followed was broken by Betsy. 'What do you mean?'

'There was no birth certificate, no death certificate, nothing. The baby was stillborn, and its body disposed of. There is no baby, whatever your Mrs Price said.' Rego kicked angrily at the mossy grass. 'You know,' he said slowly, 'I resent this. I resent going through this. I hardly know you and these are things that haven't been discussed for more than thirty years. It is insulting and disgusting, and not only that, it comes at a time when seven men have died on one of my boats, a time when I have other things to worry about. I tell you this because it seems that whoever put my sister in that grotesque situation appears to have had some last-minute stab of conscience. I would spurn it, send you packing, but maybe I can use this money to do something good. And maybe, just maybe, something can be salvaged from this whole ugly nightmare.'

Boyle was like stone, unmoving. Betsy found her distaste for him turning to hatred, which deepened when he finally spoke.

'No death certificate?' he asked.

'No!' screamed Rego. 'No death certificate! And no damn life certificate either. No record at all. Or do you want me to dig up this graveyard until we manage to find the little bones, bones you'd no doubt question even if we did.'

'That's where she's buried?' Boyle asked, gesturing at the unmarked cross.

'The child?' At last Rego spoke quietly.

'The mother?'

'Yes.'

Boyle took a step and then stopped. 'Need to think,' he said. 'Need to think about all this.' He swung away to walk down the hill, the cleric departing with bones he somehow didn't trust.

Rego was stunned. 'What about this life policy?' he shouted after him.

'Need to think.' Boyle threw up a hand. 'Sorry.'

They watched him until he reached the ledge above the graveyard and passed out of sight. Rego was so angry he trembled, incapable of speech. When at last he managed to use his voice, he screamed: 'Priest! Get out of here. Go dig William Kerr's hole as I told you. This isn't your place.' The sunshine was wildly inappropriate for the sense of loss that crushed the air.

Betsy gently touched Rego's elbow. 'Come on,' she coaxed. 'You've done all you can.'

Rego spat. 'What does he mean "sorry"? I don't get it. What the hell has that bastard got to think about?'

Tears. I find real tears on my face. When I wipe them with my hand, they smear the dirt and blood, and sting the rips in my hands. The salt stings. I sit with my back to the wall, the drop below my feet and find tears running down the face of the bodyaltar. The end is coming, for Cutter betrays the memories, causing these tears, tears that have not flowed since that first incision took them all away.

Light poured through the kitchen of Howe Hill, washing over James Rego as he slumped in a window-seat, his face turned towards the empty trees and the sea beyond. 'I

314

really don't understand,' he said. 'The more I give that man, the further away from this money I seem to be. You'd think he'd want to leave . . .'

'There's something strange,' said Betsy. 'It's got to have something to do with his percentage. It's got to be the parasite in him.' The kitchen had fallen to chaos. Rego had ceased washing up, newspapers hung on the back of chairs, their pages loose on the floor. The television had been moved to the kitchen table. 'You were one of the most fastidious men I have ever met,' she said sadly.

'Sign of decline.' The small smile that had accompanied this slipped. 'If I could just find out which bloody company he's working for. I've rung them all, but they have no record. They say they need a policy number.'

'Do you want me to get you a proper drink?' Betsy was pouring boiling water into the cafetière. 'It's almost midday.'

The assertive energy that had originally attracted her, and the violence that had then repulsed her, had fled, leaving an expression of weary honesty. He now looked his age, perhaps even older. It was this frailty that had convinced Betsy there was no danger in accompanying him home. Given the state he had been in, she had felt obliged to. In these rare moments of exposed exhaustion, he was almost placid. 'Too much to think about.'

Betsy waited for the coffee to infuse, hands on the plunger.

'Boyle the parasite?' The idea evidently pleased him.

'I hated him today,' Betsy said. 'Questioning you as if it were his right. It's horrible. I watched him come in that first night. You know, he arrived right in the middle of the storm, in that black suit he wears. When he came back up the hill, in the graveyard, he looked like, I don't know, something out of a grave, some bearer of horrible news, some sort of deathly messenger or something. And he appears in the village on that night, and what happens? The *Albatross* sinks, your life falls to pieces, the plague is all over the television . . .'

'And your life disintegrates.'

'It's like he came out of those pyres they keep showing on the news. I know this is silly, he's only a man, but it seemed a lot easier when he was away the last couple of days. I shouldn't over-egg it, he's just some parasite trying to make a cut. But I didn't like it today. I think it's something to do with not being able to see his eyes. It doesn't help.'

Rego stood and stretched. 'Perhaps you're right. We should have a drink. It would be fine to have a drink.' He went to the fridge.

They took their coffee and manzanilla through to the drawing room and settled by the window, sitting in silence, letting the sun warm them, the drink still them. Betsy had kept a distance between them, but if Rego noticed he didn't show it. She was wondering about his sister.

'She read too much.' He had caught her thoughts.

'Your sister?'

'She was very romantic, and it ended in being the death of her.' His willingness to talk could almost have been an apology. 'Romance is always to blame. I think you know that and so do I. Because we're pragmatists. Look at Helen.'

Betsy wasn't sure she felt comfortable with this. She hadn't examined her feelings of late, but she suspected she had changed her mind about romance.

'Nobody ever says you can read too much, but out here,

when there's nothing to temper it, you can. Mary was affected by all the mysticism of the area, the story of the saint and all the early evangelists, the carvings on the rocks that you find all over this area. That's why she loved the firing-range because it's full of stuff like that, untouched by tourists.' He sipped at his drink. 'She taught herself French. The local teacher at the time was fluent, but she had never managed to get anyone else to learn more than the basics. God knows what her accent was like, she was from Aberdeen. But Mary was keen, there was this old French writer she loved who wrote a book called *De l'amour*, which even I can translate. She took that book everywhere, wrote in the margins, all over the pages.' Rego looked at Betsy. 'What is it?'

Betsy was back in the graveyard, listening to Rego speak of the dead child. Boyle had probably been holding the book in his pocket. 'Nothing,' she said, shifting. 'I'm fine.' She put down the glass. 'I think I need some coffee. It's all been a little stressful.'

James leaned down to lift her mug from the floor and handed it to her. 'That was what the sherry was for.'

'Too much fresh air,' she said. 'I'll recover.'

He had been sitting on a high-backed chair but now he slipped to the floor beside her. Betsy attempted to warn him off with a look. 'You mentioned rock carvings,' she said.

'The rings the prehistoric people carved on the rocks? They're little circles, with a line drawn into the centre. Mary sought out new ones. She kept all her notes in that book, the one about love. And none of us thought much of it. We knew when the army was training because they would hoist these red flags, they were still using tanks over there then, so we didn't worry when it was quiet.

What we didn't know was that she was meeting this soldier, a man called Roberts, and they were having this thing. It must have started out as a friendship, when she was young, because it turned out she had been seeing him for a long time. It would have appealed to her sense of romance, and as she grew older . . .' He sucked his teeth '. . . well, you can probably guess the rest.'

'And Roberts is the man who left the money?'

'Presumably so.' Rego was playing with the fabric of her trousers. 'I don't know what happened but he just upped and left. She knew because she gave the book to him, and that was really that with her.'

'And she . . . ?' Boyle had said the book had come with the policy. It made some sort of sense, but Betsy had begun to fear the things she might not know. She was no longer sure she had all the facts.

'She never recovered from the baby. And when my mother found out, well, enough, let's talk about you.' His hand swept along her leg.

'The baby died?'

'No more, please.' He finished his drink. 'I'd like to have Priest throw Mr Boyle off the cliff, but I don't think it would get me the money.'

For Betsy the joke brought back the memory of the bale rolling towards her, and she shuddered. He moved closer, put an arm round her. 'Are you all right? You're shivering.'

'I had a fright yesterday. I'm fine, though.' She waited until he withdrew his arm before she told the story.

He replaced the arm, pulling her closer, the pressure meant to reassure. 'I've heard of kids doing that before, but this is the first time they've nearly killed someone. You should have called, you must have had a terrible fright.'

'I knew they didn't mean to scare me.' She kept her back rigid. 'Look, I'm fine.' She pulled away from his arm again.

'How did you know they were Bunbury's?'

She told him about using the church for William's funeral, and about discovering Bunbury clearing up.

His words slowed. 'And who decided to have the funeral at the boneyard?'

Betsy shrugged. 'It needed to be somewhere close . . .'

'But who?'

'It just sort of came up.' She was aware it had been her idea.

He said nothing. Then he replaced his arm, pulling her in. The sun had moved its beam across the room and Betsy wondered what to do. She wanted to leave, to retreat to Helen's cottage, to see the funeral, and then go. She was beginning to realize that every move she had made, all of her aid, had hidden meanings. She wondered if she had ever fully seen the scope of her acts, each interference with consequences that she had never imagined. She wondered if Boyle really had any money for Rego, or if something else was going on. The book seemed so personal, the child too sensitive a revelation. She recalled Boyle telling her that he would come back at a better moment, then her convincing him to stay. Rego reached over with his other hand, and ran it across her cheek. She was far too involved. She wanted away.

'Why don't we have an hour or two?' he whispered. 'It would take our minds off all this.'

Betsy turned her head, and he took this as encouragement, leaning in to kiss her. She waited until he pulled back. 'I think you're right,' she lied. 'I'm getting sick.'

'It's probably just stress. Come and lie down.'

'I'm going to go back to the cottage.'

'You're feeling that unwell?' His head had moved back a few inches. 'You're just wound up. In the bedroom, with the sun coming in, it'll be better.' His hand ran down her arm. 'Let me look after you.'

Betsy put a hand to his cheek. 'I'm going to go.' She sensed his concern turn, reconfiguring itself as something black and rotten.

'It would be good to lose an hour or two,' he said, failing to hide these feelings. 'All my problems disappear in the scent of you. It would be good for me, and for you. The next day or two will be difficult. Come and lie down.' This emerged as an order.

'I want to go back to Helen's.'

He had moved further off, although one hand had fallen heavily into her lap. 'I didn't think you'd turn against me,' he said.

'I'm not turning against you.'

'I wish I understood.'

'There's nothing more to understand. I'm not feeling—'

'I think it's something else. Are you tiring of us? Is it proving too much out here? Have you had enough?'

Betsy just watched him, unable to reply.

'What is it that you discovered?' The sarcasm emerged wet from his mouth. 'What was the lesson?'

Say nothing, she thought, nothing.

'Tell me, I'm interested. You were the one who believed it was all relative. How does it compare? You breaking up with your boyfriend, my losing everything, Helen losing her husband, those parents losing their boys. Is that your hierarchy of misery? Because that's what you're doing, Betsy, isn't it? Making yourself feel better. So, tell me, who feels the most like shit?'

'That's not . . . I just want to help.'

'And now you'll go back.'

'I just don't feel up to having sex.' She tried to keep the exasperation from her voice.

'I was talking about making love.'

Betsy couldn't help but smile, and it infuriated him.

'I was talking about us feeling better. Briefly better.' The anger rippled under that skin. 'So you're going to desert Helen, are you? When she has begun to trust you? What have you got to go back to, Betsy? You haven't got a boyfriend there. It's going to be tough to get your flat back. Or perhaps you're feeling ready for that challenge, now, at last?' His hand had clenched, perhaps involuntarily: he was gripping her thigh. 'And I need you. I have grown to need you.'

'James, please.'

'Isn't it safer you stay here? We've formed such a team, you and I. It seems such an irony, with all these reporters arriving, that you're right here in their midst after they've searched the whole of Scotland for you.' He relaxed his grip, and smoothed the fabric of her shirt. Betsy couldn't think of a reply. Instead, she watched him.

'I've been reading about you,' he said, quiet and self-controlled now. 'And although it was another burden, I was still glad you were here. Have you seen the photo they used? It's very old. I thought it unlikely that anyone around here would recognize you from it and I think that's how it's worked out. Well, Martha might know, but if she does, she would never say anything.' He smiled at her, picking up on a question she hadn't asked. 'I've known for ages. I was pleased, to tell you the truth, that you weren't all Florence Nightingale, that you had your own troubles.' He looked away, studying the room as if he

321

had forgotten its layout. 'I think we should go to bed, just for an hour or two. It's so exhausting, all these . . . It's better to find a little happiness wherever you can, it's the little happinesses that make you forget.' He looked back at her, his anger showing in a swollen vein that passed between his eyebrows.

'I should be getting back,' Betsy said, standing up.

'I think you'd be better keeping a low profile. All those journalists.' He rose too, his full height between her and the door.

'I'm worried,' Betsy said quietly, 'that you're threatening me.'

Rego snorted. 'There are a few things I'd hate, Betsy. For instance, I'd hate to hear that you hadn't been behind me in persuading Helen against the raising of the boat. I'd hate it if everything hadn't been done to keep the *Albatross* on the seabed.' Betsy was about to speak, but he raised his hand. 'And I'd hate it if Boyle went away without paying out on that policy. I'd really hate that. I'd blame you. And I'd hate it if bad things were said about me in the press, once these funerals are over. Again, I'd see it as a betrayal. So is this a threat? No. It would be my right, my duty to Helen, and everyone else you have used, to distract the reporters. You see, we were lovers, Betsy. It was you and me against the world but you are breaking that, going out for yourself, and your story is more interesting than mine, especially if they know that we had sex, as you say. First McFrankenstein, then me. They'd like that.' He stopped and watched her.

'What is it that they're going to find on the boat?' she asked.

He looked away, at the room Betsy had thought so beautiful at first but now appeared decayed, a sanctuary from another time. 'Evidence that William Kerr caused the deaths of six of his crewmates.' The words came fast, and seemed hardened by ice.

'I think I'll go and check on Helen, then.' She walked past him, her footsteps swift on the parquet floor, her nerves electric as she waited to hear him coming after her, but she was out of the door and into the fresh air.

As she walked back towards Helen's cottage, Betsy tried to think beyond what had just happened and imagine instead how she was going to repair her life. It didn't seem so awful when she thought about it: first, a sharp period of pain, but surmountable, even if she had to find herself another flat. Yet each step took her back to her fears: Rego revealing her whereabouts to a reporter, her ex-fiancé screaming at her boss from the gate of the laboratory, Helen's future in the village. Her concerns lay heavy in her muscles, hardening her shoulders against the world that surrounded her. She found that she was casting glances behind her, not to see if she was being followed but to study the sky to the west. Despite the blue, there was a change, as if terror was about to crest the horizon and if she didn't keep checking it would be upon her before she could get away. She knew the feeling was absurd, and fought to keep her eyes on the ground around her. There she saw a daffodil's green shoots on a verge, a lame cow in a field. Yet the feeling followed her the whole way, and by the time she reached Helen's front door she was breathless from the half-jog that had taken her the last half-mile. She pushed her way in, calling for her friend and rushing upstairs to find her gone.

Betsy searched the house, ending up in the kitchen where she stopped to look down at the turning tide. On the other side of the bay, a figure stood under the oak. She leaned down to the telescope and focused. Helen, wearing only her dressing-gown, was looking down at Priest, whose head was just visible as it bobbed from the earth. Betsy rebuttoned her coat, opened the back door and ran down the garden. Priest must have seen her because he pulled himself from the hole and scuttled off along the shore, while Helen watched his departure, still gazing after him as Betsy arrived.

'Are you all right?' Betsy asked, trying to catch her breath. 'You shouldn't be out here in your dressing-gown, it's too cold.'

'You chased him away.' Helen's voice was small, weary and sad.

Betsy tried to stop panting, her hands on her knees, the hole in front of her. Priest had found a rare spot where the earth ran deep, a crevice between two rising spear-heads of bedrock. Even so he had been crowbarring boulders from the base, and packing the walls. One of the oak's great roots crossed one end of the grave so that the coffin would have to be slipped in end first to settle flat. William Kerr would be, quite literally, buried under the tree where he had so often sat. Betsy saw care and skill in the work, Priest had lined the bottom with flat stone, which continued a short way up the sides, creating a small chamber. A black boulder, a schist, stood against the base of the tree, its surface long washed to smoothness by the sea and curiously marked by two seams of interlinking white quartz, asymmetrical but reminiscent of a lopsided cross, a little miracle of nature.

'You chased him away,' Helen repeated, her gaze melancholic and heartbreaking. Her hands, black from collecting stones, hung beside her.

324

'I was worried,' Betsy answered. 'You shouldn't be out here in the cold.'

'He was making William's grave so beautiful.' She began to walk towards the cottage.

Betsy looked again at the excavations, the thought and skill in every detail, then ran to catch up. 'I didn't mean for him to go.' Her words came out as an appeal. 'He just went. He's always seemed such a bad man, I didn't know.' Helen continued towards the cottage. 'He'll come back. I'm sure.'

'I hope so.' Helen's voice had taken on the hard edge that had shocked Betsy on the few occasions that it had emerged.

She hated the idea of calling Howe Hill, but offered none the less, saying she would talk to Rego to try to prompt Priest's return.

Helen swung, grabbing Betsy's wrists. 'Please don't,' she said. 'Don't telephone.' She held on until she had Betsy's promise.

They continued, through the kitchen door, then up the stairs. There Helen slipped out of her dressing-gown and under the sheets. Betsy perched beside her. 'What happened,' Betsy asked, 'when I went away?' She waited but there was no reply. 'I thought you didn't like Priest.'

'He brought me that beautiful stone.' Helen spoke into her pillow. Despite Betsy's efforts, she would say nothing more.

Betsy returned to the kitchen window and waited, the loneliness she had sought to avoid since her ex left now sweeping over her. Just before dusk Priest returned, appearing as a head in the hole even though Betsy believed she had kept her gaze fixed on the tree. The relief sighed out of her. She climbed the stairs to whisper the news into

Helen's ear, and although her friend said nothing, her breathing calmed, and within a minute she was asleep. For a while, Betsy looked down on Helen, and then she sat at the bedroom window, watching that strange man work until the darkness obscured him from sight.

WEDNESDAY

High tide: 02.29, 14.49
Cālm

Betsy gazed at the hands lying on the pillow in front of her. Her wrists were crossed, fists tightly clenched, forearms aching from the subconscious pressure. She tried to relax. A couple of hours' sleep was all she had managed, an exhausted and exhausting rest that had left her barely the strength to move. She lay still, waiting for Helen's tears but, unlike the previous mornings, Helen stirred, rose from the bed and walked through to the bathroom. Betsy rolled on to her back and looked at the ceiling, then pushed herself up and pulled aside the curtain to see a backlit bay, the dark prow of the ark emerging from dawn waters. She slumped back on to the mattress, listening to the taps run. 'Can I do anything?' she shouted.

There was a padding and Helen looked round the door. 'May I lean on you? Later, when we walk into the church?'

Betsy swung her legs out of the bed and encircled her with her arms. 'Of course,' she said. 'Of course. Anything at all.'

Bunting surrounds us. Yellow ribbons hanging from post to post. Men in white walk past me, through the barn, eyes impertinently showing their disgust as they gaze on the bodyaltar. A soldier speaks to Cutter, sympathetic, but once he's moved away Cutter mutters that he is a fool. It is difficult to stand: the bodyaltar is decaying, the collapse quickened by the exertions of yesterday. It has been vomiting with the pain. I watch these men and rub at the souring fat of that death-bringing ewe. Hirondelle is here, for this seemed to me the safest place. In the past, men in white oohed and aahed and sucked their teeth at her, offering rosettes, but now they ignore her and she bellows at me, her companions gathering. The cattle are nervous: this is their place, their routine, and it has been disturbed. Cutter stops and tells me what I already know, that the plague is here, that both cows and sheep will have to die. I must have lowered my eyes because he tells me not to snivel. 'It's your fault,' he says. 'That rotten fat you've been rubbing yourself in will have caused it.' He tells me they will pick a compensation price for each cow this evening, and then the killing will begin. What price, I wonder, remembering the money changing hands in the middle of the night. I wait, and watch, and find I cannot bear it. I know I, too, am dying now, and the bodyaltar will be soon gone. I don't want to see the slaughter of the stock. I watched them born. I feel. Sensations fill my head. The Saint screams from my shoulder and I can only go to him. I will pray at the cave, and there, please God, the screaming will make sense.

Betsy was in the kitchen when the doorbell rang. She was studying Helen, who had dressed in the same pale beige dress she had worn on the day the *Albatross* sailed for the last time. Although Betsy recognized the relevance of this, she didn't mention it. She just stepped forward to adjust the thin black cardigan that lay over Helen's shoulders. 'You look very elegant,' she said, truthfully. Helen had taken time to wash herself and had emerged to stand tall but ethereal, a bare step away from another world. She hadn't eaten in days and had taken on the glow of the starving before hunger finally breaks the body. Betsy tried to smile, but it was more of a grimace. She knew that Helen's sole aim was to get through the day. After that Betsy suspected she wanted nothing more than silence. 'I'll get the door,' she said.

It was Oliver Finlay. He was dressed in a dark suit that hung easily across his body, his blue eyes stark above the white shirt, black tie. Behind him was a black Ford, hired from the local undertaker. Betsy shook his hand. She had spoken to him the night before when he had called to ask whether the grave was ready.

'We have a problem,' he said now. 'Howe Hill farm has been hit by the plague, the vets are there.'

Betsy felt the profound sadness in the news, the village suffering yet another medieval horror, another blow to the already staggering community, but she put it to one side so that she could concentrate on Helen. 'James Rego?' she asked.

'He hasn't called?'

'No.' Betsy shook her head slowly. 'He was going to be here.'

Finlay took a step back. There was an undertaker in the driver's seat of the Ford. 'The grave's the other side of the bay?'

'Under that tree.' Betsy pointed. 'You can get down the left side of the cottage.' She spoke quietly, feeling removed from her own words. 'What about the church? It's in the middle of a field.'

Finlay's eyes were calm. 'To hell with it,' he said. 'We'll continue as planned.' He put out a hand. 'Sorry, excuse the language.'

'That's quite all right. I'll go and see if Helen's ready.'

With a hand on Helen's arm, Betsy led her friend towards the Ford, pausing only to watch a car pass along the road.

'Mrs Kerr?' asked Finlay, holding the rear door open. 'This is acceptable?'

Helen took the final few steps. 'Thank you,' she whispered, as Betsy helped her into the back seat. Betsy took the other side and Finlay the passenger seat, the tyres grinding down the gravel as they rolled towards the road. They slowed at the gate to let an oncoming car pass, but it pulled up, its driver waving them out ahead. 'Lot of traffic,' said Betsy.

Finlay gazed to the west. 'I think there'll be a change in the weather, but not today. Today it'll stay fine.'

Helen was looking out over the fields where sheep searched for the first shoots, her hand cold in Betsy's palm.

As they pulled towards the rise in the road and the branches of the copse showed, Betsy saw the driver glance in the mirror and nod backwards to Finlay. Betsy turned as well. There were now three cars behind them and another accelerating to catch up.

'Reporters?' she asked.

'Seems like a lot if it is.'

They pulled over the lip to find another six vehicles parked along the verge, their owners, all dressed in dark clothes, walking towards the gate.

'That Mazda,' said the driver. 'The owner's no reporter.' They pulled past a small group, who moved to the verge, smiling sympathetically as they followed Helen with their eyes. She swivelled in her seat as they fell behind, raising her hand in reply to a wave, before giving Betsy a quick look of surprise. A man in yellow overalls at the gate sprayed the tyres with disinfectant, then waved the car into the field. There, people clustered in three small bands, Helen studying each in turn. There were a few reporters but they stood a little way off, a policeman corralling them. Closer in, Betsy recognized the shopkeeper with a woman she presumed was his wife. A family stood by the now opened gate that led into the church precincts. Helen mumbled to herself as they rolled towards them.

'I missed that,' Betsy said quietly. The man had a round, lined face under short black hair, his wife stout, thick-set and immaculately turned out. They stood with their hands on twin children of maybe ten or eleven, as if being captured in a family photograph.

'The Stewarts,' Helen whispered.

Betsy fell silent. Those people had lost two sons on the *Albatross*. She had known their name, and now recalled seeing them at the memorial service, but that was all. It seemed so little.

Finlay had stepped from the car and was shaking the hands of the waiting family. Then he opened the door for Helen. Betsy gave her friend's hand a final companionable squeeze and for the first time felt strength in the response. As she stepped out herself, she looked over to see Helen standing with her arms hanging down, gazing shyly at the Stewarts who, in turn, appeared unsure. Finally the father stepped forward, raising his hand, and when Helen took it they fell into an awkward embrace. He separated with a quiet apology, while his wife moved forward and, although a good foot shorter than Helen, enveloped her. The children, who had been holding their father's hands, nodded nervously when Helen bent down to them. There was too much shared grief for Betsy to approach, so she waited, starting when she felt Finlay's hand fall on her shoulder, a gesture designed to reassure. 'I'm just going to make sure everything is ready inside,' he said.

The Ford moved away, leaving Betsy standing alone. She studied her hands, then looked up towards the road where the reporters watched. There were only three or four, and although she recognized one from the pub all those days ago, Euan, who had given her that first information on Boyle, wasn't among them. When she turned, she found Helen gazing at her with a quiet smile, holding out a hand. Betsy walked over to her, aware of the suspicion with which the Stewarts watched her approach. 'Betsy's been looking after me,' Helen said to them. 'Have you met?'

'You're James Rego's friend?' said the father.

Betsy thought of Rego dealing with the plague on his farm, and wondered if he would make it. She must have frowned because Helen answered for her: 'She's my friend.'

She was still trying to think of something to say when Finlay returned, and took her to one side. 'Perhaps you should go in,' he said. 'The minister is nervous. There are more people than expected and this field is within the infection radius. The plague vets will close the whole thing down if they find out, so he thinks we should probably get on with it.' He was eyeing the road where more cars were pulling up.

'So Helen's no longer poison?' asked Betsy.

Finlay seemed surprised. 'Was she ever?'

She could see only decency in those pale blue eyes. 'There was a rumour that William was responsible for the accident,' she said.

'It's not true. He was trying to save the boat.'

'And James Rego?'

'I think you should get Helen into the church.'

'Mr Finlay?' Betsy insisted.

'I am not an investigator. What I do know is that rumours are a terrible thing, and I will not help them.' He grasped her elbow, 'Please, take Mrs Kerr in,' and then he walked away, up towards the road.

'We should go in,' Betsy said, when she returned to Helen's side.

'Will you sit with us?' Helen asked the Stewarts.

'Of course,' said the father. 'If that is what you would like.'

Helen smiled at Betsy and linked arms with her. 'I feel a little weak,' she said.

They passed between the open gates, crossing the spot where Priest had beaten Boyle to the ground. Bunbury stood at the door of the church, his sling a white slash across a dark jacket. 'If you'll come this way, Helen,' he said, leading her towards two lines of four chairs. 'We haven't got many seats, I'm sure most people won't mind standing. But you sit here.' He ignored Betsy.

Sunlight cut lines through the gloom of the small church, the slits through which it fell focusing light on the wall but missing the plain beech coffin that stood in front of the altar, a small bunch of snowdrops on its lid. The minister had turned to greet them but Helen had stopped to gaze at the box, and he waited as she put her hand on the wood. She seemed to press with her fingertips and

333

then stepped back, the minister moving to her side. 'The weather's held,' he said.

Helen whispered to Betsy, 'It is good, you know,' she said, 'to have him back.'

'But we weren't expecting so many people,' the minister continued.

Betsy guided Helen to where the seats had been placed in front of the three gravestones. Bunbury had pointed out the chair that lay over the centre stone of the church and Helen stood beside it, turning to the Stewarts.

'We'll take the row behind,' said the father.

Betsy sat beside Helen, holding her hand and listening to the chairs scraping behind them while her companion looked up at the roof. 'What a strange place to play games,' Helen said, and Betsy squeezed, then felt the hand pull away, her friend rising to her feet. She was facing a woman Betsy instantly recognized as Jim Orr's girlfriend Cathy, heavily pregnant, an older woman beside her. Beyond them, the church had continued to fill, people waiting respectfully. But still no sign of Rego. Helen was being embraced. 'Thank you,' she murmured. 'Thank you for coming.'

'Jim is being buried tomorrow,' said the older woman. 'You'll come, we hope.'

Helen offered them the last two seats and they thanked her, Betsy noticing that a spark had touched the grey in her eyes. The two women nodded at Betsy as they sat, the greeting without the iciness of Stewart's first glance, but cold none the less. There was no smiling when Helen remembered to introduce them.

The minister, who had been leaning over the altar, straightened and stepped up behind the coffin. He cleared his throat to begin the service. There was shuffling from

334

behind. Betsy turned to find the small space behind the seats now packed, barely remembered faces poking heads round the door and, finding no room, disappearing back into the sunlight. The minister began with a prayer, then announced he planned to keep the service short. 'Only one hymn,' he said, 'and since we only have five copies of *Mission Praise*, many of you will just have to . . .' and here he grew nervous, 'well, perhaps you'll know the words.' There was no response. The minister shifted a little because the sliver of sunlight was falling on his face.

True to his word, the service passed swiftly, the minister's eulogy low on detail, his knowledge of William Kerr's life paltry, causing disquiet among the congregation. After the blessing, when he asked people to move out of the door so that the undertaker could get in for the coffin, there was more shuffling and Stewart leaned forward to speak into Helen's ear. 'Would you let us carry him?' he asked.

Betsy watched Helen's gaze run across the church as she thought about the offer. She gave a quick jerk of her head.

Stewart stood. 'Volunteers?' he shouted, his voice rich after the minister's whine. 'Will anyone help me carry William Kerr?' Betsy and Helen were both looking back into the crowd, and although it was hard to see into the ranks, hands rose above the heads. As Stewart chose his men, each stepped to the front, all short and broad. Betsy reached for Helen's hand but they were clasped together on her lap. The minister was in the corner, pushed there by the men who, at a word, lifted William Kerr's remains on to their six shoulders. 'Lock your arms under the box, boys,' said Stewart, and they adjusted their hold, faces pained under such a heavy burden.

'Minister,' Stewart said.

The minister rustled over.

'Lead us out.'

Finlay appeared at Stewart's side, and the lead pallbearer listened, then spoke. 'Boys, we're taking him all the way home. Are ye ready? Taking it from the left, step now.' With that the minister, nodding to people on either side of a passage that had opened in the crowd, began to walk ahead of the coffin towards the light. Betsy took Helen's arm, breaking her out of a daze as they rose to follow, poised to keep her steady. It was unnecessary: Helen was walking with a straight back, her eyes brushing against the returned gazes from either side of the human aisle. As the sunlight hit, they found themselves blinded, but when the white haze cleared, a community emerged, packed ranks of villagers, with more out in the field. The undertakers stood, watching the coffin pass, and Finlay intercepted Helen to ask if she wanted to ride in the car.

'I'd like to walk,' she said, and Finlay stepped back. 'It's wonderful,' she said to Betsy.

Reporters stood at a distance along the road, photographers with lenses raised and pointing. The procession turned towards the cottage, the sun warming Betsy as she followed. Despite Helen's apparent strength, Betsy kept her arm, knowing that she was half starved and very weak. Yet she was also aware that it was Helen's kindness that allowed her to stay at her side. She knew she was no longer needed, that anyone in the procession behind had more right to walk in this place than she did. The solidarity of those following continued to strengthen Helen, and although she was still fragile, death had withdrawn from her face. Betsy felt resolution rise from the march, a community showing that it was alive despite a savagery that continued to roll over it and, once again, she wondered at Rego's absence.

336

They crested the rise and met a small car coming the other way, which slowed and pulled up on to the verge. Betsy knew now that others would soon step in to look after Helen, bringing her back into a society from which she had been separated. Despite everything, Betsy was ashamed to feel a little cast off. She had believed herself to be at the centre of events, but now a sensation of being surplus swept in. She might not be the enemy of those who now followed behind, but she was a symptom of a wrong. A man had stepped from the car to kneel in the middle of the road, his camera steady as he took a photograph. Then he moved to the side to let the coffin pass, climbing the bank and changing his lens. Betsy found herself looking into the vehicle and saw Euan in the passenger seat. He lifted a hand in acknowledgement and Betsy smiled back, grateful for the gesture. Once past, she looked behind her and saw that he had stepped out to lean on the car. Her attention was brought back when Helen pointed to a hawk that was hanging over the rough ground down by the coast. It wheeled and dived from sight as two jets sliced through the distant sky with barely a whisper. The hawk reappeared, beating its way up the coast to the west.

The pallbearers were replaced as they tired. As each man fell out, Helen nodded her thanks and received a smile in return. Only Stewart remained in place until the procession reached the cottage. There Finlay waited. He had been driven round the back roads, and now he walked forward, taking up step beside Helen. 'You might want to keep it small at the graveside,' he said.

Helen looked back at the flow of people, the cars following. 'These others?' she said.

'They're with you, they've shown that, but this might

be the time for you to have your moment.'

Helen smiled and swung round to take Betsy by both hands. 'I'll see you in a little while,' she said.

'You're sure you don't want me to come?'

'I'll be fine now,' she said. 'Will you look after everyone for me?'

Betsy slowed, her feet gradually losing momentum. She watched the minister lead the pallbearers past the cottage and down to the shoreline, Helen following, her form stark against the incoming sea. Despite the mournful image, she struck a far less solitary figure than Betsy could remember, her silhouette shimmering against the water as the abbreviated procession closed on the undertakers waiting under the tree. There was a slight haze rising, the land finally absorbing the sunlight, and Betsy felt another stab of loneliness. She turned and found the whole community waiting patiently behind her, Finlay to one side.

'What do we do now?' Betsy asked.

'Wait.'

People began to pass Betsy, some heading back to the village but most watching the burial from the fence. Although the minister could be seen standing at the head of the grave, with Helen to one side, the distance was too great to make out the details. Betsy was about to go into the cottage so that she could look through the telescope but stopped when she saw Martha walking towards her. 'Helen would be pleased you came,' Betsy said.

'Good.'

'It's a pity people weren't so supportive before.' She regretted the comment at once – but she was still smarting from the sensation of being sidelined.

Martha just laughed. Betsy noticed that the landlady

was one of the few unchanged by the tragedy, hard-edged but warm-eyed. 'Actually, I was looking for you.'

'Oh.'

'Your boyfriend. He's back.'

Betsy felt a rush of embarrassment rather than fear or surprise. 'I don't suppose he said what he wanted?'

'No.' Martha was watching the events out under the oak where the bearers were lowering the coffin into the grave, leaning back against unseen ropes.

'Does he know where I am?'

'I told him I'd find you.' She glanced back at Betsy. 'I thought it better, after all the trouble he's caused.'

'So James was right. You know too?'

'I read the papers.'

'And I thought it was a secret.' Betsy realized she sounded pathetic.

'It takes practice to keep a secret in this place, Betsy.' Again Martha's eyes were on the burial. 'Why don't you go back to the village and deal with it? Perhaps you could get him to give you a lift home.'

They stood next to each other, looking out. 'What about Helen?'

'Helen will be fine.'

'I should just see how she is . . .'

'I'll tell her you won't be long, that you'll be back to say goodbye.'

'No, don't say that.' Betsy put a hand on Martha's arm, then withdrew it. 'I'll tell her that. Just say I won't be long.'

Martha's smile was kind, but as distant as the passing jets. 'I'll tell her you won't be long.'

Despite her ex-fiancé's return, Betsy found she could neither hurry nor hesitate as she walked along the road to the village. In front of her a small group of villagers dawdled in the sunshine, another group behind. She was relieved when the road came to an end and she could turn towards the harbour, but the relief dissipated as soon as she saw her ex. He was sitting with his feet hanging over the harbour edge, looking out at the boats. He spotted her and jumped up, hurrying towards her, opening his arms wide, a goofy grin masking his thoughts.

'Madness,' he shouted, embracing her despite her hands on his chest. 'What are we like? I *go* mental and you stay, here, in *this* place.' He looked around, carefully ignoring the slogan that still showed on the harbour-master's wall.

'Why are you here?'

'Why? I came back for you.' The act wasn't smooth enough to fool Betsy. She could see the nervousness on him. She wondered what had overcome his pride to bring him back. 'I was beginning to wonder if you'd got *lost*. I thought I'd better come back and get *you*.' The sentences were leaping up at the end.

In her attempt to summon up some sort of expression that would show her distaste, Betsy found that her first sensation was of violation.

'I was worried you'd gone native,' he continued.

A group of mourners had turned the corner, and would soon pass Betsy on their way to the pub. She refused to have this conversation where people could hear. 'Let's go for a walk,' she said, starting towards the pier.

'You're not planning to stay here, are you? Become a fishwife?' He was following her. 'Look, let's get in the car and go. That way we can discuss things.'

A couple who must have been on the peninsula crossed in front of them, heading towards the pier-head, closing it off as a possible spot to talk. Betsy veered towards the coastguard station and the headland. 'Is it money?' she asked. 'Because I can't help you if you've cleared out the joint account.' She could tell she had annoyed him – he was fighting the urge to bite back.

'It's not money,' he said at last.

'So, what is it?' Betsy had stopped.

He saw where they were. 'Let's keep going,' he said.

'This is quiet. There's nobody around.'

'To the point,' he said, excited. 'Let's go over there. It won't take a minute. This is so right. Let's get rid of all that's happened since then.'

Despite herself, Betsy felt the stab of this. 'No,' she said. 'This will do fine.'

'C'mon, Betsy.' He began to run up to the coastguard station. '*Betsy*,' he shouted to her.

She looked out over the sunwashed sea. The last time they had stood on the point, she had been unable to comprehend the currents that ran beneath, but now she sensed the water rippling and boiling. She looked up to the headland where gulls circled off the point, lobster-pot buoys dotting the jade, and knew that nothing could extinguish these weeks. She walked to the coastguard station, followed her ex across the small rocky chasm and scrambled up to the point. There he waited. There was little space before the black rock fell away, jagged at her feet, precarious. She found she had to stand too close to him.

'Be amazed, Betsy, because I'm going to admit it. I was *wrong*.' Still that nervous inflection, up at the end. 'Wrong about *you*.' He pressed a finger into her chest, and she looked down to the water. 'You know much more than I imagined. Look at you, you stayed down here, and I bet you've been helping people, I'll bet you've made a difference. I wanted you to know I thought that. And I want to hear all about it. That's why I came all this way. I want you to know that I understand.'

'Well, that's okay, then.' Betsy let sarcasm enrich the words. 'Can we go back to the village now?'

'I want you to come to Edinburgh with me.' He waited until she looked at him. She knew it was a management technique: he wanted to appear sincere. 'We've both made mistakes,' he said. 'But you've made your point.'

Betsy turned to the sea, gazing out at those ancient kingdoms over the water. What a place this must have once been, she thought, the adventures . . . 'Why did you go to the papers?' she asked, regretting the question at once, but it was a sop to the fury she was suppressing.

'I was angry.' He scratched the side of his mouth. 'I make no apology for that.'

Betsy finally understood, and it swept away her anger. If she hadn't been so tired she would have laughed. By staying away, by not going back to fight him, she had tortured him. He must have been horribly frustrated up in Edinburgh, the lack of any sort of engagement driving him into irrationality. The claustrophobia of their stormbound hotel room had evaporated a mirage of love in her, but distance had inflamed passion in him. It was such a cheap response she could have hooted, then wept, but there was far too much water around as it was.

'On a good day it's the Kingdom of Heaven,' she said, the sea ebbing away under a crystal sky. 'But not today.' She took a step towards the thin trail of rocks that led back to the coastguard station but he grabbed her arm, causing her to swing outwards over the edge of the cliff, one foot on rock, his hand on her wrist. For a moment she looked into his eyes and then he yanked her back on to the small space. 'Jesus,' he said. 'Be careful.'

Tired of being frightened, Betsy felt nothing. Gripping the rock, she attempted the descent again.

'You *haven't* answered me!' he shouted.

Betsy pointed towards land. She waited for him only when she reached the station. 'I wasn't proving anything to you,' she said. 'Maybe at the beginning I was trying to prove something to myself. But you were right, too, I admit it, I have plenty still to learn. It won't be with you, though.' She felt her balance return, and started for the village. He kept pace beside her.

'Well, let's talk about the trouble at the lab, then.' There was a trace of hunger in the words. 'Impressive, wasn't it? Come on. Shout at me. You must want to.'

Betsy had reached the point where she could break away along the coastal path to Helen's cottage, and she stopped. 'No,' she said. 'I don't want to. Take the car. It's yours.'

'This is nonsense,' he responded, continuing towards the harbour. 'I've just realized what your problem is. Ultimately, you're selfish.'

Betsy had already turned away, her steps swift so that she dropped out of sight before he had time to look back. Selfish? Once again she was amazed by how perceptive he could be about the faults in others. What he missed were the strengths. She had always liked to think she was the opposite, seeing the best in people, but now she questioned whether she was capable of judging the qualities in others at all.

Betsy took care to look back as she followed the coast. While she was almost certain her ex wouldn't give chase –

she had noticed he was wearing his favourite shoes and knew he would be worried about ruining them – she was determined not to draw him into Helen's life. Her confidence grew with distance, and by the time the cottage fell into view, she believed she was rid of him. The branches of the oak showed on her left and she slowed, keen to see what was going on before she barged in. A boy was working over the grave with a spade, a man at his side. A step closer, and she realized the boy was the undertaker's assistant, and the man was Euan.

'I'm on the digging,' she heard the boy say to Euan. 'The boss is on the wake.' He must have seen Euan's eyes move because he turned and saw her. 'But the likes of you shouldn't be down here,' he added apologetically.

The grave was almost filled in, a few spadefuls left. The headstone still rested beside a carefully piled stack of flat stones. Betsy perused the fields, the dykes casting shadows away from the sliding sun, and wondered if Priest was out there. 'He's right,' she said. 'You shouldn't be down here.'

'I'm just getting a little colour, getting the details right. It helps. You know, "They came to an old oak, burying him where the sea could not touch him", that sort of thing. You think the widow would mind?'

Betsy looked across at the cottage. The lights were on, people inside. 'They'll have seen you, so I suppose she's decided not to cause a fuss. Don't stay too long or you'll make her nervous.'

They stood looking at each other. 'How have you been?' he asked.

'Oh, all right.'

'Funny place to hide.'

Betsy frowned and threw a look at the gravedigger. 'Have you seen the ark?' she asked.

344

'I've been wondering about that.'

They began to walk away from the boy, Betsy giving Euan a potted history of the strange sunken boat. 'Don't take notes,' she ordered.

'Sorry.' They were now out of earshot of the boy.

'I don't want Helen thinking I'm giving you an interview.'

He put away the pad.

'Why do you say I'm hiding?'

'I guessed when I was in the car this morning.' He shook his head. 'Some reporter.' He looked at her carefully. 'I'm worried that this is a wasted trip for me. The dailies will have done the funerals, there won't be a lot left to report by Sunday.'

'So why are you here?'

'There's something else. There's more to this, I know it, I just don't know what it is yet. And, hey, if I'm wrong, there's always you. I can reveal the hideout of McFrankenstein's assistant.' He started to laugh, but stopped when he caught her expression. 'But for one problem. I'd have to admit I missed that story when it mattered. Which would be, let's say, embarrassing.' He paused. 'Did you ever find out what the story was behind the weird guy at the inn?'

'You're annoying me,' Betsy said. 'They're killing farm animals less than three miles away. What the hell are you doing off the road?' She made for the cottage.

'Wait,' he said. 'This is what I'm thinking.'

Betsy slowed and he caught up.

'You're not really a story for me. First, it's too late and second, unless you speak, there's only the sordid side of the tale and that's not really our thing, at least not overtly. And . . . I think there's a better story here. This involves lives being lost, but my problem is that I can't get anyone to speak. There's a big story to the sinking of the *Albatross*, an important story. Give it to me, give me anything, a place to start, and we forget all about you.'

The boy was walking towards them from the graveside. 'That's me done there,' he said.

Betsy wondered if Rego had finally turned up, whether he was in the cottage drinking to the memory of the drowned man, and knew instinctively he wouldn't be. He had used a similar threat, although for different ends. Again, she cursed herself for being a poor judge of character. 'I'll walk you back to the house,' she answered the boy, then turned to Euan. 'Let me think about it. Give me until tomorrow.'

'I'd prefer you didn't think about it.'

'You should be happy. Trust me. I'd gladly sacrifice myself for Helen Kerr. I wouldn't even think twice about it, but maybe soon it won't matter. Let me think about what I can tell you.'

'It's good to see you again,' he said, with a slow smile.

'Yes. You too.' Saying it surprised her.

THURSDAY

High tide: 03.07, 15.28
Stiff north-easterly, and strengthening

Helen hung on to Betsy's arm. 'Perfect, isn't it?' she said, shifting her head to avoid Betsy's hair, which was whipping across in the wind. It seemed Priest had visited in the night and covered the grave with the flat stones. A toe-high wall ran round the perimeter. The memorial, with its smooth quartz seams, rose from the head.

'Very beautiful,' agreed Betsy.

Helen loosened her grip, angling away to scale the spearhead of bedrock. She had been transformed: although mourning lingered, the suffering had gone, and she stood braced against the breeze, clothes pulling at her, hair flying. She seemed to hover, before touching down briefly at the base of the tree.

'I can sit here,' she raised her voice so Betsy could hear, 'where William and I used to sit, and though I can't see his grave, which I think is right, I'll know he's just over there.' She rose again, and returned to take Betsy's hand. 'The Orrs have asked me to their house after today's service.' She squeezed, looking again at the grave. 'Beautiful,' she said.

'I'm beginning to see why the Regos' graveyard looks so good,' Betsy commented. 'Priest must look after it.'

'What's that?' Helen asked.

'The graveyard? At Howe Hill. Priest must tend it.'

'Poor man.'

'You're coming round to him?' Betsy smiled.

'He seems bad, but his mind is ruined.' She ran her hand over the memorial.

'What happened to him? I heard something about an accident, but not the details. James said—'

'Cathy Orr said I shouldn't worry about Mr Rego any more. I think you should keep away from him too.' Her voice became conspiratorial. 'There are people who say it was Mr Rego who hurt Priest.'

'Hurt Priest?'

'I don't know very much.' Helen seemed confused by the tone of Betsy's question. 'Anything in fact.'

'But you said James hurt Priest? How?'

'You know that he's cut?' Helen appeared unsure of the reaction she saw in Betsy's face. 'Down there.' She pointed. 'Like a eunuch?' Embarrassment frustrated her. 'You understand?' When Betsy finally nodded, Helen said, 'Some people say Mr Rego did it to him.' Shame rose on her face. 'But William hated gossip.'

'Priest is castrated?'

'It all happened long before I met William. They were young. Their sister was still alive. So I really don't know.'

'*Their* sister? Are you saying Priest is James's brother?'

'Oh, no,' said Helen, shocked. 'I don't think so, do you? They don't look alike at all. No. It was Priest's sister.'

Betsy felt an unpleasant sensation in her head, like a sheet of glass straining under pressure. 'Mary was Priest's sister? But you said *their* sister. This is very important, Helen.'

'William didn't believe in gossip. Especially in a place like this.' She looked down at the tide. 'I should be getting ready for the funerals.'

Betsy tried to order her thoughts. 'Helen . . .'

'I must go.' Helen's voice dropped a tone. 'Are you wanting to come?' Betsy noticed the trace of reserve in Helen's invitation, despite the information she was now trying to digest. Helen was slipping away, seeking the friendship of those who would stay. 'Will you be all right on your own?' she asked, knowing she had to get moving herself.

'Oh, yes.' Helen spoke with confidence.

'Helen? What you were just telling me?'

'I should hurry.' She rushed off towards the cottage.

Betsy watched her go, all the while attempting to make sense of what she had just heard. The suspicion that there might be more to Boyle's visit returned: coincidences, impressions and oddities slotting together in her mind. She saw him turning up at Howe Hill with his book and his rock, his search for something precious. She saw the disappointment engulfing Rego. Betsy realized now that she had been troubled by something in Priest's face and manner: beneath the fat and filth, there was something of Boyle. She recalled Rego saying the child was dead, a declaration that had sent Boyle staggering from the graveyard.

She cut up to the road and made for the inn. The responsibility for encouraging Boyle and Rego in their coy dance clung heavily to her conscience. She hurried, although certain she would be too late. Rego might have been confined to Howe Hill by the plague, with Boyle

349

hunkered down at the inn, but patience had been running out on both sides, and either of them could have made a move. She passed people gathering outside the village church, and held a hand up to Euan when he tried to intercept her. She found Martha at the bar, alone, writing in a ledger. 'He's gone,' the landlady said, with a quiet smile. She didn't even look up.

It took Betsy a second to understand that she meant her ex, not Boyle. 'Martha, you know who Mary Rego was, don't you?'

The landlady put down her pen, and rubbed her left eye with a finger. 'Why?'

'I really need to know.'

'I make a point of not involving myself in family affairs in this village.' She sighed. 'It's a policy you should consider.'

Betsy turned and ran up the stairs. She banged on Boyle's door but there was no answer.

Martha had followed her. 'I just wanted to check you weren't going to damage my hotel,' she said.

'Let me tell you who I think Mary Rego was,' said Betsy, pointing at the door. 'I think she was Henry Boyle's mother.'

Something that must have been troubling Martha resolved itself, but not to her liking. Her expression slipped, then hardened, but she said nothing.

'He thinks James Rego's his uncle.' If Betsy hadn't been looking for the reaction, she would have missed it, because it occurred almost entirely in Martha's eyes. 'But he's not, is he?' Betsy tried the door and almost fell in when it opened under her hand. 'Henry?' she called. On the sideboard stood the glass box, now holding something ugly. The salt had dissolved, leaving the twig thin and

350

black. She watched as Martha moved to stand over it, touching the case. 'And James thinks there's money in this,' she said, to the landlady's back. 'He thinks Henry works for a life-assurance company, and that the father . . .'

'Ty Roberts,' said Martha. 'He worked on the range.'

'. . . left Mary money, not knowing she was dead. James has told Henry that *he* is the only surviving relative.'

Martha sat down and laughed, the sound low and dark. The bed was carefully made, although the room had not been cleaned for some time.

'It's not funny,' said Betsy.

'It is quite,' said Martha. 'James expects cash and gets a nephew.'

'But it's not true, is it? James and Priest, they're not brothers?'

Martha looked up. 'Not by blood, but . . .' She continued in a calm voice: 'Mary and John came up here as children during the war. For their safety. But their parents were killed in the bombing of Coventry so they were brought up by James's parents. Mary adopted the Rego name, John never did – John Priest.'

'I've got to stop Henry,' Betsy said.

'Why?'

'Because something bad is going to happen.'

Martha didn't reply. She had picked up the copy of *De l'amour* from the side-table, and laughed again.

'What?'

'It's just a name, nothing, really. The man who wrote this book, Stendhal, his real name was Henri Beyle.' She sighed, looking tired and unhappy. 'Leave it,' she said. 'Let it sort itself out. Don't interfere.'

Betsy was already heading for the door. 'I've done

nothing but interfere.' She had spoken over her shoulder. The noise of her feet rebounded off the stairs at her. She had seen Rego's anger and was convinced he was capable of any horror.

She passed the church and went into the fields, ignoring the strips of tape that ran along the fences. She walked, then ran towards Howe Hill, climbing the ridge that rose to the peak itself, traversing in to meet the wall that ran along the hill's flank. There she stopped, the wind carrying the scent of wood, creosote and something undetermined, more animal. She climbed step by step until a mound emerged, as high as a railway cottage and as long as a train. The pile of sleepers ran to the west, straw-bound and jagged with animals, the carcasses of the cows twisted and bloated, feet sticking up, heads twisted back, eyes open, the blood dry on their hides. Betsy looked on to the scene with cold awe, the men working at the far end oblivious to her presence. A digger gurgled into life, a black belch swept away by the wind. It lifted a cow by a hind leg so that it spun slowly against the sky before being laid across the pyre. Betsy backed off and, her head down, jogged a path parallel to this horror. She heard the voices of the vets and soldiers beyond the dyke but stayed out of sight. She didn't want to see this, and she certainly didn't want to spot Hirondelle.

The fires are soon to blacken the sky and I will have to see it, the bodyaltar yet to fail. I tried to break its strength by building a memory for the fisherman. A sentimental act, which leaves me confused. The sensations – guilt, shame and pity – now torture me, the Saint purifying my spirit before death. I will take my place at the top of the garden, but where the bodyaltar will rot, I do not know. Cutter brought the plague, I know that now, and the sensation of that truth cuts as warmly as that first slash. I feel it through the fire in my shoulder, the pain feeding the disease that now cripples my mind. I doubt Cutter. I doubt, finally, that his decision was right. And if he was wrong, if it was a mistake, how many other errors have there been before now? All those decisions. My life, oh, sister, our lives, were dependent on his wisdom and here, now, at last, he has shown error. I cannot remove his words from my head, the fever whispers them to me in the night. The storm was unexpected, he said, they were not supposed to die, cutting the pipe was supposed to let the water in slowly, the pump and the alarm disabled so that they would be taken off and the boat would go down easily. But then the storm came, and he tells me that I am to blame, having been the one to do the damage. The fishermen were supposed to survive. I feel the sensations now, of anger, anger, anger. The fever is in my mind and I am beginning to understand the words of the Saint. They grow clear, and speak of culpability. The pyres go up, the tankers ready to pour fuel on the animals I raised. I fear for my mind, but I am dying. I have to make a choice. I have to believe in Cutter to the end. If he was wrong, then he was wrong about everything, wrong about your child, wrong about that first cut. Then all would be lost and the flames must engulf us. We must believe and yet ... the flames still rise.

Betsy reached the top of the stairs, all but falling through the door of Rego's study. He sat behind the heavy desk, his face as ancestral as his surroundings, his hand extended with fingers arched on the wooden surface. He looked thoughtful, if disturbed by the sound of Betsy's arrival. Both he and Boyle gazed at her as she caught her breath. Boyle, more gaunt than ever, was holding a letter. The paper, yellow against the black he habitually wore, shivered in his hand.

'It's not him,' Betsy gasped. 'It's Priest. It's not James. Priest's your . . .' She saw Rego move, but nothing more.

The first thing she made out was Henry's eyes. The stained irises were large, crowding out muddy whites to accommodate his perpetually shadowed pupils. He was holding her head in his arms with great tenderness, but looking down at her without expression. The pain was shocking, sharp and tender, directly above her nose and only a fraction below the hairline. 'You there?' he asked.

Betsy nodded.

'Fingers?' He held up two but they were fuzzy and she looked away. 'Better get you to hospital.'

'Two,' she said. 'What was it?'

'Paperweight, off your head. Could have killed.'

She tried to sit up, feeling unsteady, sick. Boyle's eyes disappeared. 'Where's he gone?'

He pointed towards the door. 'Must be important? What you were saying?'

She summoned back the image of the room as she had seen it a few minutes before, Boyle holding the letter, no doubt stuttering. 'Priest is your uncle, not James.'

For once Boyle was noticeably shocked, and Betsy couldn't help but smile. 'Funny when you come to think of it, but there are similarities.' She lifted a hand to touch her forehead, grimacing at the pain. 'Did you tell him there was no money?'

'Didn't . . . get that far.' The monotone collapsed and

his voice betrayed a terrible anguish. 'How? You know . . . this . . . all . . . of a sudden?'

'Martha,' explained Betsy, pushing herself to her feet. 'He wouldn't hurt Priest, would he? If he thought he was in the way of the money?' She didn't feel strong enough to spell it out, but she realized that Rego would probably be Priest's next-of-kin.

'You.' Boyle stood with her, holding her arm. 'Unsteady.'

Betsy widened her eyes, trying to fix the shimmer that still unbalanced her. 'How long was I out?'

'Few seconds.'

'We should check. See where he's gone.' She lunged forward towards the stairs, using her momentum to grab the banister, hanging on to it as she spun down. Once into the daylight, she took Boyle's arm, running on her uncertain legs towards the outbuildings. She heard the Range Rover's horn cut the air, and saw the car as they came round the trees. Rego had jumped from the vehicle, and was crossing the fence. By the time they reached the edge of the forest, he had disappeared.

'Mr Rego!' Boyle shouted. 'No money.' His voice, although strong, hit the trees and died. 'Never any money.' Again, just the blank wall of needles. 'Only me.' These last words were spoken quietly.

Betsy squeezed his arm. 'We need to go after him.' She looked along the fence to where two army trucks were parked at the edge of the driveway, trying to settle her vision by focusing on them, a dumptruck and a tanker. True clarity had yet to return.

They crossed the stile and burst through the branches, moving fast down the track they had taken on their way out to the firing-range. They crossed firebreaks and cuts, then veered away from the original path, as Boyle searched the ground for clues. They stopped in a clearing, adjusting to the light. Betsy looked to Boyle for reassurance. In the distance they heard an engine start up.

'Mr Rego!' Boyle shouted.

'We're lost,' sighed Betsy. 'I think those are the lorries. They'll be taking them over to the pyre.' They listened, but the sound of the motor was regular, its position unchanged, making it difficult to gauge its direction.

They followed a tunnel in the spruce, scuttling along its narrow breadth until they reached a dry stream where Boyle stopped. 'Lead us back?'

'If we go the other way, the worst case is it would lead us to the graveyard,' Betsy said. 'We should try to find James.'

Boyle stepped down. They had to pick their way carefully down the two-foot-deep trench, razor-sharp branches a meshed sheet above their heads. 'Thank God it's dry,' muttered Betsy.

The trees grew thicker overhead. A broken wall came in from the side, and the stream swung to follow it briefly, then headed in its original direction. It was dark under the canopy, and Betsy looked to the places where light penetrated, a particularly bright clearing opening up to one side where the sun sliced in, darkening the surroundings further. There, cobwebs glistened, and the piercing lime of the moss was crossed by the browns and reds of fallen trunks. She had reached out for Boyle, freezing with her hand on his back, for in the middle of this sunspot, at the heart of the blinding Jacob's ladder, crouched Priest, naked and shimmering. He raised his face and looked at them.

It was only the sensation of her feet getting wet that

made Betsy look away, down into the gloom. The stream had begun to flow, a small trickling headwave pushing past her, past Boyle, and searching for gradient between the pebbles and pine-needles. She peered upstream and, at the same instant, inhaled the powerful reek of fuel-oil, the stench of petrol pumps. She looked again at the clearing but Priest had gone. Then she understood what was happening. 'That tanker,' she said. 'James is going to burn Priest out. He's pumping fuel into the stream.'

They panicked. The branches on each side were too thick to break through, and they ran down the ditch. 'We have to get out,' Betsy shouted, beating at Boyle's back. 'Out of the stream.'

'Need space.' They were trying to catch the bow-wave but, having appeared to pass so slowly, it had now gone too far.

Betsy was staggering as she ran. The image of Priest kneeling in the sunlight cut in with those of the pyre, melting together in her already concussed mind, her imagination grafting it to her terror. The fuel felt cold on her feet, the smell sickening. A branch caught her and she sprawled forward, cutting her hand, Boyle grabbing her, lifting her. She was now wet, her cuts stinging. She knew that when the rush of flames followed, they would come fast. The image in her mind re-formed with Priest at the centre of the vast pyre, the forest itself, sunlight the flames. They were hemmed in but still Betsy bounced against the serrated brush at the edge of the ditch.

'No room to run,' Boyle screamed in her ear as she fought the branches. 'No rain for days. Forest is dry. It will go up. Need a firebreak . . . to get away.'

The fuel was higher round their feet now, flowing well. Betsy listened for the sound of fire chasing the bow-wave through the wood, as she splashed down the gentle incline. The smell, the pain in her head, the fear strained the will in her. She fell again, her shirt soaking through. An arch opened up in the trees on the right and Boyle was out, reaching back for her, pulling her from the ditch as she crawled on hands and knees. She would have happily lain there, but he held her under the arms and pulled her to her feet.

'Come,' he yelled. 'Must move.'

He half carried her along the tunnel but she only lasted seconds before she threw up a hand and fell to her knees. She fought for breath against her bile, yearning for sunlight and fresh air, desperate to be out of the gloom.

'Need to move,' shouted Boyle. She held up a hand and, as if at this signal, she heard the noise, a fast passing hiss. The fire came as a brightness moving through the forest, snaking through the gloom like a will o' the wisp, and for an instant it appeared to have gone. Only then did its malign trail reach up to catch the branches and make them crackle and explode.

'Come,' said Boyle quietly, and they were scrambling down the narrow vent in the wall of brush.

With the flames behind them, shadows played ahead, twisting and flickering in the branches. Stumps underfoot tripped them, and again and again Betsy found herself grabbing for Boyle's arm, or turning to pull him from the brushwood. She thought they were winning, the shadows diminishing, but the noise remained, and the foul scent of smoke now reached them, a small deer darting in front of their feet. A clearing appeared to their left, and they turned towards it, breaking through to find a farmhouse falling towards ruin. Enclosed by four walls of pine-needles, its otherworldly qualities were exaggerated by a tower of ivy that rose smoothly at one end. Exhaustion and surprise dislodged their fear and they gazed in wonder at it. The planks under the roof had fallen away so gaping holes showed in the slate; in places boarded-up windows had been torn away. It was a home, despite its crumbling walls and ruined roof. There was a frame outside the back door, its wood stained black, and a small kitchen garden, bare under the smoky sunlight. Paths cut through the yellow grass that surrounded it. A pile of ashes rose beside various pots that were turned upside-down in the grass. Boyle took a step towards the ruined door, then faltered.

'Priest!' he shouted. 'You here, Priest?' There was no answer.

The clearing darkened as smoke smeared the sun to a white hole, the sky filling up, the fire growing louder. Betsy followed Boyle to the edge of the house. Round the corner of the building, they found that the stream ran through the backyard, the flames invisible in the sunlight. As Betsy saw that they had blundered back into the fire, flames seared along the forest wall, instantly covering the height and length of the trees, needles fizzing and popping in a single sheet of flame. Heat came off the trees in a wave.

'This way.'

Boyle pulled her towards the one corner of forest that remained untouched, but Betsy stopped. 'We can't go back in there. We'll be trapped.'

'Die here,' Boyle said. 'The heat, smoke. Kill us.'

'No.'

'Yes.' Boyle pulled her.

Betsy hesitated, and as she did, she felt a great heat on the back of her neck, perspiration running down her spine. She gave in, and let herself be led back into the trees, into the tunnel from which they had emerged. They had travelled only a few feet when the wall of needles behind them went up in a rush of oily flame. The passage gave out within yards. A thin trail showed on the left, Boyle staring at it for only an instant. 'Have to try,' he said, and turned down it.

Betsy saw flames flaring in the gloom ahead. 'We're going into it,' she screamed. 'We're going right into it.'

'Round it.' The branches hung low and they had to crouch as they scurried along the passage, Betsy no longer noticing the agony of being scratched and cut. Trees were burning up now, exploding in sap-fuelled detonations. The sucking roar of the fire was closing on them, and they were closing on it, the narrow space under the trees filling with smoke. The haze made it all but impossible to see, although the murk grew brighter from the fires. Boyle stopped, and Betsy understood she was going to burn to death.

'Back,' he said, but she stayed where she was, the heat prickling on her skin. '*Back!*' he screamed. She felt nothing. All she was aware of was the rush of oncoming death. In front of her, Boyle's eyes widened and again the irises revealed themselves. She was being pulled violently to the side, something had got hold of the collar of her coat, lifting and dragging her through a thousand small cuts.

The stench of rotten meat mixed with the smoke that had blinded her, and she understood that she was in the hands of Priest. She could hear Boyle struggling after them. At first her muscles, locked in fear, resisted Priest's strength, and then the pain of the branches tearing at her flesh forced her legs into a kind of walk. He was lifting her, so this became a paddling at the air. Occasionally she touched the earth, lurching beside him, head pushed forward, half carried, half propelling herself. The smoke cleared a little and she felt the hint of a breeze on her face, the light changing, Priest pausing. She tried to stand, but her rescuer was using an immense strength to hold her at arm's length. She lifted her head, but found she was unable to see. Even his massive body, a mere foot or two away, was just smudged flesh to her running eyes. He must have made a decision because Betsy found herself paddling again, the strobe effect of passing trees suggesting the rowan avenue, confirmed as she heard the click of Priest opening the gate of the graveyard, the air finally tasting fresh and clear.

He dropped her at a gravestone, and there she lay until the strength returned for her to rub at her eyes with her cut and dirty hands. The landscape that formed around her was caught in shadow. She peered up, the sky dark with the trails of smoke that rose from the fire consuming the forest on the cliff above. She focused on the waterfall, the stones blackened where fuel had fallen towards the sea. Her eyes rose again to follow the smoke, and she rolled back against the stone to see its trail stretch far out to sea where, at last, sunlight reached the waves. Boyle stood near the wall, bent over in the way of victims. His hands were dark and streaked with blood, his clothes torn and filthy, the stretched skin of his face crossed with cuts. She leaned back, following his line of sight to where Priest stood on bandy legs, fat and naked, his tongue between his teeth. The sight was terrible, his shockingly mutilated body was robbed of decency. A skinscape of scars covered his smeared bulk, each seeming to be of a different age and size, but all identical in shape, a dreadful aberration of split skin, reminiscent, Betsy saw at once, of the mouth of the cave in the cliff below. He was breathing deeply, watching Betsy's gaze as it fell. The castration was nothing more than an absence, his penis tiny compared with his frame. What astonished her, and removed the pain of her own injuries, was his shoulder: the skin of his chest and neck was mottled green and purple, darkening to black where a suppurating wound had gone rotten. It ran with pus, sousing the soot that covered him. He grunted under her gaze, dropping his shoulder with the pain, staggering away as if under a great weight.

Boyle crouched down beside her. 'We'll . . . get him a doctor,' he said. 'How about you?'

She lifted a hand to her forehead where her skull still ached from the paperweight. Her expression must have conveyed surprise at being alive, because he slumped beside her with a laugh.

'Own grave, I see,' he said.

Betsy turned to see her name on the stone behind her, reading the words before looking back. 'What was in the letter,' she asked, 'that you showed James?'

'From my mother. To my father. Asking him . . . to take care . . . of me. She gave him the book . . . that salt bough you liked . . . the stone, all gifts . . . from her to me. I was two days old.'

'Why didn't she . . . ?'

'Don't know. Why I'm here.'

'You changed your name?'

'Yes. Stupid name. Stendhal. Stendhal Roberts. After the author.'

'Perhaps Rego's mother made her give you up?'

'Perhaps.'

Or perhaps James Rego himself, she thought, as she looked back at the gravestone. *Betsy Gillander, Faithful retainer of the Rego family*. It was an epitaph that would have transferred perfectly if Priest hadn't saved her from the fire. Rego had asked her about the hierarchy of misery she had found in this place, wondering where her own troubles fitted in. She didn't care now. She was glad to be alive. They sat, saying nothing as she thought about this, watching Priest pick his way up the hill to crouch at his sister's grave.

'You think he's a real Priest?' Boyle asked.

'No.'

'You . . . know,' he grappled with the words. 'I . . . stayed.' He must have won because the rest came in a rush: 'Because of you.'

Betsy gazed out, at the sky and the sea, at the countries at the edge of sight. The horizon lay out there, promising all the opportunities she had once imagined, the endless opportunities for her to screw things up. She looked on to the vast space between the nations and felt her reliance on logic fall apart, passion filling the void. She was about to kick him, tell him to go and find his own gravestone, that she didn't need to be reminded that it was all her fault. She was stopped by a shadow of anticipation and dread in his expression. He had stayed because of her; it wasn't such a horrible thing for him to say, however the corollary might chime in her conscience.

A movement caused her to refocus. Beyond him, Priest climbed the wall, and jumped.

FRIDAY

High tide: 03.49, not applicable
Gales forecast

Betsy gazed out of the car window at the languid beauty of the windfarm, where vast white blades revolved against the darkening sky. The machines seemed impossibly elegant to her, futuristic in such an inhospitable landscape, and she found herself longing for the city. 'You drive very badly,' she complained.

'I'll drop you off at the next bus stop if you like.'

'No ... No, I don't think you will.' She tried not to flinch with the approaching corners. Her head still ached from the paperweight, and her hands and face were an agony of small cuts, calmed with Savlon. She had avoided hospital, although that was where Boyle had ended up. After Priest dropped from the cliff, Boyle had climbed the wall and almost fallen after him. He had begun to yell, an ululation filled with such loss that it had torn into Betsy. He had quietened only when Priest reappeared, slowly making his way across the rocks at the water's edge below. By then Boyle had become stuck half-way down the cliff. When, several hours later, the soldiers manning the pyre had fought their way through, they said Priest had been found hunched and shivering at the cave's mouth. Betsy, feeling she had been mean to Boyle earlier, had insisted on waiting until he was rescued before leaving.

After talking to the police, Betsy had spent the night at the cottage being fussed over by Helen. Her friend had been welcomed at the funerals of the other crewmen, which had fed her confidence and steadied her. To Betsy, she had seemed, at last, reassured. The goodbye, when it came, had been a long, enveloping hug. Standing on the gravel in front of the cottage, the friendship had revealed its depth in small gestures – they had picked at each other's hair and clothes, growing awkward when they realized what they were doing. When Helen had asked if she would visit, Betsy had assured her she would, asking in return whether Helen would be all right. There had been little doubt in her friend's eyes when she said she would be fine.

Shortly afterwards, as Betsy waited for her lift on the pier-side, Martha had emerged from the inn to stand at her side. This had become a sort of communication between them, and together they had gazed out at the wall of cloud obscuring Ireland and threatening the Isle of Man. It had taken a few minutes for Martha to speak, and when she did, she had started with nothing more than a commonplace. 'It will be raining in an hour,' she had said. 'And I'll be glad. There's something wrong about too much sunshine at this time of year.' She had turned, but Betsy kept her eyes on the sea. 'And you'll be gone too, and hopefully the reporters, and Mr Boyle and, eventually, this bloody plague, and we will get on with our lives.' She had waited for a response and when none came, had sighed. 'They're definitely lifting the *Albatross*. They say it had been damaged, that Rego intended to sink it for the insurance. You should remember that you flushed him out, that we had lived with him for years, all of us suspecting what he might have done to John.' The original given name for Priest had humanized him, as had the profound sadness in Martha's voice. 'They'll catch Rego, and he'll go to jail, and we will get on with our lives.' She had paused. 'By the way, I've decided to suggest a domino night in the pub.'

Betsy had smiled, keeping her eyes on the clouds.

'The maximum bet will be a pound a game.' Again there had been that pause. 'But what of you? Did you get what you wanted?'

Only then had Betsy turned to the innkeeper, but a movement in the background caught her attention and she had seen, at the other end of the street, the harbourmaster on a ladder. He was painting out the slogan that covered his wall. The 'Any' had gone, and then in a smooth sweep the S and, for a moment, as he reapplied paint to his brush, it had read, Port In A Storm. She had opened her mouth to reply when Euan emerged from the inn, spinning his keys around his finger as he approached. 'You ready?' he had asked, and Betsy extended a hand to Martha.

'You're not talking,' Euan said now, flooring the decrepit Astra's accelerator, trying to get it up the hill. 'You promised you'd talk.'

'I'm thinking,' Betsy said.

'About?'

'Where James Rego might have gone.'

'Tell.'

Betsy laughed. She had remembered Rego talking about the sherry, the town he and William had visited. He